There are some of us Gentiles who love Jesus, love Jews, love Jesus as a Jew, and realize we were drawn into an Hebraic faith when we became Christians, and we have long hoped for better literature to serve our cause. Much that is written about Jesus as a Jew is a scolding distribution of blame rather than an ennobling call to truth. Ron Cantor has changed this. He uses fiction, humor, a bit of fantasy and a time traveler's imagination to tell us a tale that ought to be told. He makes us know Jesus anew. I am grateful; and I hope he is forerunner of a new tribe on the rise.

STEPHEN MANSFIELD
New York Times bestselling author

Ron Cantor is not only married to one of my favorite people on the planet, he is also a friend and co-laborer in Messiah for well over two decades. In his book, *Identity Theft,* you will find him witty and clever as well as insightful as he shares Jewish roots from a totally unexpected angle. I was pleased to discover that *Identity Theft* is an engaging page-turner! I believe you will find this book to be pointed as well as helpful, and you might even catch yourself becoming an agent in restoring Messiah's true identity!

PAUL WILBUR
Recording artist
Integrity Music

Ron had my rapt attention from page one of the Introduction! And what a great title, as Ron effectively portrays the identity theft of the centuries—that Jesus has been robbed of His Jewishness! Tragically, many of those who professed to believe in Him would have put Him in the gas ovens of Europe had He lived during their lifetime.

DON FINTO
Author, *Your People Shall Be My People*
Former senior pastor, Belmont Church
Nashville, Tennessee

Ron Cantor's new book, *Identity Theft*, is as riveting as it is revelatory and as entertaining as it is enlightening. With the unique vantage point of a Messianic Jew living in Israel, Ron gives you a guided tour of history from the pages of the New Testament to the Holocaust and then back to the Cross for an extraordinarily powerful portrayal of the Messiah's sacrificial death. Buy a copy for yourself and one for a friend!

DR. MICHAEL L. BROWN
President, Fire School of Ministry
Concord, North Carolina
Host, national radio talk show, *Line of Fire*
Author, *Answering Jewish Objections to Jesus* series

I've known Ron for a number of years and have always enjoyed his ministry. When I read *Identity Theft* I was captivated by the story. I couldn't stop reading until I was finished. What a must-read for anyone wanting to be part of an incredible journey to faith in the Messiah!

DR. EVON G. HORTON
Senior Pastor, Brownsville Assembly
Pensacola, Florida

How ingenious to embed a powerful teaching in an engrossing novel of a Jewish man's search for the truth! Many Christians today are experiencing a longing to know more about their Jewish roots, which are so foundational to all followers of the Messiah. But to really understand Christianity's Jewish heritage together with today's Jewish culture and mindset, Christians must know both the biblical narrative and the story of the Jewish people over the past 2,000 years, as well as how it has been so influenced and even dominated by the Church. In *Identity Theft*, Messianic communicator Ron Cantor has written the book that will give you this information in unforgettable portraits from first-century Jewish believers to the tragic wanderings of the Jewish people up until today.

ARI AND SHIRA SORKO-RAM
Founders, Maoz Israel (www.MaozIsrael.org)
Senior leaders, Tiferet Yeshua Congregation
Tel Aviv, Israel

Not just dramatic, but exhilarating! An easy-to-read story that draws non-Jewish readers into Jewish consciousness and Jewish readers into Jesus's consciousness. While many novels distract people from life, this one contains a life-changing message that can transform a reader's life. Happy to recommend.

DR. JEFFREY L. SEIF
Chair of the Jewish Studies Department
Christ for the Nations Institute
Dallas, Texas

This much-needed work is important for all seekers of truth. Though I am not much of a fiction reader, I quickly found myself engrossed in Ron's manuscript and unable to put it down. *Identity Theft* is a great book for both those who recognize the Jewishness of our Messiah as well as those who've never truly considered His identity. As we enter into a season of unparalleled anti-Semitism, we must remember that our Messiah was born into a Jewish home, lived as a Torah-observant Jew, died as King of the Jews, and is returning as the "Lion of the Tribe of Judah."

SCOTT VOLK

Pastor, Fire Church

Charlotte, North Carolina

President, Hineni International Ministries

I first met Ron Cantor in our local congregation in Washington, DC, decades ago. It seemed readily apparent he would emerge in a leadership role, and this has happened. Now we serve together in Maoz Ministries (Israel), where he is the winsome televised messenger of God's good news of the Messiah.

His recent book, *Identity Theft*, artfully explains the ancient schism between Jews and Christianity. This he does not through dry theology, but rather through a captivating novel.

The book will fascinate both the Jewish and Gentile reader with its portrayal of the heartbreaking truth of the Church's treatment of God's ancient people. The robbing of Yeshua (Jesus) of His cultural identity has resulted in a terrible and lengthy tragedy to the Jewish people. Ron's book seeks to restore to Yeshua His original ethnic context. The story helps us to better understand and reveals many, many things.

PAUL LIBERMAN

President, Messianic Jewish Alliance of America

Publisher, *The Messianic Times*

Ron Cantor has written a fast-paced novel that power-fully defends the faith. It reflects the understanding of many Messianic Jewish leaders in Israel and speaks the Gospel with simplicity and clarity to Jewish people who do not yet follow Yeshua. This book will open up minds and hearts—not only for Jewish people, but for many in the Church who will be enlightened as they see the first followers of Yeshua in their historical Jewish context.

DR. DANIEL C. JUSTER
Executive Director, Tikkun International
President, Messianic Jewish Bible Institute
Jerusalem

Ron Cantor adds his voice to the still small choir singing out the truth of the story of Jesus, His Jewish life and times, and the tragic opposite effect the rewritten story has had upon the Jewish people and Christians. As an orthodox Jew, I have not been convinced by this book to change my own life, but I hope Ron is not "preaching to the choir," and Christians who feel uncomfortable with their understanding of Jesus will pick up this volume and discover biblical truths that they never knew existed. *Identity Theft* is an important milestone in the journey that Christians must take in times such as these, and by extension, it impacts Christian-Jewish relations as well.

GIDON ARIEL
Christian-Jewish friendship cultivator
Founder of the Facebook group "Jews Who Love Christians
Who Love Jews (and the Christians Who Love Them)"
and www.root-source.com

From the time I picked it up, I didn't want to put it down. Ron Cantor has ventured into "no-man's land." Is it possible that the bridge between Judaism and Christianity is where truth resides? This book will challenge Christians to reexamine their theological presuppositions and take a much different view of the origins of their faith. It will also challenge the Jewish community to reexamine their 2,000-year-old wound inflicted by Gentile hypocrisy and take a new look at this "Yeshua of Nazareth" in His real clothing!

RICHARD FREEMAN
Messianic Rabbi, Beth Messiah Congregation
Houston, Texas

Ron is a passionate communicator, teacher, and storyteller. I had the joy of serving with Ron in both Ukraine and Hungary where his teachings on Jewish roots, history, and Messianic theology blessed many. In this creative book, Ron takes you on a journey of his Jewish people's experience through the centuries. You will be enlightened and encouraged as you see the "family story" told in a very new way. I wholeheartedly recommend this book.

WAYNE WILKS JR., PH.D.
International Director, Messianic Jewish Bible Institute

If Jesus is both 100 percent deity and 100 percent human then it's essential to understand what kind of human He is. He is certainly not a blue-eyed Scandinavian as some have portrayed Him. For more than a decade, Ron Cantor has been passionately revealing the true face of Jesus to Israel and the nations. As Ron shows how Jesus came to earth as a Jew, many truths in Scripture become more comprehensible and alive. You'll be enriched by Ron's insights.

WAYNE HILSDEN
Senior pastor, King of Kings Community
Jerusalem, Israel

The emotional depth and immediacy evoked in this novel would be impossible in a theological tome with the same purpose. It's a book you will want to read at one sitting, and if you're like me, your only regret will be having to wait for the remaining two volumes of the trilogy.

Dr. David H. Stern
Translator, *The Complete Jewish Bible*

IDENTITY THEFT

IDENTITY THEFT

RON CANTOR

DEDICATION

This book is dedicated to all the indirect victims of this *Identity Theft*—the lost sheep of the house of Israel. I implore you to take a fresh and honest look at Yeshua (Jesus) the Jew. I think you will be surprised.

In defending myself against the Jews,
I am acting for the Lord. The only
difference between the church and
me is that I am finishing the job.
—ADOLF HITLER

Chapter One

THE VISITATION

It happened a year ago. He came in a vision. I have never fully shared this with anyone, except my wife, and at first, she didn't believe me, but I felt it was time to put my testimony on paper.

After all, I am a writer and He chose to send His messenger to me. People must know the truth. Christians must know the truth. And by all means, Jews must know the whole story.

Is that it?

Three words that turned my life upside down: "Is that it?" It wasn't that I was unfulfilled. On the contrary, I was extremely content. I was five years married and had two amazingly cute little girls. At twenty-eight, with only a bachelor's degree, I had risen in the ranks. I already had a daily column in the *Philadelphia Inquirer* and a well-read blog. Life was perfect.

And yet *that* was the problem—what if there was something I was missing? Maybe there was a God out there who expected something from me. Maybe not, but the truth is, *I had no idea*. What keeps my heart ticking day after day? Who makes sure that it continues to pump blood through my veins?

I had taken all of this for granted. It suddenly hit me that we spend entire lifetimes working and planning just to make sure we are comfortable when we retire, which is a very short period of time. Yet we rarely consider what happens after retirement when we die. Is that it? Six feet under and never another conscious thought? Or is there life beyond the grave? And if so, where would I spend eternity? I had no idea.

I was determined to find God. I was full of questions and I had no clue where to begin. How do you *find God?* It's not like I could just Google Him as I had learned to do for everything else.

Where to start?

Being Jewish, I began to go to synagogue and even attend afternoon prayers, the Mincha service, when I could. It felt great when nine men were waiting and I showed up to complete the *minyan* (a quorum of ten Jewish bar Mitzvah'd males required to begin the prayer service). As a last resort they might grab some poor just-over-thirteen-year-old out of his studies to reach the required number, but then I would show up, saving the day.

While that made me feel good about myself, I didn't sense any personal connection with the Almighty. It was more a satisfaction that I had performed some religious duty, than actually feeling His presence. I began to study other religions and actually began to pray—not in a formal sense like in the synagogue, but I simply asked God to show me if He was real and what He expected from me.

To be honest, I was drawn to Jesus. His message of salvation was so different from any other religion I had studied. Every single one of them put the emphasis on what I did. *Do this on Friday. Do that in the morning. Be a good person. And by all means, never do this.*

But the message Jesus preached conceded that my case was hopeless. There was nothing I could do to please God in light of all I had done against Him. That was why He came; in order to give His life as a sacrifice; to take my punishment—or so they say. It was the only philosophy that didn't stress religious obligation, but instead presented me with the opportunity to accept the fact that 1) I was a sinner; 2) I could not save myself; 3) Jesus had taken my punishment; and 4) through faith in Him, I could have eternal life.

You may be thinking, *So what's the problem? Buy into it!* It's not quite so easy. You see, being Jewish, I was convinced that to believe in Him would be to deny my faith, my heritage, and my community. Everyone knew that to believe in Yeshua was to betray the Jewish people—a people who had suffered more than any other, and had so often suffered in the name of the very One to whom I was attracted.

Also add to that the fact that the whole Jewish community knew my father was the son of Holocaust survivors. Surely they would all turn on me. And it seemed to me that they would be right. What kind of a Jew takes sides with the descendants of the Crusaders? When I went to my rabbi to confide in him, he nearly bit my head off. He told me to drop my pursuit and never bring it up again—"For the sake of your family." I was completely and utterly confused and immobilized.

And then he came. His name is Ariel. I was at Starbucks sipping on double-shot espresso. I have never been a Venti, non-fat, no-foam, no-water, six pump, extra-hot, chai tea latte kind of a guy—just strong espresso. That was all I needed to get my creative juices flowing in order to write.

I was sitting there reading the paper, getting ready to start on my column, when suddenly the entire room became white. In fact, it was so bright that *white* seems like an understatement. Everyone was gone—the girl behind the counter, the tattooed hipster listening to his iPod, the student on his computer, the couple that appeared to be going over a business plan...*all gone!*

I was terrified. Suddenly a man appeared...*an angel*. He introduced himself. "I am Ariel, an angel of the Most High." He was about six feet tall, quite fit, with dark hair, dark skin, and a short beard. He was wearing a white robe, interestingly, just as I would have imagined an angel to be dressed.

I said nothing. "David, you who are highly esteemed, consider carefully the words I am about to speak to you and the lessons you will learn, and stand up, for I have now been sent to you."

When he said this to me, I stood up trembling.

"I have been sent to give you understanding. You are a confused Jewish young man, but you have found favor in the eyes of Adonai."

I knew Adonai was Hebrew for *Lord*. Even though I had not been very religious, going to Hebrew school three times a week during much of my teen years had not been a complete waste.

He continued, "I have come to take you on a journey, to show you the past, the present, and even the future. At times you will beg me to stop, but in order for you to understand the truth and help others to understand, you must experience it—you must experience *all* of it."

I found my voice, but could not think of anything to say. Before I knew it the angel grabbed my hand, and suddenly we were flying through time. It is very hard to explain on paper, in words, what I was experiencing, which is one reason that it has taken me a year to begin this testimony.

I somehow knew that we were going back in time. It was thrilling and yet petrifying. I could see scenes in time, but from a distance. And then everything suddenly grew bigger, as when a plane lands. As though watching a timeline, I could see that we were in the second century, and then the first. Things grew really close, as if we were zooming in on Google maps. The Middle East, Israel, Jerusalem! And then, we passed right through a roof and gently landed inside what seemed like an ancient synagogue from the second Temple period. Only there were several rows of seats, like in a modern movie theater, and a massive screen. Torches lit up the room, as it was night.

There were other angels there. Two were above me and there were two at every entrance. They said nothing and Ariel didn't even acknowledge them. It appeared they were standing guard. Then I thought, *Am I in some kind of danger?* It reminded me of the first time I visited Israel. The armed soldiers at the airport made me feel safe and deeply concerned at the same time. From what and whom were they were protecting me? And now the question that plagued my mind was, *What dangerous spiritual force is seeking to bring about my demise?*

"What is going on? Is this a dream?" Words finally found their way out of my mouth. I knew this couldn't really be happening and yet I was quite sure I was awake. The only thing missing was Morpheus offering me a blue pill or a red one.

"David, your journey will begin here. You will watch events in the lives of four Jews, all from different time periods during the past 2,000 years. You see, David, you are struggling with the idea of *being Jewish and believing in Yeshua.* You don't mind if we refer to Him by His Hebrew name, do you?"

It was more of a statement than a question. He continued, "You feel that to believe would be a betrayal. But that is only because you do not know that the Yeshua you imagine in your mind is not the Yeshua who walked the streets not too far from where we are right now."

"So, we are in Jerusalem?" I asked.

"The Old City, to be exact. The year is 35 CE, a time when the Messiah was understood in the context in which the Jewish prophets described Him. The multitudes who followed Him during this period were all Jews.

"Over the years, that has changed. His message has touched nearly every nation...and that is a good thing. However, in the process, the nature and identity of the Messiah has been tampered with, even altered, by those without the authority to do so. In short, there has been an insidious case of identity theft.

"Long before computer hackers and credit cards, the most destructive, most horrendous case of identity theft occurred, and the victim was the Messiah Himself! Today, we will uncover it, and then you, young man, will expose it to the world."

This was getting interesting!

"Sit down. Let's begin," instructed Ariel.

Feeling completely confused and utterly intrigued, I sat in what was the most amazingly comfortable chair I had ever sat in, immediately forgetting the burden that he had just placed upon me—"You will expose it to the world."

I waited to see what would come next. Ariel picked up a remote, pointed it toward the screen, and pressed a button. The torches in the room faded, until it was completely dark. The film began to play.

Chapter Two

LIVING WITH SHAME

Words emerged on the screen:

27 CE, Capernaum, Galilee

Then a woman appeared and began to talk, as if she were being interviewed:

"I am a Jewess and my claim to fame is that my story, wonderful in and of itself, was recorded—at least the most important part—for posterity, by not just one, but by *three* ancient writers!"

As she continued to talk, I watched her story unfold like a movie.

"My name is Chaya. I spent my childhood playing on the shores of the Sea of Galilee. And each evening my father would come home after a day of fishing, bringing fresh tilapia with him for dinner. Now I know that the smell of fish isn't everyone's favorite, but for me it conjures up precious memories of my hardworking father who loved and provided for his family. My mother worked hard as well, taking care of the home and her children, using all her ingenuity to feed and clothe us. But no matter how hard they worked, there was never enough after paying the crippling taxes imposed by the nation's Roman overlords.

"Like most Galileans, we longed for the day when the Messiah would come and free us from the tyranny of the Romans. Every Shabbat we would go to the synagogue, in the center of our village, to hear the Torah read and to pray. It was a constant reminder to us all that God had saved our people once before when we were slaves in Egypt—surely He could do it again, and the sooner the better.

"In my late teens, around the age when many of my friends were being given in marriage, I began to bleed heavily. I went to every doctor in the area but none of them could help me. For twelve years I suffered greatly. The deepest pain of all was the social stigma, the loneliness, and the knowledge that no one would take me in marriage with this condition. I had no friends, because everyone I came in contact with would become ritually unclean. I began to realize that even if I lived a long life, I would never know the joy of having children, of holding a baby in my arms, or hearing my children's laughter at play. It broke my heart.

"Along with being emotionally drained, I was physically weak and, to make matters even worse, I was now destitute. Because I was unclean, I could never enter a synagogue to hear the Scriptures read. Over the years I had spent all I had on doctors and medicines—all to no avail. If it weren't for the fear of the Almighty, I think I would have taken my own life. *Baruch HaShem* (Praise the Lord), I didn't!

"I was in my late twenties when I first heard of the Rabbi from Nazareth. He was trained as a carpenter, they said, but He spoke like an angel—like someone who truly knew God, not just knew *about Him*. He had recently come to live in Capernaum and was invited to read from the Torah in our synagogue.

"I remember it so clearly. People were truly amazed by His words. He didn't speak like the other rabbis or the priests. He spoke with such authority!

"He created quite a stir, and several of the young men from our village attached themselves to Him. In fact, a number of them had worked with my father on the fishing boats. Jacob and John, two brothers a few years younger than I, actually became part of His inner circle.

"Before long, stories began to circulate that He could heal the sick. Suddenly, for the first time in many years I felt hope stirring within me. Could He heal me? But how could I, a woman who could hardly walk the short distance to the market, ever get close to Yeshua?

"For days I thought about nothing else. I was desperate. If He were to heal me, I could live again, maybe get married, even have children—I could have a life! But the more I thought about it, the more impossible it became. How could I, as a woman in my unclean state, ever get anywhere near the Rabbi?

"Then one afternoon, I heard a commotion outside. Because I lived so near the city square, I went out to see what was happening. Quite a crowd had gathered and I was told that Yeshua was coming, that He was on His way to the house of Jairus, one of the leaders in our synagogue. Jairus's daughter had been very sick and over the past few days had taken a turn for the worse. Earlier that day I'd heard they feared she might die. Jairus, in desperation, had begged Yeshua to come to his house and pray for his daughter.

"When I finally got to the square, I saw the Rabbi surrounded by masses of people. My heart sank. I felt so drained. I had no energy at all. Twelve years of bleeding takes its toll. And then, suddenly, I felt a surge of strength, of determination. I had to try. I knew that if I could just touch the *tzitzit*, the fringes on His garment, I would be healed. I was sure of it. I had to touch Him.

"Caught up in the crowd, I began to push and fight my way through. I am sure many were surprised that poor, quiet little Chaya was suddenly aggressively pushing her way past them. But if any were offended, I didn't notice. After more than a decade of weakness and suffering, I really didn't care. I meant to reach Him at any cost.

"In Jewish culture it is forbidden for a woman to publicly touch a man, much less a man she is neither married to nor acquainted with! Moreover, the nature of my problem deemed me perpetually unclean according to biblical law, so that anyone or anything I touched would become unclean. And yet, I was compelled, driven in my soul, to go through with it.

"Finally, I could see Him in front of me. One final charge! And just then, I was flung to the ground. The crowd was so thick that I thought I would be trampled. A foot on my hand, a kick in the back...*No!* I jumped to my feet and pushed forward until I was within reach of the Rabbi.

"*This was it.* With all the strength I could muster, I lurched forward, just barely managing to graze the fringe of His *tallit* with my fingers. And as I did, I felt such power come into me. But it was more than power...it was pure, it was clean, it was *life!*

"I knew in that moment that I had been healed, but more than that, I had been changed, radically changed. My life would never be the same. No, it wasn't that I would now be desirable to a man. At that moment, everything else was irrelevant compared to the pure joy that was radiating within me. I had found more than a husband—I had found the God I had only known from stories and traditions. Now, through this Galilean Rabbi, I was in the presence of the Almighty.

"Of course, I had believed in the God of Israel all my life. I had always celebrated the Holy Days of Passover and Yom Kippur, the Day of Atonement, Sukkot, and Shavuot. And I had hoped that the Messiah would one day come. But never had I realized that Elohim could be this close—He could be felt and experienced. And without ever realizing that I hadn't known it before, I now knew that *He loved me.*

"As all this was happening inside of me, I suddenly realized that the Master had stopped walking. He turned and asked, 'Who touched Me?' It seemed like a ridiculous question when dozens of people were touching Him as they pressed in. His puzzled disciples said as much. Yet, ignoring them, He continued to look around.

"I knew He was referring to me and I was terrified. I wanted to run, and yet I wanted to be with Him forever. The way He said, 'Who touched Me?' made me feel like I had taken something without permission. I was scared, but still I went forward and fell at His feet and confessed that it was I.

"*What had I done?* Everyone was looking at me. Barely above a whisper, I told Him about my sickness and how I felt that if I could just touch Him I would be healed. And just like that, a huge smile appeared on His face as He took my hand and said, 'Daughter, your faith has healed you. Go in peace and be freed from your suffering.'

"Those words changed my life. He called me *daughter* and despite the fact that I was nearly as old as He, I don't know that I ever experienced more fatherly love than I did at that moment. In an instant I was transformed from being unclean and undesirable, to being a woman who was healed and highly favored by the Messiah Himself."

Now I was crying, weeping with joy for this woman. My daughters had always laughed at how easily I can cry during a movie. But this was the most moving thing I had ever seen! Hollywood could never compete with Heaven!

She continued.

"You might be wondering whatever happened to the daughter of Jairus. Sadly, she died before Yeshua was able to pray for her. Yet, the Master still went to Jairus's home. When He arrived, everyone was weeping and mourning 'Why all this commotion and wailing?' He asked. 'The child is not dead but asleep.'

"But though they laughed at Him, He was not dissuaded. He threw everyone out of the house and, taking the child by the hand, told her to get up. And she did! She was brought back from death! We could hardly believe it!

"From then on He traveled from village to village through-out Galilee, Samaria, and Judea preaching the 'good news of the kingdom,' healing all who were sick and casting out demons from those who were oppressed. Oh, what an amazing time it was!

"Yet, how abruptly it all ended—or so we thought. On the eve of Passover, just a couple of years later, He was betrayed and handed over to the Romans by some of our religious leaders. Many thought that once the Romans arrested Him, He would then lead a revolt against them. But before we knew it, contrary to all expectation, the Romans crucified Him—they nailed Him to a cruel Cross! Crucifixion was the most excruciating kind of death that existed.

"Along with a number of others, I had followed Him to Jerusalem. We were all devastated. We had had such high hopes. We thought that, like Moses, He would deliver us from our enemies. But instead they killed Him. I don't have words to describe. With John by her side supporting her, His distraught mother was in agony as she watched her precious son die a torturous death. This was not supposed to happen! He was our hope.

"However, incredibly, after several days, in the midst of our despair, word began to spread that the One we had watched die, was alive. And unbelievably, it was true! He had risen from the dead. Over a period of forty days, His disciples and hundreds of other people saw Him, including me! And then, while His followers watched, He, our Messiah, was taken up into Heaven.

"In accordance with His last instructions, 120 of us stayed in Jerusalem and waited for the promised Holy Spirit. For ten days we prayed and many fasted. Then on Shavuot, while seeking Him in one of the enclaves of the Temple courtyard, without warning, suddenly, there was the sound of a mighty rushing wind and the power of Elohim fell upon us.

"Shimon, from Capernaum, left the enclave, part of Solomon's Porch, where we had been praying and ventured into the Temple courtyard. Under the power of God's Spirit he began to speak boldly to the massive crowd of Jews who were at the Temple for Shavuot. They were already wondering what was happening after hearing the sound of the mighty wind. He proclaimed to them that the Messiah of Israel lives. I had never before seen him like that. It was hard to believe that this was the same fisherman who had worked with my father. Suddenly, he had stature and passion. His words were tangible—like arrows piercing the hearts of his hearers. The thousands gathered there in the Temple courts hung on his every word as he spoke with incredible confidence and astounding authority about eternal life and their need to repent. That day our number grew from 120 to several thousand.

"That was all of ten years ago. Tens of thousands of Jews have found peace through Yeshua, their Messiah, since that day. And yes, I did find a husband, and we now have four children, all of whom, except the baby of course, have placed their trust in the Messiah, much to our delight.

"The future is bright. We know that soon Yeshua will return and this time He will set up His kingdom on earth, but first we must spread His message to the rest of Israel and to the Jews scattered farther abroad.

"Oh, and let me tell you the latest development that has everyone talking. We recently heard the strangest news from

Shimon. He claimed that Elohim told him to go into the house of a Gentile, a Roman commander named Cornelius, and to preach there. This caused something of a commotion, as we Jews would never normally go into the house of a Gentile.[1] They are saying, however, that when Shimon arrived there was a huge crowd gathered. As he began to teach, the *Ruach Hakodesh*, the Spirit of God, fell upon the people there just as He did upon us at Shavuot, and they began to speak in tongues and praise Elohim!

"Shimon thought, *If the Spirit is falling upon them as He did on us, how can we stop them from being immersed in water?* Can you believe it? We are all amazed that Gentiles are now following the Jewish Messiah and are even being immersed in water! No one is going to believe this!"

The movie ended and the lights came on. I turned to Ariel and said, "I don't understand. Why was she surprised that Gentiles were believing in Jesus? Virtually the only people I know today who believe in Him are Gentiles!"

"Let us not run too far ahead. All will be clear soon enough. Now sit down again," he gently said, "intermission is over." The lights dimmed and once again, just as before, a date and place appeared on the screen.

Note

1. To be clear, the Torah does not forbid fellowship with non-Jews, but the Pharisees placed a huge emphasis on ritual purity. Because they could never be sure if a Gentile had come into contact with something or someone unclean, it was far easier just to decree that you could not go into the home of a Gentile; that way you would know that you were not ritually unclean.

Chapter Three

"HaShem, Where Are You?"

1099 CE, Jerusalem

This time I could hear a voice, but there was no one being interviewed that I could see. "I am a Jew, and I am thirteen. My family has lived in Jerusalem for generations, going all the way back to Yehoshua (Joshua) son of Nun. But that family line is coming to an end. My name is not important since I will be dead soon. The Crusaders, of whom we have been living in dread, have finally broken into the city. They have already killed scores of Muslim soldiers. We Jews, those of us who are still alive, have gathered in the great synagogue hoping against hope for mercy, but I can already smell the smoke. Soon, we will all be dead.

"We've heard stories of these Christians who have come from every corner of Europe all the way to Jerusalem. If the rumors are true, and we pray to God they are not, the Crusaders have pillaged and slaughtered whole Jewish communities all along their way. We were told they were coming to *liberate the Holy Land* from the *Muslim infidels.* And truth be told, the Muslims have not been too kind to the Christians here in Jerusalem. Churches have been destroyed and over the centuries Muslims have murdered scores of them. The Christians had apparently had enough. But what does that have to do with me? I am not a Muslim!

"Their religious leaders, we're told, have promised them that if they die in battle, all their sins will be forgiven and they'll go to Heaven[1]—because they are serving Jesus Christ. But *where will I go if I die today?* I'm scared.

"We have always gotten along with our Muslim overlords—at least in my lifetime. They haven't persecuted us. In fact, my father Isaac and my older brother Michael fought valiantly with the Muslims to protect Jerusalem. Those Muslims are now dead—slaughtered one after another by the Crusaders as they broke into the city.

"They arrived in early June and surrounded our walls. Jerusalem is an isolated city, barely protected by its ramparts and surrounded by mountainous deserts. Once they encompassed us, we knew it was only a matter of time before they would break through. We could get no food into the city and they poisoned our water supplies. In mid-June, as I was helping the fighters on the wall, we could see them, see their large banners with huge crosses on them. That is their symbol. It's painted on their shields and sewn onto their tunics.

"Finally, two days ago around midnight, just over a month after their arrival, they broke through our defenses and took the city. While some escaped, I don't think there is a single living Muslim left in Jerusalem. As soon as they stormed through the gates, the Christians began to kill everyone around them, indiscriminately—men, women, and children, Jews and Muslims alike. There was blood everywhere. Bodies are stacked one upon another wherever you look. I have never seen anything like it—so much death. The stench is unbearable. People begged, they pleaded for their lives, but the Crusaders showed no mercy. The last image their victims saw was the vivid cross worn by their killers. It was as if these men were possessed.

"Our family, along with about 1,000 other Jews, has taken refuge in the great synagogue. Actually, the Crusaders' leader, Godfrey de Bouillon, drove us in here. This de Bouillon, it is said, is hoping to kill every Jew because he is convinced that every Jew is responsible for the death of Jesus. I don't know much about the New Covenant, but I thought it was a book about love and forgiveness, not killing and murder. Did this Jesus go around butchering women and children as His so-called followers are doing? And what does a thirteen-year-old boy, just bar Mitzvah'd, have to do with the death of a Jew over 1,000 years ago?

"Not that it matters what I think. Death has invaded our city. Hope is all but gone. They are mercilessly cruel. They have already murdered thousands of Jews throughout the city in the past twenty-four hours. We are the only ones left.

"How could it be that less than a month ago I was celebrating my bar Mitzvah at the Western Wall of the Temple Mount? I never dreamt that I wouldn't see my fourteenth birthday.

Such a day it was, reading from the Torah and chanting the blessings. They told me I became a man that day. Little did I know how quickly that would be the truth. Instead of playing with my friends or helping my father in our shop, I was supplying arrows to fighters on the walls of Jerusalem, fighting for our lives and watching Crusader arrows fly back at us.

"We had heard the stories of what they did in Europe. At first this was considered purely a war against the Muslims. But in Europe, greed and bloodlust perverted their cause. They reasoned, 'Why wait until we get to Muslim territory, when there are Jews, *Christ-killers*, all throughout Europe?' I overheard horrific tales coming from my parents—stories of rape and slaughter, stories of Jews being offered protection for money and then being killed by the very ones they'd paid!

"Inside the synagogue, I huddle together with my sisters, younger brothers, and my parents. My older brother is dead. We were told he was killed yesterday, shortly after the Crusaders broke through. He was sixteen. Will I be next? I'm too young to die. What have we ever done to these people?

"I will never grow up, never marry or be a parent. Today the Crusaders will kill me.

"Smoke suddenly makes its presence felt. Both the smell and sight of sinister tendrils of grey smoke curling their way under the heavy locked doors relay the dire extremity of our situation.

"HaShem! God!

"Flames begin licking their way in through the barred windows. It is getting hotter. The godforsaken savages are going to burn us alive. Even over the screaming inside the synagogue, I can hear the Crusaders singing hymns to this Jesus

Christ. What kind of religion is this? They are burning us to death and they sing of love? They have slaughtered nearly every human being in the city and they rejoice to the smell of burning flesh?

"The people who are praying, now increase their supplication in fervency and volume. Others collapse in shock. All are in a state of panic. Some are screaming and beating on the door. Others seek to shelter their children from the smoke as most back away from the walls, which are becoming scorching hot. The flames are now clearly visible on every side. The realization that their families and little ones really are burning to death finally becomes an inescapable reality against a backdrop of voices singing *Christ, We Adore Thee!*

"Incredibly, as the flames wrap themselves around rafters, which are beginning to collapse, and the intensifying heat causes some, mercifully, to succumb to smoke suffocation, the sound of these murderous Crusaders singing hymns to their Jesus Christ escalates.

"Yet, they say this Jesus was a Jew.

"It's inconceivable! They are singing to a Jew while they burn us alive for being Jews!

"HaShem! Where are You?"

I was angry! "Ariel, how could this happen? This is so different from the first story. What changed? What happened to healing the sick and raising the dead to life? Now they are putting the living to death! Clearly Jesus is not telling them to murder in His name, for His cause! I don't understand."

"David, it gets worse," he put a comforting hand on my shoulder. "You will have to bear with not understanding for a bit longer. In time, all will be explained." Once more the lights went out.

Note

1. Religion hasn't changed much in the past thousand years. Al Qaeda, Hamas, and other Islamic fundamentalist groups have sweetened the pot by throwing in seventy-two virgins for suicide bombers who die in the "line of duty." Yet, they have only copied the manipulative tricks of the Roman Catholic Church. How easy it is to motivate a poor peasant to fight for you when you promise him Heaven. We know from history that many of the Crusaders raped, pillaged, and killed without mercy. And yet, Church leaders went outside of scriptural authority, guaranteeing these men a place with Yeshua.

Chapter Four

IMMERSION OR EXPULSION

1496 CE, Tangier, Morocco

A young man is sitting in a chair.

"My name is Christophe. At least that is my *baptized* name. I am a twenty-three-year-old Jewish man. Several years ago we had to make an extremely difficult decision as a family. The authorities told us that if we didn't convert to Catholicism and join the Church, we would have to leave Spain.

"We were Jews, but Spain was home. Many of my father's friends had already joined the Church and been baptized. For a while they secretly continued to be our friends, but then, one by one, we ceased to see them.

"Their children were not allowed to play with us any-more. It wasn't their fault. Now that they had left Judaism, the

Church forbade them to intermix with *non-converted Jews—* we were poison. The punishment, should they be caught, might well be death!

"For many, many months my father wrestled with this decision. While many of his friends had already joined the Church and been baptized, many others had chosen to pack their bags and leave for other countries, such as Morocco to the south. However, they had to leave almost everything behind. Property was sold for a fraction of its worth. Jewelry was traded for food. We heard reports that some of our friends had been robbed and even killed on the way to their new life. My father did not want this for our family.

"One evening, he sat us all down and explained that if we wanted to survive and maintain our current quality of life, we would have to play their game. He told us that we would be baptized as Catholics, but remain Jewish in our hearts. This is what many Jewish families had done.

"We knew, and our tormentors knew as well, that this had nothing to do with religion; it was about politics. Spain was seeking to unify the country under Roman Catholicism. In fact, virtually all *non-Catholics* were suffering the same fate as we were.

"When the day came, not only were we baptized, but my father had to read a public confession denouncing Judaism as a demonic religion. He promised never to celebrate any Jewish holiday or even associate with non-baptized Jews. We were told that if we ever returned to Judaism, *in any form*, we would face severe retribution from the Church. They could confiscate our property and expel us from Spain. Even death was on the table. This was one of the worst days of my life. I felt so sick and dirty. How could we have compromised to this extent, trading in our faith for acceptance?"

This was how I felt. Although no one in twenty-first century America was threatening me with expulsion, I knew, like Christophe, that to become a Christian was to deny who I was. He continued.

"We were called *Conversos*, new Christians, or the more derogatory title, *Marranos*—meaning 'pigs'! Despite giving an appearance of welcoming us into the Church, they did all they could to humiliate us. It was clear that we would never be permitted to be one of them and yet we couldn't be who we were. We were stuck somewhere in the middle of no-man's land.

"My father reminded us many times that we were still Jews and would always be Jews, but that we must be very careful. Everything had to be done in secret. Just a refusal to eat pork was considered sufficient reason to have a person arrested. We could trust no one, as the Church had its spies. Imagine that, a religious institution hiring people to spy on their subjects to ensure truly Catholic behavior. How could such a system claim to represent God? And how did they expect such coercion to spawn true devotion? Well, of course, they didn't. This was all about Spain, not about religious devotion.

"Outside the home we maintained the facade of being good Christians while inside the home we remained God-fearing Jews. We lived this way for many years and while I carried with me a permanent feeling of uneasy guilt, we were able to remain in Spain. All that came to a very abrupt end, however, when my father was finally arrested.

"A *friend* came by to greet us on the Sabbath. Candles had been lit to welcome in the day of rest. We thought this friend could be trusted. In fact, he was a spy. In the beginning we had been much more careful—*especially* on Friday nights. Spies were encouraged to poke around the homes of *Conversos* on *Erev Shabbat*, Friday evenings, hoping to catch someone honoring the Fourth Commandment. Lighting Shabbat candles, saying the Jewish blessings, and singing the songs I grew up singing on Erev Shabbat were forbidden under the threat of death.

"Tragically, we had grown careless; we'd relaxed our caution. Three days later they came for my father. He was arrested and brought before an inquisition. The Church then tortured him until he confessed to the wretched crime of lighting Sabbath candles.

"My father was given a choice. He could repent of his deceit and take a part in a *verguenza*—a 'shaming,' in which he would be stripped to the waist in freezing temperatures (it was winter). He would then be paraded through the streets, led by monks and mocked by the crowds, suffering countless other indignities all along the way. The other option was to be burned at the stake.

"We knew additional punishments would be imposed once my father accepted the *verguenza*. They would expect him to turn in other *Conversos* who were secretly living as Jews, but he had been humiliated enough. Hadn't he already denied his faith, in public, for our protection? And now these Christians wanted to add insult to injury. No, it was too much. He would not!

"When my father declared he would not recant, he was taken back into custody and sentenced by the religious magistrates, apparent followers of this Christ, to be burned alive.

Yes, my father would be tied to a stake and endure the inconceivable agony of burning to death as the fire slowly, painfully, consumed him.

"All this in the name of their religion!

"When the day came, my family watched. We did not want him to die alone. This was it. The *religious police* were going to kill my father—take him from me because we lit candles. They brought him out with his hands bound behind his back. He was tied to a stake. He said not a word. Even when the flames engulfed him, burning his living body, he would not scream. He was telling us, without words, *'Don't give in...don't compromise...be strong...'* and then, my father died.

"After my father was murdered and all our property confiscated, we did what we should have done in the first place. We made the journey to Gibraltar and sailed on to Morocco, where we settled into a thriving Jewish community in the city of Tangier. I miss my father deeply and I will never forget his courage. I live to honor his memory and to honor Judaism, for which he laid down his life.

"Oh, and by the way, please don't call me Christophe. My name is Jacob."

"Ariel, I can't handle much more of this. I studied the Inquisitions in college, but that was just words in a book. This is different. Those poor people! How could Christians act this way?"

"Patience, David, patience."

At this point, my mind had ceased trying to determine whether I was imagining all this or really talking to an angel and traveling through time. My emotions were fully gripped by what I had just seen. All that we Jews had ever wanted was the freedom to make a life for ourselves, but it seems there was always someone seeking to prevent that and to persecute us. I thought, *My God, Hitler didn't have to look too far back in history to find a pretext for killing Jews. He needed only to look at the Church.* And then it hit me.

"No Ariel! I can't! I won't watch it! Take me back! It's too much..."

Chapter Five

HORROR!

The lights dimmed, but this time I wouldn't watch. I sought to get up in order to escape and found that I couldn't. I was literally glued to my seat. I yanked and jerked, but nothing worked. I was stuck there. Finally I resigned myself. On the screen were the words:

1945 CE, Bergen-Belsen Concentration Camp

And a young boy began to tell his story of horror.

"My name is Tuvia Lebowitz. I am sixteen years old. Today, I am free. But while my body is free my soul will ever be captive to memories and horrors too painful to utter. My mother is dead. My father is dead. My sisters may be dead. My little brother is dead. And I have not eaten a proper meal in five years.

"It all began when I was ten years old. My father was a university professor. We lived a comfortable life and I was happy. My friends were Jewish and Polish, but over time fewer and fewer of my Polish friends were permitted to play with me. I was very sad about it and so were most of them. But one day one of those boys, Jacek, came up to me as I walked home from my violin lesson, and yelled, 'You Jew! You killed Christ. You will also suffer!'

"I had no idea what he was talking about, but the anger with which he said it sent a shiver up my spine like I had never known before. The coming years, however, would bring ample fulfillment of the premonition I felt in that moment.

"The day came when all the Jews of Warsaw, nearly a third of the city's population, were required to leave our homes and move inside an area that was smaller than two and a half percent of the city. Four hundred thousand people were living in an area that was designed for just over three thousand!

"Once inside, no one was permitted to leave the *ghetto*, as it came to be called, without a work permit. And these were restricted mainly to older people. Fortunately, my father was one of the few to be granted one, although his status as a university professor was now relegated to *factory worker*.

"Over time, food in the ghetto became scarce. We were surviving on fewer than 200 calories a day. My father would sell some of our possessions to keep us from starving. It wasn't uncommon to see dead bodies on the streets. Some starved, others froze to death, and some just gave up. Hunger and disease were the two biggest killers. There were, of course, those who told us this would all pass, that we had simply to obey the rules and in time all would return to normal. *They can't kill all of us*, they reasoned.

"The day came when we were informed that trains were to transfer us out of the overcrowded ghetto. We were told that families were to be resettled in better areas in the country-side. It was a welcomed prospect and I hoped that we would be among those selected to leave this dirty, congested place for the country. But then rumors began to trickle in that the families who were leaving were not going to a better place, but to concentration camps where some were killed and others were forced to work for the Nazis. Many simply refused to give credence to these stories while the rest of us were terrified. But again, our leaders assured us that these were just rumors and everything would soon be all right.

"And then our name was called—we would be going to the countryside. We took all our belongings, which weren't many, and boarded a train. There were no seats like on the trains I used to love to ride when we traveled from Warsaw to visit my grandparents in Lodz. *My grandparents*? What had become of them?

"We crowded into the cattle cars and just when I thought I had found a place to stand, I was shoved backward. The car was already full, but they just kept herding more and more people into the car. *Where was my little brother?*

"The heat was simply unbearable and almost immediately, the complaining began: *We are going to die in here. Move. I need more room. They might as well bury us in this train as we'll never survive.* I could hardly breathe, we were packed so tightly together. It was terrifying. After a few hours, people needed to relieve themselves and with no facilities, the stench was horrible. They had told us things would get better, but they only got worse. No one could have imagined that we'd be in that cattle car for four days without food or water. Sleep was nearly impossible, but after a couple of days you fell into a state of stupor where you could be asleep and awake at the same time. I would dream that I was back at home only to be jolted out of my fantasy, as someone would faint or cry out, returning me to this living nightmare.

"After three days, a woman standing just a few spaces from me collapsed. She was dead. She didn't appear to be much older than my mother, whose sobbing could barely be suppressed as my father sought to console her.

"I had just turned thirteen. I was supposed to have had my bar Mitzvah by now. I would have stood proudly in the synagogue, chanted from the Torah, and endured the praises of my family, friends, and relatives. Instead, here I was enduring suffering like I had never thought possible. How much more of this could we take?

"The next day we arrived at a work camp. We were taken off the train and separated into different groups. When my mother was told to follow the women, she became hysterical. She grabbed my little brother and begged the guards not to separate them. They ripped him from her and when she protested, the butt of a guard's rifle found the back of her head, knocking her to the ground. I was in shock. Was this really happening? I wanted to fight, but I couldn't move.

"And then, when it seemed things couldn't get any worse, one of the other guards solved the dilemma by pulling out his handgun and putting a bullet through Chaim's head, with as much emotion and effort as he might have used pouring himself a glass of water. My little brother lay dead on the ground, blood streaming from the gaping hole in his head. The image haunts me to this day, and always will.

"No one cried, no one screamed—we were simply in shock. Surely what we had just witnessed with our own eyes didn't really happen. Chaim couldn't be dead. And yet, he was. A five-year old Jewish life was of little consequence to the Nazis.

"Father and I were herded into the men's line, while my grief-dazed mother, still in shock, was pulled into another line. We would now work for our tormentors. My two sisters, barely twelve and fifteen at the time, were placed with other girls their age. Only later did I learn what would happen to these girls. They would be used to service the Nazis. Fortunately, I was too young to understand such things. It would have been too much for me. But now I am a man. I'm sixteen and know exactly what they did to my sisters. I don't even know if they are still alive.

"My mother only survived a few months. The devastation of watching her baby, her youngest son, murdered before her eyes, robbed her of the will to live. She was inconsolable. The other women covered for her as best they could, but soon it became clear to the guards that not only was she not doing her share of the work, she no longer cared whether she lived or died. Mercifully, before she could be sent to the gas chambers or terminated, she was gone. One morning she simply didn't wake up.

"This happened three months after we arrived, but my father and I only found out a year later. I didn't even weep. By that time I was completely numb. Death was everywhere.

It had become too familiar to warrant a response. I was sure it was only a matter of time before these monsters or this godforsaken place would kill me as well. My father, on the other hand, was completely undone by this news. He held on for another year, for my sake, but in the end, hopelessness, despair, and malnutrition claimed him. Like my mother, one morning he simply did not wake up.

"At fifteen I was, at best, the man of the house, or at worst, the only one left in the house. Part of me hoped my sisters were dead. The thought of some sleazy, overweight, Nazi officer with alcohol-laden breath, laying his hands on either one of them, sickened me.

"I was transferred to Auschwitz, a death camp, in early 1944. As I passed through a gate a guard hissed at me, '*You killed Jesus Christ; now we will kill you.*' Jacek was right. They blamed me for the death of a man who died 2,000 years ago—a Jew no less, someone they themselves would have killed, given the opportunity. I was fifteen; I had never killed anyone! And I wondered, in passing, what exactly had become of Jacek. For all I knew he could be living in our house. Or maybe he'd joined the Hitler Youth, and was now training to fight for the Nazis.

"The guards obviously agreed with Jacek as they forewarned us of our fate, their retribution for our crime of killing Christ. The butt of a rifle in my stomach accompanied the threat, in this instance. How much more could I take?

"They then moved us to Birkenau, one of the camps adjacent to Auschwitz. There in a red brick building, which from the outside appeared harmless enough, they had built fake shower blocks. Instead of encountering clean water, unsuspecting victims were led into the showers and asphyxiated by poisonous gas.

"This was one of the cruelest and yet most efficient tricks of the Nazis. How do you kill thousands of people at one time and keep them from panicking, or worse, revolting? You give them a cake of soap and tell them they are going to receive the first shower they have had in weeks, or months.

"The red brick building was just one of many such death machines. Its only distinction lay in the fact that it had been the first, or so I was told. I know this because it was my job to remove the bodies. Every day, all day, I dragged the lifeless corpses of my people out of the gas chambers, loading them onto carts to transport them to the crematoria, all the while hoping against hope that I wouldn't share their fate.

"I was surrounded by death. I no longer felt human, so I guess they'd won. Clearly that was the subliminal message the Nazis transmitted by transporting us in cattle cars. In truth, I felt just like an animal seeking to survive the barren winter—only winter was now going into its fourth year.

"Finally, in January 1945, the Germans began to demolish the gas chambers. Our captors blew them up, one by one. They seemed intent on getting rid of the evidence. You could see the fear in their eyes. Was this war coming to an end? Would we soon be free? Was someone coming to rescue us?

"Our hopes of freedom, however, were soon crushed. The barely living were rounded up and ordered to march from Auschwitz to God knows where. Thousands who were too weak were simply left behind. It was freezing, the dead of winter. Tens of thousands of us marched and marched. It was nothing for someone in front of you to simply collapse. Those who couldn't walk were left for dead. I passed hundreds of dead bodies. Who knows if they were dead when they hit the ground or simply froze in the snow? What would once have shocked me had become commonplace. A dead body, even that of child, barely fazed me. What had they done to me?

"I had determined from the outset that I would survive—if not for me, in the faint hope that I might one day see my sisters again.

"Finally, we arrived at Bergen-Belsen. By April, most of the guards had fled, but the remaining ones seemed perversely intent on leaving no inmate alive. After several days with no food or water, more and more Jews began to collapse, go crazy, or simply die. Bodies were everywhere. Typhus was spreading. Surely my body would soon succumb to these deathly conditions.

"And then, yesterday, April 15, 1945, five days after my sixteenth birthday, British troops arrived and—miracle of miracles—we were emancipated!

"Now I am free. Or so they tell me. What does that even mean at this point? My parents and little brother are dead. My sisters, if alive, have been violated repeatedly for years. *What will become of me*, of Tuvia Lebowitz?"

By now I was sobbing inconsolably.

"David," the angel called out. I didn't answer. "*David Lebowitz!*" he called out again.

Chapter Six

FROM CHAYA TO TUVIA...
HOW DID WE GET HERE?

Still sobbing, I cried out, "But why?"

"I told you it would be hard, but He has a task for you, and you have to feel it deeply so that you can deliver it effectively, even though it pains you—even though you feel like your very guts are being ripped out."

I calmed down. "You know, he never told us what happened there. Not even my father knows the full story. After they came to the states, it was as if they took a vow of silence. Not just my grandparents, but my great aunts as well. My God." I sighed, "What had they suffered?"

Sobbing again, I could not get the image of my grandfather being tormented as a young Jew in Poland out of my mind. Finally, I looked up at Ariel and asked, "How in the world did a message as pure as the one the woman from Galilee shared, get so corrupted? She talked about a Man of love and immeasurable compassion, and one thousand years later, His followers are marching across Europe killing Jews as part of their devotion to Him. Help me understand!"

Ariel answered, "Indeed, these were *religious* people—but incredibly corrupted in their understanding of what true devotion to God really was. Yes, they were religious, but they were not practicing what is written in the Bible. Religion, apart from a true relationship with God, kills. Unsubmitted men will manipulate it for their own ends, be it lust for money or power."

"But didn't they read the Bible?" I asked.

"In time, David. All will be explained in time."

"In the story of the family in Spain, the Jews were being told, 'Convert or leave!' The Church there seemed more like the KGB or present-day Iran."

"You are correct, David. Those who converted were watched constantly by the Church to make sure they did not return to Judaism. *Conversos* accused of maintaining ties to or secretly practicing Judaism were cruelly punished."

I was struggling to process this.

"The Church of the Middle Ages had certainly ceased to look anything like what the Holy Spirit had birthed on that warm summer day on Shavuot, 30 CE, when the Jewish man, Simon Peter, preached so powerfully on the Temple steps, birthing a powerful revival. Instead, Rome had become a combination of greed, power, and politics dressed in the robes of religion. The good news had not merely been robbed of its

Jewish roots, but of its purity and power, its message of salvation and reconciliation to God."

Yes, I had read about Peter, the Christian evangelist, during my search for truth. But it hadn't dawned on me at the time that he was *Jewish*. But, of course he was! It all took place here in Israel.

"I am sure that you also noticed that the Jews in the first story had no qualms about believing that Yeshua was the Messiah. Not only was Chaya Jewish, but she met Him on His way to heal the daughter of one of the leaders in the local synagogue. Those first-century Jews were able to evaluate Yeshua without bias. However, two thousand years later, after the worst kind of anti-Semitism coming forth from those who claimed to represent Him, it is nearly impossible for a Jewish person to look at Yeshua without prejudice."

"We are taught, if not directly then indirectly, that one of the very definitions of being Jewish is that we don't believe in Jesus," I emphasized.

"When I was in elementary school, we had a discussion at the bus stop involving several Jewish children and Christian children. We were seeking to define the differences between our religions. After a lengthy exchange of views—our bus was always late—the 'Council of Cutshaw Avenue' concluded that the primary difference was that they believed in a man named Jesus and we did not. End of subject."

"Listen to the testimony of this rabbi." A man wearing a yarmulke appeared on the massive screen and began to speak.

> Growing up in an orthodox Jewish household, I held great antipathy toward Jesus. The very name reminded me of the suffering laid upon Jewish

communities for two thousand years: persecutions, forced conversions, expulsions, inquisitions, false accusations, degradations, economic exile, taxation, pogroms, stereotyping, ghettoization, and systematic extermination. All this incomprehensible violence and cruelty against us, against our friends and families, committed in the name of a Jew!

In my neighborhood, we did not even mention his name.[1]

"This rabbi, along with countless other Jews, could not help but factor in the Church's wide-ranging record of ungodly behavior when considering Yeshua. But what if Jewish people were able to appraise both the person and the message of Yeshua without any knowledge of either how the rabbis have viewed Him or how the Church has misrepresented Him?" Ariel pondered. "What if they could read the New Covenant without this bias?"

"I don't know that it could ever happen."

"Perhaps not, but you are with me, David, to receive an honest, accurate picture of this Man and His followers. No, it will not erase what you have learned from history, but it will give you the knowledge and capacity to discern history so that you will be able to differentiate Yeshua from religious fanatics who caused great damage to the Jewish people in His name."

Note

1. Shmuley Boteach, *Kosher Jesus* (Jerusalem: Gefen Publishing House, 2012), ix.

Chapter Seven

WHO KILLED JESUS?

Ariel continued, "While the Holocaust, unlike the Crusades and the Inquisitions, was not explicitly religious, the Church had set the stage. I am sure you have read the old axiom about Jews being called *Christ Killers*. The Nazis and others throughout the centuries have long enjoyed the employment of this claim as a satanic pretext for blood libels, pogroms, and Holocaust-scale genocide. In short, it is the excuse for nearly every perverted form of persecution that anti-Semitism has ever staged. And the enemy utilized all of this to further alienate Jews from their Jewish Messiah.

"Yes, *Christ Killer* has become a common moniker for Jews during these past 1,900 years. Under this theme, Jewish blood has flowed down the streets of not only Jerusalem, but numerous other cities as well."

"It never made any sense to me," I shared, "how an entire race of people over thousands of years of existence could be responsible for the killing of one man."

"Well David, who do you think *really* killed Yeshua?"

"I could make a case for the Romans, as Jews were forbidden from enforcing a death penalty. But I do know that it was Jewish people who handed Him over to the Romans."

Ariel helped, "Actually, David, it was primarily the Jewish *leaders*, not the people, who had a problem with Yeshua. I want you to read this."

As the words came out of his mouth, they appeared written in fire. Two passages of Scripture were before me, with some commentary in between. They were suspended in air and close enough for me to touch. I was in awe. "Go ahead, read!" I did.

> *Now when the chief priests and Pharisees heard His parables, they perceived that He was speaking of them. But when they sought to lay hands on* [Yeshua], *they feared the multitudes* [of Jews]... (Matthew 21:45-46 NKJV).

"In secret they found Him praying with His disciples at night, and only then did they dare arrest Him. In the morning, the day they planned to execute Him, the residents of Jerusalem were stunned to see this beloved Rabbi condemned. Read this next one."

Again, I read as I was asked.

And a great multitude of the people followed Him...
who also mourned and lamented Him (Luke
23:27 NKJV).

"Yeshua was taken to the home of Pilate. He was the
Roman governor over the province of Judea. Read on."

Again, emblazoned in fire I saw the Scriptures, but this
time certain words were highlighted:

Then the detachment of soldiers with its commander
*and the **Jewish officials** arrested Jesus...* (John
18:12).

*Then the **Jewish leaders** took Jesus from Caiaphas*
to the palace of the Roman governor... (John 18:28).

"While in the Greek," Ariel shared, "it merely says 'they'
in verse twenty-eight, it is understood that the 'they' in this
verse is referring to the Jewish officials in verse twelve."

"Ariel, I was told that the entire city of Jerusalem was
shouting for Him to be crucified. That would be more than
just a few leaders."

"Nowhere in the New Testament does it claim that the
entire city was calling for His death, but a crowd of people,
out of about a half a million who were in the city at the time...
and even this crowd had been worked up by the religious
leaders. But you are not the first to wrongly assume this. As
you will see on our journey, Yeshua was loved by the Jewish
masses and they came from all over the region to hear Him
teach. I want you to read a message that a Messianic Jew sent
to a Christian author on Facebook."

"*Facebook?* An angel who's into Facebook?"

"Well, I don't have my own account, but yes David, we kind of know about *everything*. Read!" Immediately, a Facebook page containing a message appeared on the screen.

Dear Martin,

My name is Avi Marks. I came across your website and I found your article, "Jesus and the Jews" very interesting; it was certainly well researched.

May I just offer one critique that will help your Jewish readers? You used the phrase "the Jews" over fifty times. Sometimes it is just part of the phrase "king of *the Jews*." But more often than not, you are referring to the group of men who brought Yeshua to Pilate. John 18:12 makes it clear that it was not "the Jews" who brought Yeshua to Pilate, but "Jewish officials," "officers of the Jews," or the "Temple guards," just to quote a few modern translations.

The problem with the way you use the term "the Jews," is that it makes it appear as if you are saying *all of the Jews*. There are a few times when you correctly say Jewish religious leaders, but for the most part you simply say, "the Jews."

It is true that in the Greek, John at certain times simply writes the phrase "the Jews" (John 18:14; 19:7,12), but there can be no doubt that he is referring to the Jewish leadership. In fact, some modern English translations, such as the New International Version, actually translate those passages using the phrase "the Jewish leaders" as opposed to "the

Jews" even though they know that is not what the Greek says. How can they be so bold?

I'll explain. Take a look at John 18:14: *"Now it was Caiaphas who advised the Jews that it was expedient that one man should die for the people"* (NKJV).

In this passage it states clearly that Caiaphas was speaking to "the Jews." However, if we turn back a few pages we can see exactly to whom Caiaphas was speaking:

> Then the **chief priests and the Pharisees called a meeting of the Sanhedrin....** *Then one of them, named Caiaphas, who was high priest that year, spoke up, "You know nothing at all! You do not realize that it is better for you that one man die for the people than that the whole nation perish"* (John 11:47,49-50).

So "the Jews" of John 18 and 19 are Jewish leaders, not the Jewish population. It would have been strange for those who flocked to hear Him teach—many of whom were healed—to suddenly call for His execution. Scripture makes it clear that a very large number of Jews followed Yeshua, even some high-profile leaders like Nicodemus.

> *When He had come into Jerusalem, all the city was moved, saying, "Who is this?" So the multitudes said, "This is Jesus, the prophet from Nazareth...* (Matthew 21:10-11 NKJV).

Many of the people believed in Him, and said, "When the Christ comes, will He do more signs than these which this Man has done?" (John 7:31 NKJV).

Nevertheless, even among the [Jewish] *rulers many believed in Him..."* (John 12:42 NKJV).

John records it was the leaders who shouted for Him to be crucified. "As soon as the chief priests and their officials saw him, they shouted, 'Crucify! Crucify!'" (John 19:6).

In the other accounts, where it mentions the crowd joining in, it seems clear they were manipulated by the leaders. As Matthew writes, "But the chief priests and the elders *persuaded the crowd* to ask for Barabbas and to have Jesus executed" (Matt. 27:20). We are not told the means by which they persuaded the crowd, but bribery would have been the common resource of the time. (They had paid witnesses to turn in false evidence at the trial the day before.) Clearly this persuaded crowd did not represent the people of Israel, as there were approximately 100,000 Jews living in Jerusalem, and because it was Passover, there could have been upward of another 500,000 visitors in Jerusalem at that time. Do you really think there were 600,000 Jews at Pilate's Jerusalem palace?

This may appear to you as nitpicking, but on the contrary, it is extremely important, because so many Jews have been falsely blamed for the death of Yeshua, even killed as part of this accusation of being *Christ-killers*. It is important therefore to make clear that it was primarily the Jewish leaders who were jealous of Yeshua who went to Pilate. The multitudes loved Him.

Thanks for your time.

Blessings,

Avi Marks

"This is crazy, Ariel. The entire Jewish nation has been blamed for the actions of a small group of jealous, politically oriented leaders and a manipulated crowd."

"I know, it is twisted and sad, but you should know not all the leaders were jealous of Him. Let the words of one of the passages that you just read, John 12:42, sink in." Again the words appeared in fire as Ariel read them:

> *Yet at the same time many even among the* [Jewish] *leaders believed in him. But because of the Pharisees they would not openly acknowledge their faith for fear they would be put out of the synagogue* (John 12:42).

"These Jewish leaders believed, but were afraid. *Nicodemus*, to whom Avi made reference, was a Jewish leader, a member of the Sanhedrin, in fact. He was initially scared to be caught even speaking with Yeshua and so met with Him in secret, but eventually he became one of His most ardent followers."

Another passage in fire appeared.

Now there was a Pharisee, a man named Nico-demus who was a member of the Jewish ruling council. He came to Jesus at night and said, "Rabbi, we know that you are a teacher who has come from God. For no one could perform the signs you are doing if God were not with him (John 3:1-2).

"David, it is entirely false to claim, firstly, that all Israel rejected Yeshua, as you will see in the coming lessons; and secondly, that the Jews, or even the Romans for that matter, were responsible for killing Yeshua.

"Let me put this dreadful argument to rest—*I know who killed Yeshua.*"

"Who?" I asked, wondering what he would say. Wars have been fought over this question and now an angel sent from Heaven itself was about to tell me. *Unreal!* I thought.

"*You* did! *You* killed Him, David!"

Chapter Eight

"ME? A KILLER?"

"What!?" I was incredulous. What was this angel talking about? "I am only twenty-eight years old. How could I have possibly killed Jesus?"

"Your sin nailed those spikes into His hands and feet," Ariel said with a holy passion, which prior to this he had not expressed. "It was your selfishness and rebellion that placed Yeshua on that Cross. Yes, David, you are the guilty one!

"But not just you, David, the whole world lies guilty before Him. It was the sin of the world—yours and that of everyone who came before you or will come after. If the world is looking for Christ's killer, it needs only to look in the mirror.

"Do you really think, David, that anyone could have killed the Divine Messiah without God's permission? Many times they tried to kill Him, but they could not, not until Yeshua allowed them to. Yeshua said it Himself. Go ahead and read, David."

The words of fire that were still there reformed into another passage and I read them aloud:

> *No one takes my life from me. I give my life of my own free will. I have the authority to give my life, and I have the authority to take my life back again...* (John 10:18 GW).

"This is in the New Testament?" I asked, astonished. He nodded. "How many Jews have been mistreated, even killed in the name of this blood libel, when all along the truth that He chose to die was plainly written in their Bible?" *I could feel myself getting angry again.*

"The Church erased the Jewishness of Yeshua and then blamed the entire Jewish nation for His death. This is why people, like you David, need to stop listening to what others tell them and do their own research. Notice that I am not teaching you anything that is not backed up by the historical account of Scripture...*and I have direct access to the Truth Himself.* When humankind has been given the divine revelation contained in the Bible, why would he then look to a human source to tell him whether or not Yeshua is the Messiah?

"Do you know how many times I have seen Jewish people, just like yourself, enter a season where the Father sends the Holy Spirit to draw them, to woo them, to attract them to Yeshua? They don't know why, but they are suddenly curious; they want to know. Seemingly out of nowhere, there is suddenly a deep concern over their soul. Is there a Heaven?

Is there a hell? Where will I spend eternity? This is how the Father brings new sheep into the fold. Yeshua Himself said when He walked the earth that 'No one can come to Me unless the Father who sent Me draws them....' It is recorded in John 6:44.

"You know what most Jewish people do when they go through that season? Watch..."

The lights dimmed as the movie screen came back to life. I was stunned to see *me* there in the video! I was walking into Rabbi Goodman's office. Oh, I remember it well. I went there to confide in him—to tell him what I was going through, spiritually. When I spoke to him about my desire to find God, he was initially happy. Even when I told him I had researched different religions from the Far East, he remained pleasant, nodding benignly. But the minute I shared with him that I was intrigued by the story of Jesus, he became agitated, even angry.

"How could you, David? Your grandfather would roll over in his grave if he could hear you talking such nonsense. Don't you know what those people have done to us in His name? *And now you want to join them!*" He was getting angrier.

"I didn't say I wanted to join them, just that the Man Jesus and His purpose intrigue me," I countered. I felt humiliated and shamed.

He warned me in the strongest terms to end my spiritual journey if that was where it was leading me. "It will tear your family apart," he warned. As I left his office, I felt like a traitor for even considering Yeshua. At this point, the movie ended.

"Now, David, God has had mercy on you. Because of His plan for you I was sent, but you know as well as I, had I not pulled you out of that Starbucks you might never have considered Yeshua again." The word *never* hit me like a sword in my *kishkas*.[1]

I felt so ashamed that I had let Rabbi Goodman's intimidation keep me from seeking truth. "I am a writer, a journalist; I am supposed to look for the truth no matter where it takes me; and here, in the most important issue of my life, I caved in."

"David," he softly said, "I have watched that same scene played out thousands of times in the past twenty years alone. Jewish people who are wrestling privately with the issue of Yeshua go to their rabbi instead of the Bible, and get shamed out of continuing their search. While it breaks my heart, please understand that Rabbi Goodman meant no harm. He cares for you and your family. He was simply seeking to protect you. But, yes, he *was* wrong. Religious leaders have always sought to control the beliefs of their constituents. Before the advent of the printing press, the poor souls were completely dependent upon their leaders to tell them what the Bible said.

"There are some, though, who have thought for themselves. Today they are called Messianic Jews."

"I have heard of them. There is a large group right here in Philly...oh yeah...I am not in Philly, am I?"

Ariel laughed, "It's time for you, David Lebowitz, to rediscover the real Yeshua, the true Man, as He lived and died and rose from the grave, in this city—as a Jew. And then, you will offer *that* Yeshua, not a distorted facsimile of Him, to the Jewish people. The Lord has a task for you, but first we will expose this multifaceted, murderous identity theft that has caused so much pain. Are you ready?" he asked. Before I could reply, Ariel, my new friend, had grabbed me by the hand and we were flying again.

Note

1.   Yiddish for "guts" or "soul."

Chapter Nine

CLASS IS IN SESSION

When we landed, we were in what I can only explain as a *high-tech, heavenly classroom*. Everything in the classroom was ancient and yet completely modern. For sure, it was the coolest room I had ever been in! There was a desk for me to sit at; it was made of Jerusalem stone. But the desktop was a tablet—I mean the desktop was a tablet as in Moses and the Ten Commandments-type tablet. But inside the stone tablet was an iPad-like interface. My tablet had a tablet!

The room was dimly lit in a yellowish-orange glow, as if lit by a torch or lantern. In fact, it wasn't unlike the synagogue in Jerusalem, except for the fact that we appeared to be suspended in space and moving though at a very slow pace!

There were no walls or ceilings, and I could see the stars and moon above me. There was a floor beneath us made of ancient, off-white marble, which made up the size of the classroom. I had the feeling that the marble was about a yard thick beneath me, but I couldn't really see.

In the front of the room was another tablet, only it was massive, about twelve feet by four feet and it had the face of a computer monitor—a very modern, large, and cool computer monitor. There was one file on the screen. It read, "DL 1.0."—my initials. *This was crazy. It had to be a dream.*

I had an insatiable desire to learn, which I can't adequately explain in human terms—especially since it was the first time I'd ever experienced it. All I can say is that I felt like my brain had been programmed to optimum absorption and I couldn't wait to start learning.

"This will be our homeroom, David. You will spend a good deal of your time here learning, but don't get too comfortable, as we will go on several journeys.

"Let me lay some ground rules. I will be showing you passages from books, encyclopedias, even websites, and of course, God's Word, so that you can prepare for your assignment. Everything I show you here will be saved on your tablet on your desktop in the classroom. You see, David, I am not going to tell you what to believe, but I am going to help you build your case, primarily based on the Scriptures, but backed up by history. I will show you the evidence, but in the end, you must decide.

"I am doing this for two reasons. First, you will use this information in fulfilling your destiny. Second, I don't want you to trust a word I say theologically, if it is not backed up by Scripture. This is how many people are deceived. Paul wrote to the Galatians that even if an angel comes to you, if it is another gospel, reject it! (See Galatians 1:8.) Mohammad and Joseph Smith are just two of the more famous individuals who were deceived by false angels. Everything must line up with God's Word.

"And, we will study history. For all you know, I could just be making up stories, but if I supply you with the documents to back it up, not only will it be credible but, back to point one, you will be better equipped to convince others."

Convince others—what was he talking about?

"Let's begin," Ariel was now dressed in professorial garb of cap and gown like in a prep school. "We will start with names. I do not deny that names are important," he began to lecture. "They are. But at the risk of contradicting myself, I would also warn you not to get too hung up on names. The Father is not looking to catch us on technicalities. Sadly, there are those who obsess over names and miss the essence of the person of Yeshua."

Ariel tapped the center of the file that read DL 1.0 and suddenly the computer within the ancient tablet came to life. Several men appeared. The first one said, "Unless you read the Bible in the King James English, you are not reading the Bible!"

The second one said, "If you are not baptized according to our church's constitution, you are not saved and you're on your way to hell."

The third and last one proclaimed, "If you don't pronounce His sacred name correctly, you will be damned."

Ariel was laughing. "Silly religious people—this is not the God of the New Covenant, who 'is not willing that any of these little ones should perish.'"

As he said this, I heard a sound, not unlike the one my cell phone emits when I get a new text message. Right on cue "No. 1: Matthew 18:14" appeared on the right side of my personal tablet.

"There is no angel at the gates of Heaven ready to say, 'Sally, we really would like to let you in. Your heart was pure, you loved people and sacrificed for the kingdom, *but* we got you on a technicality. You got a name wrong and so you're disqualified. Sorry about that!'"

Oh, so my angel is a comedian.

"No!" He continued, becoming serious again. "God is looking for every opportunity to save. People who get caught up in names, genealogies, traditions, or rituals and overemphasize their importance have a *religious spirit*, and that is not a good thing, David—it blinds them to the love of God, and sometimes to God Himself. Paul warns Timothy about those who promote controversy rather than God's love."

The text message sound and another verse appeared on my desktop, again with a number beside it: "They have an unhealthy interest in controversies and quarrels about words that result in envy, strife, malicious talk, evil suspicions" (1 Tim. 6:4).

My tablet desktop was taking notes for me. *I could've used one of these in college,* I thought.

"Sadly, there's always the danger of getting so hung up on the minutiae that we miss the very purpose of Yeshua's coming, which was, 'to seek and save those who are lost.'" A third passage appeared—Luke 19:10 NLT.

"Having said that, if we are going to understand the New Covenant in context, we are going to have to review a few names, as these name changes and translations influence how we perceive both the culture and message of certain New Covenant characters. These name revisions have resulted in both Jewish and Gentile readers completely missing the fact that these people were Jews, with Jewish names. Revisions that have tragically obscured the Jewishness of the New Covenant, communicating incorrectly to Jews that the New Covenant is not Jewish."

"D'ling," announced the appearance of Jeremiah 31:31 on my tablet:

> *"The days are coming," declares the Lord, "when I will make a new covenant with the people of Israel and with the people of Judah."*

"David, while English versions of the New Covenant refer to Yeshua by His Greek name, *Iesous*, which when translated into English becomes *Jesus*, His parents never called Him by either of those names. Joseph, His stepfather, was given very specific instructions as to what His name was to be and why." My tablet promptly displayed Matthew 1:20-21:

> *An angel of the Lord appeared to him in a dream and said, "Joseph son of David, do not be afraid to take* [Miriam] *home as your wife, because what is conceived in her is from the Holy Spirit. She will give birth to a son, and you are to give him the name* [Yeshua], *because he will save his people from their sins"* (Matthew 1:20-21).

Ariel continued his lecture, "The name *Yeshua*, in Hebrew, actually has meaning. Just about every Hebrew name has a meaning or comes from a similar root with a meaning, and the angel was very specific about the name that the Son of God, the Messiah, should have: His name was to be *Yeshua*. Pronounced slightly differently, putting the emphasis on the last syllable instead of the middle, *ye-shu-à* means *salvation*. In essence the angel told Joseph, *'His name shall be "salvation" because he will "yoshia" (verb form, save) His people from their sins.'* It is impossible to pick up on this prophetic word play in the Greek or English versions.

"And that, of course, was the mission of the Messiah, *to bring salvation to His people and to be a light to the nations.* Indeed, Simeon, the aged prophet who had been told he would not die until he saw the Messiah, prophesied as much."

Then I saw an old man on the larger tablet begin to pray, tears streaming down his face, as he held a baby in his arms. This had to be the Simeon of whom he spoke.

> *Sovereign Lord, as you have promised, you may now dismiss your servant in peace. for my eyes have seen your salvation, which you have prepared in the sight of all nations: a light for revelation to the gentiles, and the glory of your people Israel* (Luke 2:29-32).

"His name was *salvation* because He would bring *salvation*."

"The name *Yeshua* was also a shortened form of the name *Joshua*, which in Hebrew is pronounced *Yehoshua*. In later books of the Hebrew Bible we find the Hebrew name *Yeshua* and it is translated as *Joshua*. (See Zechariah 3.) Joshua means 'the Lord is salvation,' or 'the Lord saves.' Tell me David, what sounds more Jewish to you, the name *Jesus* or *Joshua*?"

"Well Joshua, of course," I answered.

"In the Greek, both Joshua and Jesus are exactly the same: *Iesous*. But when referring to the Messiah, they translated His name as *Jesus*. When Joshua is mentioned in the New Covenant, they do not translate His name as Jesus, even though in the Greek it is the same, but use the Hebrew transliteration—Joshua—leaving us to think they are two different names. As a result, we lose the Jewish character of Jesus's name. While Joshua is seen as Jewish, the Jewish Messiah has been portrayed throughout history as being something other than Jewish."

"So Joshua and Jesus are the same name?"

"Don't be so amazed, David. There is more.

"All your life you were probably told that the mother of Yeshua was a woman named Mary. In fact, millions of people actually call her Maria. Why is this significant? It's important because these names make the mother of Yeshua sound English as in *Mary* or Italian as in *Maria*, when of course she was neither. She was not the lead role in *West Side Story* or Jimmy Stewart's wife in *It's a Wonderful Life*."

"How do you know about movies, Ariel?"

"Stay focused, David."

"I always viewed Mary as a Roman Catholic teenager," I offered.

Ariel chuckled and said, "That would have been difficult, as she was born in Israel several hundred years before there ever was such a thing as the Roman Catholic Church."

"Well, what about this *mother of God* business? They worship her and pray to her in some cultures."

On the larger tablet appeared a woman, a precious woman. She began to talk to me. "David, this breaks God's heart and mine as well. I am just a woman, a very blessed one, but nothing more. The Father never intended that people would pray to me or worship me. While it is difficult to be sad when you are constantly in the presence of the Almighty, what people have made of me disturbs me greatly. And what is worse is that the very people who claim to adore me have oppressed my people. They pray that I will intercede for them, and at the same time they persecute and kill my descendants. I am an Israelite, and my name, by the way, is Miriam, *a Jewish name*—the same name as the sister of Moses."

"So why is your name printed as Mary in the New Testament, but the sister of Moses is *Miriam*?" I asked her.

"Oh, I'll let Ariel explain that. He's the expert. I shared what I needed to share. Bless you David," and the board was empty again.

"The answer is simple," said my eager angelic teacher, "and it is not as sinister as you may think, although it still confuses the identity of Yeshua's earthly mother. The New Covenant was written in Greek so her name had already been *Hellenized*—that is, conformed to Greek culture. Even in the original text, they wrote the Greek equivalent of her name rather than her actual name. And the English translation of the Greek form of Miriam is *Mary* or *Maria*. Whereas when the Hebrew Scriptures were translated into English, there was no Greek influence. Thus, Moses's sister remained Miriam.

"One more thing, David—while Miriam was correct in saying that she was not divine, I don't want to sell her short. She was chosen for a reason. She was a humble, loving, God-fearing servant of the Lord. She has taken her place next to

Class Is in Session

Sarah, Rebecca, and Rachel in the kingdom. She is a very special woman and should have been an example to young Jewish girls throughout the centuries, but like Yeshua, her identity was greatly altered, even hijacked."

"This is really new to me," I responded. "But, I have a question."

"Shoot," said Ariel.

"Okay, this *John the Baptist* character; if you are saying that the New Covenant is Jewish, who is this guy? I mean, he is a *Baptist*, for crying out loud. How could there be anything Jewish about him?"

The massive tablet came to life again and a fellow wearing some sort of caveman outfit appeared. He was laughing at me.

"Tell me something, Dave," he chuckled. "If I mentioned the name *Ezekiel* would you think Jewish or Christian?"

"Ezekiel was a Jewish prophet, so Jewish, of course."

"How about *Jeremiah, Daniel, Isaiah,* or *Haggai*?" the man asked.

"Well they were all prophets from the Hebrew Scriptures, so once again, Jewish."

"Right, Dave."

I didn't appreciate this caveman character calling me *Dave.* My name is David.

"Okay, I'll call you David," he laughed again.

"But how—I didn't say anything."

"No, but you thought it and I'm a prophet, which is not a mind reader, of course, but if the Lord allows it, I sometimes see things, and I saw that you didn't want to be called *Dave,* okay David?"

"O...kay," I uttered uneasily.

"David, getting back on point," the prophet continued, "if I mention the name *John the Baptist*, what do you think of?"

"Well Christian, right?"

Then he yelled out, *"Booooom! Gotcha!"*

I was startled. This guy was a hoot.

"My name is John, actually Yochanan in Hebrew, and I was *not* a Baptist. And here is another shocking revelation for you: *There were no Baptists at that time—although they seem like fine folk,"* he said jokingly in a southern accent. In his normal voice, he continued, "The truth is, David, I was a Jewish prophet and I died, actually I had my head handed to me on a silver platter—literally!—years before anyone had ever used the word *Christian*.

"In the manner of Ezekiel, Jeremiah, and Isaiah," he became serious, "I was honored to be the last and greatest of the Jewish prophets who proclaimed the coming of the Messiah in fulfillment of prophecy."

A sound signaled new activity and Isaiah 40:3-5 appeared on my tablet.

"Sadly, I died prior to the New Covenant, but it was important for me to get out of the way," he added with feigned annoyance, "although it would have been nicer to simply die in my sleep—and keep my head!

"David, the only difference between me and my predecessors was that my ministry was recorded in the New Covenant. They called me *the Baptizer* because when my *100 percent Jewish* followers would repent, I would immerse them in water, symbolizing spiritual cleansing. Funnily enough, the practice did not begin with the New Covenant or as a Christian tradition; immersion in water had been common practice in Judaism as a form of ritual cleansing for centuries before I implemented it in my ministry.

"In fact, outside the Temple in Jerusalem were nearly fifty *mikvot*—immersion tanks—for Jews wishing to make a sacrifice at the Temple. The ministry of immersion with which the Lord entrusted me preceded and prepared the people for Yeshua's coming. It was not something new to the people of Israel. They understood its significance. The fact that thousands of Jews 'from Jerusalem and all Judea and the whole region of the Jordan,' went out to be immersed by me attests to this fact."

Matthew 3:5 appeared on my tablet. "The fact that people now associate me and my signature with a denomination that began only five hundred years ago and that they don't see me as a Jew is truly sad, because it takes the Jewish context away from the Gospel narrative. God called me, a Jewish man, to call the Jewish people to prepare themselves for the Jewish Messiah."

The screen on the larger tablet went blank.

"I liked him, Ariel."

"I should let you know that the people you are meeting do not look as they appear to you. It was decided that for the purposes of our investigation each of these figures would appear to you as they would have appeared on earth during their lifetime," Ariel explained.

"Good to know. I was hoping people didn't dress like cavemen in Heaven!"

We had a good laugh. Ariel and I were becoming friends.

Chapter Ten

PETER THE POPE?

"Have you heard of Peter?" Ariel asked.

"Eh, yeah, he was one of the first followers of Je—I mean Yeshua, right? Wasn't he the first pope?"

I thought Ariel was smiling because I began to refer to Jesus by His Hebrew name, but he was chuckling at my assertion that Peter was the first pope.

"Okay, D'vid" he used the Hebrew pronunciation of my name, "there are two issues with Peter—his *name*, and his *function*. Let's start with his name. First of all, it wasn't Peter. The word *Peter*, or *Petros* in Greek, simply means *rock*. Peter's real name was Simon, or Shimon in Hebrew. However, on the occasion he received the revelation and declared that Yeshua was 'the Messiah, the Son of the living God...'" Matthew 16:16

appeared at the top of all the previous passages that had been sent me on my tablet. "Yeshua announced that henceforth..."

"*Henceforth*? Who talks like that?" A strong, well-muscled individual with a big bushy beard now occupied the screen. He was confident and clearly had a sense of humor. "Angel, just let me tell my story. David," he turned to me, "I really think you would rather hear it from me. I don't use any of those three-dollar words like Professor Ariel over there."

"Oh yes, you are a brilliant communicator. The problem is, you don't know when *not* to talk!" Ariel then mimicked, "Lord, it is good for us to be here. If you wish, I will put up three shelters—one for You, one for Moses and one for Elijah," reminding the man of his ill-timed words on the Mount of Transfiguration (see Matt. 17:4).

"Yeah, yeah, yeah, you can remind us of that or you could tell him about my sermon on Shavuot...or before the Sanhedrin when they told us to stop preaching the Gospel! I remember it like it was yesterday, 'Rulers and elders of the people! If we are being called to account today for an act of kindness shown to a man who was lame and are being asked how he was healed, then know this, you and all the people of Israel: It is by the name of Yeshua, the Messiah, that this man stands before you healed...salvation is found in no one else, for there is no other name under Heaven given to mankind by which we must be saved' (see Acts 4:8-12).

"In truth it wasn't that difficult. Even though He had gone, He was still with us. We couldn't see Him, but man, we could feel Him. Yeshua's presence was almost tangible. The miracle of healing we'd just witnessed—a paraplegic jumping up and down, praising God—and the fact that we were now doing what we'd watched Him do so many times, empowered us. We felt as bold as lions—not afraid of any man!"

"Okay, Fisherman, you got it right more than you got it wrong so I guess we could let you share for a bit." They both laughed.

"Where were we...oh yes, when I had the revelation that Yeshua was the Messiah, the Son of God, He gave me a new name—*Kefa*!

"*Kefa* means "rock" in Aramaic, the commonly used language of the time. It's very close to Hebrew. However, when the New Testament was written in Greek, in most places they did not transliterate my name. Do you know what that means?"

"Sure, that's when you take a word from another language and spell it with the letters of your own language to enable you to pronounce it, even though you may not know what it means," I offered.

"Exactly," said Simon Peter. "My name was rarely transliterated to Greek which would be *Cephas*. In most places, they translated it to *Petros*—the Greek word for "rock," which in English is *Peter*. Yeshua, however, never called me *Petros*, but only *Kefa* or *Shimon Kefa*."

Scripture references appeared on my tablet: John 1:42; First Corinthians 1:12; 3:22; 9:5; 15:5; Galatians 2:9,11,14.

Ariel interrupted, "The problem with using the name *Peter* is the same as with *John* or *Mary*. They are fine names; they just take away from the Jewishness of the narrative. Your average Jewish person has no idea that the man Christians call Peter is actually Jewish.

"This brings us to the second issue, regarding his *function*. When Yeshua told Shimon that He would build His Church on this *rock*, He was referring, not to Peter the man, but to the revelation Shimon had been given, that He, Yeshua, was 'the Messiah, the Son of the living God.' This revelation would be foundational to receiving salvation—and to the nature of the *Kehilah*."

"*Kehi*-what?"

"*Kehilah*. It's a Hebrew word that means community. I want you to use it when referring to the community of followers of Yeshua. Many people use the word *church*. Church comes from the Greek word *kyriakon*, which is not in the New Covenant. The word that is translated church is *ekklesia*, which means, 'called out ones' or 'those called to assemble' and comes from the Hebrew word *kahal*, which means, "audience" or "assembly." *Kehila* also comes from *kahal* and means 'community.' *Ekklesia* is a great word, because those who follow Yeshua are called out from the rest of the world and are grafted into the Commonwealth of Faith, the Father's household. No matter what you think of the word *church*, a word is only as powerful as its meaning to its hearer, and most people hearing the word church today think of buildings, not people.

"For instance, if someone said to you 'David, look at that church,' what would you be looking at?"

"A building, I guess?"

"That's correct; at least in the way the word is most commonly used today. But if someone said, 'I belong to a *community*,' you would think of people, not a building, right?"

"Makes sense."

"Okay, back on topic—the Roman Catholics misinterpreted Yeshua's words to mean that He was bestowing special authority on Kefa. From this distorted interpretation, a doctrine later emerged that taught that *Kefa* or *Peter* himself was *the rock* upon which Yeshua would build his Church.

"Centuries later, this misinterpretation extended to the Roman Catholics' claiming that Shimon Kefa was the first pope."

Shimon began to laugh, "I don't know what's crazier, that there was a pope in the first century or that he was *Jewish*! Can you imagine me, Shimon, wearing that outfit the popes wear, or letting people kiss my ring? And how about that hat?" We were all laughing now.

"It's called a mitre, Shimon, and we need to move on now," Ariel gently chided the fisherman. Still laughing, Shimon disappeared from the screen.

"Romans Catholics maintain," Ariel continued, "that Peter was the primary leader of the early believing community, and that he eventually moved to Rome and became the first bishop of Rome. Through apostolic succession, every bishop of Rome after Peter would be the head of Christianity."

"Apostolic *what*?" I asked.

"Apostolic *succession*. It is the belief in the uninterrupted transmission of spiritual authority from the apostles through successive popes and bishops. Roman Catholics mistakenly maintain that Peter passed his authority down to the next pope and so on and so forth. Many denominations believe in the idea that there has been unbroken transfer of apostolic authority from the apostles to the present, but the Roman Catholic Church additionally believes the Pope's authority on matters of faith and morals is divinely inspired and sanctioned."

"So you are saying that Peter's authority was passed down to the second pope, and then he gave it to the next one, all the way down to today's pope...and that they are therefore incapable of making mistakes?"

"No, *I* am not saying that, *Roman Catholics* say that. This bishop of Rome, or the Pope, was regarded as authoritative when it came to issues of doctrine and morality for the Church. It was maintained that, without its leaders, the Church would move into deception. Later on, they would declare that the Pope's dogmatic teachings on faith and morality were infallible.[1]

"It is true that the Father raises up leaders to guide His people..." The text message sound prompted me to look down:

> *So* [Messiah] *himself gave the apostles, the prophets, the evangelists, the pastors and teachers, to equip his people for works of service, so that the body of* [Messiah] *may be built up until we all reach unity in the faith and in the knowledge of the Son of God and become mature, attaining to the whole measure of the fullness of* [Messiah]. *Then we will no longer be infants, tossed back and forth by the waves, and blown here and there by every wind of teaching and by the cunning and craftiness of people in their deceitful scheming* (Ephesians 4:11-14).

"...But they are always subject to the authority of His Word. God never expects us to blindly follow a man, especially one who claims he is incapable of making mistakes. As the passage says, leaders are given to His followers to bring them to maturity, so they can think for themselves—not to keep them enslaved to one man's dogma."

I remembered again how I allowed my rabbi to make me feel guilty over my interest in Yeshua. I know he meant well, but he was basically asking me to trust him and not seek truth on my own.

"Either it is ridiculous," Shimon was back, "or Yeshua changes His mind a lot, because Roman Catholic doctrine has changed quite a bit over the centuries, with a number of popes contradicting the edicts of other popes. There are even examples of violence and intrigue between popes and would-be popes.

"Believe it or not, David, many of the popes were far more *political* than *pious*. The first bishop to adopt the title of pope was a guy named Saint Damasus. He was accused of adultery and led murderous raids against his enemies, killing over one hundred and sixty people! He was anything but a genuine believer.

"Another pope, Symmachus, around the year 500 CE conducted what can only be described as a holy war against his enemies. As the two groups fought in the streets, killing scores of men, one of the pope's ardent followers declared that the pope was 'judge in the place of the Most High, pure from all sin, and exempt from all punishment.' All who fell fighting in his cause, he declared, enrolled on the register of heavens.'"[2] The quote appeared on my tablet.

I responded, "Throw in a few virgins, and this sounds eerily similar to the radical Islam of today."

"You're so right," exclaimed Shimon. "Religion is religion no matter what name you give it. It is easier to get people to fight for your cause if they are willing to die, and it is a lot easier to get them to be willing to die if you promise them paradise on the other side—plus something extra to appeal to their carnal lusts, like seventy-two virgins. For a destitute, uneducated Arab teenager who doesn't see much of a future ahead of him, this promise is very attractive."

"It was the same with a lot of the Crusaders you showed me, right Ariel? Many of them were poor peasants who suddenly found purpose and identity through fighting for the Church, even if it was misguided."

"You are catching on quickly, David," responded the angel.

"Another pope, Stephen VI," Ariel was not to be distracted, "had the body of a previous pope exhumed and dressed in his Episcopal robes so he could stand trial. He was found guilty. This mock trial also declared all of Pope Formosus's ordinations to be invalid. Apparently he was not as infallible as once thought."

"This is crazy!" I maintained. "How can this be true? I see the Pope on TV and he hardly seems capable of such things."

"Fortunately the Catholic Church has changed—for the better, I might add—over the years. And to be clear David, there have always been true followers of Yeshua in the Roman Catholic Church. Many of the bishops throughout the centuries truly loved Yeshua and sought to serve Him. In fact, there were several popes who genuinely sought to serve the Lord, but this sad history, one that most Roman Catholics don't even know, did indeed take place. And David, it is important that I prepare you for your future task ahead and that requires taking an honest look at history."

"Okay guys, I've already heard this, so I'm going to leave now. David, it was an honor to meet you." And he was gone.

Future task ahead? An honor to meet me? I wasn't even sure if I believed any of this was happening—and here was Peter of the Bible telling me that he was honored to meet me!

Ariel interrupted my reflections, "Now concerning Peter or Kefa and the belief that he was the first pope..." suddenly on my tablet opposite the Scriptures, under the heading, "Notes" were listed four points.

"Read those out loud please," Ariel requested.

"Number 1. While it is clear from the early chapters of Acts that Peter—that is, Kefa—was the greater among equals, the senior leader among the apostles, it is also clear that Kefa gave himself to traveling ministry (Acts 8, Acts 10) and turned over this responsibility to James..."

"Actually, his name was Jacob," Ariel interrupted me, "but we will come to that later." I continued reading.

"...The brother of Yeshua, as he was clearly the one in charge in later chapters, both in Acts 15 where Shimon Kefa testified and in Acts 21 when Paul visited Jerusalem. Furthermore, in Galatians 2, Paul writes 'When certain men came from James to Antioch where Peter was,' proving both that Peter was sent out to Antioch from Jerusalem and that Jerusalem was the headquarters.

"Who is Paul? You mentioned him earlier," I asked.

"Soon, David, just keep reading."

"Number 2. Peter clearly wasn't infallible as we see in that same Galatians 2 passage. Here Paul rebukes Peter publicly for his hypocrisy in refusing to eat with Gentiles when certain men came from Jerusalem, though he freely ate with them before these men arrived. The tradition of the elders, which would become the oral law, forbade Jews to eat with

Gentiles. This was not a biblical issue, but one of tradition—a bad tradition.

"Number 3. There is no record in the New Covenant, or in history, of Peter ever being the bishop of Rome.

"Number 4. And last, while there is evidence Peter visited Rome, we never see him portrayed as the Bishop of Rome. And even if he had possessed this position, where is it written in the New Covenant that the Bishop of Rome would hold the seat of authority over Church doctrine—ever? Let alone, forever? If such an idea were even biblical, Jerusalem, not Rome, would have been the obvious choice, as the Acts 15 Council, the first doctrinal conference of elders and apostles, was held in Jerusalem. And of course we know that Yeshua does not return to Rome to set up His millennial kingdom, but to Jerusalem." (See Zechariah 14:1-4.)

"I know that some of these things are probably a bit confusing to you, David—'Millennial Kingdom,' 'Jerusalem Council,' etc. I realize that much of this is new, but just stay with me and it will all be clear in the end. The main point I want you to see here is that God never intended for there to be any central authority on earth that controlled the faith and doctrine of every believer. He alone holds all authority, and it is to Him and to His Word that men must come. People can, and should, read His Word for themselves."

Notes

1. This doctrine was adopted by the Roman Catholic Church in the First Vatican Council of 1869-1870.

2. G.W. Foote and J.M. Wheeler, *Crimes of Christianity* (London: Progressive Publishing Co., 1887), 123.

Chapter Eleven

NICE JEWISH BOYS: SAUL, JACOB, AND JUDAH

"David, you asked about Paul. He is the central author of the New Covenant—at least of the letters to the congregations—and his name was actually Saul of Tarsus. He was both Jewish and a Roman citizen, not to mention a rabbi of the Pharisees. He studied under Gamaliel, one of the most respected rabbinical scholars of his day. He was so zealous for God and convinced that Jewish people who believed in Yeshua were deceived that he sought to arrest Jewish believers and even approved the stoning to death of Stephen, a leader among the first Jewish believers."

Acts 7:58–8:1 appeared and I made a mental note to look it up afterward. Right now, I was hanging on the angel's every word. "However, on his way to Damascus to arrest Messianic Jews—Jews who believe in Yeshua—he was knocked to the ground and blinded by a great light. I remember that day! We angels weren't too crazy about this guy. I mean, he was throwing Jewish believers in jail and even having some killed! But the Father said, 'This man is my chosen instrument to proclaim my name to the Gentiles and their kings and to the people of Israel. I will show him how much he must suffer for my name' (Acts 9:15-16).

"At the time, I quietly thought, *He deserves to suffer all right*, but couldn't quite see how this guy would ever be preaching to the Gentiles. But, as always, Father knows best.

"Yeshua had a little chat with Saul on the Damascus road and convinced him that he was on the wrong side of the issue. After this dramatic encounter, he became a believer and actually began to share the good news of Yeshua with Jewish people. In fact, he immediately went into the synagogues and began preaching."

"Wait a minute! Are you telling me that the primary writer of the New Covenant was a Jewish rabbi,[1] and that after persecuting believers, he became one himself and actually went into Jewish synagogues preaching about Yeshua?"

"You're starting to get it, David," he said with a big grin.

"Well, why don't Jewish people know this?" I demanded.

"That is why you are here David—to answer that exact question! But not quite yet." He continued telling Paul's story. "Many years later, as he traveled throughout the known world seeking to help both Jews and Gentiles discover a dynamic, personal relationship with the King of the universe, the Bible refers to the fact that he had two names." On my screen appeared: "Then Saul, who was also called Paul..." (Acts 13:9).

"Sadly, for centuries Christians have taught that Saul changed his name to Paul after he became a believer. In other words, he had to get rid of his Jewish name and take on a Christian one."

"But Paul," I jumped in, "is a Latin name and was popular in Rome long before Christianity. If anything, it would be connected to Rome, which was pagan and polytheistic."

"Right David, and let's not forget. At the time that Paul was preaching, Rome was anything but a friend to the believing community. In fact, Rome became the primary persecutor of the body of believers, the Kehilah, for the first three hundred years."

Just then a gray-haired English vicar appeared on the screen. He was addressing his congregation:

> "The Roman emperor Nero had the believers tied to poles in the garden, covered with tar and set on fire to illuminate his garden parties. And then he would take other believers and sew them into the skins of wild beasts and set dogs on them to tear them to bits to entertain his guests. And I have stood in that garden and wondered how many believers died a horrible death for his barbecue parties."[2]

"It is highly unlikely that Saul changed his name to reflect this barbaric culture. What's more, if Saul truly changed his name from a Jewish one to a Roman one, then why did he wait so many years after coming to faith to do so?"

"Then why does it say he was also called Paul?" I asked.

"Let me ask you this," Ariel replied. "Do you have a Hebrew name?"

"Of course. Anyone who grew up in a Jewish home outside of Israel knows that it is common for Jewish people to have two names, one that relates to the culture in which they live, and a Hebrew name. Mine is Chaim."

"Ah, Chaim, a great name. It means *life*," Ariel commented, then continued. "When Saul was traveling in non-Jewish areas, he used his Roman name, Paul, and when in Israel or amongst Jews, he used his Hebrew name, Shaul. Saul is its Anglicized equivalent. Notice the passage doesn't say, 'Saul, who changed his name to Paul,' but rather, 'Saul, who was also called Paul'—as, *in addition to*, not *instead of*.

"Some of the smartest Bible teachers in the world miss this simple fact. This pastor you are about to see (a man standing behind a pulpit appeared on the flat screen but in pause mode) is an excellent Bible teacher and he loves Israel. He and his church have given sacrificially to Jewish believers. But listen to him in a recent message."

Ariel played me just one sentence. I couldn't tell you the context of his sermon but I simply heard him say: "Saul was on the road to Damascus. That is what his name was *then*."

"Here is another one. This man's messages are listened to by millions every week online." Another man appeared. "Paul, his *original* name was Saul..."

"This fine preacher, well-versed in the Scriptures, simply assumes that Shaul changed his name. If people so bright can miss this simple point," Ariel noted, "how easy has it been for the enemy to rob Saul, the second most prominent figure in the New Covenant, of his Jewish identity and thus confuse the nature of the New Covenant for Jewish people?" Ariel noted. "Earlier I mentioned James to you," Ariel said, switching subjects.

"You said his name was actually Jacob."

"Good, you're paying attention!" Paying attention was an understatement. I felt like I had a supernatural ability to absorb information. "Well I want you to meet Jacob, the physical half-brother of Yeshua."

The screen of the massive tablet lit up again and a handsome man in his thirties said to me, "Yeah, they sure did a job on my name. 'James,' for Heaven's sake! No one ever called me James, not growing up, not ever! If they had, you might assume I was the butler or the chauffeur!" James was laughing. "But nope, I'm Jewish and grew up in Galilee."

"You...grew up...with...*Yeshua*?" I tentatively asked, making sure I used the name that Jacob would have known Him by. How surreal it was to be talking to someone who actually grew up in the same house as Jesus!

"Yeah, and it wasn't easy. Try growing up in the shadow of the *Ma-Sye-Ya*!" he raised his voice for emphasis, but was smiling. "In all seriousness, it wasn't easy. It took me a long time before I believed—imagine your half-brother telling you that His other genealogical half is God! But after His resurrection, there was no denying that indeed, my brother was the Messiah. After I became a believer, others quickly looked to me for leadership, simply because I grew up with the Messiah. I resisted this at first—I had doubted Him for so many years. However, to my surprise that is exactly what He called me to do—to lead this new group of believing Jews in Jerusalem, along with Kefa and the other apostles, in following the Risen Messiah—my brother.

"I'll let Ariel take it from here. I just wanted to meet you." And he was gone.

Like Shimon Kefa, Jacob wanted to meet *me*? Who was I?

"David," Ariel continued his lesson, "in just about every other translation of the New Covenant—German, Hungarian, French, etc.—the word *James* is properly translated as *Jacob* or *Yakov*."[3]

"So why is it *James* in English?" I asked.

"Many have speculated that since King James authorized the English translation of the Bible, translators did this to honor him, but actually the names Jacob and James had been synonymous for some time. The Latin name *Iacomus* (James) was very close to the Latin for Jacob, *Iacobus*, and it appears that it was just a linguistic corruption or confusion. Nevertheless, it has been a costly one.

"The problem, once again, with this mistranslation of Jacob is that it lessens the perception of the New Covenant as a Jewish document. If a Jewish person, like you David, opened up the New Testament to the book of James, you would wrongly conclude that this James had no connection with Judaism or Israel. However, if the book, which was addressed to the twelve tribes of Israel scattered abroad, was properly entitled Jacob, your reaction would be just the opposite—you would instantly recognize that he is Jewish. It would convey and reinforce to you the Jewish context[4] of the New Covenant. I want you to meet Jacob's brother."

"*Yeshua!*" I exclaimed, terrified.

"No, He had other brothers. David, meet Judas."

A shiver went down my spine. I was afraid to speak.

"Relax, David, I am not *that* Judas."

"Who are you then?"

"I am Jacob's brother, like Ariel just said, which makes me, yes, the half-brother of Yeshua. I know that Judas Iscariot, who betrayed Yeshua, is more famous, or I should say 'infamous,' than I, but I did write one of the books of the New Covenant, albeit a very short one, creatively titled after yours truly. The problem with the other Judas, in addition to the fact that he was a thief and a traitor, is that his name has become synonymous with 'traitor' in modern vernacular and in many dictionaries."

On my tablet I saw: "Judas: *someone who betrays under the guise of friendship*, Webster's Dictionary."[5]

"But no one, thankfully, ever actually called me by that name. My name is Yehuda, or Judah in English, the same name as the fourth son of Jacob, of the tribes of Israel."

Ariel took over, "As in the case of the name of Yeshua, had they skipped the Greek and simply transliterated from Hebrew to English, my friend here and his book would be known today by the name *Judah.*

"*Judah*, or *Yehuda*, means 'praise,' from the same root word we get *Judaism*, the name of the Jewish religion. When ancient Israel was separated into two kingdoms, the southern kingdom was named Judah. Modern-day Israel still refers to the southern region of the territories that she recovered in the Six Day War as Yehudah."

"Ariel, it seems that there has been a concerted effort to make the followers of Yeshua look very *non*-Jewish. Not only has Yeshua's identity been altered, but also His first followers; even His brothers appear to have undergone a *Gentile make-over*. I didn't know any of this! And I know that my Jewish friends and family don't know it either."

"David, we are just beginning. This is only the tip of the iceberg. Here, take my hand."

We were flying again.

Notes

1. Formal rabbinic ordination did not begin until about forty years later, but *rabbi* was the term of honor given to a respected Jewish teacher in Paul's day.

2. Adapted from a message given by David Pawson at Brisbane Gateway Centre in April, 1998 entitled, *What Hope for the Millennium?*

3. *James* appears in Spanish Bible as "Santiago"; it is derived from *san* (meaning *saint*) and *Diego*, which comes from Jacob—but changed a lot along the way. Nevertheless, it has no connection to the English name James.

4. It is also interesting to note that in Jacob (James) 2:2 when it refers to the meeting place of believers, the Greek word that is translated *meeting* in the NIV and *assembly* in the KJV is *synagogē*, from which we derive the English word *synagogue*. This was not a blatant attempt to change the meaning of the word because synagogue, while associated today with Jewish houses of worship, does mean assembly. However,

if the New Covenant translators simply used the obvious English equivalent, synagogue, it would have sent a different message to Jewish people.

5. Webster's Online Dictionary, s.v., "Judas," accessed August 10, 2012, http://www.websters-online-dictionary.org/definitions/judas.

Chapter Twelve

THE LAST SUPPER OR SEDER?

Once again, we were going back in time. Above me were only stars, while below I could see time periods passing me by. They looked like scrolling movie film and I could make out the names—the Industrial Revolution, the Revolutionary War, Napoleon, and Louis the Sixteenth. And as we again drew closer to the ground, I knew we were back in Jerusalem. It was evening, and the city was bathed in soft golden light, as torches illuminated almost every courtyard.

We hovered over one home in midair and I realized we were defying gravity. We were able to see right through the roof. It was as if it were transparent. A group of people were sitting around a long table.

"What do you see?" asked Ariel.

"A dinner party."

"Look more closely," he exhorted.

"I see a Kiddush Cup, for blessing the wine, and that looks like matzah. Is it Passover? Are they having a Seder meal, the meal we eat on the first night of Passover?"

"Indeed they are, but this is no ordinary Passover Seder. Look a little closer, at the people."

"Wait a minute. I recognize Peter, I mean Kefa. Is this what I think it is?"

"Yes, it is the Last Supper; and tomorrow Yeshua will die."

"Are you telling me that the Last Supper was a Passover Seder meal?"

"What else would you expect Jews to be doing on Passover in Jerusalem—celebrating *Festivus*?"

I have an angel who knows Seinfeld jokes, I thought.

"Look on your screen." I did and saw:

> *Then came the day of Unleavened Bread on which the Passover lamb had to be sacrificed. [Yeshua] sent Peter and John, saying, "Go and make preparations for us to eat the Passover."*
>
> *"Where do you want us to prepare for it?" they asked.*
>
> *He replied, "As you enter the city, a man carrying a jar of water will meet you. Follow him to the house that he enters, and say to the owner of the house, 'The Teacher asks: Where is the guest room, where I may eat the Passover with my disciples?' He will*

*show you a large room upstairs, all furnished.
Make preparations there."*

*They left and found things just as [Yeshua] had
told them. So they prepared the Passover.*

*When the hour came, [Yeshua] and his apostles
reclined at the table. And he said to them, "I have
eagerly desired to eat this Passover with you before
I suffer"* (Luke 22:7-15)

"When you see Leonardo da Vinci's painting of the Last
Supper, you don't think *Jewish*. If I remember correctly, he has
bread on the table! It's Passover, for goodness sake; Jews don't
eat bread on Passover!"

"What do you expect from an Italian painter in 1495? The
Church had already drifted so far from its Jewish roots, no
one would have even thought to bring it to the painter's attention. In Spain they were already killing Jewish converts who
returned to Judaism. Why would Leonardo emphasize the
Messiah's Jewishness? In fact, doing so could have put his own
life in jeopardy."

"That makes sense," I agreed. "So Yeshua died on the first
day of Passover?"

"Yes, but there is more." Ariel and I were flying again. This
was a very short trip. We landed on a grassy knoll near some
large rocks. I realized later that they were tombs.

"Where are we?" I asked.

"No, '*When are we?*' is the correct question. And I'll give
you a hint—in Heaven we don't call this day *Easter Sunday*
any more than we call the Passover you just saw *Good Friday*.
Read this passage David."

This time it was a cloud that formed in the shape of letters. But it was in Hebrew. "Ariel, I can't read Hebrew. I mean, I can sound out the words but I have no idea what I am saying." Most Jewish boys in America learn how to read the Hebrew alphabet for their bar Mitzvahs, but rarely do we actually learn the language.

"Try," he said with a mischievous grin.

So I did, and I found I could both read and understand Hebrew! Amazing! The verse said: "He is to wave the sheaf before the Lord so it will be accepted on your behalf; the priest is to wave it on the day after the Sabbath" (Lev. 23:11).

"Ah...so? What does this mean to me, today?" I asked.

"David, this passage is from Leviticus 23. Adonai tells the Israelites to bring a Firstfruits offering before the Lord on the first Sunday after the first Saturday, or Sabbath, after Passover begins. On this day the priest would wave a sheaf before the Lord. It is called the Feast of Firstfruits. Shaul, remember him? He wrote this: 'but now [Messiah] is risen from the dead, *and* has become the firstfruits...'" (1 Cor. 15:20 NKJV).

This time it was in English and I was beginning to grasp the significance of what he was showing me. "Is this the day Yeshua rises from the dead? And if so," my thoughts were racing, "you are telling me that not only did He die on a Jewish feast day, but He also rose from the dead on a Jewish feast day?"

"*Bingo!* Such a good student you are," and he actually pinched my cheek in jest. "But David, this is not just any Jewish feast day! It is the Feast of *Firstfruits!* Yeshua rose from the dead, as Shaul said, as its fulfillment. He is the Firstfruits of God's harvest, and millions have followed Him. The same power that raised Him from the dead lives in them, giving them life everlasting. I imagine you would like to experience that, too?"

I could experience it, too? This was what I was looking for. Yes, I want that joy, that peace; I want that serenity I saw in Kefa, Jacob, and Judah. And they are Jews! I am not turning my back on my people. They *are* my people! This is what I have been searching for!

"Ariel, I'm ready. I want—*Ariel?* Where are you?" Finally, I was ready and my angel just disappeared. Unexpectedly there was a commotion behind me. I turned around and saw two women who looked absolutely terrified and a few Roman guards on the ground trembling with fear. Then I saw *why*. The massive covering stone had been removed from one of the tombs and two men in gleaming garments were standing beside them. No, they weren't men. They were like Ariel... wait...it *was* Ariel! At least, one of them was. As they began to speak, their words formed in little clouds in front of me. I read as I heard them say to the women:

> *...Why do you look for the living among the dead? He is not here; he has risen! Remember how he told you, while he was still with you in Galilee: "The Son of Man must be delivered over to the hands of sinners, be crucified and on the third day be raised again"* (Luke 24:5-7).

When Ariel reappeared by my side, I said excitingly something akin to, "You were...you...ah."

"Yes, I was chosen to join Alexander in announcing that the King—the King of the Jews—had risen from the dead."

I was beginning to understand that I was with no *Private First Class* angel. This dude had some clout. And what did that say about the fact that he was sent to me? What did all this mean? I'm just a writer from Philadelphia.

"That was an amazing day, that was," he wasn't even talking to me. "There was rejoicing in Heaven on a scale none of us had ever seen before; not even when Moses parted the Red Sea."

"You were in on that, too?"

"No, but I watched it."

"My rabbi once told me that the Israelites passed through the *Reed* Sea, not the *Red* Sea and that the water was only a few feet high."

"Tell your rabbi that if he's right, then an even greater miracle happened on that first Passover!"

"What do you mean?"

"All of Pharaoh's army drowned in only two feet of water!"

We both laughed out loud as he took my hand again. Being somewhat analytical, I realized that I wasn't just laughing because he was funny, but because I was with an angel, 2,000 years in the past and I was happier than I had ever been in my whole life. Happy isn't even the right word. I was beyond happy. I was ecstatic! I felt a joy beyond my ability, even as a writer, to express. Later I would find the term "joy unspeakable" in the New Covenant—and that summed it up perfectly!

We were flying again but in daylight this time. When we landed, we were still in Jerusalem, but at the ancient Temple. We hovered above the courtyard and I noticed the city was packed.

"Why are all these people here?"

"Today is the day of Shavuot, one of the feast days on which Jewish pilgrims from all over the region come to Jerusalem to celebrate. It marks the ending of the forty-nine day counting of the Omer, from *Firstfruits*, the day Yeshua rose from the dead, to *Shavuot*, the Feast of Weeks. Sadly, most Christians know this feast day only as the Day of Pentecost, a Greek word meaning "fifty." Greek-speaking Jews would also have used this word, but the difference is that they knew it was a Jewish or biblical feast day. Most Gentile Christians know it only as the day that the Holy Spirit fell upon and empowered the believers, birthing the Kehilah."

"Can you unwrap that for me further? The Holy Spirit fell? What does that mean and why is this Jewish festival important to Christians?" I asked.

"Ten days ago, forty days after His resurrection, Yeshua told His followers, about 120 of them, to wait in Jerusalem for the Holy Spirit to empower them. He told them that once empowered, they would take this message, the message of forgiveness of sin and redemption through His sacrifice, not only to Jerusalem and Judea, but also to Samaria and even to the ends of the earth. Look."

The cloud returned and I read, "But you will receive power when the Holy Spirit comes on you; and you will be my witnesses in Jerusalem, and in all Judea and Samaria, and to the ends of the earth" (Acts 1:8).

I reached out and waved my hand through the cloud. The letters scattered, but then returned to form sentences again. *Unreal*, I thought. Suddenly there was a loud sound. It seemed to come from the sky, like a windstorm, and could be heard from afar.

"Look down David," Ariel instructed.

When I did, I could see a large group, I assumed the 120, gathered in an enclosure that was part of a colonnade.[1] I saw what looked like flames of fire resting over the heads of each of the believers there, who were now praising God loudly in different languages. They seemed intoxicated with joy. "There is Shimon Kefa," I blurted out, as he made his way into the Temple courtyard, followed by the others.

"Keep watching," Ariel was smiling.

The noise like a mighty wind, the flames of fire and the spectacle of Galileans speaking in foreign languages had quickly drawn a crowd of curious Jewish bystanders, which was growing larger by the minute.

"Oh, so this is what he was talking about when he proudly referred to his sermon on Shavuot. He is going to speak now, right?"

Ariel nodded, as Kefa stood up, "Men of Israel!" he declared. Kefa was right. This was an amazing moment. I had never heard anyone speak like this—certainly not in my synagogue. With passion, authority, and insight into the Scriptures, he proclaimed that Yeshua was Israel's Messiah. His hearers were deeply moved. All these Jews, many of whom had come from other nations for Shavuot, appeared to be stunned by the rough fisherman's dynamic delivery. Even the other believers were looking at Kefa with new respect and amazement, as if to say, "Is this the same Shimon Kefa that we know?"

"This is the same Kefa who, only fifty-three days ago, denied that he even knew Yeshua!" Ariel said.

"What!?"

"I am afraid so. It was just after Yeshua was arrested. A young servant girl accused him of being a disciple of Yeshua. He swore up and down that he wasn't. Kefa was a gaffe machine! One minute he declares that Yeshua is the Messiah, then the next, he is telling Yeshua that he won't let Him go to the Cross. And then he denies even knowing Him—not just once, but *three* times!

"Afterward, he was so ashamed. But Yeshua, after His resurrection, immediately reassured Him of His love and forgiveness and affirmed that he would have a significant role to play in His kingdom—no, not as the Pope," he smiled, "but as one of the greatest communicators of Yeshua's message there has ever been!

"I'll let you in on a secret. The Father doesn't always choose the ones that others would. He took the youngest son of Jesse, David, and made him king over Israel. He chose Joseph, the hated brother of the sons of Jacob, who was sold as a slave, and made him the second most powerful leader in the world—just in time to save from starvation the very same brothers who had wanted to kill him. And here, He takes an impulsive, uneducated, burly fisherman and gives him a gift like no one has ever seen before. The Father is far more interested in a person's heart than in their talents. And Shimon has a great heart. Take a look."

After hearing his message, the men cried out to Kefa and the other apostles, "Brothers, what shall we do?"

Kefa didn't hesitate, "Repent and be immersed in water, every one of you, in the name of Yeshua, the Messiah, for the forgiveness of your sins."

The crowd began to weep, as people openly confessed their sins. It was like someone took a collective blindfold off of these Jews and they saw clearly that they were in need of forgiveness. This was nothing like Yom Kippur in my synagogue. Every year we all dress up and come to the congregation to pray. We fast for twenty-four hours—many without even water. We spend the morning reading prayers that someone else wrote, confessing our sins—but never in tears! Never like this. I wouldn't say it is a joke, but neither is it taken seriously. At least now I could see that. It wasn't unlike the state of these people *before* the Holy Spirit fell upon them. They had come to Jerusalem out of religious obedience, but hadn't actually expected to have an encounter with God.

The apostles organized the crowd and used what appeared to be a system of baths (*mikvot*), to immerse these people in water. Thousands went into the water and came out on the other side. As they did, they were glowing. They entered with tears of anguish and guilt at the realization of their sin, but emerged with tears of joy. Many were actually dancing with each other as they came out. In fact, it reminded me of the story of Miriam and the Israelites dancing on the other side, having passed through the Red Sea unharmed. The city was in an uproar. And while I could see that these people's lives were being radically changed, I couldn't understand why a Jew would be baptized.

"What is happening? Why are these Jews being baptized?" I asked Ariel.

"Remember what John told you earlier—immersion in water *began* with the Jews. These *mikvot* or immersion pools have been in existence for centuries. It was the practice of all those coming up to Jerusalem to present an offering at the

Temple to first be made ritually clean by passing through these waters.

"The problem is that most Jewish people, when they hear the Greek word *baptism*, tend to think of the Middle Ages, when so-called Christians forced Jewish people to be baptized in water, symbolizing their conversion from Judaism to Catholicism, just like Christophe in our story earlier. To the Jewish mind, baptism is not equated with coming to faith in the Jewish Messiah or seen as a sign of dying to the old nature and rising to new life, but rather it is equated with persecution, expulsion, and even physical death.

"But as you have just seen for yourself it was not like that in the beginning. Thousands of Jews, plus their wives and children, joyfully and *willingly* entered into the waters of immersion, seeing it as something entirely Jewish, which it is."

Written before me appeared an archeological reference in cloud-like letters as before:

> A series of public ritual bathing installations were found on the south side of the Temple Mount. Because of the stringent laws regarding purity before entering holy places, demand for *mikvot* was high and many have been discovered from first century Jerusalem.[2]

"The difference is that immersion in water during the Temple period was something that needed to be repeated over and over again, each time one would come to the Temple to make a sacrifice. In the New Covenant, it is something we do only once, when we come to faith—as these have done today—and it symbolizes dying to our old life and entrance into a new life with God. Just look at their radiant faces—it's so obvious, they've undergone a life-changing experience."

A passage appeared.

> *Or do you not know that as many of us as were baptized into* [Messiah Yeshua] *were baptized into His death? Therefore we were buried with Him through baptism into death, that just as* [Messiah] *was raised from the dead by the glory of the Father, even so we also should walk in newness of life* (Romans 6:3-4 NKJV).

"Unbelievable!" I was beside myself. This journey was endlessly amazing. "Ariel, do you realize that Yeshua *died* on a Jewish feast day—on Passover? And that He *rose from the dead* on the Jewish feast of Bikurim, Firstfruits. And then, He *poured out His Spirit* for the first time on His followers on the Jewish feast of Shavuot. It's almost as if God was trying to impress upon the world that this thing is *Jewish!* Am I right?"

"You're preachin' to the choir," Ariel was beaming. "However, within a few decades, the number of non-Jews who would join the *Kehilah,* the community of believers, would far outnumber the Jews, and the Father was laying a blueprint that would ensure people never forgot that salvation began with the Jews."

"But they did forget," I offered. "The Christianity in most of those stories, the movies you showed me, bears no resemblance to anything that I've seen here today. The Church changed so much over the centuries that Yeshua was no longer even recognizable as the Jewish Messiah of Israel. And it was not just His name that was changed, but

His very nature. They made it seem like Yeshua was against the Jews!"

"And," Ariel interrupted, "they conveniently forgot that He'd said that He had been sent *to the lost sheep of Israel,* and that, not only were all His followers Jewish—He was Jewish Himself! Furthermore, according Jeremiah, the New Covenant would be made with the house of Judah and the house of Israel!" (See Jeremiah 31:31.)

"Even baptism," I jumped back in, "they managed to turn into something altogether foreign to Jews. Nor was it ever emphasized, if the Church was even aware of it, that all these powerful milestones of Christianity, like His death and resurrection, took place on Jewish holidays.

"And another thing—why do Christians worship on Sunday when the Sabbath is clearly from Friday evening to Saturday evening? If this all started with Jews, why would they change the Sabbath?"

"You wanna go there? Okay then, I guess we can take a look at it." The angel *stretched,* feigning exhaustion. "But we will need to return to the classroom first. Hold on to me."

Instantly, we were flying again. *I would never get tired of this!*

Notes

1. While it has been a longstanding view that the 120 were at the Upper Room, many modern-day scholars, including Daniel Juster and Richard Longenecker, as well as the NIV Study Bible authors, not to mention the 19th-century scholar Adam Clarke (Clarke's Commentary on the Bible) and many others believe the disciples were in the Temple,

probably in an enclosed area as part of Solomon's Portico or porch.

"When, moreover, we bear in mind the fact (which appears both from the Scriptures and from other contemporary records) that the Temple, with its vast corridors or 'porches', was the regular gathering place of all the various parties and sects of Jews, however antagonistic the one to the other, it will be easy to realize that the Temple is just the place—both because of its hallowed associations, and also because of its many convenient meeting places—where the disciples would naturally congregate. Edersheim says that the vast Temple area was capable of containing a concourse of 210,000 people; and he mentions also that the colonnades in Solomon's Porch formed many gathering places for the various sects, schools and congregations of the people. In commenting on John 7 this trustworthy authority says that the gathering places in Solomon's Porch 'had benches in them; and from the liberty of speaking and teaching in Israel, Jesus might here address the people in the very face of his enemies.' It was, moreover, and this is an important item of evidence, in Solomon's Porch that the concourse of Jews gathered which Peter addressed in Acts 3 (see verse 11). Hence there can be little doubt that one of the assembling places to which Edersheim refers was the 'house' where the disciples were 'sitting' when the Holy Spirit came upon them." (Philip Mauro, The Hope of Israel: What Is It?, 1922, accessed August 10, 2012, http://www.preteristarchive.com/books/1922_mauro_hope-israel.html#CHAPTER_X.)

Let us also consider that this was on the morning of Shavuot, one of the most significant days of the Jewish year. It was the custom of the disciples to worship and pray in the

Temple courtyard daily—how much more on Shavuot? Luke records: "While he was blessing them, he left them and was taken up into heaven. Then they worshiped him and returned to Jerusalem with great joy. And they stayed continually at the Temple, praising God" (Luke 24:51-53). This passage refers specifically to the ten days immediately after the ascension leading to Shavuot.

Furthermore, the Upper Room, at least the place where it is believed to have been, is a good twenty-minute walk from the Temple Mount and the immersion pools. The throng of Jewish pilgrims who witnessed the outpouring would have been at the Temple on Shavuot, as that is why they had journeyed to Israel. At the very least, if it was a home, it had to be adjacent to the temple.

2. "Southern Temple Mount," Excavations (BiblePlaces.com), Mikveh, accessed November 17, 2012, http://www.bibleplaces .com/southerntm.htm.

Chapter Thirteen

CELEBRATE THE SABBATH AND FORFEIT YOUR SALVATION!

Back in the classroom, the lesson began...

"In the year 364 CE, at the Council of Laodicea, the Church formally declared Sunday as the Lord's Day, the day of worship and rest, effectively changing the Sabbath from Saturday to Sunday—at least in their minds. The pervading sentiment of the Council is given expression in this quote from Canon XXIX:

> Christians shall not Judaize and be idle on Saturday, they shall work on that day; but the Lord's Day they shall especially honor; and being Christians,

shall, if possible, do no work on that day. If, however, they are found Judaizing, *they shall be shut out from Christ.*[1]

"These believers were not merely discouraged from celebrating the Jewish Sabbath, they were *commanded not* to do so. If they *did*, they would be 'anathema from Christ,' as another English translation of the same quote says. That means they would be, in the eyes of the Church—but not the Father's, mind you—cut off from the Church and the Messiah—in short *excommunicated*."

"How could they do that if it is not expressly written in the New Covenant? Where did they get the authority to do such things?" I asked.

"That goes back to the Kefa debacle. Remember when we talked about how the Roman Catholic Church misinterpreted Yeshua's comment to Kefa?"

"Yes," I said, marveling that my capacity to absorb information here was at least ten times what it had been when I was in university. "Yeshua was saying that the rock He would build His Kehila on was *the revelation that He is the Messiah, the Son of the living God*. Roman Catholics believe that Kefa *himself* was the rock, and that is why they assume he was the first pope."

Ariel added, "From there they somehow concluded that Kefa, 'the first pope,' had special authority when it came to issues of doctrine, and so every pope after him had this same authority. This really gave them *carte blanche* when it came to dogma. They could basically make up whatever served their purposes, whether it was in the Bible or not, and then declare that it was binding—not because God had said it, but because He had given them the authority to do so. In fact, later they would claim that not only did the Pope have permission to establish doctrine, but that he could not err in doing so—he was infallible. He was preserved by God from error. It is taught that this was an expression of God's love to protect the Church from deception, which is in fact why we have His Word. In truth, this was invented so that the Church could control the people and the Pope's authority over doctrine was drilled into them. For example, in *The Convert's Catechism for Catholic Doctrine*, the question is asked, 'By what authority did the Church substitute Sunday for Saturday?' The answer: 'The Church substituted Sunday for Saturday by the plenitude of that divine power which Jesus Christ bestowed upon her.'[2]

"The Scriptures are the highest authority for the body of believers. Yet they base this change not on the authority of Scripture, but upon their own misguided reasoning that the Father had given them authority *beyond* Scripture," Ariel concluded. "Over the centuries the Church has abused its authority, using it to manipulate those dependent upon its leadership for guidance."

"That's horrible. How does God react to people who take their own ideas and turn them into hard and fast doctrine? They don't even give scriptural support for their ruling because they claim, 'The Church has authority.'"

"Well David, He gets downright *langry!*"

"*Langry?*"

"Yeah, I made it up, it means that first He laughs at how utterly ridiculous it is for mere men, His creation, to pretend that they speak *for* Him without first speaking *to* Him—and then He gets angry.

"In Psalm 2, when speaking about the nations' attitude toward Yeshua and Jerusalem, He also gets *langry*." My tablet signaled new activity, as Psalm 2:1-6 materialized.

> *Why are the nations so angry? Why do they waste their time with futile plans? The kings of the earth prepare for battle; the rulers plot together against the Lord and against hHis anointed one. "Let us break their chains," they cry, "and free ourselves from slavery to God." But the one who rules in heaven* **laughs***. The Lord scoffs at them.* **Then in anger he rebukes them, terrifying them with his fierce fury.** *For the Lord declares, "I have placed my chosen king on the throne in Jerusalem, on my holy mountain"* (NLT).

"I always picture the United Nations when I read that passage. All those little people wielding too much authority, pretending that they can out-vote God. You humans are something else, you know—heads of nations parading around with their entourages, feeling very important. From our vantage point, they look like ants—ants who talk too much!

"You see David, Yeshua's idea of leadership is so totally different from man's."

The board flickered and, as on a movie screen, I saw Yeshua and His disciples. I was fascinated by what I witnessed. The meal was ending as Yeshua got up from the table. He took off His outer garment and wrapped a towel around Himself. *What was He doing?* I noticed that the faces of His disciples were equally mystified as He took a large washbowl and carefully filled it with water. Then placing it on the floor beside Him, He knelt down and started washing their feet.

What impressed me most was the manner in which He did it, showing all the tenderness and love with which a mother would wash her infant child. Don't get me wrong, the man I was watching was 100 percent masculine; His hands were strong and angular. *The hands of a carpenter*, I thought. Hadn't Chaya shared in her story earlier that He was a woodworker by trade?

Having carefully washed the feet of each one of them, Yeshua was resisted by Peter alone, who at first protested and then consented to the act of servanthood and affection. Yeshua then drew the towel from His waist and, exhibiting the same gentleness, dried their feet...at which point the image faded from view.

"Impressive, huh?" said the angel.

"Wow." I wiped a tear from my eye. "Such love and humility," I marveled. This short scene really touched me. "But why did Kefa object?" I asked.

"Kefa felt like many of us would—he felt it wasn't right for someone of Yeshua's standing to lower Himself and do the work of a servant, but that was exactly the point He wanted to make. To be a true leader you had to be willing to be a servant. He was setting an example.

"That is the model of New Testament leadership," Ariel shared, "but rarely does a man lead from love. Most aspire to leadership for reasons of selfish ambition; to boost their ego, to have control or to compensate for some lack in their own self-esteem. But Yeshua said that to be a leader you must be the servant of all, and He set the example, not only by washing the feet of His protégés, but by laying down His life for all humankind.

"Here is one of the most ancient creeds of the first believers."

> *Who, being in very nature God, did not consider equality with God something to be used to his own advantage;* **rather, he made himself nothing by taking the very nature of a servant,** *being made in human likeness. And being found in appearance as a man, he humbled himself by becoming obedient to death—even death on a cross!* (Philippians 2:6-8)

"Good leadership will always be accompanied by a deep concern for the welfare of those under their authority. Because of His great love, He left Heaven—He left the Father's side—to come to earth.

"Furthermore, when human leaders make decisions without consulting God's Word, or that are contrary to God's will, they invariably end up doing more harm than good. They fail to see the big picture, and can only guess at how their actions or decisions might affect those who will come after them. It was the same with this Council. They thought changing the Sabbath was harmless back in 364 CE, but now, with the benefit of hindsight, we can clearly see how the edict not only provided the groundwork for future persecution of the Jews but sadly erected an insurmountable barrier to Jewish people even considering Yeshua."

A new passage appeared on my tablet: "But as he came closer to Jerusalem and saw the city ahead, he began to weep" (Luke 19:41 NLT).

"Luke records that Yeshua was weeping over Jerusalem because they hadn't recognized the day of their visitation. But," Ariel expanded, "His weeping was not for that generation only."

As the scene unfolded before me, I saw Yeshua gazing down upon Jerusalem as He made His way down the Mount of Olives. His soul was in anguish as He saw the suffering of His people down through the centuries; suffering which could have been averted had they only recognized and welcomed their Messiah

As He began to weep, it was as if I were seeing what He saw. And together we watched a series of scenes unfold, one after the other:

First, I saw the Romans destroy the city in 70 CE, the Temple being destroyed and the city burned. Thousands were massacred—men, women, and children.

Then I saw the Romans crush the Bar Kokhba revolt in 135 CE Those murdered were too numerous to count. For ten years, the Jews were not allowed to bury their dead. Jerusalem was renamed Aelia Capitolina, referencing false gods, and Judea was renamed Palestine, as the Emperor sought to disassociate it from the Jewish people. Jews were barred from Jerusalem. Then I saw a series of blood libels, where Jews were accused of kidnapping Christian children and using their blood in the making of matzah (a patently ludicrous accusation in light of the Jewish food laws which prohibited the eating of blood). Tragically, countless numbers of Jews—whole communities, were killed.

Next, I saw the Crusaders overtaking Jerusalem, butchering almost the entire city.

This was followed by Inquisitions—Jews being tortured, forced to convert, or expelled from their countries.

Next I saw a Ukrainian man, whose name I instinctively knew was Bohdan Khmelnytsky. This leader and instigator of hundreds of pogroms murdered tens of thousands of Jews in the most vicious and sadistic ways, most of whom had previously fled other nations where they were not welcome to come to Poland, a nation considered a safe haven for Jews until Khmelnytsky came on the scene.

"Stop!" I screamed. "I can't take anymore!"

"You made it further than most. Still, it's a drop in the bucket compared to the burden that Yeshua carries. He sees it all, past, present, and future. When He wept over Jerusalem, it wasn't merely for the Jews of that time. He was able to see the terrible persecutions that awaited them in the future, both in Israel and in the Diaspora...*and it broke His heart.*"

The Messiah's image faded from view as I wiped beads of sweat from my brow. "I thought we were talking about Sunday worship. How did this get so intense?"

"Interesting you should say that, because those responsible for the seemingly innocuous act of changing the day of worship didn't realize either that it would lead all the way to murder and even genocide.

"Okay. Are you ready to continue now?"

"Can you promise to keep it light?"

Notes

1. John Nevins Andrews, *History of the Sabbath and the First Day of the Week* (Washington, DC: Review & Herald Publishing Assoc., 1912), 409.

2. Rev. Peter Geiermann, *The Convert's Catechism of Catholic Doctrine* (St. Louis: Herder Book Co., 1946), 48.

Chapter Fourteen

"THEORY" TRUMPS "COMMANDMENT"?

"Other well-meaning Christians have bought into different theories about why the Sabbath was changed or should be changed, but that's all they are, theories. None of them in any way abrogates Exodus 20."

> *Remember the Sabbath day by keeping it holy. Six days you shall labor and do all your work, but the seventh day is a Sabbath to the Lord your God. On it you shall not do any work, neither you, nor your son or daughter, nor your male or female servant, nor your animals, nor any foreigner residing in your towns. For in six days the Lord made the*

heavens and the earth, the sea, and all that is in them, but he rested on the seventh day. Therefore the Lord blessed the Sabbath day and made it holy (Exodus 20:8-11).

"It would seem to me," I offered, "that to change something so explicit—one of the Ten Commandments—you would need an equally explicit command."

"Exactly. There are of course those who hold the view that since we are now no longer under Law but under grace, that we no longer need to keep the Sabbath. If followed to its logical conclusion, this argument would remove any obligation to keep the other nine of the Ten Commandments as well—Heaven forbid that believers embrace adultery, thievery, and murder because they are 'no longer under the Law.'

"Another commonly held idea is that because the resurrection occurred on the first day of the week and is referred to as the Lord's Day, another error which we will cover in a few minutes, it now supersedes the Sabbath as the day of worship or celebration."

"But there is actually nothing in the new Testament that specifically says the Sabbath was changed to Sunday." I reiterated.

"Nothing! Now that doesn't mean that there are not a few passages that have been misinterpreted. For instance, Yeshua appeared to His disciples as they were gathered together on the Sunday on which He rose from the dead."

"But they weren't having a service, were they? They had just two days earlier witnessed their leader being executed. I imagine they spent most of their time together after that."

"Yes, you are right, David, but some say they were together on Sunday, when Yeshua appeared to them again a week later, according to John's Gospel."

The white screen hummed to life and a character I'd not yet met appeared.

"Hello David, my name is Toma, some call me *Doubting Thomas*, but that really isn't fair. It was just the one time and you have to admit, it had been a rough few days for all of us."

"Really? What about when you blurted out on the way to raise Lazarus from the dead, 'Let's go, too—and die with Yeshua'?" Ariel was laughing.

"That wasn't *doubt*, Angel; that was *courage*. I was willing to die. So I misunderstood the mission. But still, I was ready to pay the ultimate price. And concerning His first appearance, don't forget I hadn't seen Yeshua and the others had. I'd arrived late that first night He appeared to them, and missed seeing Him. So naturally I was pretty skeptical about it all. Who wouldn't be? It had been an extremely stressful time. I thought they were probably seeing things. You know, lack of sleep and all that. Anyway, I am here because I've got a message for my Jewish brother here. You ready, David?" Toma asked.

"Sure." I liked his personality.

"Okay. Even though I missed the first meeting, I made sure I was there for the second meeting—not that we knew when He would come back. I just made sure that I stayed close to home. And as it turned out, my brothers weren't so crazy after all."

A passage appeared on my tablet that read, "A week later his disciples were in the house again, and Thomas was with them. Though the doors were locked, Jesus came and stood among them and said, 'Peace be with you!'" (John 20:26).

"I nearly jumped out of my skin!" exclaimed Toma. "I was standing there talking when I felt a tap on my shoulder and turned around. And there He was, smiling the biggest smile. You could tell He was enjoying it.

"'Peace be with you,' He said. *Peace?* I nearly fainted."

Ariel interrupted him, "What day of the week was that?"

"If you knew Greek," Toma became more serious, "you would know that it doesn't actually say a week later, but *eight days* later! Now I know that some have argued that the counting included resurrection Sunday, but *I was there!*"

"Well?" I asked, "Which was it—Sunday or Monday?"

"Let me ask you something first," said Toma.

Oy, these people are always answering questions with questions, I thought.

"If you were going to refer to a week from now, would you say, 'in seven days' or 'in a week'?" asked Toma.

"'In a week,' of course," I answered.

"Right, so if someone chooses to say 'eight days,' they probably don't mean a week, because if they did, they would simply say 'a week,' not 'eight days.'

"But honestly, *who cares?*" Thomas shouted, throwing up his hands. "It doesn't matter. Of course we were there! We were there on Sunday and Monday and even on Tuesday—we were *living* in the Upper Room. We were not Judeans, but Galileans. Our homes were several days away—and we didn't have cars, trains, or buses back then. We were holed up in the Upper Room, wondering what in the world to do.

"In both accounts, if you noticed, the doors are locked. That was pretty uncommon in those days, if you were at home—and we had eleven men there. Why would eleven men hide behind locked doors? I'll tell you. *We were scared!* Even though the other brothers had had that one encounter with Yeshua a week, or 'eight days' earlier," he winked, "we had not seen Him since. And remember—they *did* kill Him. So yeah, we were still scared, pretty nervous, and shaken up."

Chapter Fifteen

Saturday Night's All Right

"Furthermore," Toma continued, "the Kehilah had not yet come into being. The last thing on our minds was devising some new order or routine for meeting. We were so broken; we had no idea that we would even stay together as a group, much less meet every week. Kefa was still so ashamed that he had denied that he ever knew the Messiah. However, after Shavuot everything changed.

"We did begin to meet. Would you like to know on what day? Read these two passages."

I read.

> ***Every day*** *they continued to meet together in the temple courts. They broke bread in their homes and ate together with glad and sincere hearts, praising*

God and enjoying the favor of all the people. And the Lord added to their number daily those who were being saved (Acts 2:46-47).

"This next one is right after we were beaten because we refused to stop preaching in Yeshua's name!"

The apostles left the high council rejoicing that God had counted them worthy to suffer disgrace for the name of [Yeshua]. And every day, in the Temple and from house to house, they continued to teach and preach this message: "[Yeshua] is the Messiah" (Acts 5:41-42 NLT).

"Every day, David, *every day!* In the Temple and from house to house. It was an amazing time, looking back. We had miracles and signs and wonders and best of all, the presence of God. Yeshua was so close to us. It was simply the best time..." As Toma was reminiscing, he faded from the screen.

"David, remember the passage I shared with you in the beginning; it should be number three on your list."

"Yeah, I've got it here." I read it aloud. "'The days are com-ing' declares the Lord, 'when I will make a new covenant with the people of Israel and with the people of Judah'" (Jer. 31:31).

"With whom is He making the New Covenant?" asked the teacher.

"With Israel and Judah."

"You understand that at that time, when Jeremiah gave the prophecy, the people of Israel were divided into two kingdoms, Israel in the north and Judah in the south. So in essence, He is making this New Covenant with all of Israel, right?"

"Right," I agreed.

"Now tap twice on the passage," Ariel requested. When I did, the entire thirty-first chapter of Jeremiah opened up. "Read verse thirty-three please."

> *"For this is the covenant I will make with the house of Isra'el after those days," says Adonai: "I will put my Torah within them and write it on their hearts; I will be their God, and they will be my people"* (Jeremiah 31:33 CJB).

"Now, what is the difference between the two Covenants?"

"He says that this time, He will write the Torah on our hearts; He will put it inside us."

"Exactly! So the Father promises a New Covenant with Israel, then just over five hundred years later He pours out the Holy Spirit on Jerusalem, after Yeshua's death and resurrection, of course. He promises in this Covenant to write the Torah, His Law, on the hearts of His people.

"Does it make any sense at all that one of the first things He commands His fiery new Jewish devotees to do is to delete the fourth commandment—one that has just been written on their hearts, 'Remember the Sabbath day by keeping it holy' (Exod. 20:8), and replace it with something that centuries later, Gentile believers would use in order to excommunicate not only Jews from their communities, but also Gentiles who sought to honor the Jewish Sabbath?"

"It would be highly unlikely," I agreed.

"Another passage people use to say God has changed the Sabbath is Acts 20." *D'ling.*

> *On the first day of the week we came together to break bread. Paul spoke to the people and, because*

he intended to leave the next day, kept on talking until midnight (Acts 20:7).

"First of all, it does not say that it was their custom to meet on the first day of the week, just that they were meeting. Toma already told us that in Jerusalem they were meeting every day. And it is quite possible they had gathered in order to hear Paul, who was their honored guest, speak.

"But even if this were their normal time to meet, let's think it through. They came together on the first day of the week to break bread. The idea is that believers chose Sunday because of the resurrection. So, assuming that they had their worship service in the morning as He rose 'early on the first day,' that would mean Paul spoke from breakfast until midnight! It is highly unlikely that Paul either spoke that long or that they listened that long!"

"Why don't you let me tell you how it was?" another personality emerged from the larger tablet. "My name is Eutychus and I was there. If you keep reading the passage you'll find out that I died—yeah, I really did. I fell right out of a window. Fortunately, Paul was there with the faith to raise me from the dead. The meeting had gone on for hours and I found myself nodding off a few times and then I must have fallen backward, out the window to the ground. Probably wasn't the wisest place to sit. The next thing I know, I am waking up on the ground and Rabbi Saul has his arms around me, praying for me and telling me, 'Don't be alarmed.' Try not to be alarmed when you have just fallen three floors to the ground with enough force to kill you."

"Eutychus, I think you were going to share something with us about the Sabbath," Ariel reminded him.

"I was and I will. David, when does the Jewish Sabbath start?"

"Friday evening."

"So when does it end?"

"Saturday at sunset."

"So when does a new week start?"

I was about to say Sunday, when I realized his point. "Ah, Saturday night."

"You're catching on. So doesn't it make sense that when Luke wrote in Greek, the 'first day,' he really meant, the end of the Sabbath? Jewish believers still went to synagogue on Saturday morning to hear the Scriptures read. Remember, people didn't have Bibles back then, and a good number of us didn't read. The New Testament had not been written! So we were dependent on the Jewish believers to tell us what was written in the Hebrew Scriptures. Then in the evening, as the new week began, we would all break bread together, worship and hear the Word taught."

"That makes much more sense," I agreed. "In Judaism, the day always begins at sunset. We always celebrate the beginning of Jewish holidays in the evening.

"I remember back to the month I spent in Israel during college and how weird it was for me that the week began on Saturday night. When you would see people on Saturday morning, you would greet them with the words *Shabbat Shalom*. However, if you did that on Saturday night, people would think you were strange. The Sabbath is over—the day is over. On Saturday night when you saw people, you would greet them with the words, *Shavuah Tov*, 'Have a good week.' On Saturday evening in Israel, there was a sense that you had left one season and entered into another. Stores that closed for the Sabbath reopened in the evening. Kids got ready for school, which started on Sunday. A new week was beginning."

"Well, I guess I'm no longer needed. Adios, fellows!" And Eutychus was gone.

"And David," added Ariel, "all the Jewish believers living in Israel in the first century, before the destruction of the Temple, would've been going to work on Sunday morning because, just like in Israel today, the Jewish professional work week began Sunday morning. That would have been a difficult time to meet for a worship service.[1]

"Dr. David Stern—one of the foremost Messianic Jewish scholars and an authority on the Jewish roots of the faith—in his *Jewish New Testament*, translates Acts 20:7 like this: 'On *Motza'ei-Shabbat*, when we were gathered to break bread, Sha'ul addressed them. Since he was going to leave the next day, he kept talking until midnight' (Acts 20:7 CJB).

"*Motza'ei shabbat* refers to Saturday night. *Motza'ei* is the Hebrew verb 'to take out,' meaning that we are 'coming out' of Shabbat.

"You would do well to buy a copy of his translation,"[2] Ariel suggested.

"Why don't you just download it to my tablet and save me some money?" I joked.

"Funny, David," Ariel continued. "Now there is something I want you to be very clear about. The Father has no objection whatsoever to people gathering to worship on Sunday. They can worship on any day they want. No one is saying everyone must assemble for worship on the Jewish Sabbath—that's legalism and will produce death. No, the point I am making is that God has never changed the Jewish Sabbath."

"Why didn't God just say, 'Hey, I want everyone to meet on this day?'" I asked.

"Because there is no set day for worship!" Ariel half shouted. "The New Covenant is *purposely* silent on this issue because the Gospel would be proclaimed in many nations and received by many different cultures. Believe it or not, many cultures don't use a seven-day week. Much of the Roman world lived by an eight-day week. However, in 321 CE, Emperor Constantine abolished the eight-day week in favor of the seven-day week. And in some areas of Africa, they still use a six-day calendar. So while the message of the Gospel—that Yeshua, the sacrificial Lamb, died and rose again so the world through Him can receive forgiveness of sins and eternal life—is unchangeable, the day and manner of worship of believers is not *written in stone*...no pun intended. Besides, the Sabbath was not given to the Church, but to Israel.

"The problem is not 'Sunday worship' per se," Ariel continued. "A concerted demonic effort to detach the Church from her Jewish roots has played a significant role in all this confusion. The Council's edict to change the day of worship from the Jewish Sabbath to what some refer to as the Lord's Day, exposed the deep anti-Jewish feelings in the Church which could be seen as early as the second century. This carried the unavoidable consequence of alienating Jewish adherents from joining the Church. It has bred a deep distrust of the Church in the hearts and minds of the Jewish people ever since, covering the truth that the New Testament is as much a part of Judaism as the Torah. Sunday worship and the outright rejection of the

Jewish Sabbath confirmed, in the Jewish mind, Christianity's status as another religion altogether."

"Where does the phrase 'the Lord's Day' come from anyway, if it isn't in the New Testament?"

"Oh but it is, my friend. And I should know; I am the one who wrote it!" The face of an elderly gentleman with a long gray beard took center stage on the screen of the large tablet.

Notes

1. Many scholars do believe that the first followers of Yeshua actually met on Sunday night after work. This is a valid view, and even if it is accurate, it in no way invalidates the Sabbath—in fact, it strengthens it. Why didn't they meet on Saturday morning when they were already enjoying a day off from work? Because they were committed to being in the synagogue or Temple courts worshiping and listening to the public reading of the Word alongside observant Jews. Nevertheless, Saturday night still seems more plausible than Sunday night, as it was already a day off—synagogue in the morning, rest in the afternoon, and then the coming together for worship as believers in the evening.

2. Dr. Stern's translation of the Bible can be read free at: http://www.biblestudytools.com/cjb/.

Chapter Sixteen

MESSIANIC JEWISH ATHEISTS?

"Hello David, my name is John—not the John you met earlier. I wrote of that John and his revelation that Yeshua was the Lamb of God in my account of the life of the Messiah. I am John, the disciple whom Jesus loved. We were very close, actually best friends. Even before I understood who He was, I looked to Him as an older brother—a mentor. After a long night in prayer, He chose me and eleven others to be His closest associates and then He spent the next three and half years training us.

"The amazing thing about the Master is that even though thousands followed Him, He always found the time to be alone with us and focus on our training. Most people, who have even a fraction of the charisma and wisdom of Yeshua, seek to use it to take advantage of people. Yeshua did just the opposite. He shunned popularity and focused on leadership training. We didn't understand it at the time, but He was raising us up to lead the Jerusalem revival once He left. And it could not have been easy for Him.

"We were a quarrelsome bunch. My mother once asked Him if my brother, Jacob, could sit on His right hand and I on his left in the Messianic Kingdom. This led to all kinds of backbiting, gossip, and jealousy among the disciples.

"Meanwhile, He always spoke of being a servant. Yet it wasn't until He washed our feet, just as a servant would, that we finally began to understand. And not a moment too soon, as just a few hours later He was nailed to an execution stake showing us the full extent of His servant's heart.

"I was able, *Baruch HaShem*, to outlive all the other apostles. It wasn't easy, mind you. Emperor Domitian, who hated believers in the Messiah, commanded that I be *boiled alive* in oil! Roman guards seized me in Ephesus and extradited me to Rome. I was nearly ninety years old, in an age when most men barely made it past fifty. And what was my crime? Atheism, of all nonsense!

"I stood before a man who claimed to be God, as they accused me of being a heretic."

"How could you be an atheist? You were a believer," I asked, puzzled. "Goodness, you wrote the book of John!"

"And Revelation and the Epistles, uniquely titled First, Second, and Third John," he added with a smile. "The one religion that covered the entire Roman Empire during those years was Caesar worship. Every emperor after Caesar was thought to be divine. So those who wouldn't worship Caesar were considered atheists or heretics. The punishment for this depended on the ruling emperor of the time. When I was on trial, Domitian was Emperor of Rome. He was referred to in his public documents as *Our Lord and God* and he took his divinity quite seriously. He was one of the most vicious men in history. In 96 CE, he put to death his own cousin for being an atheist. Of course he was actually a believer in Yeshua, but any refusal to worship the emperor as God earned you the title of atheist. And you are going to be amazed at how he came to faith! Just wait."

A quote, though not from the Bible, appeared on my tablet. I was reminded that Ariel had forewarned me that he would be downloading information from a variety of sources.

> He informed all governors that government announcements and proclamations must begin, "Our Lord and God, Domitian, commands"...They must call Domitian God—or die. Thus the issue was clear. It was a matter of gods. Either the Lord Jesus Christ or the Emperor of Rome was Lord-God. It was Jesus or Caesar.[1]

"I was brought before the Emperor to be judged. We were in a full coliseum-turned-courtroom, and he asked me, 'Is it true you are an atheist, and refuse to declare that Caesar is God?'"

"I serve Yeshua, the Messiah, the King of Israel, Savior of the world."

"*Whoa!* Dude, that is impressive! What did he do?" I asked.

"He got a little upset." John smiled, clearly understating the event.

"The great Domitian responded," John now assumed a grand imperial tone, "'You understand that the penalty for atheism is death?'

"I was in my eighties, David. What was he going to threaten me with, *Heaven?* I was more than ready to join all my friends who had gone on before me, each one of them dying for the cause. Now it would be my turn, or so I thought. Domitian was, in essence, doing me a favor. I can't tell you that I was too excited about being *boiled in oil.* But David, God will always give us grace for anything He permits. In that moment I thought of Stephen."

"Who is Stephen?" I asked.

"Stephen is one of my heroes. He was one of our disciples in Jerusalem and a true servant. When the first apostles were feeling overwhelmed by all the administrative duties involved in serving such a large and growing body of believers, we appointed a group of godly men as servant leaders who were suitable for the task."

"Like Yeshua, when He washed the feet of the disciples?" I turned to Ariel who smiled and nodded assent.

"Stephen not only served the people with compassion and humility," John continued, "he was also a mighty and effective communicator of the good news. People would listen to him mesmerized at his ability to explain their need for salvation. Through him, God did many mighty miracles. Blind eyes were opened and the lame walked. At the time, the Kehilah was growing rapidly. Even many Jewish leaders had come to faith. Something the Jewish ruling council was none too happy about.

"God was using Stephen powerfully to bring many Jewish souls into the Kingdom. At that time we were only reaching out to Jews—mostly from Jerusalem, but the message of salvation and forgiveness was also touching many Jewish visitors to the Holy City. Stephen had a supernatural power of persuasion that I have not seen since, and being backed up by signs and wonders, opponents found it difficult to argue with him. He was so full of the love of God that many who sought to hate him ended up following Yeshua. He would lead them to Yeshua and then they would return to their hometowns or homelands as believers in their Messiah, taking the good news back with them.

"Some of these Jews who had come to Jerusalem from other countries began to argue with Stephen. They mistakenly assumed that they could easily defeat him in debate, as they were far more learned than Stephen. They were confident that once the bystanders saw how 'baseless' Stephen's arguments were, they would abandon this 'nonsense that the Messiah had come, and had risen from the dead.'

"Well, their scheme didn't go quite as planned. They were the ones who invariably ended up looking foolish as Stephen skillfully countered their every argument. He simply amazed everyone with his quick-wittedness and knowledge. You would have thought he was wearing an earpiece and someone was feeding him the answers. It was as if the Spirit of God was simply telling him what to say. He was a young man speaking to men who were twice his age and who had studied the Hebrew Scriptures all their lives.

"Of course, this is exactly what Yeshua said would happen:

Be on your guard; you will be handed over to the local councils and be flogged in the synagogues. On my account you will be brought *before governors and kings as witnesses to them and to the Gentiles. But when they arrest you, do not worry about what to say or how to say it. **At that time you will be given what to say, for it will not be you speaking, but the Spirit of your Father speaking through you*** (Matthew 10:17-20).

"Those leaders were flabbergasted and infuriated when they couldn't stand up to Stephen's Holy Spirit-inspired wisdom. So they moved to Plan B. It is amazing to what depths men with wounded egos will stoop. Humiliated by Stephen, they produced false witnesses who accused Stephen of speaking blasphemous words against Moses and against God. This was then reported to the Sanhedrin, the Jewish ruling council, and Stephen was arrested.

When Stephen began to testify in his own defense, the people listened as if entranced. It was supernatural. He stood before those who clearly wanted to kill him, and spoke as if he were an invited guest lecturer. It was obvious to all that he was far more concerned about their well-being and their eternal destiny than he was in defending himself. He used his last chance to defend himself to seek to bring other Jewish men to Yeshua—to salvation.

"It was as though he was seeing deep into the soul of every man there. Take a look."

I did, and saw Stephen testifying before a makeshift court; his face was glowing, like that of angel, as words spilled from his mouth. The members of the Sanhedrin were growing ever more furious. But Stephen, clearly full of the presence of God, was not concerned. He looked up to Heaven and cried out:

"Look, I see Heaven open, and the son of Man standing at the right hand of God."

This so provoked the crowd that with a scream they rushed at him. It was as if the presence of God, which produced such peace in Stephen, had the exact opposite effect on his hearers. They recognized that the more he spoke, the more convincing and powerful he became, but their hearts were so hard; they just wanted to silence him.

They dragged him outside the city and formed a circle around him. Then stones started flying, as one after another hurled rocks at Stephen, gashing his face so badly that blood poured from an open wound on his forehead and from his nose. One missile hit him directly on his left ear, slicing it in half. I could hardly bear to watch as rock after rock found its target. They were killing him. And yet, I couldn't turn away either. Amazingly, despite facing death and being surrounded by a frenzied mob, Stephen remained as calm as any man I had ever seen. No hysterics, no begging for his life. He seemed almost detached...and then I saw why.

As rocks continued to slam him from every direction, he prayed—he actually prayed: "Lord Yeshua," he cried out, "receive my spirit." Then he fell to his knees, and cried out again, one final cry, "Lord, do not hold this sin against them." And he died.[2]

Even in his final seconds, he was more concerned for his killers than himself. I was truly in awe.

I turned to John, *They killed him!* he could see the tears in my eyes.

"Actually David, Stephen has never been more alive! When he gave up his spirit, he simply left his body and went to receive his reward. In fact, all of Heaven was cheering when he arrived!"

Notes

1. Patrick M. Jones, *Revelations from Revelation* (Brushton, NY: TEACH Services, 2008), 19.
2. You can read the full account of Stephen in Acts 6 and 7.

Chapter Seventeen

BOILED ALIVE!

"It was that peace that you have just witnessed in Stephen that gave me the courage I needed as I stood before Domitian. I trusted that God's presence would cover me in the same way.

"That demented dictator, Domitian, continued to rant like the madman he was, 'Bow before me, heretic, and declare, "Domitian is god!"'

"I shouted in Hebrew, then in Greek, '*Shema Yisrael Adonai Elohanu, Adonai Echad.*'"

"Hear, O Israel: the Lord our God, the Lord is one," (Deut. 6:4). In English I quoted from memory the Shema—one of the most sacred creeds in Judaism.

"Yes," said John, "and this infuriated him even more. 'Death to the atheist!' he shouted. The crowd joined in. 'Boil him alive! Death to the heretic Jew! Feed his boiled flesh to the lions!' In your day, David, people rail against Hollywood for making ungodly forms of entertainment—and rightly so in most cases. But in my day, there were no movies or reality TV competitions—this was the entertainment. Coliseums would fill to capacity just to watch a man being torn apart by lions, or burned alive or, as in my case, boiled in oil.

"Anyway, as the crowd clamored for my execution or boiling, I stood there enveloped in the peace that passes all understanding and I thought, *This is it. I am finally going to be with Him. Reunited with my best Friend! No more sadness, no more pain, just forever in His presence*—until my thoughts were rudely interrupted by Roman soldiers, men who had been turned into bloodthirsty savages by the inhuman nature of their work, violently grabbing me. They dragged me over to the vat of oil as the crowd followed, eager for a spectacle, and then they hurled me over the top. My body plunged into the massive pot, my eyes closed to keep the oil out, and as quickly as I could, I stood up. The oil, dripping from my head and clinging to my beard, came up to my armpits.

"'Light the fire!' came the command. A flame ignited the dry brushwood beneath the pot. Within minutes I could see tongues of fire rising higher than the massive pot of oil in which I was standing. As the flames burned higher, I knew it would only be a matter of time before the oil would heat up and begin to boil.

"*Time for one last sermon*, I thought, knowing they wouldn't kill me quickly because that would put an end to the show. I opened my mouth, for what I assumed was the last time on earth, and shared as passionately as I knew how about the love of God and His desire that all would be saved. Rather than plead for my life, I exhorted the crowd to turn to Yeshua. 'No emperor can save you. He is not God. No man is divine, but One. Yeshua is the only One who can give you eternal life!'

"David, it simply didn't matter anymore. The worst they could do was kill me, and they were already doing that. I discovered in that moment that when you have nothing to lose, you lose all inhibitions. There's nothing to hold you back. I knew it was my last opportunity in this life, and I was determined to make it count.

"I continued, 'Fear not them that can merely kill the body, but fear Him who can cast both body and soul into hell! (see Matt. 10:28). Turn from your sins and find forgiveness in Yeshua.

"In time, to the delight of the emperor, who I am sure just wanted me to shut up, the oil did begin to boil. David, have you ever been burned by oil?"

"Actually, yes, I have. On my last wedding anniversary, I took my wife to a beach house in Delaware. I had the bright idea of making her dinner—pan-seared tuna. However, I didn't realize how hot the oil had become or what would happen when I placed the fish in the pan. Flames shot up everywhere and boiling olive oil flew out of the pan and onto my hand. For hours my hand throbbed in pain and many months later, I still have the scars on my hand to remind me of it. Of course, that can't be compared to what you went through."

"But still, you have a reference," said John. "You understand boiling oil is lethal. However, even as the oil boiled around me, I felt no pain. In fact, it was just the right temperature—therapeutic even to my old bones!

"Domitian was furious, but the people—they were half terrified, half incredulous. How was it possible? How can a man be put in a pot of boiling oil and survive, and more than that, seem impervious to the experience? Like Shadrach, Meshach, and Abednego, who were thrown into a fiery furnace and were not harmed, I was protected by the Lord. It was quite surreal, to be honest. They threw me in, expecting me to die, but I simply stood there and continued speaking. No burns, no pain...nothing. No one seemed to know what to do. Everyone just stood there staring in confused disbelief. So, finally, I simply climbed out. Even the formerly hardened guards were too terrified to do anything, wondering, *Who is this man? What kind of man could withstand such a lethal punishment?*

"Then I thought, *Well, I'll just leave.* And since no one tried to stop me, that's what I did. I could hear the emperor shouting to his guards to stop me, but they were simply too frightened to respond. I later learned that many who were there that day turned to the faith—*including the cousin of Domitian.*"

"Ah, so that is how he came to believe in Yeshua. And then Domitian later had him executed for being an atheist."

John nodded, "Eventually, because Domitian could not kill me, he had me exiled on the Island of Patmos and that is where I wrote these words."

I heard the familiar sound from my tablet, and read: "On *the Lord's Day* I was in the Spirit..." (Rev. 1:10).

"Many Christians, even some of my own disciples, wrongly assumed that I was referring to Sunday. While I understand why people might assume that, I was actually referring to a specific day of the year on the Roman calendar.

A reference anyone reading the prophecy at the time would have understood.

"As I said, Domitian took the idea that he was deity very seriously. Other religions were tolerated, as long they did not conflict with Caesar worship. This became a problem for the believers as well as for religious Jews who did not believe in Yeshua." Another quote appeared on my tablet.

> Once a year, everyone in the empire had to appear before the magistrates in order to burn a pinch of incense to the godhead Caesar and to say: "Caesar is Lord." ...To refuse to say, "Caesar is Lord," was treason.[1]

"This yearly event was known to be *the Lord's Day*. This is what I was referring to, not Sunday. Believers, knowing my history with the emperor, defying him and surviving, understood the significance of the Lord giving this revelation to me on that specific day. It was meant to highlight the theme of the book of Revelation, which can be found over and over again within it pages: Stand firm in the faith, even unto death. I was chosen to write the book because I had already chosen death over capitulation. In addition to being thrown into a vat of oil, I was on the island because of my faith.

"Consider these verses." *D'ling.*

> *I, John, your brother and companion in the suffering and kingdom and patient endurance that are ours in* [Yeshua], *was on the island of Patmos because of the word of God and the testimony of* [Yeshua] (Revelation 1:9).

*Do not be afraid of what you are about to suffer. I tell you, the devil will put some of you in prison to test you, and you will suffer persecution for ten days. Be faithful, **even to the point of death**, and I will give you life as your victor's crown* (Revelation 2:10).

*To the one who is victorious and **does My will to the end**, I will give authority over the nations* (Revelation 2:26).

*They triumphed over him by the blood of the Lamb and by the word of their testimony; **they did not love their lives so much as to shrink from death*** (Revelation 12:11).

"If anyone is to go into captivity, into captivity they will go. If anyone is to be killed with the sword, with the sword they will be killed." This calls for patient endurance and faithfulness on the part of God's people (Revelation 13:10).

This calls for patient endurance on the part of the people of God who keep his commands and remain faithful to [Yeshua] (Revelation 14:12).

"It was no accident that God chose to give this revelation to me on the very day that virtually every believer under Roman rule—many of them my children in the faith—would be confronted yet again with this crucial test of loyalty: *Caesar or Yeshua?*—a test which for some, could mean death.

"Those believers understood both the reference and its implication."

Another quote appeared on my tablet, "...Many Christians were thrown to the lions, charged with atheism for refusing to sacrifice to the Emperor who claimed to be God."[2]

"You have to understand, David, that to publicly confess, 'Yeshua is Lord,' was to put one's life and family in serious peril. Sadly believers, especially today, miss the point of what my brother, Saul, wrote to the Romans at the seat of Caesar worship: 'If you declare with your mouth, "[Yeshua] is Lord," and believe in your heart that God raised Him from the dead, you will be saved'" (Rom. 10:9).

"That's it? Really? Just confess Him and believe?" I asked.

"Actually, it was a bit more complicated than that for the believers living under Roman rule.

"Once you understand the background of Caesar worship and the persecution it entailed, you suddenly realize that to do this—to publicly confess that Yeshua was Lord—was in essence to say, 'I am willing to die for my faith in Yeshua.' What Saul is doing here is indirectly confronting the issue of commitment, because to confess that you were serving Yeshua was equivalent to confessing that Caesar was, in fact, *not* your Lord. And that could earn you a one-time lunch date with a lion in a Roman coliseum—where *you* were the lunch!

"Still today, believers are suffering for their faith all over the world. In Muslim nations, even nations that tolerate Christianity, they will not allow one of their own to leave Islam. It is a crime punishable by death."

On the board I saw the pictures of two men. One was an African man, the other Middle Eastern. Half of the African man's face was horribly disfigured and his right eye was gone. Under his picture it read:

> Umar Mulinde, 38, apostle, Uganda: ex-Muslim who preaches Yeshua to Muslims and supports the state of Israel. Two Muslim extremists threw buckets of acid in his face.

Under the Middle Eastern man it read:

> Youcef Nadarkhani, 34, pastor, Iran: ex-Muslim pastor in Iran who was charged with apostasy and sentenced to death. Awaiting execution.[3]

"It saddens me, David, that so many people have missed the central theme of the book, hidden in that verse. The Lord's Day reference was a reference to persecution, something that Youcef and Umar both know well."

"This is fascinating," I whispered, stunned by what I was learning. "So you weren't referring to Sunday at all?"

"No, David, I wasn't. Just think about it. What makes more sense? I am receiving perhaps the greatest prophetic visitation that any human has ever received and I mention—*oh, by the way, it's Sunday.*

"Now, I do understand that Sunday was more significant than Tuesday or Thursday, as Yeshua did rise from the dead on a Sunday, but still, Sunday occurred fifty-two times every year—it wasn't that uncommon. However, doesn't it make more sense that I am referring to the one day of the year when the faith of every believer in the empire would be tested to the hilt, as I am writing a book to encourage them to overcome, persevere, and not give in to persecution?"

"Completely! This is awesome!"

"I am pleased to see that you are grasping this, David. The Master has chosen well."

"Chosen? For what?"

But John was gone. The board was totally blank, but not me. I was high! That is the only word I can think of to describe it. I felt like someone was waking me up, and then I would wake up again, to ever newer levels of knowledge. I don't think there are any words in English to explain it.

"John was amazing, wasn't he?" I rhetorically asked Ariel. "He is my favorite so far. I miss that guy already."

"You can see now why he and Yeshua were so close. Of course He loved them all, but John was a special younger brother in the faith to Him. And David, let me say this one more time before we move on. This is key, and I don't want there to be any misunderstanding. The Lord delights in His people when He is worshiped—no matter what day His people come together to worship Him, and Sunday is just as good as any day. But what I do want you to understand is that Sunday never displaced or replaced the Sabbath. And for Jewish believers in the Messiah, He still expects them to honor the Sabbath—not as a condition to receiving eternal life, but as a matter of identity and calling."

Notes

1. Jones, *Revelations from Revelation*, 19.

2. Ibid.

3. Umar Mulinde and Youcef Nadarkhani are actual 21st-century persecuted believers.

Chapter Eighteen

YESHUA THE LIBERATOR!

"This stuff is so completely Jewish. I can't understand why the Jewish people rejected Him."

"But did they, David? After untold centuries of false doctrines that *authorized* the Church to persecute the Jewish people, it is no wonder that *today* Jews have learned to stay away from the Church. But it was not like that in the beginning. In fact, if the Jewish people had indeed rejected the Messiah, the message would never have been taken to the nations. The fact that *Jesus* is a world-renowned name today and His followers number in the billions is irrefutable evidence of the faith, commitment, and success of those early Jewish believers to whom Yeshua entrusted His message of salvation. It was Jewish messengers who spread His message to Africa, Europe, and Asia.

"Let's go back to the days immediately after Yeshua ascended into Heaven. Take my hand."

We were heading back in time, once again. I loved this part! And again scenes from history flashed below me as we journeyed back through time. When we arrived, it was night.

We gazed once more into the room where Yeshua had celebrated Passover with the disciples. But now the room was filled with men and women who were praying. Ariel began, "Remember, David, how Yeshua, just before He ascended into Heaven, told these people not to return to Galilee but to wait in Jerusalem for what the Father had promised—the Holy Spirit. And as you can see, they are obeying Him even though they don't really know what to expect. They spent their days in the Temple courts and nights back at the Upper Room, constantly seeking God for His promise. There are over one hundred people in that room worshiping Him, and every single one of them is Jewish.

"Let's fast-forward a few days to Shavuot."

And within seconds we were viewing a sea of humanity in the Temple courts on the morning of Shavuot. In one of the enclosures off the courtyard, I could see the 120 gathered here, waiting and praying. This was the same scene he had shown me earlier.

"David, they had no idea what was about to happen. Read this verse." I saw this passage illuminated and read:

> *When the day of* [Shavuot] *came, they were all together in one place. Suddenly a sound like the blowing of a violent wind came from heaven and filled the whole house where they were sitting. They saw what seemed to be tongues of fire that*

separated and came to rest on each of them. All of them were filled with the Holy Spirit and began to speak in other tongues as the Spirit enabled them (Acts 2:1-4).

He was filling their mouths with praise and worship and in a multitude of languages!

We watched, and I was fascinated that it was only the *sound* of a mighty wind. There was no movement as the Holy Spirit visibly fell on each one. It was a sound that could be heard far beyond the reaches of the place where they were and the strange phenomenon quickly drew a huge crowd. These Jews were not only from Israel but from all over the known world. They had come up to Jerusalem on pilgrimage to celebrate Shavuot.

Imagine their amazement at hearing God's praise going forth in their own languages. We couldn't help but smile as we watched Kefa stumble from the enclosure into the Temple court's public area. The Jewish worshipers were staring at him and the others. Seeing this, Kefa took the opportunity to explain what was happening. He boldly preached his first sermon under the power of the Holy Spirit to an enormous crowd.

"By the end of the day, David, three thousand men had believed in Yeshua and were ready to be immersed in water." (See Acts 2:41.)

"I remember this," I said. "They were immersed in the mikvot pools surrounding the Temple."

"Let's take a look," Ariel said as he leaned forward, and in seconds we were watching another amazing scene. There was great joy amongst the crowd as thousands of new believers in the southern sector of the Temple were being immersed in water.

"Ariel, that looks like more than three thousand to me!"

"Indeed you are right. They only counted heads of households back then. In truth, there were over ten thousand new believers—and again—all of them were Jewish! And consider, David, many of these men had not traveled with their families. So, while many of them arrived in Jerusalem feeling spiritually broken and beat up, seeking to survive under Roman rule, they returned home as new men. Their wives were stunned as their husbands radiated a new respect and love for their spouses, something that was uncommon in the world at that time.

"Let me take a few minutes to explain something to you and then we will get back to Shavuot. While many people falsely think that the New Testament restricts women, nothing could be further from the truth. Until this time, there had been no document more liberating for women than the New Testament. You have to understand that very few marriages at that time were based on love and mutual respect. Virtually every marriage was arranged. In many cultures women were viewed as property. In Roman cultures women were treated very poorly, often viewed merely as objects for sexual gratification and reproduction. A good many women died in childbirth.

"In richer families, the women were expected to bear children as quickly as possible, with little rest between pregnancies. In fact, many girls were doomed at birth. Boys were preferred, as they could carry on the family name, and for a girl the father would have to provide a dowry to her husband upon marriage. At certain periods in Roman culture, fathers were permitted to *expose* their newborns if they chose. Exposing a child meant that the child was thrown in a river or allowed to die naturally from starvation. This fate, in most cases, fell upon girls."

I was sick at hearing this!

"In most cultures, women could not receive an education, testify in court, socialize in public, or talk to strangers. Young women were usually secluded until marriage and married women, especially in the larger cities, wore veils in public. Men, generally, looked down on women, seeing them as inferior.

"Despite the fact the wives of the Patriarchs are honored in Jewish prayers—Sarah, Rebekah, Leah, and Rachel—it rarely translated into true honor between and husband and wife in the first century. The marriage hardly resembled a modern Hollywood movie, but was a contract between families. I am sure you remember the play *Fiddler on the Roof.* Tevye the Milkman was obsessed with finding suitable matches for his daughters, and that was based on Russia in the early nineteen hundreds. Things have changed rapidly in the last 100 years.

"Yeshua, however, broke all the rules, and treated women as equals in a time when such things were unthinkable. To be clear, we all have defined roles to play in our lives—for instance, you're never going to have baby, David!"

"I hope not!" we laughed.

"The Father has created men and women uniquely different to complement each other in their relationships as they raise families. Men tend to be more disciplinary, while women are more nurturing. Yes, men and women are different, but equally valued and loved by the Father.

"And while on earth, Yeshua frequently challenged the status quo. On His way back from Judea to Galilee, He and His disciples passed through Samaria. While the disciples went into town to buy food, He did the unthinkable. He talked to a woman in public! John recorded the whole story in chapter four of his biography of Yeshua.

"When the disciples came back they were clearly surprised and bewildered to see the Master talking to a woman alone—especially a Samaritan woman!

"Let me show you another example." Ariel snapped his fingers and a portable version of the tablet appeared before me, like a flat screen TV, and a movie began to play.

Yeshua was at the Temple courts teaching a group of eager listeners, when He was approached by an aggressive group of men. They appeared to be religious leaders. Two of them violently pushed a bound woman in the direction of Yeshua. She was scratched and bruised, clearly their prisoner. Her hands were bound. As they pushed her forward, she fell and they made a half circle around her. Then the ringleader turned to Yeshua.

"Teacher, this woman was caught in the act of adultery. In the Torah, Moses commanded us to stone such women. Now what do You say?"

Oh my goodness, they were going to stone her, like they did Stephen. It would have been one thing if this were merely a movie. But Ariel was showing me something that really happened.

"No!" I blurted out. "They can't!" Ariel was smiling. "Ariel, how can you smile? This isn't funny!"

He just looked at me and said, "Keep watching."

I continued to watch, as they asked Yeshua if they should stone her to death. Their accusations and calls for her to be stoned were met with silence. Some of them even appeared to be giddy as they put the weight of this woman's life upon Him.

Yeshua gazed at them intensely, but said nothing. Finally, He bent down and began to write with His finger in the dust on the stone floor.

Ariel interrupted, "David, this was far more than a man writing in dust. In fact, He was essentially saying, 'I am Divine.' It was the finger of God that emblazed the Ten Commandments on the stone tablets. Now here, the Divine Son, humbled by taking on the form of humanity, revealing Himself not as the One who parted the Red Sea or spoke the world into existence, but as a servant, He has a divine message for this woman's accusers."

As he bent down I could see what He was writing, and despite that it was in Hebrew, I understood it. "Pride, deception, manipulation, shame, judging, jealousy...." Even as He wrote they continued to badger Him with questions.

At last, He stood up and, looking them straight in the eye, gently said, "Let the one among you who is without sin be the first to throw a stone at her." And then He resumed writing on the stone floor as they pondered His rebuke. "Lust, greed, hypocrisy...."

His confronters were suddenly very uncomfortable, embarrassed, and clearly outwitted. No one was laughing now as, one by one, starting with the oldest, they all crept away.

Yeshua then untied the hands of the woman. She was weeping, overcome with relief at the sudden change in the course of events. She was sure that stones would soon be digging into her flesh and now she was free. Yeshua asked her, "Where are your accusers? Is there not even one to condemn you?"

"No, Lord," she said.

Yeshua looked at her with eyes of compassion and said, "Neither do I. Go and sin no more."

The tablet went blank.

"You see David, they knew they had no legal authority under Roman law to kill her, and that is why they sought to trap Yeshua. They knew if He said, 'Stone her!' He would be in trouble with their Roman overlords. However, if He was unwilling to pronounce a death sentence over her, they would tell the people that He didn't obey Moses. Instead, He exposed their own sinfulness and guilt. Yeshua, making them look like fools, revealed that their sin was just as evil as hers."

"Is this story in the New Testament?" I asked.

"Yep, that and many more that reveal how counter-culture the teachings of Yeshua were. If you read what Shaul wrote to the Ephesians, it probably won't seem so earth-shattering."

I looked to the tablet and saw: "Husbands, love your wives, just as [Messiah] loved the [Kehilah] and gave himself up for her" (Eph. 5:25).

"That's a beautiful passage," I remarked.

"Sure it is—*for you*—a twenty-first-century American husband. But for the Ephesians and the rest of the known world at the time it was revolutionary. It was not the norm for a husband in those days to regard his wife in this way—as someone to be cherished, protected, someone for whom he would be willing to die. You have no idea how radical this teaching was. Asking a man to express unconditional love and affection for his wife was unheard of. Western culture has Yeshua to thank for this shift. Without the teachings of the New Covenant, the West would never have become as civilized as it has.

"Of course, the belittling and devaluing of women went on for centuries, because the Church did not emphasize these teachings and forbade people to read the Bible for themselves. Even in Jewish circles women continued to be treated poorly. Josephus, the great first century Jewish historian noted, 'The woman, says the Law, is in all things inferior to the man.'[1] Here are a couple more quotes from both Jewish and Christian sources." I looked to the tablet:

> Rather should the words of the Torah be burned than entrusted to a woman...Whoever teaches his daughter the Torah is like one who teaches lewdness.
>
> —ELIEZER BEN HYRCANUS[2]

> What is the difference whether it is in a wife or a mother, it is still Eve the temptress that we must beware of in any woman...I fail to see what use woman can be to man, if one excludes the function of bearing children.
>
> —ST. AUGUSTINE OF HIPPO

"While so much has changed in the West in regard to how women are viewed, much of the world still treats women as objects or property. Hold your stomach and watch this."

A video played on the tablet. A Muslim sheik was teaching on the proper way to beat one's wife. I looked at the angel incredulously. He was not smiling. "If the husband wants to use beatings to treat his wife, he must not do it in front of the children. It must remain between him and her....”[3]

The video ended quickly. “This is sick!” I roared, “Religious leaders giving instructions on the *godly* way to beat your wife!”

“Oh David, if you knew how many horrible and tragic events take place every day on your planet. Women are raped, sold into slavery, and forced into prostitution in nearly every country, every day.[4] Evil men line their pockets with money, as their consciences are seared. They feel no guilt or remorse as they use and abuse these creations of God, whom He made in His image.

“This is why Yeshua was so radical in His treatment of women—He hates the way men have used physical strength to take advantage of women. On another occasion when a woman with a notoriously promiscuous past came and wept at His feet, He did not send her away. He was actually in the home of a religious leader at the time and everyone there judged Him for letting her touch Him. But Yeshua rebuked them. In truth there was no difference between them and her—they were all guilty of sin before God. The only distinction was that the woman recognized she was a sinner, while the smug, self-righteous ones present misguidedly trusted in their own virtue for salvation.

“No one in history has contributed more to the liberation of women than Yeshua,” Ariel said emphatically.

Notes

1. Josephus, *Against Apion Book II*, 201.
2. Rabbi Eliezer, “Mishnah, Sotah” 3:4.

3. Wife beating in Islam—The Rules, http://www.youtube.com/ watch?v=Wp3Eam5FX58.

4. The Richmond Justice Initiative (www. richmondjusticeinitiative.com) is a great resource to get educated concerning human trafficking and sexual slavery in the U.S. and around the world. It is headed by Sara Pomeroy, a former student of mine.

Chapter Nineteen

TENS OF THOUSANDS OF MESSIANIC JEWS

Returning to the subject of the Jewish revival that began on Shavuot 30 CE, Ariel continued, "So these men who were giving their lives to the Messiah returned home as changed men. In most cases, their wives were so affected by the new respect with which they were now treated that they, too, quickly became followers of the Messiah."

I looked at the scene as one after another entered into the mikvot—the immersion pools.

"Rising up out of the water is a picture of the resurrection life—the new life in the Spirit that Yeshua gives to all who ask. And three thousand is a very significant number."

"Why?" I asked.

"Well, Shavuot, traditionally, is the holiday on which Israel celebrates the giving of the Law to Moses at Mount Sinai. On the day Moses brought the tablets of the Law into the camp, the people's sin was so flagrant, Moses threw down the tablets, breaking them—and three thousand men were put to death" (see Exod. 32:19-28).

"So, three thousand people died when the law came, but with the coming of the Holy Spirit three thousand people received new life!" I added.

"Precisely! Shaul wrote to the believers in Corinth, 'He has made us competent as ministers of a new covenant—not of the letter but of the Spirit; for the letter kills, but the Spirit gives life' (2 Cor. 3:6). The letter kills because it only reveals the problem. However, when one receives Yeshua, he now has power to live out God's plan. It was the beginning of a whole new way of relating to God—now the Torah would be written on their hearts.

"And this number quickly grew," the angel continued. "In Acts 4:4 it states that the number of *men* grew to about five thousand—and when you count the rest of the family members that number was closer to twenty thousand, *and*, need I say it...?"

"...*All of them were Jewish!*" I finished his sentence.

"Indeed they were, David, and it wasn't merely the uneducated or the unwanted, though the Lord loves them greatly, who were placing their trust in Yeshua. Acts 6:7 says, 'So the word of God spread. The number of disciples in Jerusalem increased rapidly, and a large number of *priests* became obedient to the faith.'"

"What kind of priests? Catholics?" I asked.

Ariel laughed out loud. "No, there weren't any Catholics yet, David. These were Jewish priests!"

"We have rabbis," I said, "but I have never met a Jewish priest."

"It's true, David. If your typical Jewish person were to read that second part, they would probably all think that these priests were Catholic. Why? Because there is no such thing in modern Judaism as a *priest*. The spiritual leaders in post-temple Judaism are called *rabbis*, which means *teachers*. Without a Temple, last destroyed in 70 CE, there was no need for priests anymore, as the job of the priests was to offer sacrifices to God in the Temple on behalf of the people. Even when there were Jewish priests, they would not have used the word *priest* but *cohen*, which is a common family name even today among Jewish people. The fact that a large number of these men, the *cohanim*, who worked in the Temple had come to faith, shows that the good news of Yeshua was reaching *every sector* of Jewish society."

Ariel snapped his fingers and a rather serious-looking man addressed me from the tablet screen.

"And that included Jewish society outside of Israel as well. Shaul, who once imprisoned Jewish believers, made it a point of principle everywhere he traveled to seek to reach the Jewish people first."

"David, meet Lukas. Everyone up here calls him Dr. Luke."

"Hello, David. What a pleasure to meet you."

Despite his stern demeanor, his voice was warm and his manner friendly.

"Hi...eh...Dr. Luke."

"Dr. Luke was the first historian among the early believers. He traveled with Shaul for some time, always taking notes. Eventually, when Shaul was imprisoned in Caesarea for two years, he began to put together an account of their travels. And he collected information from others, *firsthand accounts*, so he could write a history of the Kehilah, going as far back as the birth of the prophet John. There is no one up here, other than God and Shaul himself, who knows more about Shaul than Dr. Luke.

"I think Shaul would agree that I know more about him than he knows about himself. He was brilliant, but he really could have used a smartphone," laughed Luke. "He was so focused on his task that he would often wear two different types of sandals, forget to eat, or even have his tunic on backward for half a day until someone finally had the courage to tell him. Of course he would always laugh at his absentmindedness. The first thing he would ask me every morning was, 'What city are we in?' It became a running joke between us, even when he was imprisoned for two years in Caesarea, waking up in the same place each morning. The authorities allowed me almost constant access to Shaul during that time.

"But let's talk about Shaul's commitment to reach the Jewish people even while he was called to the Gentiles," said the doctor. Before me lay two passages:

> *I am talking to you Gentiles. Inasmuch as I am the apostle to the Gentiles, I take pride in my ministry in the hope **that I may somehow arouse my own people to envy and save some of them*** (Romans 11:13-14).

> *For I am not ashamed of the gospel, because it is the power of God that brings salvation to everyone*

*who believes: **first to the Jew**, then to the Gentile*
(Romans 1:16).

"This next passage may shock you as it did me when I heard Shaul dictate these heartrending words to Tertius, his scribe. We were in Corinth at the time and Shaul was greatly concerned for the believers in Rome. Emperor Claudius had expelled the Jews, both Messianic and non-Messianic, from the city in 49 CE. Midway through the next decade they were allowed to return, however the non-Jewish leaders of the Roman *kehilot* had falsely believed that the exile of the Jews had been a sign that God had rejected them permanently. Upon their return they were treated poorly—as second-class citizens. Much of the book of Romans was written to counter this false theology, with chapters nine through eleven, in particular, being devoted to the topic of God's irrevocable covenant relationship with His people, Israel. And I recall Shaul, weeping unashamedly, sharing God's heart for his brothers after the flesh—Israel."

I speak the truth in [the Messiah]—I am not lying, my conscience confirms it through the Holy Spirit—I have great sorrow and unceasing anguish in my heart. For I could wish that I myself were cursed and cut off from [Messiah] for the sake of my people, those of my own race, the people of Israel. Theirs is the adoption to sonship; theirs the divine glory, the covenants, the receiving of the law, the temple worship and the promises. Theirs are the patriarchs, and from them is traced the human ancestry of the Messiah, who is God over all, forever praised! Amen (Romans 9:1-5).

I was stunned by what I'd just read. "Yes, David, he was willing to give up his place in Heaven, in the Messianic Kingdom, if by doing so more of his people could know the Messiah and receive eternal life. He carried this burden with him until the end. While false historians have portrayed Shaul as an enemy of Israel, I never met anyone who loved the Jewish people more. Despite his calling to the Gentiles," continued Dr. Luke, "the principle, *to the Jew first*, was always foremost in his mind. Take a look at these passages." Scriptures appeared again as clouds in the air; only this time they were scrolling as I read them. Certain words were in boldface. This was to highlight the fact that Shaul's priority, in every city he visited, was always to seek out the Jewish people and tell them the good news of their risen Messiah:

> *When they arrived at Salamis,* **they proclaimed the word of God in the Jewish synagogues.** *John was with them as their helper* (Acts 13:5).

> *From Perga they went on to Pisidian Antioch.* **On the Sabbath they entered the synagogue** *and sat down* (Acts 13:14).

> *At Iconium* **Paul and Barnabas went as usual into the Jewish synagogue.** *There they spoke so effectively that a great number of Jews and Greeks believed* (Acts 14:1).

> *On the Sabbath we went outside the city gate to the river, where we expected to find a place* [where Jewish people met for] *prayer. We sat down and*

began to speak to the women who had gathered there (Acts 16:13).

*As was his custom, **Paul went into the synagogue**, and on three Sabbath days **he reasoned with them from the Scriptures*** (Acts 17:2).

*As soon as it was night, the believers sent Paul and Silas away to Berea. On arriving there, **they went to the Jewish synagogue*** (Acts 17:10).

***Every Sabbath he reasoned in the synagogue**, trying to persuade Jews and Greeks* (Acts 18:4).

*They arrived at Ephesus, where Paul left Priscilla and Aquila. **He himself went into the synagogue and reasoned with the Jews*** (Acts 18:19).

***Paul entered the synagogue and spoke boldly there** for three months, arguing persuasively about the kingdom of God* (Acts 19:8).

"We see from Acts 14:1, where it says, 'as usual,' and Acts 17:2, which states, 'as was his custom,' that this was something Shaul always did. I was with him during much of this time, and the moment we arrived in a new city, his first question was always, 'Where's the synagogue?' If we'd had a GPS back then, he would have had it programmed to locate every synagogue!

"In many of these places, numerous Jewish people came to faith; in others, there would be persecution. More often than not, it was a mixture of both.

"Everything originates with the Jewish people in God's scheme of things. The Jewish people gave the world the revelation of the one true God, His Word—the Bible—and ultimately the Messiah, Yeshua Himself. In addition to *instant messaging* and *Starbucks*," Luke said with a smile.

Then becoming serious again, he added, "And the children of Abraham have paid a heavy price for being God's chosen vessel—persecution, hatred, even attempted genocide, have pursued them to this day. Without Israel, there is no Messiah, and no salvation. And since the New Covenant was made with the house of Israel and the house of Judah, and salvation is of the Jews, it should come as no surprise that Heaven decreed the good news would be preached to the Jewish people first, and then to the nations. And this proclamation was not without effect! Far more Jewish people than is realized received Yeshua in those first two centuries! And today, again, more and more Jewish people in Israel and all around the world are embracing Him.

"I remember when Shaul returned to Jerusalem," Luke continued. "I believe the year was 58 CE, almost three decades after the birth of the first community of believers. The Gospel by that time had gone all around the known world.

"And surely, you would have thought, by now the Jewish revival in Jerusalem would have died down. But it was not so, David. The movement had continued unabated. When we arrived in Jerusalem, Shaul met with Jacob, the brother of Yeshua and senior leader of the Jerusalem community."

Luke turned to Ariel, "I'm assuming you have explained the Jacob/James name debacle. Such nonsense!"

"Nope, I let Jacob do that himself," Ariel responded with a wink.

"Good. Jacob and the elders," Dr. Luke continued, "gave a great report concerning the work of the Gospel in Jerusalem."

Another verse formed before me.

...Then they said to [Shaul]: *"You see, brother, how many **thousands of Jews** have believed, and all of them are **zealous for the law**"* (Acts 21:20).

"There are two eye-openers here and a mistranslation." I could see that Dr. Luke loved to teach. "First, they report to Shaul that the revival is continuing in power and bearing much fruit. However, it is even better than what you read David, because the Greek word translated "thousands" is *muriades*. Do you know what that word means in English?"

"*Muriades*," I thought aloud. "Clearly, by context, it is an amount. It sounds like *myriads*."

"Right, David. Do you know the meaning of *myriad?*" asked Dr. Luke.

"I don't know. I guess it means *a lot*."

"One myriad is ten thousand. Myriads, plural, are *tens of thousands!*"

A verse formed in front of me as Ariel jumped in, "Dr. Stern's translation of this verse is more accurate."

I read, "...They also said to him, 'You see, brother, how many tens of thousands of believers there are among the Judeans, and they are all zealots for the Torah'" (Acts 21:20 CBJ).

"Not only does Dr. Stern's translation bring out the fact that tens of thousands of Jews or Judeans—Jews who lived in the areas surrounding Jerusalem—had embraced Yeshua, but it suggests something that would have sent shockwaves throughout the Middle Ages during the Crusades and Inquisitions—that these tens of thousands of Jewish believers were 'zealots for the Torah!' Oh, that those so-called Christians who outlawed the Sabbath, forced Jews to deny Judaism and be baptized, among other atrocities, could have simply read this book instead of listening to the lies and half-truths that abounded!

"It destroys the myth that Yeshua came to start a new religion apart from Judaism. Jacob, here, is clearly not reporting this to Shaul as a problem, but as something good. In Yeshua, the Law had meaning. Ezekiel and Jeremiah both prophesied that one day God, who had written His Law on tablets of stone, would one day write it on their hearts!"

> ...I will put My law in their minds and write it on their hearts... (Jeremiah 31:33).

> I will give you a new heart and put a new spirit in you; I will remove from you your heart of stone and give you a heart of flesh. And I will put my Spirit in you and move you to follow my decrees and be careful to keep my laws (Ezekiel 36:26-27).

"Somehow many Christians today have come to look at the Torah, the Law of God given to the Jews, as a bad thing. It was bad only in that it could not produce life—but it was never intended to. The Law itself was given as a revelation of God's righteousness, and thus it exposed man's sinfulness. The Law of Moses not only showed us how to live, it served another role in that it revealed our inability to actually keep the Law—it revealed our need for a Redeemer.

"Shaul, speaking of the Torah in Romans, says: 'So then, the law is holy, and the commandment is holy, righteous and good.... We know that the law is spiritual...' (Rom. 7:12,14).

"These were Jewish believers on fire for God and zealous for the Torah. Now keep in mind, when people today think of the Torah, they often conjure up images of black hats, long black coats, and endless, tedious ritual. Most of modern-day Judaism is not following the Torah per se, but traditions built upon the Torah and a *supposed* secret Oral Law,[1] which Moses was given on Mount Sinai, in addition to the written Law.

"But goodness, what is more *Torah* than the Ten Commandments? Take a look at them—they are God's practical instructions for righteous living, far removed from rote tradition! They are in fact responsible for all that is good in Western civilization. Our constitutions, legal codes, and court systems all find their source in the Law of Moses. The only thing remotely close to ritual is the keeping of the Sabbath, and who can argue with the fact that we all need time off for rest, reflection, and rejuvenation?

"And, David, here is something you may have overlooked. While Shaul had written some of his letters to individual congregations by this time, there was as yet no New Testament. All that the new believers had were the Hebrew Scriptures— the Torah, the Prophets, and the Writings."

"So even the Gentiles of the day were almost solely reliant on the Old Testament?" I asked.

"David—there was nothing else!" Luke asserted. "In fact, when Shaul wrote to Timothy that 'all Scripture is God-breathed,' he was referring to the Old Testament! (See 2 Timothy 3:16.)

"To further illustrate this point, take a look at what Jacob and the other leaders were concerned about." A passage formed as clouds before me.

[The Jewish believers] *have been informed that you teach all the Jews who live among the Gentiles to turn away from Moses, telling them not to circumcise their children or live according to our customs. What shall we do? They will certainly hear that you have come, so do what we tell you. There are four men with us who have made a vow. Take these men, join in their purification rites and pay their expenses, so that they can have their heads shaved.* **Then everyone will know there is no truth in these reports about you, but that you yourself are living in obedience to the law** (Acts 21:21-24).

"Some of the Jewish believers were concerned by rumors that Shaul was teaching a heresy, saying Jews who embraced Yeshua should 'turn away' from the Torah. Furthermore, it confirms that Shaul himself was 'living in obedience to the Law.' The funny thing is the very idea that caused deep concern among the apostles eventually became Church policy in the Middle Ages. The believers were alarmed that Shaul may have rejected the Torah, but by the Middle Ages, not only were Jews who came to faith *not encouraged* to continue to live as Jews, they were *forbidden* to do so! Acts records that Shaul, Jacob, and the other apostles affirmed that it is wrong to teach Jewish believers to forsake Jewish life and calling, but the Church of the Middle Age made it doctrine!

"Some, even today, teach that Shaul left Judaism. But I can show you, just from what I wrote in Acts, that he continued to follow the Torah.

"In Acts 18:18, Shaul cut his hair because of a vow he had taken. What kind of vow do you think would require you to cut your hair?"

"I am not sure." I responded, wishing I had been more attentive in Hebrew school.

"In Numbers 6, Moses receives special instructions for a man or a woman who wants to make a vow of dedication to the Lord. It is called a *Nazirite vow*. During the vow, you would not cut your hair, but at the end of the vow, you would shave your head completely, and Shaul did that.

"Another example is in Acts 27. Let's use Dr. Stern's translation for this: 'Since much time had been lost, and continuing the voyage was risky, because it was already past Yom-Kippur...' (Acts 27:9 CBJ).

"Shaul specifically mentions the Fast, referring to Yom Kippur, the Day of Atonement, here. But why did he not just say, 'because fall had arrived'? Had Shaul truly disassociated himself from Judaism, as some claim, he would not still have been referencing the Hebrew calendar.

"Further evidence is provided when Shaul is on trial in Acts 23:6. He appeals to the fact that he is *a Pharisee and the son of a Pharisee*. Notice he doesn't say that he was, but that he is, as in, 'the present tense,' a Pharisee. People today think the word *Pharisee* means hypocrite, and yet here was one of the most honest, true-to-yourself, theologians in the world saying, 'I'm a Pharisee!'

"Okay. Let's get back to Shaul in Jerusalem; I remember it well! Jacob and the other leaders came up with a plan to show clearly that Shaul continued to live as a Jew. So that everyone would know that he 'was living in obedience to the Law.'

I recorded it in Acts 21. And Shaul, who was nobody's push-over—and I know that better than anyone—went along with the plan just to prove that it was true, that he, while 'not under the condemnation of the Law,' still sought to live according to God's pattern for Israel—the Law of Moses.

"Take it from one of Shaul's closest companions for many years, David. He never stopped living as a Jew."

"Hang on there, Luke. Remember our instructions. Everything must be backed up with Scripture, not commentary. Only then will he be prepared," Ariel interrupted.

"And what do you think I have been doing for the past half hour?" remarked the doctor. "David, I wish you great success on your journey. I trust that something I said will prove useful."

And with that, he disappeared from the screen.

Note

1. The Oral Law or oral tradition is believed to have accompanied the written Torah which Moses received on Mt. Sinai. The Oral Law was supposedly given in order to know how to live out the written Torah. It is believed that Moses passed this down to Joshua and from Joshua to future generations, all the way until it was codified in the Talmud, beginning around 200 CE. However, there couldn't have been an Oral Law because in the time of King Josiah, they had lost the written Law and didn't even know what Passover was, much less an oral tradition. When the book of the Law was recovered, they had to start from scratch. If there had ever been an oral tradition, it had long been gone. Strangely, the Oral Law has now been written down in the Mishna and Talmud. It is probable that the religious Jews in the time of

Yeshua did not actually believe that the Oral Law came from Mt. Sinai, as it was merely referred to as *The Traditions of the Elders*. Yeshua Himself rebuked the Pharisees for putting these traditions above the Word of God (see Mark 7:9).

Furthermore, concerning the idea of an Oral Law, we find in Exodus 24:3-4 that, "When Moses went and told the people all the Lord's words and laws, they responded with one voice, 'Everything the Lord has said we will do.' Moses then wrote down everything the Lord had said...." This passage says that God shared all His laws and Moses wrote them down. There was no secret Oral Law. The children of Israel were told to obey all that was written (see Deut. 30:10; 31:9,24,26; Josh. 1:8). For deeper study on this subject see Michael L. Brown, *Answering Jewish Objections to Jesus: Traditional Jewish Objections*, Volume 5 (San Francisco: Purple Pomegranate, 2010).

Chapter Twenty

BREAKING NEWS! FIRST-CENTURY ORTHODOX JEWS PROVE YESHUA IS MESSIAH

"Wait! Rules? Prepared? Journey? What are you all referring to?"

"Soon, David, soon." Ariel reached for my hand and we were flying back to the classroom.

Seated at my desk with Ariel standing in front of the massive tablet, he began to sum up this last visit with Luke. "So, you see, not only was there a massive revival in Jerusalem with signs, wonders, and miracles, but these Jews continued to live as Jews. If you had walked up to Yochanan (John), Jacob, Kefa or any other of the leaders of the Jerusalem revival and said, 'Praise God! How does it feel to be free of the Torah and Judaism and to now be a Christian?' they would have stared at you blankly. They wouldn't have known what you were talking about. All they understood was that they, as Jews, had met their long-awaited Messiah. What could be more Jewish than that? What they may have asked, is, 'What is a Christian?' as they referred to themselves simply as *believers* in those early days. The term *Christian* to describe believers in the Christ, which is merely Greek for Messiah, was first coined by unbelievers many years later, in Antioch, a Greek-speaking city.

"After the Shavuot outpouring, do we see Kefa and John going to a church building to pray? No, of course we don't. Look at your tablet."

I read, "One afternoon at three o'clock, the hour of *minchah* prayers, as Kefa and Yochanan were going up to the Temple..." (Acts 3:1 CBJ).

"They were praying the afternoon *minchah* Jewish prayers," I offered. "Just like I do sometimes at our local synagogue. This is mind-blowing! I never pictured the followers of Jesus praying from the Siddur, the Jewish prayer book."

"Well, the Siddur came later, but make no mistake, they were going to the Temple to pray the afternoon *minchah* prayers. The New Covenant doesn't actually use the word *minchah* in the Greek, but the phrase *the time of prayer,* which for a Jew would have been at three in the afternoon. Clearly they continued in this tradition after coming to faith in Yeshua.

"David, Luke showed you all those passages about Shaul going first to the synagogue whenever he would enter a new city. Do you think he walked in and said, 'Hey, my name's Paul, used to be Saul. Can I share a little bit this morning during the service about a new religion we have started called *Christianity*?'"

"Based on what I learned today, that would be highly unlikely," I admitted, smiling at the very thought.

"Precisely; the Rabbi Shaul's objective was to tell his people that their long-awaited Messiah, the Messiah of whom the prophets of Israel spoke, had come—and that through Him they could have eternal life.

"However David, if you really want to know whether Yeshua was the Jewish Messiah, you don't even need the testimony of Shaul, Kefa, or the prophets. In truth, all you have to do is look to the Jewish leaders of Yeshua's day—the Sanhedrin."

"I don't understand. It was members of the Sanhedrin who handed Yeshua over to the Romans. How could they and why would they prove that Yeshua is the Messiah?"

"Well, they didn't do it on purpose! Watch."

As the tablet flickered and came to life, a scene began to play before me.

I could see a gathering where the high priest, his entourage, and all the Sanhedrin were present. These were the elders of Israel. Then a stunned jailer ran in, shouting, "They're gone! They're gone! Those rebel-rousers have escaped! The jail door was locked and the guards were there, but when we opened it up, they were all gone!"

A buzz traveled throughout the room as the high priest and the captain of the Temple guard tried to figure out what was happening. They were visibly shaken.

Then someone else ran into the room and announced, "The men you put in jail are back in the Temple courts teaching the people!"

Several of the Temple guards went immediately with the captain to investigate. Sure enough, there were Kefa, John, and the others, boldly proclaiming that Yeshua was the Messiah. The captain appeared worried. He could see that the people loved the apostles and what they had to say. If he arrested them by force, the people might revolt. But Kefa and the others simply turned to him and said, "Relax, force won't be necessary. We will come with you."

Once again they were brought before the Sanhedrin. The high priest stood and began to question them in an angry, smug and intimidating tone. "We gave you strict orders not to teach in this name...yet you have filled Jerusalem with your teaching and are determined to make us guilty of this man's blood" (Acts 5:28).

Kefa spoke for the other apostles as he boldly proclaimed, "We must obey God rather than any human authority. The God of our ancestors raised [Yeshua] from the dead after you killed him by hanging him on a cross" (Acts 5:29-30 NLT).

I was reminded again that while the Jewish masses—who came from all over the country to hear Yeshua—loved Him, it was the religious leaders, out of jealousy, who had asked the Romans to execute Him.

"Then God elevated Him to the place of honor at His right hand, as Prince and Savior," Kefa continued with holy boldness. "He did this so the people of Israel would repent of their sins and be forgiven. We are witnesses of these things and so is the Holy Spirit, who is given by God to those who obey Him" (see Acts 5:31-32 NLT).

The high priest and the others were so incensed, they could barely restrain themselves. They wanted to kill the apostles. They were frustrated and jealous that these uneducated Jews from Galilee had the whole city listening to their message. It was clear that they were determined to stop them at any cost, lest they lose their power over the people.

Then one of them, clearly a respected member, stood up. He asked that the apostles be sent outside so they could discuss the issue at hand. Then he raised his voice and said:

> *Men of Israel, take care what you are planning to do to these men! Some time ago there was that fellow Theudas, who pretended to be someone great. About 400 others joined him, but he was killed, and all his followers went their various ways. The whole movement came to nothing. After him, at the time of the census, there was Judas of Galilee. He got people to follow him, but he too was killed, and all his followers were scattered.*
>
> *So my advice is, leave these men alone. Let them go. If they are planning and doing these things merely on their own, it will soon be overthrown. But if it is from God, you will not be able to overthrow them. You may even find yourselves fighting against God!* (Acts 5:35-39 NLT)

Fortunately, his reasoning swayed the majority. The disciples would not be stoned to death...at least, not yet. They were brought in and these arrogant, self-serving demagogues had each of them lashed with a whip and again ordered not to speak in the name of Yeshua. But the apostles, in stark contrast to what you would expect of prisoners who had just been beaten, left rejoicing, and as they did, the tablet screen switched off.

"Wow! What a story. Why does Hollywood waste its time on vampires and Harry Potter? This is far more compelling!"

Ariel asked me, "Do you know the name of the man who stood up and convinced the Sanhedrin not to kill the apostles?"

"No," I answered.

"His name is Gamaliel, remember? I told you earlier that Shaul studied under him. I am sure you have heard of Hillel."

"Of course. He was one of the greatest Jewish scholars ever. Without him, there would be no Mishna or Talmud. Hundreds of universities and every major one in the United States have a *Hillel House*, a place for Jewish students to maintain their Jewish culture and identity while away from home. I would occasionally eat Shabbat meals there when I was in college."

"Gamaliel was Hillel's grandson and also a very respected Jewish voice of his time. He was a senior member of the Sanhedrin. There is no doubt that it was his lineage and respected position that kept the other elders from executing the apostles that day. And what was his argument?"

Like Neo learning martial arts in the Matrix, I could recall everything with vivid detail. "He told them that if Yeshua was not from God, they had nothing to worry about—He would soon be forgotten. That other would-be messiahs had arisen yet they had come to nothing and no one remembered them. However, he warned, if Yeshua was the Messiah then they would not be able to stop His message from spreading and could find themselves in the uncomfortable position of fighting against the very One they claimed to represent."

"Very good, David. Let me ask you something. Did Yeshua's message spread abroad? Do people still follow Him? Do they still talk about Him? Or, like those others, Theudas and Judas, to whom Gamaliel referred, has He been forgotten?"

I didn't even have to answer the question.

"So according to the wisdom of one of the greatest Jewish leaders of the first century, Yeshua must have been sent from God. Amazing! I remember reading, while growing up, that John Lennon once said that The Beatles were more popular than Jesus and that Christianity would eventually vanish."

"Oh, they were popular..." Ariel broke in on my train of thought *"...for a minute,"* he said with a hint of angelic sarcasm. "But Yeshua has had staying power for over two millennia. I think it is safe to say that John Lennon had a tendency to *imagine.*"

My funny angel.

"You know, David, Orthodox Judaism testifies to the validity of Yeshua's sacrificial death in another quite profound way."

"Really? How so?"

"You are familiar with the *Talmud,* yes?"

"Familiar? I know what it is—the Oral Law written, the *Mishnah* and the commentary on it, called the *Gemara.* But no, I am not a student of it."

"Tell me what you know about Yom Kippur—the Day of Atonement."

"It's the holiest day of the year for Jews. We confess our sins and fast in the hope that God will forgive us."

"Do you sacrifice a goat as well?"

"*No,* what are you talking about?"

"Before *fasting* became the central element on Yom Kippur for the Jewish community, it was all about the sacrifice. Aaron, the first high priest, the brother of Moses, was to sacrifice a goat before the Lord. Actually there were two goats. The second goat was the goat upon which the high priest would lay his hands, placing all the sins of Israel upon it." A passage lit up my desktop tablet:

> *When Aaron has finished making atonement for the Most Holy Place, the tent of meeting and the altar, he shall bring forward the live goat. He is to lay both hands on the head of the live goat and confess over it all the wickedness and rebellion of the Israelites—all their sins—and put them on the goat's head. He shall send the goat away into the wilderness in the care of someone appointed for the task. The goat will carry on itself all their sins to a remote place; and the man shall release it in the wilderness* (Leviticus 16:20-22).

"This is where we get the term *scapegoat*—when someone is made to suffer for, or is accused of, another's crimes."

"Why don't we still do this?"

"Because the Temple was destroyed in 70 CE and all sacrifices ceased. Over time, the emphasis was shifted to fasting, which was also commanded in the Torah, as a sign of acknowledgment of and repentance for sin. But fasting can never take away sin. The whole idea of a sacrifice was that you cannot atone for your own sins and live. That was why a substitute, in this case an animal, had to die in the nation's place—our place."

"So why do we fast then?"

"That's a good question, David. Why *do* you fast?" He paused to give me to time to digest the question and then answered himself, "Imagine that you were caught red-handed breaking the Law. Let's say you were going 100 miles per hour through a busy neighborhood. You are arrested and given a court date. How would you present yourself to the judge? Would you wear torn jeans and a dirty T-shirt before the court?"

"Of course not! I would wear a suit and tie. I would probably get a haircut as well!"

"Why?"

"He is the judge. My fate is in his hands. I would want to communicate to him that I was sorry for what I did in hopes that he would extend mercy. To present myself to him in a disrespectful way would ensure maximum punishment."

"Very good David, but tell me, can wearing nice clothes take away what you did?"

"No, I suppose not."

"In the same way, fasting was never intended to take away sin. It was merely the posture of humility in which the people of Israel presented themselves before the Lord. While the high priest was presenting the offering before the Lord and imparting the sin of the nation onto the scapegoat, the people waited outside in hopes that God would forgive them.

"Now, imagine if, while Aaron was carrying out his ceremonial duties on the Day of Atonement, the people treated it just like any other day—they worked, they ate, they played, they laughed. What would that have communicated to the Lord?"

"That they were not serious or that they didn't even believe they needed to be forgiven," I replied.

"Exactly, but if the people didn't work, or eat, and humbled themselves, that would communicate something entirely different to the Lord. It would convey, 'We are serious. We have sinned. Please accept the sacrifice.'

"And that brings me to my point. Did God always accept the Yom Kippur sacrifices?"

"I don't know. I never really thought about it."

Ariel replied quickly, as if he was eager to share a great insight, "Well, the rabbis and sages over the years thought quite a bit about it! In fact, the Talmud itself, which in the eyes of the Orthodox Jews is equal to Scripture, states as a matter of fact that God rejected the Yom Kippur sacrifices from 30 CE to 70 CE. This can be found in tractate Yoma 39b.

"According to the Talmud, there were several signs that would testify as to whether or not God had received the sacrifice and forgiven the people.

"First, the priest would draw lots from an urn. One of the lots had written on it *LaHashem* or 'For the Lord'. The other lot had the words *LaAzazel*. If the priest drew the lot *LaHashem* in his right hand, that meant that God accepted the sacrifice. However, if it showed up in the left hand, it meant the opposite."

"Well that is just a 50/50 chance. How could the people pin their hopes on such odds? I mean, there is nothing supernatural about that. I could just flip a coin."

"Not so; we are talking the same result over forty years. The chances of flipping a coin just five times in a row with the same result are 3 out of 100! Imagine 40 times in a row!

Believe or not, that could happen only once in 1,099,511,627,776 times—and yet the Talmud claims that it did happen in the first century.

"Another sign was that a crimson thread, which was tied to the horn of the scapegoat, would supernaturally turn white. Actually, part of this thread was taken from the goat and tied to the temple doors. That way the people would be able to see for themselves if it turned white, and this also failed to happen even once during those forty years.

"There were other signs as well. However, the main point is that according to the most respected post-second-Temple period Jewish document—the Talmud—the God of Israel rejected the Yom Kippur sacrifices every year after 30 CE. However, what the Talmud fails to reveal—whether through ignorance or conspiracy—is what took place in 30 CE when God began to reject the offerings."

"The death of Yeshua!" I blurted out.

"Exactly! And of course we know that the reason the counting ended at 70 CE was not because God suddenly began to accept the sacrifices, but..."

"...Because the Temple was destroyed by the Romans!" I finished Ariel's sentence. "There were no longer any sacrifices after that. I never knew this! Jewish people need this information! You are telling me that according to Judaism's most trusted source, from the time of Yeshua's death until the destruction of the Temple, the Yom Kippur sacrifices were not accepted. Unreal!"

"I don't know if you know it, but there are two versions of the Talmud—one, written in Judea called the Jerusalem Talmud and one that was compiled in exile, called the Babylonian

Talmud—and both of them agree on this point." Two passages appeared on my tablet, which I read out loud.

> Forty years before the destruction of the temple, the western light went out, the crimson thread remained crimson, and the lot for the Lord always came up in the left hand... (Jacob Neusner, *The Yerushalmi*, p.156-157).

> Our rabbis taught: During the last forty years before the destruction of the Temple the lot ['For the Lord'] did not come up in the right hand; nor did the crimson-colored strap become white... (Soncino version, Yoma 39b).

"Ariel, the Jewish people—non-religious ones like me, or like I was—don't know this. Someone needs to tell them!"

"Yes, David, someone must tell them, indeed," he stated with a twinkle in his eye.

Chapter Twenty-One

Communion Is Jewish!

"Come on, David, I want us to return once again to Yeshua's last Passover. It'll be a short visit. Are you up for another flight?"

"You need to ask?" I responded as I stretched out my hand. Instantly we were soaring. As we neared the first century, Ariel began to descend. Live scenes flashed past us as though rewinding a film. The closer we got to our destination, the slower they scrolled. We passed the Day of Shavuot. I could see Yeshua speaking with His disciples. It was followed by a scene where He appeared to a large group of people—more than 500. They were looking at Him in amazement, knowing that this Rabbi had just recently been crucified. Now He was cooking fish on the shores of the Galilee and I could see Kefa jump into the water from a boat and wade to shore. Next, we flew over the open tomb, the rock, and the angels. And finally we returned to the scene of that last Passover.

This is the same room in which Kefa and the other disciples received the Holy Spirit on Shavuot. The meal appeared to be over. Yeshua picked up a piece of unleavened bread, and as He broke it, He said:

> *"Take, eat; this is My body which is broken for you; do this in remembrance of Me"* (1 Corinthians 11:24 NKJV).

Then He shared it with them, each one taking a piece.

"Was that the Afikomen? At our Passover Seder that is the very last thing we eat."

"Keep watching David. I will explain everything in just a minute."

Next, Yeshua picked up a cup of wine and said, "Drink from it, all of you. This is my blood of the covenant, which is poured out for many for the forgiveness of sins" (Matt. 26:27-28) and they drank.

"Wait a minute! Communion was instituted at a Passover Seder? Unbelievable!" I found myself saying that a lot. "When I think of communion, which I hardly ever do, I always envision Roman Catholics lining up to receive a wafer and a sip of wine from their priest. I definitely don't associate it with Passover!"

"David, the blessing of bread and wine has been a Jewish tradition for millennia. You just did not make the connection with the Lord's Supper because the Church has so religisized the practice that it hardly bears resemblance to a Seder meal and the fellowship and warmth of friends sitting around a dinner table. But yes, the Lord's Supper was inaugurated at the last Seder that Yeshua enjoyed before He gave His life as a ransom for all humankind."

"Eh... religisized. Is that a word?"

"I'm an angel. I can make up words. Haven't you ever heard of the tongues of men and angels? Ah, forget it. What I mean is that they so dressed it up in religion, that it hardly resembles its original intent or context. There is so much more I want to unpack with you concerning this subject. I think we need to take this back to the classroom." Ariel's voice trailed off—and this time, instantaneously, I found myself back in my heavenly-ancient-techno classroom.

Ariel just picked up where he had left off, as though we hadn't just traveled two thousand years in time—assuming I was back in the twenty-first century. "During the Passover Seder meal, it is customary to remove the middle piece of the three pieces of matzah from the white linen covering and break it in two. Tell me what happens in your home, David."

"Well, my father, who still leads our Seders, takes his role very seriously, even highlighting in each *haggadah*[1] for every participant (and we usually have around thirty people!) exactly when and where they have to read. He would take one half of the broken piece of matzah, the *Afikomen*, and wrap it in white linen—normally a napkin. He would hide it somewhere in the house and the children would search for it after the meal. The finder would return it to the leader and then we'd all partake of it.

"As a kid, that was the most exciting part of the Seder. My sisters and my cousins and I would run around the house after the meal, tearing our home apart looking for it. The winner got two dollars! Now my girls do the same thing with their cousins, though the going rate is now five dollars." I was smiling. Passover was always a wonderful time in the Lebowitz home. "But what does the tradition of the Afikomen have to do with the Passover? I had never thought to ask."

"The rabbis say it is to remind you of the sacrificial Passover lamb. How right they are! Sadly they don't know who the Lamb is. It can only be understood in light of Yeshua. He was the Lamb of God. He took the matzah, gave thanks and broke it, and gave it to them, saying, 'This is my body given for you; do this in remembrance of me' (Luke 22:19). Clearly the bread He broke was unleavened, as it was Passover. Leaven is often compared to sin in the Bible. Shaul reinforces this when writing to the Corinthians. Read from your tablet."

> ...Do you not know that a little leaven leavens the whole lump? Therefore purge out the old leaven, that you may be a new lump, since you truly are unleavened. For indeed [Messiah], our Passover, was sacrificed for us. Therefore let us keep the feast, not with old leaven, nor with the leaven of malice and wickedness, but with the **unleavened bread** of sincerity and truth (1 Corinthians 5:6-8 NKJV).

"Only Yeshua could say, 'This is My body,' because only He was 'a lamb without blemish or defect' as is stated in First Peter 1:19—He was sinless! Even during the original Passover, the Lord said that lamb had to be 'without defect' (Exod. 12:5). That was because, even though they didn't know it, the lamb pointed to the Perfect Lamb of God, Yeshua."

All these passages were being highlighted on my tablet.

"Amazingly, many churches today serve *leavened bread* for the Lord's supper! They seem to have entirely missed the point that the reason the bread is without leaven is to symbolize that Yeshua was sinless—the only Man without sin.

"Let's listen to how the prophet John, whom you recently met, describes his cousin, Yeshua."

John appeared on the tablet but not in real time, as in our earlier conversation. This was more like watching a video on YouTube. As Yeshua came toward him, John said for all to hear: "Look, the Lamb of God, who takes away the sin of the world!" (John 1:29).

"But in order for Him to be the Passover Lamb," I interrupted, "He would have to—woah—He would have to die!"

"That's right, David. Just like it's depicted in the Seder with the middle matzah, His body was broken. After He was killed, He, too, was wrapped in white linen and hidden for a time. And just as the matzah is found and returned for all to eat, He too returned to life, and those who believe partake of Him."

"This is all so Jewish. I can hardly believe it!"

"It really is! And yet Jewish tradition," continued the celestial professor, "has no clear explanation as to what the Afikomen is, where it came from, or why it is broken. The practice actually predates the first century.[2] This special piece of matzah represented the Messianic hopes of the Jewish people. Even as Moses rescued the children of Israel, the Jewish people looked for the One of whom Moses spoke when He said, 'The Lord your God will raise up for you a prophet like me from among you, from your fellow Israelites. You must listen to him' (Deut. 18:15).

"The Afikomen represented the Messiah. Yeshua, His disciples, and all first-century Jews knew this. When He took the matzah and said, 'Take, eat; this is My body,' let's be honest—it would have seemed very strange if they didn't understand that the broken piece represented the Messiah. However, because they were familiar with the Messianic tradition, they understood His meaning. By taking *that* piece of matzah and saying, 'This is My body,' He was in essence saying, 'I am Israel's Redeemer.'

"Sadly, the rabbis who came after Yeshua sought to disassociate Judaism from the idea that a human being could perform the divine function of redemption. In fact, Moses himself, the central figure of the Passover, was completely removed for this reason! His name is not even mentioned in the Haggadah!"

"That's crazy," I protested. "Of course Moses is mentioned in the Passover Seder—he's the protagonist!"

"Really? Where?" The angel challenged me. And as I thought about it, I realized he was right. I couldn't think of one place in the entire Passover ceremony where Moses was mentioned.

"How can Moses not be part of the Passover celebration? That would be like celebrating the Fourth of July and not mentioning George Washington!" I argued.

"It is all about control, David, and sadly, leaders in virtually every religion do it—whether it is fanatical Islamists telling would-be suicide bombers that they will soon be in paradise, or Catholic bishops creating purgatory in order to raise money for their buildings. They will use any means necessary to keep people from thinking for themselves. However, let's not dwell on that right now, but return to the Afikomen.

"In the Passover, Yeshua, the divine Son, was broken, then wrapped in linen and buried, ultimately conquering death itself, by rising to life.

"The very word *Afikomen* symbolizes the coming of Yeshua."

"What does it mean?" I asked.

"Well, interestingly enough, it isn't a Hebrew word. In fact, it's Greek," the angel explained. "And in the first century it was pronounced in its future tense *Aphikomenos*, which means, 'He is coming!'"

"Amazing. Then there could have been no doubt as to who He was claiming to be!" I exclaimed.

"Of course, there is another equally significant meaning in the hiding of the matzah. Despite being Jewish and coming from Israel, Yeshua has been largely rejected by the Jewish world since the first century. However, the day will come when the Jewish people will return to Him—but only when they search for Him, as children do the matzah."

A passage lit up my tablet and I read aloud, "You will seek me and find me when you seek me with all your heart" (Jer. 29:13).

"You are here today, David, because you chose to seek Him out. But a day is coming when far more than a Jewish writer from Philadelphia will seek Him—all Israel will long for Him. The Father has promised."

Another passage appeared:

> *For the Israelites will live many days without king or prince, without sacrifice or sacred stones, without ephod or household gods. Afterward the Israelites **will return and seek the Lord their***

God and David their king. *They will come trembling to the Lord and to his blessings in the last days* (Hosea 3:4-5).

"But that says they will return to David?" I asked.

"King David was a type of the Messiah, and Yeshua being in the lineage of David was called the Son of David. As you and I know, King David is dead, but Yeshua rose from the dead, and Israel will one day return to Him. In fact, many already have!"

Notes

1. The *haggadah* is a special book which contains not only the story of the Exodus, but the structure and the ritual of the Seder (Seder means "order"). It is read aloud at the Passover Seder.

2. To be clear, there are many valid views on when the *Afikomen* was introduced into the Passover Seder. Some believe it was started by first-century Jewish believers (as it so clearly resembles the Messiah) and was later adopted by the greater Jewish community. The fact that Jewish tradition is so vague and unclear regarding the ceremony lends credence to this view.

Chapter Twenty-Two

THE BLOOD OF THE LAMB ON THE DOORPOST OF YOUR HEART

"Let's move on to the wine," suggested Ariel. "On Passover, Jews drink four cups of wine."

"Right, the Cup of Sanctification, the Cup of Deliverance, the Cup of Redemption and—ah—help me out, Ariel."

"Praise, David, the Cup of Praise."

"Right, the Cup of Praise."

"They each symbolize something powerful. But let's focus in on the third cup, because that is the cup of wine we drink directly after we share the Afikomen—the *Cup of Redemption.* This is the cup that Yeshua took when He said..."

A passage appeared that read, "This cup is the new covenant in my blood, which is poured out for you" (Luke 22:20).

"I get it!" I yelled. "At last, I see it! I don't need to feel guilty because I am Jewish. It is totally Jewish to believe in Yeshua. It couldn't be any more Jewish! He is our Passover Lamb. The perfect, sinless..." My revelation was interrupted by the arrival of another passage on my tablet:

> *For you know that it was not with perishable things such as silver or gold that you were redeemed from the empty way of life handed down to you from your ancestors, **but with the precious blood of [Messiah], a lamb without blemish or defect*** (1 Peter 1:18-19).

Ariel elaborated, "Kefa, after describing Yeshua as the Messiah who would suffer as an innocent Lamb, likens His blood to the blood of the Passover lamb which had to be placed on the doorposts of their homes. His blood would serve a similar, yet even more powerful purpose."

"His blood," I proclaimed, "covers the doorpost of my soul. In the Passover story, the blood of the lamb on the doorpost of one's home kept the Angel of Death at bay. However, Yeshua's blood, and I'm only now just grasping this, protects us for all eternity. The Passover is a picture of what God wants to do spiritually for everyone."

"Right, David!"

"The blood of the spotless Lamb of God is impenetrable. The enemy, Satan himself, cannot touch you once you apply it to your life. It is not merely effective for one special night in Egypt, *but for all eternity.* On that great Day of Judgment, those who believe will be pardoned, exempted from judgment, just as the firstborn male was on Passover, because of the blood of the Lamb."

"Right, David! But there is more. At 9:00 AM, the very hour that Yeshua, the Lamb of God, was nailed to the Cross, the first Passover sacrifices were being offered in the Temple. And when He breathed His last breath and cried out, 'It is finished!' it was 3:00 PM, the exact time of the second Passover sacrifice."

"He truly was the Lamb of God," I whispered.

"And He still is!"

"There is so much more I want to tell you, David, but you must be getting tired by now."

I should have been exhausted, but I was totally alert. "Not at all! *Please*, tell me more!"

"Okay then..." my angel, only too willingly, conceded.

Chapter Twenty-Three

LAMB OR RAM?

Ariel continued, "The Lord laced the Hebrew Scriptures with prophetic hints, pictures, clues, illustrations, and examples, going all the way back to Adam and Eve—all to help us arrive at the truth. Here is one of those hints that points to Yeshua. See if you recognize the story."

In rugged terrain I saw on the larger tablet screen an old man on a donkey accompanied by a young man and his servants. They stopped. The old man was quite obviously giving instructions to his servants who were nodding assent. He seemed to be assuring them that they would return. Then, leaving his donkey with the two servants, he and the young man set off up the mountain. They journeyed together in silence, the young man shouldering a heavy load of wood while the old man bore a heavy heart, but never faltered in his step.

"Is it Abraham and Isaac?"

"Not bad! Now let's listen in." Ariel tapped the massive tablet in the lower right-hand corner and immediately we were able to hear their conversation.

Isaac spoke first, "Father?"

"Yes, my son?" Abraham replied.

"The fire and wood are here," Isaac said, "but where is the lamb for the burnt offering?"

Abraham answered, "God Himself will provide the lamb for the burnt offering, my son" (see Gen. 22:6-8).

I watched as Abraham and Isaac arrived at the place God had showed Abraham and together they built a low altar. And then, after arranging the wood Isaac had carried up the mountain, on the altar, Abraham—*to my shock* (yes, I already knew the story, but actually *seeing* it was different!)—bound his son and laid the compliant boy on the wood.

Was he really going to do it?!

Isaac was clearly confused and questioning, yet without a word he obeyed his father, trusting in his father's perfect love for the son he doted on. Abraham turned away, not wanting Isaac to see the tears which now flowed freely. It was clear that he was struggling with what he knew he must do. I found myself *hoping* he wouldn't do what I already knew he had to do. He turned back to his son and kissed him. His tears falling on Isaac's face and hair, Isaac felt his heart and lungs constrict with fear. Terror gripped him. The unimaginable suddenly became a reality when his father took out a knife!

I wanted to scream, "No. Don't do it!" but I knew it would be to no avail. As Abraham, eyes stricken, raised the knife high to plunge it into his son's heart, suddenly a voice, not mine, was heard.

"Abraham! *Abraham!*" An angel called to him.

His hand frozen in midair, Abraham replied, "Here I am."

"Do not lay a hand on the boy," he said. "Do not do anything to him. Now I know that you fear God, because you have not withheld from me your son, your only son" (see Gen. 22:11-12).

My heart was still pounding. I was actually sweating. I knew the story, but when I saw the knife raised and Isaac tied to the altar, helplessly submitting to his fate, I was beside myself.

"It's okay David..." Ariel assured me. "All this happened a very long time ago. Now focus, David, because I want you to see what's still to come."

I watched as Abraham looked up, but saw no one. He looked around to see who was calling him, but instead saw a ram caught in the thicket. So Abraham sacrificed the ram that God had supplied in place of Isaac, his son. The tablet went into hibernation as the screen went blank.

"Did you see what took place there, David?"

"Yes, he almost killed Isaac!" I blurted out.

"No, David. Something else. Remember when Isaac, on their way up the mountain, asked his father where the sacrifice was? What did Abraham say?"

"He said God Himself would provide a lamb."

"Exactly. So where is the lamb?"

"They found him caught in the thickets," I responded.

"No, David, look at your desktop and read it to me."

"Okay," I looked down and read, "'Abraham looked up and there in a thicket he saw...a *ram*.' Okay, he didn't find a lamb. So? What's the difference?" And then, as if someone flicked on a switch, "Ohhhh!" I said, indicating that I now understood. "Because *Yeshua* is the Lamb!"

"Bravo, David, Yeshua is the Lamb to whom Abraham referred. He didn't know it at the time, but when he said, 'God will provide the Lamb' he was speaking prophetically. And another prophet, John, whom you now know, publically announced his arrival calling Him 'the Lamb of God who takes away the sin of the world.'"

"Yes, I remember!" I exclaimed. "This is amazing."

Ariel continued, "Isaac was a *type* of Yeshua. A *type*, in the Bible, is a person or a prophetic event that predicts or foreshadows something in the future. Isaac, the son of promise, was a prophetic type pointing to Yeshua, who was also a promised Son." A passage popped up on my tablet as I heard the familiar chime.

> *For to us a child is born, **to us a son is given**, and the government will be on his shoulders. And He will be called Wonderful Counselor, Mighty God, Everlasting Father, Prince of Peace* (Isaiah 9:6).

"Think about it. God had an only Son and Abraham had an only son. Yes, he had Ishmael too, but that had been his own doing. Isaac was the long-awaited *promised* son whose birth was supernatural, in that Sarah was not only barren but far beyond the age of child bearing."

"And Abraham," I jumped in, "was willing to give to God his dearest possession, his only beloved son. In turn, two thousand years later, God reciprocates by providing the Lamb of which Abraham spoke, the One most dear to Him, Yeshua—His only Son!"

D'ling! John 3:16, written in huge letters, filled the screen:

> *For God so loved the world that he gave his one*
> *and only Son, that whoever believes in him shall*
> *not perish but have eternal life* (John 3:16).

"There were multiple prophecies foretelling just about every aspect of Yeshua's life and ministry. I don't know how anyone could have missed them," Ariel added.

"The problem is that most of us aren't looking. It was only recently that I found myself concerned about the fact that I don't know what God expects from me. I am twenty-eight years old, and this is the first time in my life that I am taking God seriously. I never thought to study the prophecies. I couldn't see what they had to do with me. I think most Jewish people are like me. I am not speaking of Orthodox Jews, but secular, cultural Jews. I mean, my life is good. I make a good living, I am healthy, I love my wife, and have two wonderful daughters. It simply never occurred to me, *until now*, that there might be more."

"Oh David, there is more...so much more," Ariel reassured me. "And it was always there for you, if you had simply searched. For instance, the prophet Isaiah foretold the Messiah's mandate seven hundred years before He came."

The passage from John faded as the prophet Isaiah himself took center screen and began to recite portions from the ancient prophecy. He was clearly well along in years and squinted as he read from a very ancient-looking parchment.

As he read, the passage scrolled across my desktop tablet, with certain words highlighted:

> Just as there were many who were appalled at him—His **appearance was so disfigured** beyond that of any human being and His **form marred** beyond human likeness—He was **despised and rejected by mankind**, a man of suffering, and familiar with pain.

> ...Surely he **took up our pain** and **bore our suffering**, yet we considered him punished by God, stricken by him, and afflicted. But he was **pierced for our transgressions**, he was crushed for our iniquities; **the punishment that brought us peace was on him**, and **by his wounds we are healed**. ... And the **Lord has laid on him** the iniquity of us all.

> He was oppressed and afflicted, yet **he did not open his mouth**; he was led **like a lamb** to the slaughter, and as a sheep before its shearers is silent, so he did not open His mouth. ...**For he was cut off from the land of the living; for the transgression of my people he was punished. He was assigned a grave with the wicked, and with the rich in his death**, though **he had done no violence**, nor was any deceit in his mouth.

> **Yet it was the Lord's will to crush him and cause him to suffer**, and though the Lord makes his life **an offering for sin**, he will see his offspring and **prolong his days**, and the will of the Lord will prosper in his hand. After he has suffered, **he will**

*see the light of life and be satisfied; by his knowl-edge **my righteous servant will justify many, and he will bear their iniquities**. Therefore I will give him a portion among the great, and he will divide the spoils with the strong, because **he poured out his life unto death**, and was numbered with the transgressors. **For he bore the sin of many, and made intercession for the transgressors*** (Isaiah 52:14; 53:3-12).

As Isaiah disappeared, I protested to Ariel, "But that's not in the Tanach,"[1] I protested, "that's got to be from the New Testament!"

"Look it up for yourself," he said.

"Seven hundred years *before* Yeshua," I pondered aloud. "How could that be? He describes everything!

"He would be rejected. He would suffer for us. He would be sinless and ultimately He would die for us, willingly bear-ing the punishment for our sins, and then come to life again. But why does it say He would see His *offspring*? Yeshua didn't have children."

"He didn't? There are over one billion people on earth who claim Him as Savior and Messiah. You don't think they qualify as children?"

"Ohhh, I see. It's talking about *spiritual* children!" The familiar chime directed my attention back to the screen. I read out loud: "Yet to all who did receive him, to those who believed in his name, he gave the right to become children of God" (John 1:12).

"And Isaiah also prophesied that He would die a sinner's death—in His case, that was crucifixion, 'He was pierced for our transgressions'—and that He would be buried with the rich. This was fulfilled when Joseph of Arimathea, a wealthy man and a member of the Sanhedrin, the ruling council among the Jews, donated his own tomb for Yeshua's burial. What he didn't know, of course, was that He wouldn't be needing it for long."

"Yeah, because Yeshua would rise from the dead. Like Isaiah said, 'He will see the light of life again.'"

So much! So much to take in! I was finally feeling like I was nearing overload. *Yeshua, the Jew...our elder brother...He was the Passover Lamb...He gave His life willingly for me...like Isaac, He was the Son who was sacrificed...this is it! This is what I have been longing for...this is what has been missing in my li—*

Suddenly, lights and colors were going in every direction, and I was flying out of control, with no angelic escort. "Ariel!" I shouted. Where was Ariel!? *"Ariel!"* I shouted louder.

I was spinning in circles. I was terrified. What was happening?

Note

1.   *Tanach* is an acronym for *Torah, Writings, and Prophets.* It refers to the Hebrew Scriptures.

Chapter Twenty-Four

CARRYING HIS CROSS

I hit the ground with a thud and knew somehow that I was back in Jerusalem, *but where?* There was shouting coming from what looked like a palace courtyard. So I walked in the direction of the noise, curious to see what all the commotion was about. As I did so, I felt a strange draft around my legs. Looking down, I saw I was wearing sandals, and...what? *Was I wearing a dress?*

On closer examination, I realized I was arrayed in the typical garb of a first-century Jewish man. Even my arms and legs, I noticed, were darker and hairier. *Sweet*, I thought—this was a nice change from my normal, fair, European-Ashkenazi complexion. Then I had another thought, *How cool would it be if...* I touched my face. Yes! A full beard! Now that was something I could never do before. I was smiling, but not for long.

I walked inside the palace courtyard and standing before a loud and angry crowd was Yeshua, bloodied and bruised, beside someone who looked to be an important Roman dignitary, or ruler.

As I stood there, an order was given and He was taken away by soldiers into the palace, and not gently. I followed behind, amazed at my own fearlessness. The whole company of soldiers surrounded Him. They took His hands and tied them to a post. Another soldier produced a whip that had multiple leather tails, and near the end of each tail were tied lethal shards of lead and glass. *My God! They're going whip Him with that thing!*

Just before they did, everything froze in time and a screen rose up from the ground. It was the size of a widescreen TV. A man appeared on the screen. He was not speaking to me but to a lecture hall of students. He was in his late thirties, and while I was sure he was a Bible teacher, he wasn't dressed in religious attire at all—just jeans, a T-shirt and a sports coat. He didn't talk like a religious person, either. He was a regular guy. I liked him already.

> A flogging was such a barbarous, intense, horrendous mode of suffering that many men simply died from it. They stripped the victim almost naked, which is very shameful in Eastern Jewish ancient culture. The man's neck and shoulders and back and legs and buttocks would be exposed and bare. And on each side would stand a professional executor and he would have

a cat-of-nine-tails. It was a handle from which preceded straps of leather. At the end of each strap was a ball made out of stone or metal and with spikes or bone protruding. The metal would tenderize the man's body and the hooks would sink deeply into the man's flesh.

Then the executioner would take a tug on the cat-of-nine-tails to make sure that the hooks were sunk deeply into the man's flesh. And then he would literally rip the flesh off the man's body. The flesh on the man's back would look like ribbons. He would be a bloodied mess. His body would be absolutely traumatized and thrown into shock.[1]

As the screen retracted I heard a loud *snap!* as the first lash was laid. The sharp and deadly thongs of the whip dug deep into the flesh on Yeshua's back as the soldier violently jerked the whip back, "*No!*" I shouted, but no one heard me, as the crude weapon continued to rip His back apart, as it was laid upon Him again and again. The soldiers were laughing. They were actually enjoying this! Only when the count reached thirty-nine did the torment finally end. Yeshua remained upright only because His arms were tied to the post.

A couple of soldiers went to untie Him. "Smack!" one of the Roman guards struck Yeshua in the face with all his might, drawing blood. The blow was followed by another one, as they continued to goad and mock Him. Yet Yeshua did not retaliate. He just looked at them with compassion. I was stunned. Isaiah's words drifted through my mind as if the prophet were whispering them to me.

He was oppressed and afflicted, yet He did not open His mouth; He was led like a lamb to the slaughter, and as a sheep before its shearers is silent, so He did not open His mouth.

The soldiers then took some thorny branches and proceeded to twist them crudely into a wreath, forming a makeshift crown. As they roughly thrust it upon His head, the long sharp thorns dug deeply into His scalp, causing Him to visibly wince and draw in breath as blood trickled from His punctured brow. Then they covered His nakedness by adorning Him in a purple robe. They began to mock Him, "Hail King of the Jews." Still, He didn't respond.

Those fools! They had no idea that they were beating the very One who gave them life, as again and again, they struck Him over the head and spat on Him. Then, they knelt down before Him in mock homage. Finally, tiring of this charade, they removed the robe and put His own clothes back on His bloodied body. I thought I was going to be sick.

At this point, He was handed over to another garrison who led Him out and laid a heavy wooden cross upon His raw and lacerated back, strapping it to His body. After all this, they were going to make Him carry His own execution stake—the cross on which He was to be impaled! Written on a sign that they would later fasten to the cross were the words, "King of the Jews" in Aramaic, Latin, and Greek (don't ask me how I knew!). The Jewish leaders protested, but the Roman centurion, who appeared to be running the show, refused to have it removed.

Suddenly, they were steering Him in my direction. *Should I run? Should I hide?* But actually, I did neither. I simply froze. A man next to me huddled with his two boys, probably visiting

Jerusalem for the Passover. He certainly hadn't brought them here to see this! They appeared just as stunned as I was.

As they neared, Yeshua collapsed under the weight of the massive cross, slamming His already beaten body against the stone pavement, crushing Him and then pinning Him to the ground. He was physically unable to get up. One of the soldiers started to say something to the man next to me, but when he noticed his sons, he turned to me instead and said something in Greek. Amazingly, I understood him and then realized that the guards had also been speaking in Greek this whole time, and I had understood.

"You! Carry His cross!" He barked at me. Surprisingly, I wasn't scared. I didn't hesitate. I ran to Yeshua and with great exertion, I unstrapped and lifted the heavy beam off His body. It must have weighed well over one hundred pounds. Tears were streaming down my face as this innocent Rabbi lifted His head. His face was half covered in dirt and gravel that now clung to the blood on His check.

And then He looked up at me—or should I say *in me* or *through me*. *Love* personified gazed into my soul and His eyes penetrated my very being. I felt totally exposed before Him. In that instant, I knew that He knew every wicked thing I had ever done—every time I had secretly looked at pornography, yelled at my wife, or disrespected my parents. He saw. He knew every time I had lied or cheated. He could see every petty grudge I'd ever held, how jealous I was of more successful writers and bloggers, and the pride—oh, the pride of life that consumed me!

In light of what He was suffering, my selfish ambition seemed so absurd. I suddenly felt guilty for joining in with the other students and bullying Rudy Green in Hebrew school. And then, I felt horrible shame for pressuring Beth Sanger to sleep with me in high school, taking her virginity, assessing its value at about the same level as taking a friend's pencil for a test. *What had I done?* I then heard these words in my mind:

> *For the word of God is alive and active. Sharper than any double-edged sword, it penetrates even to dividing soul and spirit, joints and marrow; it judges the thoughts and attitudes of the heart. Nothing in all creation is hidden from God's sight. Everything is uncovered and laid bare before the eyes of him to whom we must give account* (Hebrews 4:12-13).

Laid bare...yes, that was exactly how I felt. He could see everything. I was surrounded by a thousand Roman swords, but the worst they could do was pierce my flesh. The eyes of Yeshua dug deep into the darkest recesses of my soul, leaving me utterly exposed and without excuse.

I thought my heart would burst. I wept for my sin. I wept for those I had hurt. *He* was suffering today for *my* sins. In the past, if I did something that I knew was wrong, I might feel a tinge of guilt, but ultimately would justify my behavior. *What's the big deal? Everyone does it.* Every successive time, it became easier and easier—always less guilt than the time before, and finally—no guilt at all.

Now I was seeing that my sin was indeed a big deal. My sin was doing this to Yeshua. This was not a lamb, bull, or goat at the Temple—this was the Messiah, God's Son, and He was going through this hellish ordeal in order that I might be pardoned! How could I resist love like this any longer!?

Again, I heard Isaiah's voice in my mind:

> *But He was pierced for our transgressions, He was crushed for our iniquities; the punishment that brought us peace was on Him.*

I could not break His gaze. All this time, I'd thought that David Lebowitz was a good guy. *What had I done that was so evil,* I would reason, *I am not as bad this one, or that one.* My problem was that I only compared myself to those around me—my friends and co-workers. But now, looking into the very essence of righteousness, I realized how desperately short I had fallen. Even my good deeds were invariably motivated by pride and ambition.

Isaiah's voice was almost audible:

> *All of us have become like one who is unclean, and all our righteous acts are like filthy rags; we all shrivel up like a leaf, and like the wind our sins sweep us away* (Isaiah 64:6).

At which point another voice broke into my consciousness:

> *The fool says in his heart, "There is no God." They are corrupt, their deeds are vile; there is no one who does good. The Lord looks down from heaven on all mankind to see if there are any who understand, any who seek God. All have turned away, all have become corrupt; there is no one who does good, not even one* (Psalm 14:1-3).

I was experiencing the rudest of awakenings! I was two thousand years in the past on the dusty streets of Jerusalem, with the dying Messiah only a few inches away. I was seeing myself for the first time and it was true—David Lebowitz was not a good guy at all. He was selfish, petty, unforgiving, and corrupt, just like everyone else. I deserved God's judgment.

Then I heard in my spirit:

> *Oh, what a miserable person I am! Who will free me from this life that is dominated by sin and death? Thank God! The answer is in* [Yeshua the Messiah] *our Lord...* (Romans 7:24-25 NLT).

> *For what one earns from sin is death; but eternal life is what one receives as a free gift from God, in union with the Messiah Yeshua, our Lord...* (Romans 6:23 CBJ).

Yes! He is my only hope. He is anyone and everyone's only hope! Despite His knowing everything there was to know about me, I felt no judgment—only indescribable, unsurpassable love and compassion. Despite all the pain, the beatings, and flogging that He had endured, a slight, but undeniable smile that expressed a brotherly affection that I had never felt before appeared on His face as He looked at me. He seemed to be telling me that everything would be okay. He was actually in control.

Note

1. Material based on information taken from Mark Driscoll, "Jesus Died" (sermon, Mars Hill Church, Seattle, Washington, April 1, 2012), accessed November 20, 2012, http://castroller .com/Podcasts/MarsHillChurch/2831461.

Chapter Twenty-Five

"Surely, This Man Was the Son of God!"

"Ahhh!" I cried out as a big Roman boot found my stomach.

"Get up!" the soldier hissed.

The pain brought me back to the harsh present reality, stealing me from His holy gaze. In fact, had it not been for that Roman boot, I don't think I could have broken away from His stare. While it had only been a matter of seconds, it had felt like eternity. So much had been communicated in that brief fragment of time. With another heave, I shouldered the cross and they marched us a little over a quarter mile, outside the city walls, to the place where they would crucify Him.

I was finally ordered to stop and I lowered the heavy cross-beam to the ground. The dreaded moment had arrived—but just before they would nail Him to the wooden beam, the tablet came forth again from the earth as the young Bible teacher returned on the flat screen. Everything and everyone around me froze. The teacher said:

> The ancient Jewish historian Josephus called crucifixion the most wretched of deaths. They could hang for upwards of nine days, going in and out of consciousness, stripped almost, or altogether, naked. It was done publicly; it was state-sponsored terror, meant to instill fear in any other would-be lawbreakers. This would be like crucifying people in front of a local mall, or a store or a park, the kind of place where people frequented often and large crowds would gather.
>
> The body is in such trauma and shock at this point that men are weeping; they are in and out of consciousness, and dripping off of their bodies would be tears and blood. For some this was sport. They thought this was entertaining.[1]

The flat screen descended into the earth and the crucifixion began. I wanted to turn away, but I also wanted these soldiers to know that I would be a witness to their vile deed. No, I would watch it all, I decided as a soldier grabbed Yeshua's arm and held it down on the crossbar, while another soldier pulled out a massive nail, resembling a railroad spike—it was at least six inches long—and placed it firmly against the right hand[2] of Yeshua. A mallet was produced and without wasting any time, with a loud grunt, he brought the head of the hammer down firmly on the center of the nail, pushing deep into the center of the Messiah's hand, between two bones. Yeshua winced, but said nothing. Another strike and it appeared that the spike made its way clear through His flesh, into the wood. A few more blows of the hammer and Yeshua appeared to momentarily lose consciousness as His hand was fastened to the wood. And then the other hand was secured to the beam in the same manner.

The soldiers then moved to secure His feet to the vertical beam. They placed one over the other, and then pounded a single nail through the center of His feet, causing agony beyond description. Once done, they levered the cross into position using ropes and dropped it into a hole about three feet deep in the hard ground, jarring Yeshua's entire body. At the sound of the jolt the onlookers involuntarily shuddered, as the impact pushed His body first upward, then downward on the nails through His hands and feet. The pain He felt would have divided time as He hung there between Heaven and earth.

Thankfully, the scene transformed at this point, as I didn't know how much more of that I could watch. The flat screen reemerged and this time the setting was a university lecture hall where a professor was delivering a clinical, forensic analysis of death by crucifixion to a class of students.

A death by crucifixion seems to include all that pain and death can have of the horrible and ghastly. Dizziness, cramp, thirst, starvation, sleeplessness, traumatic fever, tetanus, shame, publicity of shame, long, continuous torment, horror of anticipation, mortification of untended wounds, all intensified just up to the point at which they can be endured at all but all stopping just short of the point which would give to the sufferer the relief of unconsciousness. The unnatural position made every movement painful. The lacerated veins and crushed tendons throbbed with incessant anguish. The wounds inflamed by exposure gradually gangrened. The arteries, especially at the head and stomach, became swollen and oppressed with surcharged blood and while each variety of misery went on gradually increasing, there was added to them the intolerable pang of a burning and raging thirst. And all these physical complications caused an internal excitement and anxiety which made the prospect of death itself, of death, the unknown enemy at whose approach man usually shudders most, bear the aspect of a delicious and exquisite release.[3]

Hung completely naked before the crowd, the pain and damage caused by crucifixion were designed to be so devilishly intense that one would continually long for death, but could linger for days with no relief.

According to Dr. Frederick Zugibe, piercing of the median nerve of the hands with a nail can cause pain so incredible that even morphine won't help, "severe, excruciating, burning pain, like lightning bolts traversing the arm into the spinal cord." Rupturing the foot's plantar nerve with a nail would have a similarly horrible effect.[4]

In crucifying someone, one thing is for sure—
no one was concerned with a quick and painless
death. No one was concerned with the preserva-
tion of any measure of human dignity. Quite the
opposite. Crucifiers sought an agonizing torture
of complete humiliation that exceeds any other
design for death that man has ever invented.[5]

As the lecture ended I was returned once again to the most
amazing history lesson I had ever had. I looked at the Man
hanging from the Cross—He was unrecognizable. The flogging alone had bloodied and torn His flesh from His bones.
The beatings and the pulling out of His beard had so ravaged
His face as to make Him unrecognizable. Again I heard Isaiah's voice in my mind.

*...his appearance was so disfigured beyond that
of any human being and his form marred beyond
human likeness...* (Isaiah 52:14).

The soldiers who had removed His clothes before, placing His naked body on the Cross, were now, like this whole
thing was a game, callously casting lots to see who would get
His garments.

I thought of the movie I had seen as a teenager, *The Robe*,
where Richard Burton plays the Roman tribune who not only
oversees Yeshua's crucifixion, but wins His seamless robe.
The robe brings a curse on him until he finds peace in Yeshua.
But this was no movie. I heard a whisper in my mind: "They
divide my clothes among them and cast lots for my garment"
(Ps. 22:18).

Was this also foretold? I wondered.

Some among the crowd cruelly mocked Him. Even passers-by hurled insults, saying, "If You are the Son of God, then prove it. Come down from the Cross."

I remembered the words that Ariel shared with me when he quoted Yeshua: "No one takes my life from me. I give my life of my own free will. I have the authority to give my life, and I have the authority to take my life back again" (John 10:18 GW).

Even some of the religious leaders taunted Him, "He saved others, but He can't save Himself! He's the King of Israel! Ha! Let Him come down now from the Cross, and we will believe in Him," they laughed. The Roman soldiers joined in.

Astonishingly, a man was suffering a torture unlike anything I had ever seen and they acted as if it was nothing more than a show. They had no idea who they were messing with! *He should destroy them!* Call down fire from Heaven! My blood was boiling! Don't they know that He is doing this for them!? My anger *at* them was suddenly overridden by my fear *for* them. This was the Messiah, the Son of the living God, they were daring to crucify.

I would find out later that He could indeed have destroyed them. For when Kefa had sought to prevent His arrest in Gethsemane by lashing out with a sword, Yeshua told him: "Do you think I cannot call on my Father, and he will at once put at my disposal more than twelve legions of angels?" (Matt. 26:53).

A couple of soldiers offered Him some vinegar on a sponge to quench His thirst, laughing and mocking as they did so. I didn't know what was in it, but I soon found out, as the screen emerged again. The young Bible teacher was back and this time he shared something that literally made me gag:

> During a trip to Greece, Israel and Turkey, in one archeological dig, we saw seating from an ancient public restroom. And people would sit on marble slabs and water would roll underneath as a sort of shared bathroom. And underneath the seat there was an opening, so I asked one of the archeologists, "What was that for?" They said that the servants would be paid to take a stick with a sponge on the end and use it to clean the person while they were seated upon the toilet. But then they found that as they reused the sponge people would get sick and they would develop infections. So they began dipping it in wine vinegar as an antiseptic to kill the germs.
>
> I literally, in that moment, lost it. I just sat down and started tearing up and fighting back complete weeping. It dawned on me. When they took the stick with the sponge on the end, dipped it in wine vinegar and tried to shove it into the mouth of Jesus on the cross, they used a soldier's ancient toilet brush. It was the kind of thing he had used to clean himself on the battlefield. And he took that and tried to shove it into the Messiah's mouth, to silence and shame Him.[6]

The tablet reentered the ground and I felt nauseated. As they offered Him the vinegar-filled sponge, the soldiers laughed at Him and shouted, "If You are king of the Jews save Yourself."

And then, looking heavenward, Yeshua cried out for all to hear, "Father, forgive them, for they do not know what they are doing."

My God, they have beaten Him, ripped the flesh from His body, hit Him in the head repeatedly, shoved a crown of thorns on His brow and now, hanging from a cross by His hands and feet, in excruciating pain—*He forgives them!*

I began to weep. *Who is this Man who so generously pardons His tormentors?*

His friends and family looked on in utter anguish. His mother, Miriam, being supported by a young man as she sobbed—wait!—he looked familiar. It was a younger version of the old man John I had met earlier. Yes, he'd been at the Passover meal as well. He did say he was one of the original twelve. Standing with them were several other women.

Suddenly darkness came over Jerusalem—and possibly over the whole world. It was around noon on what had just been a cloudless spring day. In a matter of minutes, it became so dark I could barely make out the Cross. Then in my spirit, a voice recited a prophecy.

> *"In that day," declares the Sovereign Lord, "I will make the sun go down at noon and darken the earth in broad daylight"* (Amos 8:9).

My God! It was as if Elohim wanted to reinforce the fact that we were extinguishing "The Light of the World" when we crucified Yeshua.

I looked straight at Him. He was in agony as He hung there. The whole weight of His body was being brought to bear on the single spike driven through the middle of His feet. There was no little platform for Him to stand upon, as has so often been depicted in movies and paintings. No, His full weight came down upon that rusty nail, sending every nerve of His body into spasm.

Every breath brought searing pain, as He had to push up from His feet using only the spike for leverage to inhale, while His back—which was bloodied and raw, the nerves exposed—would drag against the crudely hewn wood inflicting excruciating pain.

It came as no surprise to me, therefore, when I later discovered that the very word *excruciating* is derived from the word *crucify!*

For six endlessly long hours He hung there as a sense of abandonment and desertion pervaded the hearts of those who kept vigil that day. It must have been the middle of the afternoon, as an eerie foreboding hung over the city, that Yeshua emitted an anguished cry in Aramaic, *"Eli, Eli, lema sabachthani?"* Which, translated, is, "My God, my God, why have you forsaken me?" (See Matthew 27:46.)

As I heard these gut-wrenching words, I was engulfed with a feeling of utter despair, of anguish, of horror, and questioning desperation. I didn't just cry, I groaned. Such a feeling I had never imagined possible. Again, I was reminded of what Isaiah had said, "Yet it was the Lord's will to crush Him and cause Him to suffer...."

I yelled out loud, "How? How could this be God's will?"

Again, the prophet's voice: "...and the Lord has laid on Him the iniquity of us all."

I couldn't stop crying. *He was doing this all for me.* He was taking my punishment.

"You killed Him, David," Ariel had said.

I wept for my sin. I hated what I was. I looked up to find the Messiah's glazed eyes resting on me, as He uttered the words, "It is finished," and exhaled His final breath.

At that very moment, the earth shook violently. I could hear the sounds of rocks splitting as the very ground beneath us heaved and cracked. The soldiers, even their commander, seemed to finally understand that they had committed a terrible crime against Heaven. Cries of terror and fear accompanied the awful realization of everyone that they had perpetrated a horrible evil that day.

In the ensuing stillness, the inner conviction that had fallen upon all present was encapsulated in the centurion's solemn summation, *"Surely, this man was the Son of God!"*

Notes

1. Driscoll, "Jesus Died."

2. I understand that there is much debate as to whether Yeshua was pierced in the hands or the wrists. In my research I found strong arguments on both sides, but at the end of the day, who cares? The focus must remain in the fact that He went to the Cross for us. While it is fine, even commended, to study out these issues, to place too much focus on them obscures the greater issue. He died for us. Nevertheless, if you would like to discuss this, please go to http://on.fb.me/itheft.

3. Frederick W. Farrar, *The Life of Christ* (Dutton, Dovar: Cassell and Co., 1897).

4. As quoted in Paul S. Taylor, "How Did Jesus Christ Die?" Christian Answers Network, 2003, http://christiananswers. net/q-eden/jesusdeath.html (accessed August 11, 2012).

5. Farrar, *The Life of Christ.*

6. Driscoll, "Jesus Died."

Chapter Twenty-Six

WAR!

The verdict was out, but even as the centurion pronounced those words, I felt myself being ripped from the scene—pulled back heavenward. However, this was no casual flight through history with my angel—there was *violence* in the air. I was being forcefully pulled back through time. The images I now saw were no longer below, at least not at first, but above.

This was war.

Angelic beings took their stand against one another. I saw one, a general, dressed in battle armor—instinctively I knew his name was Michael. He was tall, and valiant, and he commanded the respect of all. On Michael's side in the battle were orderly rows of huge angelic beings, warrior angels ready to fight for the cause. Thousands lined up; their devotion to Him was evident.

The demons they fought against all had other names connected to regions. A hideous being, equally muscular and grotesque at the same time, was named the Prince of Persia, while another was called Caretaker of Jerusalem.

But the one that really nauseated me was the king of Rome. He was dressed, not in armor, but in religious garb. He was grossly overweight, reminding me of Jabba the Hut of *Star Wars* infamy. He would eat until he would vomit, and then eat the vomit. He seemed to enjoy every form of perverted behavior there was. Their foot soldiers were a disorderly but vicious crew of demons. They would fight with one another for rank, as ego and arrogance governed them, and yet hate and fear bound them together in a perverse unity.

Below them, how far I could not tell, men fought—first with words, manipulation, and deception and then with weapons. The scenes were clearly *parallel*. Whatever war was being unleashed on earth was also being fought in the heavenlies.

Why was I being shown this? I wondered. *And where was Ariel?*

The battles below were not merely military. Multitudes of conflicts were being waged. I saw a white man in Africa. He stood on a large platform before millions of people sharing passionately about the very things I had just witnessed—that Yeshua the Messiah gave His life for them and through Him they could escape God's wrath and have eternal life. Above the preacher, a spiritual battle ensued—demons desperately seeking to maintain their hold on the people, while angelic beings simultaneously fought for their freedom. So many of the people had chains visibly upon them, like prisoners. I could see that even as the war waged above them, smaller demonic entities had their talons buried deep within many of the hearers. Their names were *witchcraft, adultery, bitterness, shame, abuse,* and the like. The forces of God, both angelic and human, were fighting for the souls of men!

One by one, as the people came forward answering the preacher's call, angelic beings would swoop down, like a smart bomb seeking its target, dislodging these demons' hold upon their captives. The people would respond with tears of joy as they discovered their newfound freedom; some were jumping up and down with excitement. The weight of guilt and sin was gone; the demonic control, broken.

What was clear to me in all of this conflict was the centrality and importance of what Yeshua had accomplished in His death. The absolute power of His blood, the blood of an innocent Lamb, to set the captives free and to authorize angelic intervention on behalf of the souls who believed in Him was in evidence everywhere.

It was absolutely clear to me that the critical factor in all of this was the decision of the person to go forward—to believe in the Messiah and accept what He had done for them. At that moment, they became new people—I could see it—delivered out of Satan's cruel domain into the Kingdom of God. I could tell the difference between those whose sins had been taken away by the Lamb's blood and those who were still under Satan's control.

It was evident that there were other spiritual dynamics at work here as well—the words that came from the preacher's mouth were set on fire by God's Holy Spirit and appeared to me as fiery arrows of Life going forth, literally piercing the hearts of his hearers. I remembered what Luke wrote about the Jewish men who heard Kefa—"They were cut to the heart."

Behind the stage were hundreds of people of whom the crowds were completely unaware. They were engaged in a spiritual war, it seemed, crying out to God for the gathered souls to find freedom and salvation. Some were pacing, others were kneeling, but all were praying. These prayer warriors might have been dressed in normal clothes outwardly, but spiritually, I could see that each one of them was fully dressed in battle armor. As their prayers ascended I could see the spiritual atmosphere around the meeting visibly clearing as the enemy was driven back. With some, tongues of fire were released as they prayed; for others their prayers in the form of incense traveled upward toward Heaven making intercession before God. These people *knew* they were at war.

Still, among all the elements at play here—the preacher's words, the angelic intervention, the believers' prayers and the conviction of God's Holy Spirit—I could see that the pivotal factor remained the decision of the individual either to believe and receive the salvation that Yeshua offered or not. Nothing determined the outcome more than that decisive first step toward Yeshua, taken individually by those in the crowd.

This was all absolutely amazing. As I marveled at everything I had witnessed, at what I had been so privileged to see and hear and know, I felt something dark invade my space, and the next thing I knew, I was being ripped away from the arena of spiritual warfare.

Fear filled my consciousness; it was so tangible I could smell it as I spun out of control in utter darkness. I thought I was going to be sick. Then a cold shiver went up my spine as I recognized that I wasn't alone. I was in the very presence of evil.

After several minutes, I found myself back in the classroom, but I was not prepared for what I witnessed there. Ariel was on the ground; a demonic being had his foot on his neck, keeping him from speaking. Other demonic creatures—the most hideous beings I had ever seen—filled the classroom. A horrible stench emanated from them.

One of them began to move in my direction. I was terrified, but had nowhere to run. I was paralyzed with fear. Then, as he approached me he slowly transformed into another being altogether—so beautiful! So attractive! The most appealing creature I had ever seen.

"David," he said in a voice like velvet that brought with it all the comfort of a mother's tender love, "we have come to rescue you. What happened to you today could have destroyed you, your family. Your father..."

Just then Ariel yelled out. I had almost forgotten him as the beautiful being was blocking him from my view, or at least was trying to. "David!" he yelled, "these demons will masquerade as angels of light, but they want to ki..." (see 2 Cor. 11:14). The demon's foot pushed harder against Ariel's throat, silencing him once again. The beautiful angelic creature momentarily reverted back to its former repulsive appearance as he turned in the direction of the demon guarding Ariel and communicated with a look that could have killed. "Keep him quiet you idiot! We don't have much time!"

As he turned back to me, the transformation reoccurred, becoming more angelic with each degree of the turn. Until once again, I came under his hypnotic appeal—an empathetic love that made me want to just melt in his presence. His silken voice and tender tone mesmerized me, draining me of all resistance. I was no longer afraid of him, but drawn to him, as if enchanted by a spell.

"David," his voice seemed to envelop me, "you are safe now. They cannot confuse you anymore. Can you imagine what this foolish decision—to become a *Christian*—would have done to your family? Your father? Embracing Jesus would kill him!"

I felt the worst guilt I had ever experienced—no, *shame* was a more accurate term. He was right. What was I thinking?

"Do you really want to lose your friends, your family, your standing in the community? Do you want to be labeled a fanatic? Do you want your children to be treated as pariahs by other children? Parents would have warned their children to stay away from yours—that is assuming Lisa hadn't left you and taken the kids with her. Of course you wouldn't want to put them through that."

He was right. I didn't.

"And David, let's be honest. There is nothing wrong with you as you are. You're a wonderful person. Sure, you've made some mistakes, but nobody's perfect. God knows that. He made you from dust, after all. He doesn't expect you to be flawless. And the things you've done wrong, you can make up for by simply doing good deeds. Eventually your good deeds will blot out your sins. You don't need someone else to die for you. You can save yourself, David. That is the beauty of truth—it is all up to you. That is the purpose of religion, to give you a way to make up for your misdeeds.

"Your rabbi was right, David. You are a great writer, but you have never studied religion. How could it be that you, in such a short time, should have discovered a truth that your rabbi, who has devoted his entire life to the study of God, hasn't seen? Thousands of years of sages and rabbinical scholars making it clear that Jesus could not have been the Messiah, and you, a novice, figure it out overnight? It's crazy, David. That is *why* you have a rabbi—to lead you and guide you so you will not be deceived.

"David, it is time to go home now. Don't go and throw away all you have on something that's a lie. You have a great life. You are well respected; you have a beautiful family, a good job, and lots of friends. What more do you need? Moreover, your future is bright. You will write books, successful books. Other authors will quote you. I see a Pulitzer Prize coming your way. I can give you all this. You just need to stop pursuing this nonsense that something is wrong with you."

He made so much sense. What had I been thinking? I almost threw my life, career, and family away. I didn't want to lose it all—to be mocked behind my back as some religious fanatic. How horrible it would be to not be welcomed at our synagogue or the Jewish Community Center, where I not only exercise, but lecture every year. We would have had to move. I couldn't imagine raising Hope and Ellie in an environment where they would surely suffer and be rejected—and not for anything they did—but for what I did. What kind of a father was I? How selfish I had been.

I was drifting now—into semi-consciousness, the feeling one gets in the final moments before anesthesia takes effect. Only I wasn't falling asleep—I was enjoying this barely-awake, dreamlike state. It was wonderful. I didn't even need to think, as thoughts were unconsciously being fed to me.

This beautiful creature had saved me. Embracing Yeshua—I mean, Jesus—would have ruined my life. I continued to drift in and out of consciousness, feeling released from all I had been through. My life was fine. I should be happy, not searching for hidden meaning for my existence.

And just like that a wave of guilt came over me as I had a vision of my father. He was weeping and asking, "David, how could you do this to us? How could you humiliate your mother and me like this?" The shame over what I had almost done was overwhelming. "Thank God your grandparents are not alive to see this! They lost everything in the Holocaust and you want to become a Christian?"

Next I saw my wife—she was hurt and angry. "I am not going to be married to a Jesus freak. Just leave!" she yelled as she pointed to the main door of our house where two packed suitcases had already been placed.

In the scene that followed, my rabbi and I were planning a funeral. "David, I told you this Jesus nonsense would kill your father!" Fear gripped my soul. I was coming out of this perfect sleep into a horrible panic. *My father is dead? I killed him?* My heart was racing.

I felt myself, once more, spinning into space.

Chapter Twenty-Seven

ARIEL!

I abruptly woke up. I was back in Starbucks and I was in a panic. Was that a dream? Had it all been a dream? My heart was racing, like coming out of a nightmare. *My father!* I thought, *Oh, thank God, he's not dead. It was all a dream.* I quickly surveyed the coffee shop to see if anyone noticed me. What a strange morning this had been. I just came in to get some work done and somehow I must've dozed off—right in the middle of the café. But what a dream! It was so real, but here I was safe and sound back in the Starbu—*whoa!*

Apparently it wasn't a dream or I hadn't yet woken up yet, I thought, as I was sucked out of my body, like a vacuum was angrily pulling me back into the heavenlies. Once again I was back at the classroom, but the scene had changed dramatically.

Ariel was no longer Ariel, the *professor*, but Ariel, the *warrior*. His muscles were bulging through his battle gear. He was massive and he was determined, and the situation was completely reversed. Ariel now had that same demon, who'd earlier had his foot on Ariel's throat, on the floor and was returning the favor. Gasping in his mighty grip was my once-beautiful "angel," only now exposed for who he really was, a revolting, hideous creature—a demon.

Other equally huge angels filled the room, each in possession of a cowering demon. Apparently reinforcements had arrived after I left.

Ariel looked directly at me. I felt so guilty for ever having doubted him. "David," he said. His voice was the same and yet completely different. The teacher was gone—the general had arrived. "Did you not understand the meaning of the vision? These creatures are deceitful beyond anything you can imagine. They will disguise themselves as truth, but they remain what they are—hideous, conscienceless, fallen angels." The demon attempted to break Ariel's vice-like grip, but was only squeezed tighter for his trouble.

"In the vision, you saw the battle being waged over the souls of men. A man proclaimed the truth while others prayed, but it was only as each one made a decision to trust in Yeshua that freedom came. But make no mistake, David. There is a battle waging over *your* soul, too. The evil powers of darkness will lie and manipulate with guilt and fear to steer you away from eternal life. They are bent on evil and devoid of conscience. They want to take you with them to their final abode—the lake of fire (see Rev. 20:15). They will play on your emotions, pander to your ego, promise you whatever you want, and then reel you in. They are not unlike me in their desire to shape your mind—except I'm offering you life, while they seek your death."

I spoke but no words came out. I cleared my throat and tried again. "But they said my wife would leave me, and Ariel, I saw my father's funeral. The rabbi said that I killed him! I was told I would lose the respect of my colleagues and my friends would all turn on me."

"And they may," Ariel said with an authority that sent shivers down my spine. "And John the apostle was boiled in oil, John the prophet was beheaded, and Kefa was crucified *upside down*. Thousands of others have suffered an equal or worse fate for the Master, and every one of them has received their reward.

"I understand your concerns, David, but you wanted the truth. And tell me, David, was Yeshua not willing to suffer for you?"

A dagger in the gut! Ariel was right. I had witnessed exactly what He did for me. I saw how they tortured Him without mercy. Goodness, I carried His Cross after it collapsed upon His beaten body! He endured all that for me.

Ariel continued, "Recall the vision, David. When did the demons lose authority over the people?"

"When they finally responded to Yeshua," I answered. "The moment they did angels soared down out of Heaven and set them free as demons were dislodged. The blood of the Lamb broke the power of Satan over them."

"Yes, David, remember what you read earlier in the Torah—the life is in the blood.

"As I said, there is a battle waging for your soul right now. The Holy Spirit has people praying for you, people who don't necessarily even know who you are. They are simply praying in obedience to His prompting. That is how we gained the upper hand over these demons today—through the intercession of His people. You can read later how Daniel the prophet prayed and fasted for three weeks, strengthening Michael and his forces so they could defeat the Prince of Persia and deliver a message to the prophet. In your case, their prayers have released an immense portion of prevenient grace[1] in your life. Prevenient grace is what God uses to draw people to Himself. However, most do not receive what you have received, and one day you will give an account.

"But David, after all is said and done, the decision remains yours. It doesn't matter how many people pray for you; if you harden your heart, as you started to do moments ago, you will cut yourself off from this prevenient grace and the convicting presence of the Holy Spirit. As powerful as the blood of Yeshua, the Passover Lamb, is, it is only effective to those who believe—who surrender to God.

"You must decide, young man. Do you want truth, freedom, and eternal life, or the respect of friends, most of whom, by the way, already gossip about you behind your back? Would any of them even come close to doing what Yeshua did for you? Would any of them be prepared to die for you? Would they allow themselves to be beaten or flogged until their backs had been ripped open? Would any of them allow themselves to be tortured to death for you, as Yeshua was?"

The question was rhetorical. *Of course not; no one would ever do for me what He did,* I thought.

"David, you have a window of opportunity. God is drawing you to Yeshua. But if you choose not to respond, then there is no guarantee He will ever draw you again. You may live the rest of your life and never give it a second thought. This demon right here will seek to make sure of that." At which the demon began to struggle again to get free, but could not.

"He and his friends will feed you every lie you want to hear to keep you blinded. Yes, they will promise you the world, even the coveted Pulitzer."

Oh, how foolish I felt! I'd been ready to trade eternal life for temporary fame and the praise of men. Oh, my deceitful pride.

"Yes, David, they will do whatever it takes to keep you lost and blinded to the truth."

"Blinded!" I exclaimed, "That is exactly what I'd been as I drifted out of here before, escorted by, um...him," I pointed to the demon. "Like I was being lulled into a beautiful lie, one that made sense but would keep me from the truth." I turned toward the demon. I was angry, as I understood how he'd sought to deceive me. He hissed at me in frustration, but unlike before, he was now powerless.

"David, once you give your life to Yeshua, you will not have to worry about these demons. Yeshua will give you authority over them. They'll still be around and they'll never give up trying, but you'll trample them under your feet. Most people are terrified of them, but the truth is, this pathetic being is absolutely terrified that you will receive Yeshua, and then use your authority against him."

The defeated demon writhed, furious that his cover was being exposed. Just a few minutes earlier he had been so strong, so confident and convincing. Now he was weak and wretched, even pitiful, in Ariel's tight grip.

"David, it really is time to go home now. Just like in the vision, you have the option—to choose freedom, to choose Yeshua, or you can remain friends with this guy," nodding in the direction of the demon. "Remember, you initiated this when you began your search for the truth. Instinctively, you knew that there must be more. And now that you've found it, you must decide. That part, no one else can do for you. But the moment you choose Yeshua—the moment you confess that you believe, you will know that you are free—just like the Jews in Jerusalem you saw on the day of Shavuot; just like the ones you witnessed in Africa. You will be free...*and you will know it!*"

Almost as if on cue, I felt myself again being sucked back, this time into a tunnel which reverberated with the words: "If the Son sets you free, you will be free indeed...if the Son sets you free, you will be free...if the Son sets you free, you will be...free...free...free..." (John 8:36).

Note

1. Prevenient grace, "is divine grace that precedes human decision. It exists prior to and without reference to anything humans may have done. As humans are corrupted by the effects of sin, prevenient grace allows persons to engage their God-given free will to choose the salvation offered by God in [Yeshua the Messiah] or to reject that salvific offer." Wikipedia.com, s.v. "prevenient grace," http://en.wikipedia.org/wiki/Prevenient_grace (accessed August 11, 2012).

Chapter Twenty-Eight

DECISION TIME!

I opened my eyes and again I was back in Starbucks. Drool from my half-opened mouth was seeping onto the newspaper I'd been reading, the other half of which lay on the floor. I checked the clock. It was 9:30 AM. Only half an hour had passed. The tattooed hipster was gone, the same young lady was working behind the counter, the student was still pecking away at his keyboard, and the couple by the window discussing business was still discussing business. Nothing had changed apart from the fact that a few more people had entered, and no one, seemingly, had noticed the drooling dude, asleep in the corner.

I stood up...and then quickly thought better of it and sat back down, wondering if this journey was truly over or whether I might not find myself at any moment flying or spinning through time again. Like an accident victim slowly beginning to move his hurting limbs to see if anything is broken, I mentally checked myself. What had just happened? Was it real, or just a dream? Dreams do feel real while you are dreaming, but once you are awake, you realize that it was just a dream. Well, I was now awake. So why did my dream still feel entirely authentic?

Did I just watch Yeshua die? Was I really in Jerusalem? And did I just witness an angelic battle over my soul? Was that even possible? Furthermore, did I just spend what seemed like days—though actually, only thirty minutes—with an angel? Or did I imagine it? Did I just doze off and have an incredibly bizarre dream or did I really meet biblical characters? I smiled as I remembered how they'd interacted with me. Am I Dorothy, finally back in Kansas—or in my case, downtown Philly?

Or did God just answer my prayer—my yearning to know the truth?

Well, there was one sure way to find out. I could simply do a little research on the Internet to see if what the angel told me was true. Was Peter really Kefa, was John the Baptist actually Jewish and was he beheaded, and was James actually Jacob? The subjects I could check on were endless. Was the Last Supper actually a Passover Seder? Were there really immersion pools in the Old City of Jerusalem? Were there really tens of thousands of Jewish believers in Jesus in the first century? And how about all that Caesar worship stuff that John talked about? Google and I would clear this up in five minutes.

I bent down and pulled my laptop from my backpack and opened it up, excited to see if any of this was true. As I clicked on my web browser, I heard a *ding,* signifying that I had new email. I immediately thought of the chime that my heavenly tablet made each time a new passage would appear and I smiled, more convinced than ever that this was all some crazy dream. My research could wait a minute, I reasoned as I opened my mail program to see what email had arrived. My heart skipped a beat.

The new email sender's name was *Ariel!*

I nearly fainted. I stared at the screen of my MacBook Air, mouth wide open in stunned disbelief. *Oh...my...God!* I waited a few seconds, just to give my heart a chance to slow down and organize my racing thoughts. Then I clicked on it.

> Shalom D'vid,
>
> I thought you might need this. See attached. We'll be in touch.
>
> Your celestial mentor,
>
> Ariel :-)

Unreal, I thought. *Can't be!* I just sat there frozen; unable to move for about ten minutes. *So, it was real! It was completely and entirely real! And if he was real, then everything he taught me is true. And...that means...Yeshua is real!*

As I emerged from my state of shock, I began to feel that same feeling that I'd sensed earlier with Ariel. It was an amazing feeling, but so hard to put in human terms. Joy like I've never known. Peace that was beyond description. And with it, revelation and understanding!

Yes, I understood why He came, who He was, and why He had to die. I watched Him exhale His last breath. I carried His

Cross! And I witnessed Him ask God to forgive the very ones who were killing Him. And right there in the café, tears began to flow as I thought of my sin, just as they did when He fixed His gaze upon me. But now I knew He would forgive me. I just needed to ask.

Realizing people were beginning to notice my now uncontrollable display of emotion, I grabbed all my stuff and moved to a more private area where I could further digest what had happened and what was happening to me.

As I sat down again, I realized, *Yes, I believe and nothing will ever be the same.* "I believe," I said out loud, and as I did I felt something—*tangible joy*—leapt inside of me. A weight lifted off of me, and I knew I was different.

I remembered what Ariel had said to me just before I left the classroom this last time: "But now, you must decide. The moment you confess that you believe, you will know that you are free—just like the Jews in Jerusalem that you saw on the day of Shavuot; just like the ones you witnessed in Africa. You will be free...*and you will know it!*"

I was, and I did!

I had found what I was looking for—it was Him, Yeshua, the Messiah, the Jew from Galilee. He loved me! He loved me so much that, in all my confusion, He'd sent *an angel* to open my eyes. Love for Him flooded my consciousness. Tears began to well up again. I craved Him; I wanted more. I wanted to see Him again. I wanted to express to Him what I was feeling. And then, suddenly I remembered the attachment with the email. I turned back to my computer and clicked on it. It opened up into some kind of multimedia encyclopedia program. And everything was there—all I'd learned—everything that had been downloaded to my heavenly desktop was now on my earthly one. *Too much!*

Suddenly, I missed Ariel. He rescued me from that slithering, lying demon. Would I ever see him again? I looked down at the email and reread the words, "We'll be in touch." Yes, I would see him again. *I can't wait!* I thought.

I felt so full of love at that moment, I feared I would burst out sobbing right there in the Starbucks. I jumped up, put my laptop away, left the newspaper, and walked quickly to my car. As I got into my Camry, I was again overwhelmed with emotion—feelings I had never known before. I finally did burst into tears. I cried more that day than I think I had in the past ten years. Not since my grandfather's funeral had I been so overcome with emotion. But that was grief; this was something else. I had never been so happy in my life. My name was written in Heaven and I had become a son of God.

After fifteen minutes or so, I finally turned on the ignition and began my drive home, having no idea what the future would bring. I thought of my wife, my girls and, my goodness, my father, the son of Holocaust survivors. How would they react? I would have to keep this quiet for a while—*but how could I?* They will surely notice the change. Either way, eventually I'll have to tell them. But they hadn't had the advantage of time traveling with an angel. They still viewed Yeshua as we had been taught—a Jew, yes, but one who'd started a new religion, a religion that had persecuted our people in the cruelest of ways for centuries. Fortunately, Ariel had equipped me to answer every question.

I turned onto my street. I was still basking in His presence. Tears were still welling up, as I was filled with such gratitude and deep satisfaction. I had never experienced such peace and contentment in all my life. Yet, it made no sense. My life was about to get crazy. When the Jewish community of Philadelphia discovers that *David Lebowitz*—son of Harvey Lebowitz and grandson of Holocaust survivors Tuvia and Edith Lebowitz, the *Philadelphia Inquirer* columnist—now believes that Yeshua is the Messiah, they are *not* going to be happy. And yet, there I was in my car, just as unworried as one could possibly be. While I didn't want to lose any of these relationships—I loved my wife and my parents—I had found the meaning of life. I later found this passage that described perfectly my new willingness to sacrifice everything in order to have my name written in His book of life:

> *The kingdom of heaven is like treasure hidden in a field. When a man found it, he hid it again, and then in his joy went and sold all he had and bought that field. Again, the kingdom of heaven is like a merchant looking for fine pearls. When he found one of great value, he went away and sold everything he had and bought it* (Matthew 13:44-46).

I had found Life itself and He was a Jewish man. I watched Him suffer as no one has ever suffered. Yes, it will be hard, but how can I turn my back on the One who would do that for me? I was willing to lose everything; friends, family, career... if it ever came to that.

And then I heard His voice speaking inside of me.

> *Whoever wants to be my disciple must deny themselves and take up their cross daily and follow me. For whoever wants to save their life will lose it, but*

*whoever loses their life for me will save it. What
good is it for someone to gain the whole world,
and yet lose or forfeit their very self? Whoever is
ashamed of me and my words, the Son of Man
will be ashamed of them when me comes in mis
glory and in the glory of the Father and of the holy
angels* (Luke 9:23-26).

No, I will never be ashamed of Yeshua, I thought. Then,
as if an alarm had just gone off, I suddenly I remembered
something. The entire time I was with Ariel, he and others
kept telling me that I had a special purpose—a particular
task. What is it I am supposed to do? Am I to tell other
Jewish people about the Messiah? Will I write books about
this? *I am a writer—a trained journalist. Would anyone pub-
lish me?*

I chuckled at the thought of asking my Jewish bosses to get
behind such a project. Well, whatever His purpose for me was,
I was willing. I hope no one will try to boil me in oil. I smiled,
knowing that was a very unlikely scenario in Philadelphia, but
whatever comes my way, I trust He will give me the strength
to deal with it.

Who would have thought when I woke up that morning,
with the grand plan of going to Starbucks, reading the paper,
and working on my column, that I would meet an angel—not
to mention John the Baptist and Shimon Kefa—that I would
travel through time and watch Abraham almost kill his son,
listen to Isaiah prophesy, and witness the Last Seder and resurrection of the Jewish Messiah? Not to mention, having a
ringside seat to the spiritual battle over my own soul and getting a Master's degree in *truth*. Yet, the most amazing event

of all that I witnessed was the act of selfless love that divided history, that was planned even before Abraham became father to Isaac—Yeshua's death on the Cross as our Passover Lamb.

As I neared my house, a peace flooded my soul and I recognized that life as I knew it was over. I also knew my quest was over. Ariel was right. The moment I said those words, *I believe*, something changed inside of me. I would later read this passage: "Therefore, if anyone is in [Messiah], he is a new creation; old things have passed away; behold, all things have become new" (2 Cor. 5:17 NKJV).

Yes! I was a new creation! I am sure that if God had opened my eyes, I would have seen an angel swoop down and cut me loose from the darkness I had walked in all my life. Maybe it was Ariel himself—my angel, my teacher, my friend. The blood of the Passover Lamb was now on the doorpost of my soul.

The spiritual battle for my soul might be over, but a new battle was about to commence once it became public knowledge that David Lebowitz was now a friend of Yeshua. I knew my faith could not remain a secret. I had to tell others. I also knew that it would touch every area of my life, from my family to my vocation.

Yes, it was beginning to make sense. God clearly had something special for me to do—an assignment. I again recalled how Kefa and Jacob seemed excited, even honored to meet me. What was this assignment? Something about exposing the *Identity Theft*, the angel said. *All in good time,* I thought. *For now, I just want to enjoy every second of being in His presence.* At that moment, I assumed I would be enveloped in that peace the rest of my life. *I was wrong.*

I turned into my driveway to find my wife, Lisa, frantic, running to the car, tears streaming down her face.

"David, where have you been? We have been calling you! *There's been a horrible accident!*"

CUT OFF FROM MY PEOPLE

"Don't you ever say that you *used to be Jewish! You are still Jewish and always will be!*"

Like an Old Testament prophet, complete with boney finger in my face, Ziva, an Israeli believer, rebuked me, because when I greeted her, I said, "I also *used to be Jewish.*"

I was a brand-new believer and Ziva was the first other Jewish believer I had met. Until this time, I had considered myself cut off from Judaism. It was a painful price to pay (and one I would discover later that I didn't even have to pay!), but Yeshua had radically changed my life and I loved Him for it, no matter what the cost.

Erroneously, I assumed that to believe in the Jewish Messiah was to renounce Judaism—my religion, my heritage, my culture, and my people. The very statement seems strange, right? If He is the Jewish Messiah, why would I consider myself *cut off*? To understand that, you need to know what it was like to grow up Jewish.

Mr. and Mrs. Christ?

"I was about twelve years old when I first learned that Jesus was Jewish," writes Dr. Michael Brown in his book *The Real Kosher Jesus*.[1] In the same chapter he also shares the story of our mutual friend Jeff Bernstein, who grew up thinking that Jesus was the son of Mr. and Mrs. Christ![2]

I can relate to both of their experiences. I too thought for the longest time that Christ was simply Jesus's last name. We are taught, if not directly, that one of the very definitions of being Jewish is that *we don't believe in Jesus.*

I have a strange memory of a phone call I made when I was about ten years old. I saw a sign on a car that read, "I found it!" In fact, if memory serves me correctly, I had seen this phrase in different places around Richmond; however, this time I jotted down the phone number and called it when I got home. I was curious to discover just what he had found.

The person on the other end of the phone was excited to inform me that he had indeed found Jesus. I hung up the phone. Had I been cleverer at the time, I might have quipped, "I didn't know He was lost!"

When I did "find" Him for myself in 1983 as an eighteen-year-old freshman in college, I assumed I had "left" Judaism. I was now a Christian. I didn't like this term, mostly because everyone I grew up with—except for my Jewish friends—claimed to be one and yet it didn't seem like any of them lived like Christians. It didn't take long for me to realize there were *cultural Christians* and *true believers.* There were people who claimed to be Christians because they grew up in homes where their parents told them they were Christians or because they went to a church on Sundays—and there were those who truly had a relationship with the Living God. In fact, growing up, most of the Jews I knew simply defined Christians as non-Jews.

Even though I did not dare call myself a Christian, I was still quite sure I was now separated from my people, my religion, and my heritage—cut off. If there was one thing I had learned growing up Jewish, it was that Jesus and Judaism don't mix! I couldn't explain everything we believed as Jews, but I could sure tell you exactly what we didn't believe! In my mind, I was now outside the camp.

I Am Still a Jew?

However, when Ziva shared those amazing words with me—*You are still a Jew!*—it changed my life! This was a revelation to me. I am still Jewish? I am still part of the people of Israel?

Of course this would have seemed a very strange revelation to the very first followers of Yeshua, whose Jewishness was never in question. They struggled with the question, "Do Gentiles have to become Jewish in order to believe in Jesus?"—not their own Jewishness. (See Acts 10 and 15.)

Ziva also told me of congregations of Jewish believers who met on the Jewish Sabbath and worshiped Yeshua. Again, I couldn't believe my ears. Jewish synagogues where they believe in Jesus? One year later when I walked into Beth Messiah Congregation in Rockville, Maryland, tears filled my eyes as I saw the largest number of Jewish believers I had ever seen worshiping the Messiah.

For a guy who grew up thinking Mary was Catholic, John was a Baptist, Peter was the first Pope, and the New Testament stories took place in Rome, I was stunned. I began to read the New Covenant for myself. The more I read it, the more astonished I became at how *Jewish* it was. This story didn't take place in Rome, there is no mention of the Vatican or a pope, and the word "Christian" can only be found three times in the entire book! These people were not starting a new religion— they were Jews who believed they had found their Messiah.

Moreover, I discovered:

- Jesus's Hebrew name is Yeshua, which means "salvation."

- Mary was an Israelite called Miriam, a Jewish name, like the sister of Moses.

- John was a not Baptist, but a Jewish prophet in company with Ezekiel, Jeremiah, and Isaiah.

- Paul was actually a Jewish rabbi named Shaul.

- Peter was not a pope, but one of the greatest Messianic Jewish communicators in history.

In fact, I was shocked to discover that Gentiles didn't even begin to believe in Yeshua until many years after He was raised from the dead—and virtually the entire early Church was Jewish!

I have a litmus test on how to come to the right conclusion on controversial theological issues. I ask myself a simple question: If I were untainted by either view, and I was given a Bible and locked in a room, what conclusion would I come to? So let's apply that test to the nature of the person of Jesus.

If a Jewish person, unspoiled by the anti-Yeshua bias in modern Judaism, were locked in a room and given the Gospel narratives to read (Matthew, Mark, Luke, and John), would that person come out of that room concluding that Yeshua was a Gentile, anti-Semitic, or the father of a new religion apart from Judaism?

I contend not only would the person not see Him in that light, but the person would fall in love with Him! He or she would see Him as a hero who stood up to the religious establishment of His day (like Jeremiah and the other prophets did) as well as the political rulers, and ultimately demonstrated His love in the greatest way possible. And that is why I wrote this book—to present the real Yeshua, a Jewish Man from Israel, to my people. But not only that! Gentiles have much to unlearn as well.

The Church's guilt in obscuring the Jewish nature of this Man from Galilee is well documented. Church fathers taught their followers the most bizarre and unscriptural doctrines, such as:

- God hates the Jews.

- It is your duty to hate the Jews.

- The Jews are cursed and will never return to be God's people.

- The Church is the new Israel.

- The Jews must suffer as a nation for the killing of Jesus.

- No one can be both Christian and Jew.

They changed the Gospel and they changed the Savior. The tragic result is that Jewish people see Yeshua "through a glass, darkly," but they must see Him "face to face" (see 1 Cor. 13:12). *Identity Theft* seeks to do that; to allow my Jewish brothers and sisters to see Him as He truly is—King of the Jews. And for my non-Jewish brothers and sisters, get ready to meet your Savior in a new and honest way.

I originally wrote this book in three parts. The first was to:

- Show you emphatically that neither Yeshua nor the New Covenant writers ever intended to start a new religion;

- Explore the Jewishness of the first Messianic believers;

- Prove that there has been a demonic conspiracy to rid the New Covenant of its Jewishness—to ethnically cleanse the faith.

The second was to:

- Expose the roots of Replacement Theology— the idea that the Church has replaced Israel as God's chosen, Covenant people;

- Take a look at history and discover how the Jewish identity of the New Covenant was stolen.

And the third was to:

- Share the history of the miraculous return of the Jewish wing, if you will, of the Body of Messiah;

- Reveal how believers can have an impact in bringing revival to the Jewish people and the world and show God's plan for Israel in the future.

Why Jews Are Simply Not Interested

Apart from the issue of sin itself, there are two primary reasons why Jewish people reject the Gospel:

1. The horrible witness of the historic Church toward the Jewish people, which includes the murderous Crusades, forced baptisms, and expulsions from one's country, all which made the Holocaust plausible.

2. The Gospel message presented today has been cleansed of its Jewish roots, so that it appears to the Jew to be altogether foreign to and distinct from Judaism, when in fact it is a Jewish story.

As Messianic Jews, we are often accused of dressing up Christianity in Jewish garb, when in fact just the opposite is true. Messianic Judaism, the faith of the first century Jewish believers, was stripped of its Jewishness in favor of priestly robes of Rome. I wrote *Identity Theft* in the hope that Yeshua, in His truest form, would be presented to the Jewish people.

Enjoy the journey on which you are about to embark.

RON CANTOR

May 9, 2012

Notes

1. Michael L. Brown, *The Real Kosher Jesus* (Lake Mary, FL: Frontline, 2012), xv.

2. Ibid., xvi.

FINAL THOUGHTS

Thank you so much for reading *Identity Theft*. I would love to discuss with you, online, the content or any issues it raised for you.

If you feel that others would benefit from learning the truths found in this story, tell your friends about the book. Share on Facebook and Twitter, and don't forget to include the link to purchase *Identity Theft:* www.IDTheftBook.com.

Like *Identity Theft* on Facebook: www.facebook.com/identitytheftbook.

Alternatively, you can go to www.amazon.com and search for "Identity Theft Ron Cantor" and leave a positive review.

And if through reading *Identity Theft* you came to faith in the Messiah, find a great Messianic congregation or church that loves Israel so you can grow. If you need help, just email me at ron@cantorlink.com.

Thank you again for reading *Identity Theft*. Part 2 is coming.

RON CANTOR

STAYING IN TOUCH WITH RON CANTOR

Ron leads a ministry in Tel Aviv called Messiah's Mandate, the focus of which is:

- Raising up young Israeli Messianic Jews into leadership.

- Organizing outreach trips to revival hot spots in Third World countries (e.g., Nigeria and Uganda) through the Isaiah 2 Initiative. (www.MessiahsMandate.org/Isaiah2) During their last trip to Nigeria, their team of Israeli believers saw 67,000 people make professions of faith. Now, they are planning an outreach to Uganda in 2013.

- Opening the eyes of believers around the world to the Jewish roots of the faith.

Ron is also part of the leadership team of Tiferet Yeshua, a Hebrew-speaking congregation in the heart of Tel Aviv. In addition, he serves Maoz Israel, led by Ari and Shira Sorko-Ram, by writing a regular blog and producing influential and informative videos. Check out www.roncan.net/MAVugT and www.roncan.net/MavMv2.

Ron blogs four to five times a week at RonCantor.com focusing on a number of different areas:

- History of Israel/Palestinian conflict

- Life as a Messianic Jewish immigrant in Israel

- The Jewish roots of the New Covenant

- Teaching to build up your faith

He also posts updates from the Isaiah 2 Initiative.

To be sure of not missing any of Ron's posts, you can subscribe via RSS or email. Those who subscribe will be sent Ron's e-book, *7 Keys to Overcoming Fear.* This book will equip you with the tools you need to take hold of God in any situation. Learn the four words that will keep you from letting others hold you back. Ron also teaches you how to recognize manipulation and intimidation and to crush it. And it's all *free* by just subscribing to RonCantor.com.

ACKNOWLEDGMENTS

There are several people I would like to thank in making this project a reality. Christy Wilkerson was the first to read this manuscript, and alerted me to the fact that it needed work. Pastor Ed Crenshaw added some great insights that I had missed. Wende Carr, living in Beirut, also did a great job of editing and would often send, with her edits, notes of encouragement that she felt that this book was going to have an impact.

However, one person stands out. Susette McLachlan from New Zealand put almost as much time and dedication into this book as I did. She volunteered to edit *Identity Theft* and I don't think she fully understood how deeply she would get involved. This is a better book because of her hard work. She would sometimes stay up all night working on it. Thank you, Susette!

I want to also thank my daughter Danielle who, from the first time she understood I was writing a new book, never stopped encouraging me and showing interest.

Dr. Daniel C. Juster and Dr. Michael L. Brown, both scholars, authors, and personal mentors to me, made valuable contributions in helping me to present what I believe is an accurate portrayal of the first century believers.

I wish to thank Ari and Shira Sorko-Ram who have graciously given me a platform to share my heart through Maoz Israel.

And I would be remiss not to acknowledge the sacrifice of my sweet Israeli wife, Elana. When I made the decision to rewrite this book as a novel instead of a teaching, I had to get it done in a matter of weeks. I disappeared—physically and emotionally. Even during a ministry trip to Germany, Austria, and Switzerland, Elana was often out sightseeing by herself, while I was confined to my hotel room with my MacBook Air. Thank you, sweetheart, for being so patient and understanding. I promise to take you somewhere amazing just as soon this book hits the printing press! I love you!

Lastly, I want to mention my Hero, my Champion, my Source of encouragement and creativity, Yeshua the Messiah, who pursued me when I had no regard for eternity. *Identity Theft* is His story.

ABOUT RON CANTOR

Messianic Jewish Communicator Ron Cantor embraced Yeshua as an 18-year-old, drug-using agnostic. He then attended CFNI in New York, and Messiah Biblical Institute where Ron received his degree. Ron served on the pastoral team at Beth Messiah Congregation in Rockville, Maryland, before heading overseas to Ukraine and Hungary where he and his wife, Elana, trained nationals for Jewish ministry. Ron then served on the faculty of the Brownsville Revival school of Ministry teaching and mentoring young leaders.

Ron travels throughout the U.S. and abroad sharing passionately on the Jewish roots of the New Testament and God's broken heart for His ancient people Israel. Ron has been privileged to take the Jewish roots message to Brazil, Ukraine, Switzerland, France, Russia, Hungary, Israel, Germany, Argentina, and most recently to Uganda and Nigeria.

In June 2003, Ron and Elana returned with their three children to the Land of Israel where they now live and minister. During this time, Ron has served as the associate leader of King of Kings Community in Jerusalem, as well as the interim senior leader. Ron heads the Isaiah 2 Initiative, an Israeli-based vision to see the Good News go forth from Zion to other nations. In their trips to Nigeria and Ukraine they have seen tens of thousands of people profess faith in Yeshua.

Ron also serves with Maoz Israel, blogging and making informative videos about life in Israel. He and Elana are part of the leadership team at Tiferet Yeshua, a Hebrew-speaking congregation in the heart of Tel Aviv. They have three daughters, Sharon, Yael, and Danielle.

Below are the links to social network sites related to *Identity Theft*:

- Join the FB discussion group: www.on.fb.me/itheft

- Like the book: www.facebook.com/identitytheftbook

- IT on Twitter: #IDTheftbook

- Follow Ron Cantor on Twitter: www.twitter.com/RonSCantor

- Friend Ron on Facebook: www.facebook.com/roncan

- Ron's website and ministry in Israel: www.MessiahsMandate.org

- Ron's blog: www.RonCantor.com

Inviting Ron to Speak

If you would like Ron Cantor to come and speak to your conference or congregation, please go to: www.MessiahsMandate.org/invite-ron. Ron makes three trips to the U.S. each year from Israel and would love to minister at your conference, congregation, or event.

Keep up to date on what God is doing in Israel! And get my book, *7 Keys to Overcoming Fear,* absolutely *free* when you sign up for our newsletter at www.MessiahsMandate.org/Updates.

I want to send you my monthly newsletter free of charge so you can:

- Stay informed concerning what is happening in Israel.

- Know how to pray for Israel.

- Continue to grow in your understanding of the Jewish roots for the faith.

When you sign up, in addition to the *free* book, you can also ask to receive the Maoz Israel Report every month, also free of charge! This is one of the most reputable Messianic publications coming out of Israel.

In the right hands, This Book will Change Lives!

Most of the people who need this message will not be looking for this book. To change their lives, you need to put a copy of this book in their hands.

> *But others (seeds) fell into good ground, and brought forth fruit, some a hundred-fold, some sixty-fold, some thirty-fold* (Matthew 13:8).

Our ministry is constantly seeking methods to find the good ground, the people who need this anointed message to change their lives. Will you help us reach these people?

> *Remember this—a farmer who plants only a few seeds will get a small crop. But the one who plants generously will get a generous crop* (2 Corinthians 9:6).

**EXTEND THIS MINISTRY BY SOWING
3 BOOKS, 5 BOOKS, 10 BOOKS, OR MORE TODAY,
AND BECOME A LIFE CHANGER!**

Thank you,

Don Nori Sr., Founder
Destiny Image
Since 1982

PRESBYTERIAN WORSHIP

PRESBYTERIAN WORSHIP

A GUIDE FOR CLERGY

J. Dudley Weaver Jr.

Geneva Press
Louisville, Kentucky

© 2002 J. Dudley Weaver Jr.

Scripture quotations from the New Revised Standard Version of the Bible are copyright © 1989 by the Division of Christian Education of the National Council of the Churches of Christ in the U.S.A. and are used by permission.

Book design by Sharon Adams
Cover design by Night & Day Design
Cover illustration: © CORBIS

First edition
Published by Geneva Press
Louisville, Kentucky

This book is printed on acid-free paper that meets the American National Standards Institute Z39.48 standard. ♾

PRINTED IN THE UNITED STATES OF AMERICA

02 03 04 05 06 07 08 09 10 11 — 10 9 8 7 6 5 4 3 2 1

Library of Congress Cataloging-in-Publication Data is on file at the Library of Congress, Washington, D.C.

ISBN 0-664-50218-0

For Mary,
who taught me the meaning of grace

Contents

Acknowledgments

*M*y experience of Christian worship began as a child sitting sandwiched between my parents in the family pew Sunday after Sunday. The love of worship was nurtured within me by that first congregation who took me up in baptism, loved me, taught and led me until Christ was formed within me. It has continued through a number of congregations with whom I have shared life and have been graced to share in the work of Christian liturgy. I am especially grateful today for the members and staff of First Presbyterian Church, Portland, Oregon, with whom I am pleased to worship and serve.

My late father-in-law, William H. Schutt, for thirty-three years minister of music for Grace Covenant Presbyterian Church, Richmond, Virginia, was the first to help me understand and to appreciate fully the integral role of music in Christian worship. It is a gift I will forever cherish. I am grateful also to the members of First Presbyterian Church, Savannah, Georgia, who bore with me, encouraged me, and grew with me when I served as their pastor and began to explore the riches of our Reformed and church catholic liturgical heritage. My wife, Mary S. Weaver, not only carefully read this manuscript and offered thoughtful advice and suggestions, but has for more than thirty years of marriage always encouraged me and supported me, and shared with me the gift of her insights, her honesty, and, most valued of all, her love.

Chapter 1

Defining Worship

Christian worship joyfully ascribes all praise and honor, glory and power to the triune God. In worship the people of God acknowledge God present in the world and in their lives. As they respond to God's claim and redemptive action in Jesus Christ, believers are transformed and renewed. In worship the faithful offer themselves to God and are equipped for God's service in the world.

The Directory for Worship

*I*t was the Sunday after Pentecost, and our seminarian in residence had taken her place with the children of the church on the chancel steps for the "time with children." In an attempt to continue a lesson on the seasons of the church year, she reminded them that the previous Sunday had been "a very special day," and then asked: "Who remembers what it was?" One little girl, without a moment's hesitation, shot her arm straight up into the air and called out loudly: "It was stay-at-home-Sunday!" Her parents, both of whom sang in the choir and were sitting in full view of the congregation, flushed a bright shade of red. They had moved the week before, and, while their little girls slept, much of Saturday night and the wee hours of Sunday morning had been spent unpacking boxes and getting things arranged in the new house. Weary but happy to be in their new home, they had collapsed in exhaustion on a mattress on the floor for only a short while before their two little girls came bouncing into the room and woke them up, eager to go to church. "It's stay-at-home Sunday," their dad said as he rolled over and went back to sleep. For a family who rarely, if ever, missed worship, "stay-at-home Sunday" was indeed a very unusual day.

Sunday after Sunday, year after year, the people of God gather to worship. What is it that draws us together in our places of worship? Obedience, perhaps. God has commanded this of us. Habit, maybe. Going to church is a part of the routine for many of us, and breaking that routine leaves us feeling out of sorts, incomplete, for the rest of the week. Being with friends may be another draw. For many of us our closest and dearest friends are a part of our church family. Maybe it is for the music or the preaching or the peace and quiet. Maybe it is out of a sense of duty. You sing in the choir, play the organ, serve on the worship committee, or do the preaching. To be sure, a number of different things draw us together, but there is one thing common to us all, I think, and that is that we have heard something there, felt something there, found something there in the worship of the Christian community that draws us back again and again both in times of joy and in times of sadness, in times of success and of failure, in times of hope and of disappointment. It is because God is there—in the gathered presence of the people; in the hymns, prayers, readings, sermon, sacraments; in the moments of shared silence—that we gather to worship the God who has lifted burdens of heavy guilt; who has walked with us through valleys of deepest darkness; who has brought us peace in the midst of turmoil, hope in the shadows of growing despair, strength in days of weakness; who has brought and continues to bring us *life*.

Almost without exception we gain something when we gather for worship; but it is not primarily the hope of gain that draws us together. Rather, it is the gratitude born of having already received. It is God's identification with us in Christ, God's suffering beside us and for us in Christ, God's immersion into our death and God's victory over death for us in Christ, that elicits our worship and our praise. The primary aim of Christian worship is not entertainment, or spiritual renewal or moral transformation, or even evangelism, but doxology. We go to church not merely to have our spiritual batteries recharged, or to get the lift we need to see us through another week, or even for some new insight and understanding, but we come together as the church to praise God in Jesus Christ for what God has already done and is in the process of doing in our lives. Donald Wilson Stake writes that "worship is literally 'ascribing worth' to God. What we do in worship represents an awareness of the relationship between ourselves and God. We are creatures and God is the Creator of us and our world. We exist at the will of God, and we are confident that God's will is for our good. So we worship God, affirming our faith in God as the ultimate value in life. Worship is our encounter with God in response to God's promised presence in Jesus Christ."[1] While worship may do something for us, ultimately it is not for us that worship is done. To worship God is to praise God. It is to acknowledge God's ultimate value in our lives and the poverty of our lives apart from God. And so we pause, we turn, and together we offer our praise and thanks to the One who has created us, who redeems us, and who sustains us in every day of life.

Worship, though, is more than a matter of what we do together in the sanctuary. Ultimately it is the giving of ourselves in answer to God's own self-giving to us in Christ. It is the offering of ourselves to be renewed by the grace of God in Jesus Christ and the power of God's Holy Spirit, that we may live what we profess with our lips and feel in our hearts. Worship and life can never be neatly separated. Authentic Christian worship bears fruit in Christian living. As the apostle Paul put it: "I appeal to you therefore, brothers and sisters, by the mercies of God, to present your bodies as a living sacrifice, holy and acceptable to God, which is your spiritual worship. Do not be conformed to this world, but be transformed by the renewing of your minds, so that you may discern what is the will of God—what is good and acceptable and perfect" (Rom. 12:1–2). Worship begins with God, but its end and goal is the transformation of human life so that the image of the God who is worshiped in Jesus Christ may find expression in the life and conduct and relationships of the worshiper. Lowell Mason's hymn reminds us that "Love so amazing, so divine, demands my soul, my life, my all."

That is why the way we plan for worship and what we do in worship is so critically important. "Worship forms subtly influence the kind of people we are becoming," writes Marva Dawn. "All aspects of our worship . . . nurture in us a specific kind of character. We must therefore be constantly asking how our worship reveals God and what kind of people we are becoming, because the perspectives and understandings about God and the specific attitudes and habits of being that are created by all the elements of worship services affect how we think, speak, and act as we worship in the rest of life."[2] Sunday after Sunday, year after year, the Scriptures we read, the hymns we sing, the prayers we offer, the sermons we hear, the sacraments we share shape our understanding of God and our understanding of ourselves.

As in many times in the past, exactly what constitutes the right worship of God in Jesus Christ is the subject of no little discussion. Today more than one pastor and congregation find themselves embroiled in debates, sometimes battles, over how worship will be structured and offered. "Worship wars" is what some have called them. Some in the church resist any change. "We've *always* done it this way," they say, "and we aren't about to change now!" Tradition, though, sometimes has a rather short history and is little more than a euphemism for personal preference and individual experience. What may be tradition for one can be quite novel, even threatening, to another. When someone says, "Let's sing the old hymns," it is best to inquire exactly what period and what hymns are meant. The "old hymns" for some might be the Phos Hilaron from the third century or the Genevan psalm tunes from the sixteenth century. Or they may be the songs and hymns made popular by the nineteenth-century Sunday school and revival movements. Tradition is often quite relative. What is new for one may well be "old hat" for another. And, for that matter, just because we've always done something in a particular way does not mean that it needs to be done that way forever. Some things outlive their usefulness and need to be relinquished. But because they have been useful to the church in its worship, they deserve a decent burial. Change never comes easily, and it never comes without a price, the price of what is familiar and comfortable, what we may even cherish, and so sometimes, perhaps often, we resist it, even when the old is no longer working, because any change, even a change for the better, threatens our sense of stability and security.

On the other hand, others argue for radical and immediate change. The traditional forms of worship are no longer culturally relevant. The world has changed and the church has not changed with it. "Few leaders would suggest using a North American denominational hymnal when planting a church in Africa or Mexico," writes Tim Wright, an Evangelical Lutheran Church pastor and advocate of contemporary worship forms. "Such services would only erect barriers to effective outreach. The language and styles of worship would be culturally irrelevant and religiously unintelligible. Instead, missionaries need the freedom to develop styles of worship that grow out of the needs of the people. One of the largest mission fields in the world is right here in the USA. Yet many insist that congregations should continue to use traditional styles of worship in speaking to today's culture."[3]

The truth is that the traditional language of Christian worship is no longer a language in which even a majority of American people are easily conversant. The rites, music, and traditions with which we are so comfortable and familiar are totally alien to many. There was a time, not long ago, when ours might have been considered a "churched" culture. The laws of the land, social customs, public education, all cooperated with the church to teach and to reinforce a basic knowledge of the elements of the Christian tradition. The school day began with prayer and Bible reading and students even memorized some passages of Scripture along with their school lessons. Those days, however, are past. "The translation task," as Gail Ramshaw reminds us in her book on liturgical language, " is never over for Christians. The very words we speak change in connotation, even denotation, year by year, and in order to proclaim the incarnation, we must speak the gospel in words that the shepherds in our fields can understand."[4] But what language might that be?

Advocates of contemporary worship argue that it is the language of the marketplace. More and more of the people who come through the doors of our churches, both visitors and increasing numbers of members, see the church not so much as a community to which one belongs and in which one makes a commitment, but as a provider of services from which one may purchase a product—just another shop in the mall. "What's in it for *me?* How did the service make *me* feel? Did *I* enjoy it? Did it meet *my* expectations? Was it fun?" David Butchelder, in an article in *Reformed Liturgy & Music,* points out that "the quest for individual enrichment is influencing an industry that samples public opinion for what people want from worship. Armed with this data, churches make changes to give customers what they want. . . . Worship that is shaped by a consumerist mentality becomes dependent on exit polls to see if its people will continue to want its product. In a 'feel-good' culture people want less emphasis on sin and sacrifice and more on blessing and abundance. Failure to deliver what people want will mean they shop elsewhere."[5] We don't want them shopping elsewhere—with our competitors, that is—and so we are tempted, sorely tempted, to give them what we are told they want. Replace the organ and traditional choir with a group of musicians—jazz, blues, country, depending on the tastes of your customers; toss the hymnals and replace them with the simple, and often simplistic, words of praise songs and choruses that can be projected on a screen at the front of the "worship center"; crank up the volume and pick up the pace—eliminate those moments of quiet, "dead spots" they are called; watch out for "religious" jargon, and take care to exclude anything that might threaten the worshipers' self-esteem, such as prayers of confession. Granted, a distinction is often made between "seeker services" and "believer services," but the focus in each is the same: the consumer and the product that is offered. In and of themselves there may not be anything *wrong* with many of these practices. Just because something is new and different doesn't make it bad, but neither does being new and different necessarily make it good. The question is "Who is being worshiped here?" If worship is a commodity sold on a competitive market, then what the consumer wants has to be the primary consideration, but if worship is understood as the response of a grateful people to the love and mercy of a gracious God, then the formative question is not what the worshiper wants out of worship, but what God wants of us, for us, and from us when we gather to worship in the name of Jesus Christ and then disperse to serve him in the world. In one, *I* am the focus; in the other, *God* is the focus. In one, it's what *I* get out of it that matters; in the other, well, in the other *I* am not the one who matters. One is an hour that is shaped by *my* desires, what I understand to be *my* needs. The other is an hour in which I come face to face with God's desires for me.

It may be that the most significant challenge facing the church as we begin this new millennium is not that of learning to speak the language of the "shepherds in the field," the language of the culture, with greater fluency, but rediscovering who we really are. In many respects, in recent years, rather than having failed to speak the language of the shepherds, we have spoken it so well that we have blurred the distinction between the church and culture and have lost sight of our unique identity in and for the world. We have, from the beginning, been called to be *in* the world, but not *of* the world. We have been summoned out to live as the first sign, the foretaste, of God's new creation in Jesus Christ and sent back to serve as the instrument of God's transforming purpose in the world. As such the church's language, while certainly informed and to some degree shaped by the culture in which it lives, is nonetheless a language uniquely its own. An alternative reality requires an alternative language. Stanley Hauerwas and William Willimon suggest that "to be Christian is to submit ourselves to the discipline of learning how to speak a foreign language. The church's language is not a natural language, but it is a language that requires the self to be transformed to be part of that language." They remind us that language is not merely a matter of words but "a set of practices." "That is why translation of Christian practices or terms (such as *eucharist* and *sin*) into more relevant and acceptable ideas is always such a doubtful business. . . . Just as you can't learn French by reading a French novel in an English translation, so also you can't learn the gospel by hearing it translated through the language of self-esteem (I'm okay, you're okay) or the marketing jargon (God is your CEO) of American capitalism."[6] The language that we speak, the words and actions of our worship, shapes who we are, our beliefs, values, perspectives, our ways of relating. From the beginning, the challenge for the church has been how to *enter* into the marketplace where Christ has called us to witness and serve without *becoming* the marketplace.

The language we employ must be both intelligible and faithful—in touch with the church's tradition and awake to the problems, the challenges, and the needs of the contemporary world. Time doesn't begin with us. The church doesn't begin with us. We are, each of us, only a part of a story that began long before us and will continue long after us. Understanding that story helps us understand more clearly who we are. Without an understanding of our past we are in danger of losing our sense of identity and purpose, but the opposite is also true: Without a vision for the future, we are in danger of losing our way. "In liturgy we interact with the past. To fail to do so leads to faddy, trendy worship, worship that soon grows thin and unsatisfying. It can neither judge nor redeem, for it tells us what we already know. When we use, and repossess as our own, elements that have come to us from previous generations, believers of the past join our prayer and praise. They bring what we would not find from our own resources. Our faith grows by their participation in it. . . . But indebtedness to the past does not mean that all that needs to be said has been said. History, as it moves, does produce real newness; many features of our contemporary experience are without precedent. We are entitled to replicate the past—not by doing in our time only what was done in past times, but by being as resourceful and innovative in our time as the best creators in the past have been in other times."[7] Faithfulness requires both memory and vision, tradition and innovation, for innovation without tradition becomes merely faddish and shallow, and tradition without vision is ever in danger of becoming little more than a lifeless idol. It is not so much a matter of either/or but of both/and. The question is not *if* we will change the ways in which we seek to order our common worship of God in Jesus Christ, but *how*. We live in the midst of a changing world. Change sooner or later is thrust upon us, but change is also basic to our tradition as Reformed Christians. It is not simply something that we cannot avoid, but something in which we choose to engage. The *Book of Order* reminds us that "The church affirms 'Ecclesia reformata, semper reformanda,' that is, 'The church reformed, always reforming,' according to the Word of God and the call of the Spirit."[8]

Chapter 2

The Changing Language of Worship

*W*hile genuine Christian worship maintains as its central focus the praise and adoration of God, the liturgy, the forms used by the church for expressing that praise and adoration, is anything but fixed and unchanging. It has and continues to be shaped by the living experience of those who belong to the Christian community; the language, customs, and art forms of the culture in which the church lives; and the needs of the world in which the church seeks to bear witness and to serve. Don E. Saliers points out that "Liturgical celebrations, both festive and ordinary, employ cultural modes of communication to address God and to address human beings. In a sense this is simply a tautology: Christians have no other language and gesture, no other music and bodily actions than the human ones we have received and within which we dwell. We must wear the clothes we have and breathe the air where we live. . . . The words we use in liturgy, whether in prayer, reading, singing, or preaching, are dependent upon the cultural 'languages' for their sense and point. Yet, we do change styles of clothing and we monitor the air for pollution, aware of our dependency and complicity. So liturgy lives in cultural modes of communication, but uses these to critique the inherited religious assumptions that become worn out or toxic."[9] The Christian liturgy did not begin last Sunday or the Sunday before, or even with the generation before us. It did not spring into being spontaneously or from the laborious work of a special committee appointed for that purpose, but has evolved over two millennia.

Many things have helped to shape the church's liturgy, beginning with the Jewish synagogue service. Our earliest mothers and fathers in the faith, being Jewish Christians, continued the practice of synagogue worship on Saturdays and supplemented that with their own peculiarly Christian assembly on Sunday. Indeed, the genesis for the two major divisions of Christian worship—the service of the Word and the service of the Table— may be traced to the practices of Jewish worship. The service of the Word has its roots in the synagogue service, which centered on the Scriptures, with readings from the Pentateuch and from the Writings or the Prophets, perhaps intoned. Each of the readings was followed by one or more psalms. The congregation confessed their faith in the recital of the ancient Shema. Prayers of intercession were made, and there was a sermon or lesson based on the readings. The service of the Table can be traced to the Jewish family meal, which was more, much more, than simply a time for feeding a hungry stomach, but was a time of worship and learning as well. Specifically, the service of the Table has its inception in the family meal shared by Jesus and his disciples on the eve of his betrayal and arrest. The meal was customarily preceded by a blessing that included the breaking and sharing of a loaf of bread. Dinner was then eaten, and the meal was followed by a special cup of wine, which was blessed and shared among the family members. The prayer over the cup was usually longer than the one with which the meal began. Thanks were given for the food that had been eaten; God's covenant with the people of Israel was remembered; and the fulfillment of God's promises to the people was faithfully anticipated.[10]

The New Testament does not give us a fully developed Christian liturgy, but only glimpses of the rites and practices that served as the foundation stones for the liturgy that would develop over the next two millennia and which continues to develop today. Acts tells us that the earliest Christian believers lived in a communal fellowship, devoted themselves to the apostles' teaching, to prayer (perhaps services of daily prayer), a common meal, which included the Lord's Supper, and participation in the synagogue service (Acts 2:42). The baptism of the Ethiopian eunuch by Philip (Acts 8:26ff.) gives us a description of an early Christian baptism. Of course, the New Testament also contains the institution narratives of the Lord's Supper (Matt. 26:26–29; Mark 14:22–25; Luke 22:15–20; 1 Cor. 11:23–26). There are, as well, examples of early Christian canticles and hymns: Mary's Magnificat (Luke 1:46–55), the Canticle of Zechariah (Luke 1:68–79), the Canticle of Simeon (Luke 2:29–32), perhaps the *kenōsis* passage in Philippians 2, and Paul's beautiful hymn of love in 1 Corinthians 13.

A letter from Pliny the Younger, who served as governor of Bithynia and Pontus (A.D. 111–12), to Trajan, the emperor, reporting on his dealings with the Christian community, gives us a glimpse into the worship practices of the church at the beginning of the second century.[11] The governor reported that the Christian communities in his district assembled twice each Sunday. The first gathering was in the early morning, perhaps just at dawn, since Sunday was still just another workday. The morning service was basically a service of the Word, which may also have included the sacrament of baptism. The evening service, which followed at the end of the workday, was for a congregational dinner (an Agape meal or "love feast") and included the celebration of the Lord's Supper. In time, in response to decrees from Rome forbidding suspicious gatherings after dark—and the Christian community's worship practices were considered rather suspicious, with rumors of cannibalism and strange sexual rites—the church was forced to move its evening meal to the morning assembly. The regular meal was dropped, but the celebration of the Lord's Supper was retained.[12] It is clear that from the beginning, the Lord's Day service included both the service of the Word and the service of the Table. Word and sacrament formed a unity.

The *Didache,* a collection of teachings from the first half of the second century, provides, in addition to rules for fasting, for the work of bishops and deacons, and directions for administering the sacrament of baptism, two brief descriptions of the Lord's Supper. The first focuses on the prayers for the sacrament.

> Now about the Eucharist: This is how to give thanks: First in connection with the cup:
> "We thank you, our Father, for the holy vine of David, your child, which you have revealed through Jesus, your child. To you be glory forever."
> Then in connection with the piece [broken off the loaf]:
> "We thank you, our Father, for the life and knowledge which you have revealed through Jesus, your child. To you be glory forever.
> "As this piece [of bread] was scattered over the hills and then was brought together and made one, so let your Church be brought together from the ends of the earth into your Kingdom. For yours is the glory and the power through Jesus Christ forever."[13]

A second prayer of thanks followed the meal. Of special interest in this service is the fact that the blessing and sharing of the cup preceded the fraction and sharing of the bread, and the words of institution are totally lacking. In fact, there is no mention of the Lord's body and blood whatsoever. The didachist, however, does admonish that "you must not let anyone eat or drink of your Eucharist except those baptized in the Lord's name."

The second reference to the Lord's Supper in the *Didache* has to do with the moral character and relational health of those participating in this central event of the Lord's Day service.

> On every Lord's Day—his special day—come together and break bread and give thanks, first confessing your sins so that your sacrifice may be pure. Anyone at variance with his neighbor must not join you, until they are reconciled, lest your sacrifice be defiled.[14]

One's "worthy" participation in the sacrament was not so much a matter of correct theological understanding as it was honest self-understanding: the humility born of the awareness of one's own sin and need for divine mercy, and one's willingness to extend to others the same gift of forgiveness offered in the sacrament.

Justin Martyr's *First Apology* gives us yet a clearer picture of the Lord's Day service during the Patristic period. Justin was born in Samaria in the early part of the second century and, after investigating a number of world religions, became a Christian in A.D. 130. His *First Apology* was written about twenty years later for the purpose of defending the Christian faith to non-believers. The writing, which contains seven chapters related to liturgical matters, features this description of the Lord's Day service:

> On the day called Sunday there is a meeting in one place of those who live in cities or the country, and the memoirs of the apostles or the writings of the prophets are read as long as time permits. When the reader has finished, the president in a discourse urges and invites [us] to the imitation of these noble things. Then we all stand up together and offer prayers. And, as said before, when we have finished the prayer, bread is brought, and wine and water, and the president similarly sends up prayers and thanksgivings to the best of his ability, and the congregation assents, saying the Amen; the distribution, and reception of the consecrated [elements] by each one, takes place and they are sent to the absent by the deacons. Those who prosper, and who so wish, contribute, each one as much as he chooses to. What is collected is deposited with the president, and he takes care of orphans and widows, and those who are in want on account of sickness or any other cause, and those who are in bonds, and the strangers who are sojourners among [us], and, briefly, he is the protector of all those in need. We all hold this common gathering on Sunday, since it is the first day, on which God transforming darkness and matter made the universe, and Jesus Christ our Saviour rose from the dead the same day.[15]

The reading that began the service was taken from the Old Testament prophets or the writings of the apostles, which was to become our New Testament, and the lector "read as long as time permits," which was to say as much as possibly could be read, leaving adequate time for the discourse and Communion, before the congregation had to depart to begin the day's work. After the discourse or sermon, the congregation stood for the prayers, which was the common posture for prayer in the early church. The prayers were probably offered in a litany form in which the people all participated. The newly baptized joined the assembly for the prayers of intercession and petition, after which all joined in the holy kiss or kiss of peace. The men of the church kissed one another, and the women did likewise. Today we "pass the peace," giving each other a handshake or embrace, but the meaning is the same. The kiss of peace provided a transition from the service of the Word to the service of the Table, and it was at this point that the nonbaptized were dismissed from the assembly. A curtain of sorts fell around the holy assembly at this point, excluding any who had not passed through the waters of baptism. Only the baptized were allowed to be present and to participate in the Eucharist. The bread and wine for Communion, as well as gifts for the poor, were received at this time. The table was prepared and the president, or presiding member, offered up "prayers and thanksgivings to the best of his ability." The Great Thanksgiving was an extemporaneous prayer, but clearly a prayer of thanksgiving following a Trinitarian pattern. The people responded with an audible "Amen" to add their assent to the words of prayer spoken on their behalf by the president, and all (including baptized children) communed. Interestingly, the words of institution are not mentioned in this liturgical commentary, perhaps because they were not included at all or because they were included as a part of the prayer, which would be in keeping with later and current practice in most traditions. The celebrant would have led the worship from behind the holy table, facing the people.

It is from Hippolytus in the third century that we find the clearest statement on the church's worship and what would become the normative pattern for the liturgical practice of the Christian community for the first thousand years of its life. This work of Hippolytus has served as the paradigm for nearly all the liturgical revisions made by the major bodies of the Christian community in the last three decades.[16] The *Apostolic Tradition,* which dates from about A.D. 215, is a manual for church order and worship, which contains detailed instructions for daily prayer, the sacraments of baptism and the Lord's Supper, ordination rites, and burial practices. We are especially indebted to Hippolytus for his description of the eucharistic prayer. The opening dialogue of the prayer continues in use in many traditions today. The words spoken responsively between pastor and people join our voices to the voices of countless saints who have gone before us.

> The Lord be with you.
> *And also with you.*
> Let us lift up our hearts.
> *We lift them up to the Lord.*
> Let us give thanks to the Lord.
> *It is right and proper.*

In the prayer that follows, God is praised for God's creative power at work in the incarnate Word; the saving work of Christ is recalled; and the presence and power of the Holy Spirit are invoked. The prayer, while it includes the epiclesis and anamnesis, does not include the Sanctus, which is based on Isaiah 6:3 and Revelation 4:8. It may be that Hippolytus assumes its inclusion and felt it unnecessary to mention. Most liturgies after his time include this song of holy praise, even as it continues to be sung or recited in the eucharistic prayer of thanksgiving in most traditions today. The words of institution are included as a part of the prayer, and the people respond with the great "Amen." Noted American liturgical scholar James F. White explains the importance of Hippolytus in these words: "What Hippolytus gives us is the prototype of the central prayer of the central act of Christian worship. The eucharistic prayer was in his time and for several centuries afterward the most common theological statement of the Christian faith. In thanking God, the church followed the Jewish custom of summing up its faith in what God had done. The prayer is largely a recital of the *mirabilia Dei,* God's saving acts. It is proclamation and creed rolled into one. The structure is basically trinitarian: thanking God the Father, commemorating before God the Father the work of God the Son, and invoking God the Father to send God the Holy Spirit. The whole is then concluded with a doxology praising all three members of the Trinity."[17]

The liturgy generally in use in the late third or early fourth centuries, while still quite fluid, would have looked something like this:

Liturgy of the Word

Scripture readings (Gospel read last with the people standing)

Psalms (sung in between the readings, led by cantors)

Alleluias (sung before the Gospel reading)

Sermon or sermons

Prayers (litany for those being dismissed, led by a deacon)

Dismissal of the unbaptized

Liturgy of the Table

Prayers (litany for the faithful, led by a deacon)

Kiss of peace

Offertory: collection of gifts

Presentation of elements

Preparation of the table

Prayers of thanksgiving (eucharistic prayer)

Sursum Corda

Preface: Thanksgiving for creation, and so on

Sanctus

Thanksgiving for redemption in Christ, and so on

Words of Institution

Anamnesis

Epiclesis

Intercessions

The Lord's Prayer

Fraction

Elevation

Communion

Post-Communion prayer of thanksgiving

Reservation of bread for the sick and absent

Dismissal

The Scripture would have been read from a lectern by readers from among the people. As a sign of special reverence, the people would have stood for the Gospel lesson. The sermon was preached from the sanctuary steps. When the elements were distributed, the celebrant(s) would have received first, as an example for the people, then the other clergy, the "religious," the men, and lastly the women and children. The number of clergy participating varied, and the practice of concelebration (more than one clergyman, reciting the liturgy in unison) was common. The work of deacons during the service included providing general direction for the people in the service, leading in some of the litanies, guarding the doors, receiving the offerings, reading the lessons, and serving the elements to the people.[18]

In the second decade of the fourth century, after three centuries of marginalization and periodic persecution, the church moved from the fringes to center stage. The Edict of Milan, which was issued in 313 under Constantine, granted religious freedom to Christians and pagans alike. In 321 Constantine declared Sunday an official day of rest for all judges, city dwellers, and business people. Finally, in 380 Emperors Gratian in the West and Theodosius in the East proclaimed Christianity as the only true and legitimate religion of the state.

The impact on the church's worship was significant. The church moved out of the homes of believers into large, public buildings (basilicas) constructed at public expense by the emperor and members of his family, as a rush of new believers made their way into the church. The liturgy itself expanded in order to accommodate the larger congregations in larger spaces. An increased use of devotional material, primarily psalmody, was employed to cover movement in the liturgy: the entrance of the clergy, the procession with the gifts, and the serving of the elements to the people.[19] The opening rite was expanded to include the introit (a psalm), the Kyries, the Gloria in Excelsis, and a collect. The special recognition accorded bishops also served to expand the liturgy. Bishops were now extended the same courtesies and recognition as civil magistrates. Like their secular counterparts in the imperial court, the bishops were escorted as they entered their basilicas by lesser ministers bearing lights and incense, and were seated in what was now termed the bishop's throne. The royal treatment did not end there. They were also accorded the same courtly obeisance as the emperor and the realm's highest officials: bows and *proskynesis* (prostration with the forehead touching the floor).[20]

By the sixth century two main liturgical streams or families had developed in the West: the Roman rite (which was limited primarily to the city of Rome and surrounding area) and the Gallican rite, which spread over the rest of Europe and was much more varied in its local forms. During the next several centuries each influenced the other. With the rise of Rome and the emergence of the power and authority of the Roman See, efforts were made to "Romanize" the Gallican liturgy. In the ninth century, the latter dropped from general use, and by the authority of Pope Gregory (1073–85) the Roman rite became the liturgy of the land. This liturgy, however, was radically different from that of the fourth or fifth century, as it bore the mark of Gallican influence and included Gallican material.[21]

As the church entered its second millennium, the liturgy continued to evolve, but the evolution left the people behind. The role of the clergy was significantly elevated, while the role of the laity was reduced to that of mere observers. All that had previously been done by the deacon, the lector, the choir, and the people came to be seen as roles and prerogatives of the clergy. Neither the people nor the choir—not even music—was required for worship. The priest, assisted only by a server, *said* Mass. By the late Middle Ages, the low Mass or private Mass had gained public acceptance as the normal way of celebrating Eucharist. If the people were present, they watched the action up front or involved themselves in their individual and private devotions. The vast majority of the celebrations of the Mass omitted them altogether. The focus of the liturgical action shifted from a single table with the celebrant facing the people to an altar shoved against the rear wall of the sanctuary, with the priest celebrating the Lord's Supper with his back to them. The language in which the prayers were offered, the Scriptures read, and the sacraments celebrated was Latin, so even if the people were present and could hear, they could not understand what was being said. An already elaborate ceremonial became even more elaborate with the addition of a variety of signs, genuflections, beatings of the breast, kissing the altar, and so on.[22] Allegorical meanings were attributed to every part of the rite. The elevation of the elements came to be understood as the high point of the Mass, and many thought it sufficient to be present only at that moment. In some places, the faithful were known to rush from one mass to another in order to be present for this one moment. A penitential and introspective focus began to dominate, and the spirit of thanksgiving and the sense of eschatological anticipation, so much a part of the Lord's Supper from its very beginning, simply disappeared. From a celebration of God's forgiving and renewing grace in Jesus Christ, the Lord's Day gathering and its central liturgical focus came to be seen as a sacrifice offered in the hope of securing grace and forgiveness. The bread and wine of the Eucharist began to be seen by the people, not as God's gifts gladly and mercifully given, but as powerful objects in and of themselves to be feared. Between the twelfth and the fourteenth centuries, the wine of Communion was more and more withheld from the people because of the fear that they might accidentally spill it, and the people's own fear kept many of them from Communion at all. In response, the Fourth Lateran Council (1215) decreed that the faithful must commune at least once a year, even if it was for them a frightful thing to do, but in bread only. The once-weekly celebration of the Lord's Supper became for them an annual event, and the people were left behind.[23]

With the privatization of the Mass and the general exclusion of the people from participating in worship, preaching all but disappeared, in spite of some significant efforts to restore it to a place of prominence in the church. A late Middle Ages innovation, "prone," provided for a service in the vernacular, including a sermon, as a kind of unofficial addition to the Sunday mass. It was inserted into the liturgy right after the Gospel, and included not only a sermon but bidding prayers, the Lord's Prayer, the Ave Maria, the Apostles' Creed, the Ten Commandments, a general prayer of confession that included absolution, and even a time for congregational announcements.[24] The practice did not last, however, and by the time of the Reformation the sermon was no longer even considered a normal part of the Sunday service. Over a period of a number of centuries, a transition was slowly made from the liturgy's being something that the people did together before God to something that was done for them. Their role was reduced primarily to that of observers, who could busy themselves with private devotions while the Mass was being said.

The need for reformation was both urgent and critical. Martin Luther led the way in 1520 and was joined by Huldrych Zwingli in Zurich, Martin Bucer in Strasbourg, John Calvin in Strasbourg and Geneva, John Knox in Scotland,

and Thomas Cranmer in England. While principal leaders of the Reformation on the Continent varied in the degree of their reforms, and while they never reached consensus about the meaning of the Lord's presence in the sacrament, they were in agreement on these basic matters: (1) Worship should be in the language of the people; (2) prayers should be spoken clearly and audibly so that all could hear and understand; (3) all sacrificial elements should be removed from the liturgy; (4) full Communion by all the people should be restored; and (5) preaching should be restored to a place of prominence in the daily and Lord's Day services. With the exception of Zwingli, the Reformers also sought to reestablish the celebration of the Lord's Supper as a regular part of the weekly Sunday service. John Calvin, the principal leader of the movement that came to be known as the Reformed (Presbyterian) branch of the Reformation argued in his *Institutes of the Christian Religion:* "What we have so far said of the Sacrament abundantly shows that it was not ordained to be received only once a year—and that, too, perfunctorily, as now is the usual custom. Rather, it was ordained to be frequently used among all Christians in order that they might frequently return in memory to Christ's Passion, by such remembrance to sustain and strengthen their faith, and urge themselves to sing thanksgiving to God and to proclaim his goodness; finally, by it to nourish mutual love, and among themselves give witness to this love . . . in order that none of us may permit anything that can harm our brother, or overlook anything that can help him, where necessity demands and ability suffices."[25] While Calvin was committed to a weekly celebration of the Lord's Supper as an integral part of Christian worship, he was ultimately unsuccessful in his efforts. He did succeed in obtaining permission from the Geneva City Council for a quarterly celebration, but when Calvin sought to schedule these quarterly services in such a way that the sacrament would be observed on different Sundays in different churches, thereby increasing the frequency of its celebration, the city fathers set the time for all churches at Christmas, Easter, Pentecost, and Harvest-tide.[26] The reformer nonetheless constructed the liturgy for use in his church with the celebration of the Lord's Supper as a regular part of the weekly service.

The service began with opening sentences from Psalm 124: "Our help is in the name of the Lord, who made heaven and earth." This was followed by a prayer of confession and then by a biblical word of comfort and an absolution. "Let each of you truly acknowledge that he is a sinner, humbling himself before God, and believe that the heavenly Father wills to be gracious unto him in Jesus Christ. To all those that repent in this wise, and look to Jesus Christ for their salvation, I declare that the absolution of sins is effected, in the name of the Father, and of the Son, and of the Holy Spirit. Amen."[27] This worked well enough in Strasbourg, but in Geneva the people showed their objection to the practice of absolution by jumping to their feet before the end of the confession to avoid the absolution. Calvin gave in to their objection. There followed the singing of the Ten Commandments, sometimes done in two segments with a prayer in between, but whether in two segments or one, the use of the Decalogue here conforms to the third understanding of the law as a guide for righteous living. (The other two purposes of the law are for the conviction of sin leading to repentance and for the maintenance of public order.) Up to this point, the service had been led from the Communion table. Now, either during the singing of the second table of the law or during the singing of a psalm, Calvin took his place in the pulpit, from which he would offer a prayer for illumination, read the lesson for the day, and preach the sermon. On Sunday mornings, the reformer ordinarily preached through the Gospels or the Acts of the Apostles. The Old Testament psalms or a New Testament epistle provided the text for sermons at Sunday vespers, while weekday mornings Calvin preached through Old Testament books. There were also services each weekday evening.

Following the sermon, the preacher offered a lengthy prayer of intercession known as the Great Prayer, which concluded with the Lord's Prayer, except on Sundays when the Lord's Supper was observed. The Apostles' Creed was said or sung at the conclusion of the prayer. The creed marked a transition in the liturgy, a response to the Word read and proclaimed. The table was prepared with bread and wine as the creed was sung or said. The Communion invocation, or Prayer of Humble Access, appears at various places in Calvin's liturgies, but he seems to have preferred it here, following the creed. The prayer, which was in three parts, began with an invocation or epiclesis, asking that the people might receive the grace promised in the sacrament. Thanksgiving for God's redemptive work in Jesus Christ followed, and the prayer concluded with a renewal of covenant vows. The Lord's Prayer followed. The words of institution were then said. The Reformed tradition is almost alone in separating the words of institution from the Great Thanksgiving. The Roman Church had declared the power of the priest to effect an actual change in the bread and wine by speaking these words, and Calvin understood otherwise. So the words were separated from the prayer and read as proclamation and warrant for the sacrament. An exhortation and excommunication came next. This was actually a short sermon setting forth the benefits of the sacrament, warning the unrepentant to stay away, and inviting the faithful to come to the table to renew the covenant vows. It ended with the call to "lift up your hearts and minds on high where Christ is seated in the glory of his Father, whence we expect his coming at our redemption." The people came to the table for the distribution of the elements. The ministers served the bread and the deacons the cup. Psalm 138 was sung by the congregation during the distribution. After all had communed, there followed a prayer of thanksgiving in which the people dedicated themselves to live out their lives to the glory of God and the well-being of their neighbors. The Canticle of Simeon or a psalm of thanksgiving concluded the service, and the people were dismissed with the benediction.

Service of the Word

Call to Worship

Prayer of Confession

Absolution

Ten Commandments or Psalm

Prayer for Illumination

Scripture

Sermon

Service of the Table

Collection of Alms

Great Prayer (Intercession)

Lord's Prayer

Apostles' Creed

Prayer of Humble Access

Words of Institution

Exhortation and Excommunication

Distribution of Elements

Psalm 138

Prayer of Thanksgiving

Canticle of Simeon or Psalm

Benediction

It should be noted that Calvin, Bucer, Zwingli, and Knox all produced full liturgies for use in the church. Each contained some discretionary freedom, but each laid out rather clearly what was to be said and what was to be done. They were also liturgies that involved the people: as listeners through the use of the vernacular in reading Scripture, preaching, and leading the liturgy; as verbal participants through singing the metrical psalms, the creed, and at least one biblical canticle; and as active, moving participants, by walking to the table and taking their places there for the Lord's Supper. Still, Reformed worship was noted and would continue for several centuries to be noted for its sense of somber restraint. Only that which the Scriptures required or which could reasonably be deduced from Scripture was allowed a place in worship. There was little to entice the eye or ear in places of Reformed worship: all statuary had been removed and murals painted over; only the psalms and a few other biblical texts were sung; all singing was done in unison—no harmonies or soaring descants; and all singing was done without accompaniment—no organ, brass, or strings.

Like Calvin, John Knox, who brought the Reformed tradition to Scotland, also developed full liturgies. In 1564 the Church of Scotland adopted Knox's *The Forme of Prayers,* which was based on Calvin's liturgy, as containing the form of service to be used in all its churches. The original and full name of the book was *The Forme of Prayers and Ministration of the Sacraments, &c., used in the Englishe Congregation at Geneva, and approved by the famous and godly learned man, John Calvin.* It eventually became known as the *Book of Common Order* and was the standard for the Church of Scotland until the middle of the next century. Freedom was given for some improvisation, but the patterns were firmly fixed.

The Westminster Directory for the Publique Worship of God, a document produced largely by English Puritans, completed in 1645 and shortly thereafter adopted by the Church of Scotland, replaced the *Book of Common Order* (Knox's *Forme of Prayers*) and guided the shape of Presbyterian worship for the next three centuries. It abolished the service books with their full liturgies, which had been an essential part of the Reformed tradition since the Reformation, and offered instead a directory for guiding worship. It provided no forms for prayers, but gave directions and lists of topics for clergy to consider in formulating prayers. The Directory also replaced the ancient pattern of the liturgy followed by the Reformers by assuming that the sermon should be the climax of the service rather than its center. The basic order was:

Call to Worship
Prayer of Approach (adoration, supplication for worthiness, illumination)

Old Testament Reading (one chapter in course with exposition allowed)

New Testament Reading (one chapter in course with exposition allowed)

Metrical Psalm(s) (before and/or between lessons)

Prayer of Confession and Intercession

Sermon

General Prayer

Lord's Prayer

Psalm

Benediction

If Communion was celebrated, it followed the Lord's Prayer in this fashion:

Offertory (table prepared as psalm is sung)

Exhortation and Fencing of Table

Setting Apart of Elements

Words of Institution

Exhortation

Prayer of Consecration

Fraction

Communion

Exhortation to a Worthy Life

Post-Communion Prayer

Metrical Psalm

Benediction

In time, because so much discretion was allowed and because there were no "forms," much was lost. John Leith writes that "the Creed, the Gloria Patri, and even the Lord's Prayer were increasingly dropped from worship. The Directory presupposed that the minister was a converted man who could and would pray and lead worship out of his Christian experience. For a highly disciplined community and ministry such a practice was very effective. With the waning of discipline a voluntary liturgical order and free prayers became the occasion for much trivia, senseless repetition, and personal idiosyncrasy."[28]

The Scots brought the Directory with them to this continent, and until 1788 it was the only guide available for Presbyterian worship in America. In 1786, in preparation for the first American Presbyterian General Assembly, a committee was appointed to begin the work of revising the Directory. Initial drafts from the committee indicated a movement back toward the pre-Westminster

Assembly tradition by offering a suggested liturgy and prayers in place of the Directory's list of topics to be included in prayer. The drafts also provided more direct instructions for how worship should proceed. The committee's recommendation, however, did not make it past the draft stage. The Directory approved by the 1788 Assembly continued the pattern set by the 1645 document. The worship of a typical Presbyterian church of the period may have followed an order much like this:

Prayer of adoration, invocation, and preparation

Scripture reading

Singing of praise (a metrical psalm or later a hymn)

Long prayer of adoration, confession,
    thanksgiving, supplication, and intercession

Lord's Prayer

Sermon

(Lord's Supper when celebrated)

Prayer

Psalm

Offering

Blessing[29]

Prayers were long (twelve to twenty minutes), and the traditional posture for prayer was standing. Kneeling was the posture for prayer at home. If the Lord's Prayer was said, and many Presbyterians objected to the use of any unextemporaneous prayer, only the minister would have spoken it. Sermons were longer yet and, for the most part, well constructed, didactic, and concerned with the edification of the congregation in right doctrine. The music was unaccompanied and sung in unison without a printed text. Each line was "lined out" by a precentor, and the congregation sang in response.[30] This pattern of congregational song, which had originally been allowed as a way of enabling all, both the literate and the illiterate, to participate in the voice of the church's praise, became, of course, an established tradition in time. The consequence for the music itself was that tempos slowed considerably, until sometimes singing a single note could take more than one breath. The precentors, without the restriction of a printed musical text, took elaborate liberties with the melodies, making it difficult for people to respond with what they heard. As a result, people sang loudly and frequently did not sing the same thing. Thomas Walter (1696–1725), a New England pastor, wrote that congregational songs were "miserably tortured, and twisted, and quavered . . . into an horrid Medly of confused and disorderly Noises." It was, he said, "something so hideous . . . as is beyond expression bad."[31] There were, of course, no hymns, only metrical psalms. The metrical psalm/hymn battle was only beginning to be waged, and it would be many decades yet before the use of hymns would be commonly found in most Presbyterian churches.

While the sixteenth-century Reformers had sought to reform the church's worship in light of biblical principles and the practice of the early church, the actual participation of the people in the liturgy, at least by the time of the American church experience, had once again been reduced primarily to that of observers. Daniel Stevick notes that "the *Roman* liturgy had been said in Latin for centuries, and the people were left with little more than private, rather individualistic devotions to occupy them while they watched and listened. Although large numbers attended Mass, only a few received communion. They had learned nonparticipatory ways, and hardly thought to complain of them. *Protestant* worship, for its part, was, with the important exception of the congregational hymns, a monologue by the clergyman before an interested, but silent congregation. Protestants had less to watch than Catholics did, but they became very good listeners—and supposed that listening was what Christian worshipers were expected to do."[32]

The Scots not only brought the Westminster Directory for Worship with them, but they also brought the custom of sacramental seasons, which like the Directory, would have a profound formative influence on Presbyterian worship in America. In many places on the isolated American frontier, these periods of preparation, which preceded the quarterly celebration of the Lord's Supper, became for scattered friends and neighbors important times of social gathering. Families could go for months without seeing anyone but one another. Consequently, the seasons became a time when neighbors, regardless of their Christian faith or lack of it, could get together. The presence of an increasing number of "unconverted" persons in these religious assemblies (persons who were not eligible to participate in the sacrament), and the evangelistic wave washing across the nation gradually caused the focus of the seasons to shift from the sacrament to the sermon (directed to the unconverted), and the sacramental season evolved into the revival-oriented camp meeting.

The protracted meeting, rather than the camp meeting, answered the need for an evangelistic tool among many churches in more settled and urban areas. These meetings were held in the sponsoring church and were conducted by the pastor, sometimes assisted by a visiting preacher. Charles Finney, a lawyer turned preacher and a Presbyterian until he joined the Congregational Church in 1836, was a prominent leader in the protracted meeting movement and an ardent proponent of innovations in worship that appealed to the emotions and called upon the unconverted to turn to Christ.[33]

The consequence of the revival movement's encroachment on the traditional worship of the Presbyterian Church was "a further erosion of historical consciousness among Presbyterians and a discarding of almost everything particularly characteristic of Reformed worship in favor of American revival patterns."[34] The focus of worship shifted from the glorification of God and the edification of the worshiper to the conversion of the unconverted. Use of new measures such as the "anxious bench," altar calls, and the selection of hymns and the use of organs for their emotional effect on the worshiper underscore the shift in focus. Thomas Troeger notes that "the revival meeting was designed to climax in a sermon and an altar call so that the preacher became the central actor in the drama of the service. Revivalism rebuilt the order, style, and even physical setting of the service. The questioning and debate that followed sermons in many colonial churches was eliminated to make room for the altar call. The prayers and offerings were moved to the beginning of the service so that they no longer represented the people's response to the declared Word of God. The action was not among the people but up front where the preacher held forth. And up front was in some cases a new location because the insides of churches were often redesigned to accommodate the revival style. While the congregation once sat on three sides around the Lord's table, they now all faced in the same direction and looked at the minister who was on a raised platform."[35]

Not all were willing to go along with the innovations. Worship styles among American Presbyterians began to develop in two separate paths with the 1837 Old School/New School split in the church. The Old School continued to hold to the Presbyterian-Puritan approach of the past, insisting that every act of worship be backed by scriptural authority and be marked by the decorum of a people who sought to do all things decently and with order. New School Presbyterians, on the other hand, were much more attuned to the dynamic changes taking place in American culture and could and would relinquish tradition, even decorum, for evangelistic effectiveness. What worked was what mattered.[36] In time, the two schools of thought found a common ground. Old School Presbyterians relaxed some of their rigidity. The Old School understanding of worship's scriptural foundation was reinterpreted in such a way as to provide that acts of worship, rather than being derived from Scripture, should conform to the "spirit of the gospel" (in other words, principles such as order, seriousness, simplicity, and reverence), which opened the way for innovations in what had become traditional Presbyterian worship in America. New School Presbyterians moderated their position as well, shifting their focus from a preoccupation with the conversion of the unconverted to the nurture of the faithful who sat in the pews Sunday after Sunday. The place where the two schools of thought eventually met was the stage of decency and order.

Revivalism had helped soften some of the austerity ordinarily associated with Presbyterian worship and opened to many Presbyterians an appreciation for the role not only of the mind but also of the senses in the worship of God. Swept up in the rising tide of Romanticism in American life and culture, many Presbyterians longed for services marked not simply by decency and order and even emotional appeal, but by beauty and color as well. Some were drawn to the Episcopal Church in large part because of the beauty of its liturgy and its places of worship. Indeed, there were those who feared a large exodus from the Presbyterian fold and argued for changes to help stem the tide. One of the problems confronting liturgical revisionists of the time, however, was that there were no readily available Reformed liturgies to guide them in their work. American Presbyterians had almost completely lost touch with their pre-Westminster liturgical roots.

Charles Baird sought to remedy this with the publication in 1855 of *Eutaxia, or the Presbyterian Liturgies: Historical Sketches.* The book included liturgies from John Calvin, John Knox, the French Huguenots, Richard Baxter, the Dutch Reformed Church, the German Reformed Church of the Palatinate, and some of the prayers prepared for the 1787 draft of the American Directory. Baird argued in his book that there were four ways in which Christians have historically sought to order their worship of God. Two were rejected outright as inappropriate for Reformed use: a fixed, inflexible liturgy such as the Book of Common Prayer, and a liturgy designed entirely at the minister's discretion without the guidance of any directions or the assistance of suggested forms. The Reformed tradition, according to Baird, had utilized two more moderate approaches: a discretionary liturgy with suggested forms for optional use, and directions for worship without any suggested forms. The first, he said, represented the approach of the Reformers and the second that of the Westminster Directory for Worship.

Others put their hand to providing suggested forms of prayer for use in Presbyterian worship. Parker and Smith's *Presbyterian Handbook of the Church,* published in 1861, included a small collection of prayers and a suggested order of service. In 1867, Charles W. Shields published *The Presbyterian Book of Common Prayer,* which was generally greeted with apathy. On the other hand, Archibald Alexander Hodge's *Manual of Forms* found a more popular reception. In 1893, the General Assembly of the Presbyterian Church in the United States (the southern church) approved a new Directory for

Worship, the first revision since 1788. The Directory was the last of three revisions in the constitution of the church. In 1866 the General Assembly had appointed a committee to prepare a revised Book of Church Order. After thirteen years, a revised Form of Government with Rules of Discipline was adopted in 1879. Attention was then given to revisions to the Directory for Worship. Concerns had been expressed for improvements in the church's worship since as early as 1864. Some argued that the movement calling for change grew out of the slovenly manner in which worship was conducted in many of the churches, and that the answer could be found in providing ministers with some suggested forms for their use in worship, forms that would also include the congregation in a more participatory role than as listeners to the sermon and singers of the psalms. Others argued that there was no need for any additional participation by the people, and that the movement toward greater variety and improved aesthetic beauty in worship violated a fundamental principle of Presbyterian worship—that nothing may be included in worship that is not expressly or implicitly provided for in Scripture. Consequently, while the new Directory did not provide a service for the Lord's Day, it did provide certain optional forms for use in the church. These included questions for baptism and admission of persons to communing membership. An appendix included a simple marriage ceremony and two funeral services.[37]

In 1897, the Church Service Society of the Presbyterian Church in the U.S.A. was organized, and undertook a survey of worship practices in that denomination's churches, as well as a study of the liturgical education provided ministers. The "Statement of Principles" for the society declared that it was the society's intention "to follow this study of the present conduct and past history of the worship of the Church by doing such work in the preparation of forms of service in an orderly worship as may help to guard against the contrary evils of confusion and ritualism, and promote reverence and beauty in the worship of God in His holy House, unity and the spirit of common praise and prayer among the people." The results of both studies underscored the need for more direction and resources. The variety of liturgies followed in the churches was so diverse that it was impossible to classify them according to any common theme or structure. As the editors of *The Presbyterian Enterprise* assessed the situation, "American Presbyterian worship under the influence of Puritanism, the frontier, and revivalism had by mid-nineteenth century moved from 'purity' to outright slovenliness."[38]

In 1906 the Presbyterian Church in the U.S.A. approved the *Book of Common Worship* for voluntary use in the church. The volume included complete worship services for morning and evening of the Lord's Day. Also included was a collection of prayers for both corporate and personal use, an order for the celebration of the Lord's Supper, and services for Baptism and Profession of Faith. There were also a psalter and a number of ancient hymns and canticles included in the book. Presbyterians had come a long way since 1788. The *Book of Common Worship* was revised in 1932, and in 1941 the General Assembly established a permanent committee for revising the book as needed. Another more exhaustive revision was made in 1946. In the mid-1950s the need for a new revision was noted, but also noted were the discrepancies between the *Book of Common Worship* and the Directory for Worship, which had been only slightly revised since first being adopted in 1788. The General Assembly approved the drafting of a new Directory prior to any future revisions to the *Book of Common Worship*. The new Directory led not to any revision of the existing book of worship, but to the publication of an altogether new resource. *The Worshipbook* was published in 1970 as a joint venture of the Presbyterian Church in the United States, the United Presbyterian Church U.S.A., and the Cumberland Presbyterian Church. Within a decade the United Presbyterian Assembly approved an overture calling for an entirely new book of worship. The other two denominations soon approved participation in the project as well. With the publication of the *Book of Common Worship* in 1993, Presbyterians joined ranks with Methodist, Lutheran, Episcopal, and other mainline Protestant denominations in the preparation of new service books. The Preface to the 1993 *Book of Common Worship* states that "during the past thirty years the Christian churches throughout the world have seen a reformation in worship unequaled in any other century. While styles vary between traditions, the shape of the liturgy among the various Christian traditions is witnessing a remarkable convergence."[39]

From the time of the Reformation in the sixteenth century until the latter part of the nineteenth century, Protestant and Roman Catholic liturgical developments continued in complete isolation from each other. At the time of the sixteenth-century Protestant Reformation, the Roman Church itself sought to reform the liturgy. The answer, the Council of Trent believed, was to rein in both reform-minded leaders and those who were guilty of abuses by imposing on the church an unwavering liturgical uniformity. The work of this council was handicapped, however, in two important respects. The first was that there existed little or no knowledge of the liturgy as it was prior to the tenth or eleventh centuries. The second was the theological assumption that the Mass was a work of the priest and not of the people—something offered on their behalf, but not by them. The 1570 missal fixed the texts and the rites of the church, and the Sacred Congregation of Rites was established to enforce the liturgical rules. "And so from 1570 the liturgy entered a period of stagnation. Nothing in the liturgy itself could be changed or developed. Every word

printed in black had to be uttered, every action printed in red had to be performed. Thus, and thus only, was the Mass to be celebrated, and a vigilant
Sacred Congregation of Rites ensured it was so. A special branch of knowledge was developed for this purpose—the science of rubrics."[40] From 1570
until 1962 nothing changed, but then everything changed! *The Constitution
of the Sacred Liturgy* (1963), the product of the Second Vatican Council
(1962–65), opened the door to radical change in the Roman liturgy: the use
of the vernacular in the Mass; the involvement of the people, especially in the
gift of congregational song; a renewed emphasis on preaching; the introduction of a three-year Sunday lectionary; and significant changes in the rites for
baptism, weddings, funerals, and ordinations. The council "showed the
Church of Rome to be not the monolithic monarchy many thought it to be but
rather a living body capable of remarkable change, renewal, and renovation—
a model for the rest of Christianity. Moreover, the churches of the Reformation . . . saw in the working and the documents of the council an acceptance
of basic principles of the sixteenth-century Reformation: the primacy of
grace, the centrality of Scripture, the understanding of the church as the people of God, the use of the vernacular language."[41] The consequences of the
council for the Roman Catholic Church were revolutionary and served to
draw the Roman Church into the current, if not the head of the current, of liturgical change in this century. James F. White writes that "if the postwar period
was a time of Protestant ideas coming to the forefront in Roman Catholic
thinking, the post-Vatican II era has been a time of Roman Catholic ideas
shaping Protestant worship. Protestants have now returned the compliment by
borrowing much that is new in Roman Catholic worship. Indeed, new service
books from Roman Catholic, Methodist, Lutheran, Reformed, and Anglican
traditions seem to be similar recensions of a single text."[42] This can be attributed to a higher level of ecumenical cooperation than in previous years, but
also, and primarily, to the rediscovery and the employment of a common liturgical heritage from the worship practices of the early church. The discovery
of the *Didache* and the *Apostolic Tradition of Hippolytus* provided the
resources for doing precisely what the sixteenth-century reformers sought to
do—reform the church's worship in light of the biblical witness *and* the practice of the ancient church.

Chapter 3

Liturgy:
The People's Work

Christian worship is the response of a grateful heart to God's own self-giving in Jesus Christ. That doesn't change. It is the same in every age, but the liturgy, the medium by which that worship is rendered, as we have seen has changed and developed throughout the ages. Through the liturgy God speaks and we respond; through the liturgy we call and listen for God's response.

The Greek word from which we derive the English word liturgy (*leitourgia*) is actually a combination of two other words: the words for *people* and for *work*. The liturgy is, quite literally, the work of the people. It is something that we *do* together in the presence of God. It is something that involves us all and is all-involving, as it calls us to commit heart, soul, mind, and strength in this work of hearing and responding, receiving from and giving to God anew in Jesus Christ. "To call a service 'liturgical' is to indicate that it was conceived so that all worshipers take an active part in offering their worship together. This could apply equally well to a Quaker service and to a Roman Catholic mass, as long as the congregation participated fully in either one. But it could not accurately be applied to worship—whether a mass or a preaching service—in which the congregation was merely a passive audience. . . . Liturgy is the essential outward form through which a community of faith expresses its public worship."[43] We sometimes equate a "liturgical" service with printed prayers, spoken responses by the people, a more formal atmosphere, and a "nonliturgical" service with a less structured service, marked by more spontaneity and informality. At one end of the spectrum is the prayer-book tradition, and at the other is the free-church tradition. The forms, music, preaching, and physical environment may be radically different, but worship in both is rightly termed "liturgical" as long as it involves the people in some active capacity: singing hymns, choruses, or refrains; reciting the creed; saying a prayer; responding with an "amen" at the conclusion of prayer or spontaneously in the course of the sermon. It may be a liturgy prescribed by a prayer book or a liturgy shaped by local custom and tradition, but all Christian worship is intended to be liturgical, a work of the people. Everyone, from the oldest to the youngest, has a part to play.

Nineteenth-century Danish theologian Søren Kierkegaard's analogy of worship to the theater is most helpful in understanding this intention of worship. Most of us, he said, tend to regard the minister as the actor, God as the prompter, and the congregation as the audience when we think of worship. It is something that we go to church to watch, something that is performed for us. However, it really is the other way around, according to Kierkegaard. God is the audience, the minister is the prompter, and the members of the congregation are the actors in this divine drama. The liturgy is something that we go to church, come together as the church, not to *watch* but to *do*. By the grace of God and the work of God's Holy Spirit, we take something away with us from every liturgy—a new insight, a renewed sense of peace, a deeper devotion, a question to ponder—but the focus in worship is not so much "What did I get out of it?" as "What did I bring to it?" We do this work of liturgy, first of all, not for ourselves but for God.

There are three major liturgical traditions or streams. The prayer-book stream, represented by the Roman Catholic, Orthodox, Anglican, and Lutheran traditions, holds to a prescribed liturgy for all churches. For the most part, the same prayers, lections, and sometimes even hymns are offered in all the churches. Little room is given for innovation or deviation. The unity of the liturgy serves as a symbol of the unity of the church and as a defining, if not *the* defining, principle of each tradition's identity. At the opposite extreme is the free-church tradition, in which there are neither a prescribed liturgy nor any rules for governing the content and conduct of worship in a local congregation. This is entirely a matter of local concern and decision, and largely a matter of each individual minister's opinions, desires, and personal style. Presbyterians are in the middle. We are neither entirely bound nor are we entirely free. We have at our disposal the suggested liturgical forms of the *Book of Common Worship,* which we are free to use or not to use. We can pick and choose as it fits our needs, employ liturgies of our own design and composition, or even borrow from other sources and traditions. Our liturgical freedom, however, is not absolute, as in the "free church" tradition. We may not do whatever we please, whatever feels right at the moment, or even what *most* of the people may sometimes say they want. Our liturgical freedom is exercised within the parameters of the Directory for Worship, which provides not only suggestions but also directives for our worship. The Directory tells us that "In worship, the church is to remember both its liberty in Christ and the biblical command to do all things in an orderly way. While Christian worship need not follow prescribed forms, careless or disorderly worship is both an offense to God and a stumbling block to the people. Those responsible for worship are to be guided by the Holy Spirit speaking in Scripture, the historic experience of the Church universal, the Reformed tradition, the *Book of Confessions,* the needs and particular circumstances of the worshiping community, as well as the provisions of the Form of Government and this directory."[44]

Some of the guidance provided by the Directory for Worship is permissive, while some is mandatory. For instance, the Directory requires that these actions be included in the Lord's Day service: the reading of Scripture, the interpretation of Scripture through a sermon or other form of exposition, prayer, the sacrament of baptism when requested and approved, the sacrament of the Lord's Supper "regularly and frequently as determined by the Session," and the offering. This is the "canon" of the liturgy—those things that are required. A Presbyterian congregation of our denomination may do more, but it may not do less. It is hard to imagine, but music is not required for worship, at least not by the Directory. Music *may* serve as a means of presenting and interpreting the Scripture, as a response to the Gospel, as a form of prayer through psalms and canticles, hymns and anthems, spirituals and spiritual songs, but neither vocal nor instrumental music is *required.* Times for gathering, greeting, and calling to worship; for sharing common concerns; for blessing and sending the people forth; fall into the *should* category, as do special services for receiving new members; commissioning, installing, and ordaining members; services for making and renewing covenants; and services for recognizing life transitions.

This freedom-within-limits approach to worship extends to the responsibility for choosing the parts, determining the proportions, and maintaining the properties of the worship space as well. The Directory for Worship carefully spells out who is responsible for what. Some things are uniquely the prerogative of the minister, some of the session, and some are held in concert. It is important for pastors, elders, and worship committee members to be clear on their respective and mutual responsibilities. The session, the Directory tells us, "is to provide for worship and shall encourage the people to participate fully and regularly in it." In particular, the session has responsibility to *make provision for* the regular preaching of the Word, the celebration of the sacraments of baptism and the Lord's Supper, corporate prayer, and the offering of praise to God in song. The music of worship—hymns, psalms, biblical songs, anthems—are the sung prayers of the church. The session has the responsibility for making sure that these elements of worship are provided for, which would include both the appropriate persons and the physical properties necessary for each. The session has the *authority* "to oversee and approve all public worship in the life of the particular church with the exception of those responsibilities delegated to the pastor alone" and "to determine occasions, days, times, and places for worship." For instance, the pastor may think that a footwashing service on Maundy Thursday is important and worthy of celebrating, but the session must give its permission. Furthermore, the session is *responsible* "for the space where worship is conducted, including its arrangements and furnishings, . . . for the use of special appointments such as flowers, candles, banners, paraments, and other objects of art, . . . for the overall program of music and other arts in the church, . . . [and] for those who lead worship through music, drama, dance, and other arts."[45] Thus, if a Sunday school class wishes to take on the project of making liturgical banners for use in worship, the session must approve the banners, their design, and their use. If the choir, or minister, or personnel committee would like to combine the positions of choir director and organist, the session must approve.

The minister has some responsibilities that are uniquely his or her own: "the selection of Scripture lessons to be read, . . . the preparation and preaching of the sermon or exposition of the Word, . . . the prayers offered on behalf of the people and those prepared for the use of the people in worship, . . . the music to be sung, . . . [and] the use of drama, dance, and other art forms."[46] So, while the session is responsible "for those who lead" in music, drama, and other arts, the pastor is responsible for the content, placement, and proportions of each in the liturgy. While a pastor may assign responsibility for choosing hymns to a music director or organist, the pastor has the final word and the ultimate responsibility for the hymns that are sung by the congregation, and even for the music sung by the choir.

The liturgy itself, "the sequence and proportion of the elements of worship," is "the responsibility of the pastor with the concurrence of the session." The tools of liturgy (the selection of hymnals, song books, service books, Bibles, and other materials for the use of the congregation) are the responsibility of the session with the concurrence of the pastor and, where appropriate, in consultation with musicians and educators who are available to the session and pastor. The provision and planning for worship is a shared responsibility of pastor and session, musicians, and educators. Knowing who is responsible for what, striving to keep lines of communication open, and respecting the gifts, abilities, and particular authority of each is crucial for the church's worship and work.

The shape and sound of corporate worship may well vary, and often does, from one Presbyterian congregation to another. That, in part, is a consequence of being a "directory church," and it is, in part, a consequence of the tension we have historically sought to maintain between freedom and form in our worship practices. There are, however, some basic emphases that have historically characterized Reformed or Presbyterian worship. One, and perhaps the most important of all, is that *Reformed worship focuses on the praise and adoration of God* and not on the experience or satisfaction of the worshiper. Worship is first and foremost for God. This conviction is revealed in the hymns we sing, the prayers we render, the sermons we preach. Everything is secondary to this most important conviction.

Another emphasis in Reformed worship is that *it engages the people* as participants and not merely as spectators. The Reformers returned worship to the people by insisting that the service be conducted in the language of the people and that all parts of the service be audibly spoken; by insisting that the people participate fully in the Lord's Supper; and by the introduction of congregationally sung hymns and metrical psalms. The level of participation by the people may vary from congregation to congregation, but Presbyterian worship is always worship that involves the people as participants.

Another distinction of Reformed worship is that *it is a Word-centered liturgy*. The sixteenth-century Reformers set out to reform the church and the worship of the church in light of the practice of the ancient church and the teaching of the Bible. Acts 2:42, "They devoted themselves to the apostles' teaching and fellowship, to the breaking of bread and the prayers," was for the Reformers the key biblical paradigm for worship. They understood it as describing not a liturgical order, but the essential components of worship. Consequently, there are some things we do in worship—most of them, in fact—because the Bible tells us to do them: reading Scripture, preaching sermons, singing psalms and hymns, saying prayers, and celebrating the sacraments. There are other things that we do in accordance with biblical principles. For instance, Scripture commands that we baptize in the name of the Trinity, but we pour, sprinkle, or even immerse on the basis of the biblical principle that baptism is a washing with water. And some things, as long as they don't violate biblical teachings, are simply a matter of local choice and custom. Equally as important is the presence of the biblical Word in various acts of worship: in the number of lessons read, the use of Scripture for calls to worship, assurances of pardon, invitations to the Lord's Table, and so on.

Presbyterian worship has also been *characterized by an emphasis on preaching as a means of grace*. These words are not simply the preacher's words, but by the presence and power of God's Holy Spirit the word that is proclaimed may become for us God's word to us, a word that has the power to change us. Preaching is more than speech; preaching is an event, an occasion in which we are encountered by God. John Leith wrote that "the power of preaching as the Word of God does not reside in the sound of the words themselves, or even in their meaning. The power of preaching is the act of the Holy Spirit, which makes the words, the sound and their meaning, the occasion of the voice of God."[47] And what we hear is a word of grace, for preaching is ultimately the announcement of the good news of what God has done and is doing in Jesus Christ.

Reformed or Presbyterian worship is also worship that *is marked by order, dignity, and decorum.* Presbyterians may at times laugh in a service and Presbyterians enjoy worship, but Presbyterians have traditionally understood their worship as something rendered before the very throne of God, and we are not people who are inclined to hop and skip with abandonment before the Holy One. God is, we believe, a God of order and not chaos, and the worship we offer up to God is marked by order rather than confusion.

Whatever the forms may be that we employ, the liturgy is ultimately more, much more, than what we do and say and sing and hear. It is more than the liturgical text. "A liturgical text is rather like a printed play or a musical score. The volume of Thornton Wilder's *Our Town* or of Franz Schubert's songs makes the drama or the music possible. But the printed form is not the play nor the songs. These only come into being when they are performed; they come into being fully when they are performed very well."[48] Or, as C. S. Lewis so aptly put it: "As long as you notice, and have to count, the steps, you are not yet dancing but only learning to dance. A good shoe is a shoe you don't notice. Good reading becomes possible when you need not consciously think about eyes, or light, or print, or spelling. The perfect church service would be one we were almost unaware of; our attention would have been on God."[49] That, of course, is not merely a matter of our familiarity with the liturgical text or the artistic skill and integrity with which we can lead and participate in the liturgy, but it is the work of the Holy Spirit, whose presence and power can neither be commanded nor coerced, but only prayerfully sought and faithfully anticipated.

Chapter 4

Preparing for the Service

*C*ommon worship requires planning. It doesn't just happen or come together magically at the last moment. The liturgical texts (call to worship, prayers, invitation to confession, the Eucharistic Prayer, etc.), the choice of hymns, the choir's anthems, the setting of the psalm for the day, the organist's prelude and postlude, assignments for lay readers, special arrangements for children's choirs, and so on, all take planning and coordination. As King David said to Araunah the Jebusite, who offered his threshing floor at no cost to the king when David asked to buy it as a place to offer his sacrifice to the Lord, "I will not offer burnt offerings to the LORD my God that cost me nothing" (2 Sam. 24:24b). This weekly service, and any others for which we have any responsibility, should cost us something—the time, the energy, the creativity, the thought, the study, and the prayer necessary to make this offering to God the best that we have to bring.

Worship is a work of art like drama, dance, or music. It lives, breathes, moves. It flows with a sense of rhythm that is unhurried and yet forward moving. Its tempo quickens from time to time, but it can also slow almost to a stop. There are moments of loud, joyful, triumphant praise, but also moments of holy awe so hushed that you can nearly hear yourself breathe. Its colors are both bright and muted, but all the pieces fit together to constitute a whole. Choosing those pieces, preparing and putting those pieces together, is an art, and like any art it takes study, practice, and effort; prayer helps too.

The place to begin is with the lesson or lessons for the day, which means that you will have read, given some thought to, and studied the lections in preparation for the task of putting the service together. The texts, their content, their context in Scripture, set the mood, determine the flow, and suggest the theme or themes that will shape the liturgy. The liturgical season also helps shape the Sunday service. During Lent the note of self-examination and penitence will be sounded in the hymns and responses that are sung and the prayers that are offered; the Fifty Days of Easter that follow will be markedly different, with that season's unrestrained praise of victory won. During Advent a sense of hopeful anticipation will pervade the liturgy; at Christmas, the joy of promises fulfilled.

There are, of course, a wide variety of resources to assist the worship planner in his or her work, but one's own experience and knowledge are not to be underestimated. As you study the text in light of its season, jot down the names of hymns that come to mind, as well as related biblical passages that might provide images useful in the preparation of prayers and other liturgical texts. Of course, don't neglect the riches of the text in hand. For hymn selections, be sure to refer to the index of hymns by scriptural reference in the back of the hymnal, as well as the topical index. There are also at least two much more exhaustive indexes for *The Presbyterian Hymnal* available. Resources for prayers abound. The *Book of Common Worship* is the first place to begin. Other denominational books of worship also provide a rich treasury of useful resources. Beyond that, there are a multitude of other resources available through church and religious publishing houses. While they are readily available and many are well written and biblically and theologically faithful, do not allow your reliance on them to impoverish the development of the gift of prayer that is your own. As you nurture your own spirit through worship and daily prayer, as you read and study the prayers of others (especially the hymns of the church), your own gift for writing prayer for congregational use will mature. There are books, tapes, and computer programs that will plan a service for you and with a push of a button print one out for you to duplicate. These may be helpful resources, but avoid the temptation they offer to short-cut the work, the art, of crafting the liturgy. You know your congregation best. God has called you and they have called you to lead them in the work of ministry, and the work of worship is the principal work of the church. Do not offer less than *your* best.

There are other considerations as well.

The Worship Space

One of the first considerations in planning for worship is the space in which the liturgy will be offered. The space itself will shape the liturgy by allowing for some liturgical actions and disallowing others. The space will also influence how the liturgy is experienced by those who participate. A sanctuary flooded by natural light and a sanctuary in which the light is filtered through beautiful stained glass will "color" the same liturgy in different ways, so that it will be understood and perceived differently. For that matter, what works in one does not always work in the other. The same liturgy is not always easily transferable from one setting to another. Don Saliers points out that "the places where people assemble have always had a profound influence upon the elaboration and simplification of the rites. . . . The axis of a cruciform Gothic cathedral permits, even invites, solemnity in movement and a slow rhythm of speech and song. A storefront church with acoustic tile in the low ceiling requires electronic amplification and lively, rhythmic musical forms"[50]

Consider the space in which you will be working. Leading parts of the service from behind the Communion table has much to commend it from our historical liturgical practice in the Reformed tradition, and while that may be a wonderful idea, it is not always practical. In many smaller sanctuaries the space around the table is very limited. Preaching from a pulpit that is wrapped by pews on the left and right and the front is quite different from preaching from a pulpit facing a long nave with the pews stretching out for as far as the eye can see. In a large physical setting, gestures in preaching and liturgical leadership will by necessity be broader, even a little exaggerated, while in the smaller setting such sweeping movements would look absurd. The use of liturgical banners can be a wonderful asset to the worship of the community of faith, especially when those banners are designed and prepared by members who have studied the meaning of the symbols employed, but not when they overwhelm the worship space, giving a sense of clutter and distraction, or when they are themselves overwhelmed by the immensity of the space. Consider the space in which you will be working, its limitations and its possibilities and the propriety of what you plan to do. Daniel Stevick notes that "shaping good liturgy is a craft. Rather than being a science, it is an art, calling for taste, judgment and design. It requires practical sense of the possibilities and limitations of one's spatial and musical resources. It, like good and spontaneous-seeming dance or drama, may require timing and practice."[51]

Minister and Musician

While the minister has primary responsibility for planning the service, he or she cannot plan in a vacuum. There are other people whose roles in liturgical leadership need to be considered and whose gifts, insights, and expertise need to be a part of the planning process. One of the most important of these is the church musician. "There are varieties of gifts," to be sure, and some of the most important gifts for worship are possessed by those who stand before the choir and sit at the organ console or piano keyboard and give leadership to worship through the gift of music. As pastor and musician develop a close and mutually respectful working relationship, as pastor and musician explore together their respective understandings of the meaning of worship and liturgical leadership, as pastor and musician strive to work together for a service that is cohesive in all its parts the worship of the congregation will be strengthened and enhanced.

A major portion of the responsibility for initiating and facilitating this collaborating falls to the pastor, who has overall responsibility for the service. When the pastor and musician plan in isolation from each other, the result can be at best a disjointed service, and at worst a service whose parts work in opposition to one another. It is crucial that the minister and musician work from the same page, and the best page from which to begin planning is the biblical texts for the day. Since the choice of lessons read in worship is the prerogative of the preacher, it is the preacher's responsibility to communicate this information to the church musician, and since church musicians working with volunteer choirs find it necessary to plan and rehearse music well in advance, it is incumbent on the preacher to plan the texts from which he or she will be preaching at least several months in advance. If the preacher routinely follows the Common Lectionary, the matter is much simpler, in that the musician has the texts already in hand and can study and plan in advance. Ideally, the minister and musician will spend some time together, perhaps also with any lay readers and others who may participate in the leadership of the service, reading and studying the Sunday lessons. When this is not possible, it is imperative that the pastor clearly communicate with the musician. It is also imperative that the musician communicate clearly and completely with the pastor. If an unusually long anthem is planned, or if the youth choir is planning to sing an anthem that incorporates liturgical dance, the pastor needs to be consulted. Whatever the case, the place to begin is with the text or texts for the day. The theme that emanates from the texts or the primary text for the sermon can help shape the prayers for the day, the hymns that are selected, the choral anthems chosen for the choir, and the organist's music for the day.

The pastor may choose the hymns for the service or give that privilege to the church musician, or the two may work together in hymn selection, but however this is done, the hymns need to be chosen with care. Hymns are not merely "filler" for the service, but function as the sung prayer and praise of the people. They need to be selected with a view to their theological content, singability, familiarity, and appropriateness to the day. Occasionally the text of a hymn will simply cry out to be sung in a particular service, but the tune is totally foreign to the congregation. There are several options. One is to plow right ahead and catch everyone by surprise. Another is to sing the hymn to a more familiar tune of the same meter, though that does not expand the congregation's repertoire. We can pass over the unfamiliar hymn, or we can teach the new hymn to the congregation. The hymn may be rehearsed prior to the beginning of the service; the choir can sing a stanza, if appropriate, as an introit; or the organist might introduce the hymn, playing the melody line only, after which the choir might sing the first stanza alone, with the congregation joining in the rest. On a Sunday when a new hymn is introduced, it is wise to be sure that the other hymns chosen for the day are familiar to many, if not most, in the congregation. When little or none of the music is familiar, it presents an impediment to the congregation's sung prayer and praise, and stands as an obstacle to their worship.

The textual content of hymns, anthems, and service music is critically important for worship leaders to consider, not only in terms of their appropriateness to the day, but simply for their appropriateness. No one leaves church humming a sermon, but the words and music of our hymns stay with us, lingering in our hearts and minds, there to be retrieved, there to surface, sometimes quite on their own, in our times of need and our times of joy. The music we sing shapes us—our understanding of God, of ourselves, of God's will and purpose for us. "Text and tune, when combined together, have a particular power over our minds and emotions. The shapers of the early church, such as Chrysostom, as well as the reformers of the sixteenth century, such as Luther, Bucer, and Calvin, saw that the power of text and tune could be intensified if the text was taken from Scripture and the music was thus made to be a bearer of the Word of God. The new hymns and metrical psalms of the Reformation era were therefore not considered to be simply songs to be sung by the people of God, but Scripture done into meter and rhyme and set to appropriate tunes—nothing less than theology expressed in poetry and music."[52] Our music shapes us from our earliest years. Consequently, it is critically important that those who have responsibility for choosing the music for worship give careful attention to the texts that are sung. What they say is as important as how they sound.

The same careful consideration should be given to the music. Trivial music trivializes the object of its praise. While using styles of music popular in the secular culture may seem appealing, such music may have the drawback of being associated with values that are contrary to the faith. When adapted for use in worship, contemporary secular music may unintentionally communicate cultural values, rather than the values of the gospel. The Doxology can be sung to the tune of "Hernando's Hideaway," and while that might be amusing, it does not direct one's attention to the one "from whom all blessings flow." Rather, it brings to mind other images and experiences.

Introducing Change

One of the freedoms enjoyed by those who stand within a worship-directory tradition is that of innovation in liturgical practices. This freedom, however, like any freedom, carries with it certain responsibilities. In this case, the responsibility is that of acting with theological and biblical integrity, in conformity with the provisions of the church's constitution, and with a concern for the intelligibility and usefulness of the innovation for the whole community of faith. As you depart from historical forms and practices, recast traditional forms in more contemporary shapes, reclaim liturgical practices abandoned by previous generations, appropriate practices from other Christian traditions, or begin from scratch, consider the motives for your creativity. Will it edify, inspire, and build up the community of faith, or does it "dumb down" the church's worship in order to appeal to the largest number of people? Not everything is worthy of inclusion in worship or even appropriate for inclusion in worship. Does the change point worshipers in the direction of God, or does it draw their attention primarily to your own creativity, innovation, and ingenuity? Consider, too, whether it is in keeping with the provisions of the Directory for Worship and with the theological tradition in which you stand. Have the appropriate persons or groups been consulted prior to the implementation of the change or addition? Has the congregation been adequately informed, so that they understand the rationale for the innovation and are prepared for their participation in it? Is it appropriately placed in the liturgy? Does it contribute to the overall movement of the liturgy, or is it disruptive? Does it make sense? Not all good ideas are usable or even doable.

There are two basic ways of introducing liturgical change in the church. One works; one doesn't. The first is to "just do it." Of course, the downside is that people are caught by surprise, may not understand what is being done, and consequently will, more often than not, resist it. The other, more successful, way is in conversation with the people. Any substantive change or addition to the liturgy needs to be shared and discussed with the members of the session's worship committee. When the members of this group give their endorsement and support, each becomes an interpreter and advocate. Their review and consideration may also serve to identify potential hazards not previously seen, and their suggestions may well help make a good idea even better. Another way to converse with the people is through the use of worship forums in which issues regarding the church's corporate worship may be discussed, questions may be asked, and concerns may be aired in a nonthreatening environment. These forums might be sponsored by the worship committee.

Whatever the case, before you introduce any new liturgical practice, tell the people ahead of time what it is that you plan to do and why. If singing psalms in worship is being introduced, for instance, begin with an article in the church's newsletter or weekly bulletin about the history of psalmody in the church and the special contributions of the Reformed tradition to this ancient music of the church. The pastor or music director might teach a Sunday school class or set aside some special time with the choir to teach them about psalmody in Christian worship. Announce a week or two ahead of time that on a coming Sunday the congregation will sing the psalm appointed for the day as a response to the Old Testament lesson. The week before the metrical psalm is used, have the congregation and choir read the psalm for the day antiphonally. Then on the appointed Sunday sing a melodic, easy-to-sing metrical setting of the psalm. Include information in the bulletin about the psalm, the music, the author of the metrical paraphrase, and the composer of the music. The next several Sundays sing a variety of metrical psalms. Then introduce a responsorial psalm—one that is singable, memorable, simple, and short. Begin by reading the verses of the psalm and having the congregation and the choir sing a response chosen from a favorite hymn. On a subsequent Sunday have someone intone the psalm and the congregation and choir sing the refrain.

In introducing and implementing changes in the liturgy, be clear about what is being done and why; give plenty of advance notice; obtain ownership by key leaders early in the process; be sure to follow whatever process is appropriate constitutionally and/or traditionally in your congregation; and don't try to do too much at one time. Keep it simple.

Personal Preparation

Liturgical leadership requires not only coordination and critical judgment in the planning stages, but also careful personal preparation to ensure thoughtful, confident leadership. The one presiding in liturgy needs to be very familiar with the liturgical texts for the day so that he or she can lead with confidence and a sense of authority. "A deer caught in the headlights" look on the face of a worship leader is the last thing a congregation needs to see. If we are to lead the people of God before the very throne of God, we ourselves need to know the way both within our souls and with the texts in hand. Read the lessons for the day. Familiarize yourself with them so that you can look up from the page, give the appropriate emphasis, and read with the appropriate tone. (Jesus speaking to the men gathered around him ready to stone the woman caught in adultery will sound different from Jesus speaking words of forgiveness to the woman.) Read the unison prayers as you would leading fifty or five hundred other people in prayer. Where are the natural pauses? Are there any typographical errors in the prayers printed in the Sunday bulletin? Computer programs that verify spelling will not note the difference between *our* and *your,* but the difference can be very important if one is meant and the other is printed. If a moment of silence is kept after the prayer of confession and before the Kyrie is sung, has the organist been apprised of how long a moment of silence is desired?

Liturgy is not something that any of us can simply pick up and do on a Sunday morning. It is something for which we prepare by immersing ourselves in the liturgy that is to be led. Familiarity with the text, the details, the movements of the service will help us lead with a sense of confidence and with a sensitivity for the flow and rhythm of the service. Yme Woensdregt wrote that "the work of presiders is to help worshipers enter wholeheartedly and single-mindedly into the new creation that God is fashioning in our midst. As such, they are artists. They bring their own unique gifts and skills, their own unique artistry to this work. It is necessary to be profoundly aware of this dimension of the work of presiding. An actor, for example, cannot simply show up on the night of the performance and expect to present a riveting performance. In order for an author's work to shine through the actor's performance ('being transparent'), a great deal of preparation is required. Skills must be honed. Texts must be memorized. Actions need to be blocked out on the stage. As the artist prepares for this dramatic presentation, the author's intention begins to be realized ('made real'), and the actor becomes a more and more transparent vehicle. The audience sits spellbound because Juliet and Romeo have come to life again on the stage, not because the actor points to herself or himself."[53] Familiarity with the texts, the special needs of the day, and one's own spiritual preparation and centering help equip the liturgist to lead in such a way as to draw attention to the message rather than the messenger.

In leading the liturgy, aim for an economy of words and gestures. Such an economy in relation to the elements of the service serves to draw the attention of the people to the God before whom we bow rather than to the worship leaders and the mechanics of the service. An actor succeeds when he draws attention away from himself and his acting, and enables the audience to identify with the character he is portraying. A musician succeeds when she is able to shift the attention of the audience from her performance and free them to be drawn up into the music itself. Likewise, the liturgist and other worship leaders succeed when they draw attention away from themselves and the mechanics of the service and to the God who is being worshiped. While awkward pauses that indicate a lack of preparation are to be avoided, an unhurried pace allows worshipers to feel a sense of God's presence. A pause after the invitation to pray allows the worshipers the opportunity to focus their thoughts on the work of prayer. A worship leader who abruptly or quickly jumps up to continue the service as soon as the choir has sung the last note of the anthem shatters the moment of holy awe as the last sounds reverberate or the sound of silence hangs suspended in the air where music flowed only moments before. There are times when activity—the lining up of a children's choir or the movement of a number of readers in succession—needs to be cloaked. The point is to avoid drawing attention to yourself.

As abrupt and unnecessary movement is to be avoided, so is unnecessary chatter. If, for instance, the page numbers of the hymns are printed in the service bulletin, they don't need to be announced. If announcements have been printed in a bulletin information sheet, they don't need to be talked to death in the service. If a period of silence is to precede a unison prayer, rather than explaining it in detail, simply print "A brief silence is kept" just above the prayer and then, following the silence, call the people to pray in unison by saying, "With one voice we make our common confession," or "Together we give our thanks, saying . . ." Worship is like a work of art with varying colors, hues, and shades, or like the music of a symphony orchestra or vocal ensemble in which the sounds of the various instruments or voices blend to form a harmonious whole. Each part, each movement, every moment is important to the whole and needs to be coordinated and conducted in such a way that the integrity of the service is kept in view.

Technical accuracy, poise, dignity, rhythm, visual contact all play a role, but the greatest asset that a worship leader has is the inner conviction that what is being done is of utmost importance. "The primary, essential ingredient is passion. If a liturgical leader does not communicate that she believes that what she is doing is important with all that she is—heart, body, soul, and mind—others will also come to understand that worship is simply one more option among a host of others. Passion has to do with commitment. To be passionate about something is to commit oneself to it. It is to understand and communicate that we are about a task that makes a difference in the world."[54] This is holy time in the presence of the Holy One. Not just any old thing will do. This demands the best that we have to bring—no less and no more.

Most of all, remember to pray, and to bring your best self to this service. Enter the sanctuary feeling rested, prepared, and focused. You cannot lead God's people in worship that is orderly if you are yourself internally scattered and stressed. There is also a kind of energy, I think, that should characterize our worship leadership. Calm and composed leadership is not the same as somnambulant leadership. How can one lead God's people before the throne of grace and not feel within a sense of energized anticipation and excitement? This too deserves to be communicated. And finally, be yourself. Don't try to be something or someone you are not. It is *you* God has called to this service: you with the gifts that are yours, the voice, the look, the personality that is yours. Strive to develop your gifts, improve your voice, your presence, but be the best that *you* can be. Forgeries sooner or later reveal themselves.

Chapter 5

Leading the Service for the Lord's Day

While the Directory for Worship lays out the principles, responsibilities, and requirements for worship in a particular Presbyterian congregation, the *Book of Common Worship* provides the forms that put flesh on the skeleton provided by the Directory. Between 1984 and 1992 seven separate liturgical resources were developed and published for trial use in the church. These seven "Supplemental Liturgical Resources" were the basic components for what would become the *Book of Common Worship,* published in 1993. The book includes an order for the Service for the Lord's Day with suggested texts; a large number of texts appropriate to the various seasons and special days of the liturgical year; orders for the sacrament of baptism, for the affirmation of baptismal vows, for marriages, for funerals, for pastoral liturgies; a lectionary of daily readings and a three-year-cycle lectionary for Sundays and festivals; orders for daily prayer; a collection of prayers; and a Psalter with the psalms marked for intoning.

The Directory for Worship and the *Book of Common Worship* restore the liturgical pattern of the early church and the Reformation as the normative pattern for the Service for the Lord's Day: gathering in adoration and confession; the reading and proclamation of the Word; responding to the Word; sealing of the Word in the sacraments; and the sending forth of the people to live out their worship of God in the world.

Gathering

As the people gather, it is inevitable and also desirable that they greet one another and engage in conversation. Together we are the body of Christ, a people who share a common faith, a common love, a common life; a people whose diversity of gifts and abilities is seen as a prerequisite for the body's unified and healthy functioning. It is not right that we should act as strangers to one another, surrounding ourselves with walls of silence. Congregational announcements and concerns, if they are not printed and must be verbalized, may be made at this point. This is also a good time to rehearse liturgical actions or music which may not be familiar to the congregation, so that when the service has begun worshipers may engage in the liturgy with a sense of confidence, attentiveness, and a minimum of verbal instructions.

A Liturgical Greeting

The use of liturgical greetings drawn from the Scriptures is much preferred to the "Good morning" one would be just as likely to hear at a meeting of a civic club or school assembly. "The Lord be with you," spoken by the leader, "*And also with you,*" spoken by the people, clearly indicates that this is no ordinary gathering but a gathering of God's own people. The use of the salutation reaches back to the earliest church. It was the greeting that Christians extended to one another in daily life, and only naturally became the greeting spoken by the bishop or presiding minister to the gathered assembly in worship. It soon became the traditional invitation to prayer. Carol Doran and Thomas Troeger note that "many congregations favor the worship leader who is chatty and intrusive on the spirit of prayer, and who will customarily begin a service with a cheery 'Good morning, how are you?' instead of a call to worship or a remembrance of our sins or a hymn of adoration. We may think that this is a small matter, that to disparage the use of 'Good morning' is picky and ungracious. But, in fact, major issues are at stake here, not only for the vitality of worship, but also for the health of the world. There is a hunger for mystery that will not go away. If the church fails to satisfy this hunger by treating worship as nothing all that special—all we need to begin worshiping the Creator of the universe is a cheerful 'Good morning'—then people will seek mystery in other practices."[55] Christian worship is special time, set-apart time, and these greetings used by Christians throughout two millennia remind those who assemble that they stand not only in one another's presence but in the presence of the living God.

The Call to Worship

A musical prelude helps to gather the people's attention and to shift the focus from the exigencies of the last week or congregational concerns and announcements to the worship of God in Jesus Christ. If announcements have been made or liturgical actions rehearsed, the minister or the one leading this time may conclude by saying, "Let us worship God." Now is the time for conversation to cease and for worshipers to allow the music to serve as an aid to centering their thoughts and preparing their hearts for the work of liturgy that is to follow. The entrance of the clergy and choir, the ringing of bells, the bringing of the Bible into the church by an elder or other member followed by the clergy, or simply the worship leader approaching the table signals that the service is beginning.

The people are called to worship with sentences taken from Scripture. This summons to worship is a summons from God, not an invitation from the worship leader, and God's Word is much more appropriate than any words a leader may be able to devise. This is not a time and opportunity for us to state or to be instructed in our purpose for gathering, but a time for us to rise in obedience to God's call in Jesus Christ to render our worship and praise. The *Book of Common Worship* offers ten generic calls to worship as well as opening sentences tied to the lections for the day for each Sunday in the church year. The psalms of the Old Testament, of course, are an extremely rich source as well. A choral call to worship should never be allowed to substitute for this biblical summons. If it is deemed important for the choir to sing some short piece as worship begins, this can be done just prior to the sentences of Scripture, as an introit. The opening sentences may be spoken by the worship leader only, but it is preferable that they be shared by all in a responsive form. This indicates from the beginning that what follows involves everyone—not just the person up front.

Collect for the Day

The call to worship may be followed by the collect for the day, a brief prayer that reflects the biblical theme of the service or the particular day in the church year, or a general prayer of adoration may be spoken. The collect is a summary form of prayer, and ordinarily has a single point, though that point may be rather complex. It usually begins with a brief address, which is followed by a descriptive clause citing some aspect of God's nature, such as "Almighty God, you are more ready to hear than we are to ask." The prayer then concludes with a brief petition[56] such as "Open our eyes to recognize our need, our hearts to know your mercy, and our voices to proclaim your praise."

The Hymn of Praise

The hymn that follows the collect or prayer of adoration continues the theme of praise and adoration. We begin our worship of Almighty God not with a whimper, but with a glad shout of thanksgiving and praise to the God who has made us, redeemed us, and reconciled us, and is at work to renew us in Jesus Christ. This is true even during the more somber seasons of the year. The praise of God may be jubilant and unrestricted, but praise may also be marked by a restrained sense of holy awe and reverence. The words and music of "O Sacred Head, Now Wounded" are as much the praise of God as "To God Be the Glory." Marva Dawn points out that "so many new compositions dumb down our perception, knowledge, and adoration of God. A principal cause of such dumbing down is the contemporary confusion of praise with 'happiness.' Some worship planners and participants think that to praise God is simply to sing upbeat music; consequently, many songs that are called 'praise' actually describe the feelings of the believer rather than the character of God."[57] The call to worship and collect focus our attention on God. The hymn is our response to the majesty, love, and mercy of the Holy One.

An Act of Confession

The movement to confession in this first part of the service follows almost naturally. We cannot stand in the light of God's holiness and remain unaware of our own sinfulness. In other traditions confession is a separate rite or brief service, often held just before the beginning of the full service. Because Presbyterians do not provide for such a separate rite, an act of confession is included as a normal part of the Lord's Day service. Calvin's liturgies included the prayer at this place, and it was followed by words of absolution and the singing of the Ten Commandments. The prayer of confession may also be placed just prior to the celebration of the Lord's Supper, as an act of preparation for the sacrament. This option may be particularly appropriate during the penitential season of Lent. The prayer is offered, however, only once.

Invitation to Confession

The people are called to confession with a biblical word that acknowledges both the sinfulness of humanity and the mercy of God, who desires to forgive. This summons to acknowledge our sin and to receive the gift of forgiveness is God's invitation, not the pastor's. Words of Scripture are more appropriate than anything the liturgist might devise.

The Prayer of Confession

This general prayer of confession is precisely that—general. While it may reflect themes from the Scripture passages of the day or the particular season of the church year, this prayer purports to speak the confession of the whole people of God. This is not a time for instruction or moral lecturing. This is a time to give expression to the conviction that none of us is worthy to stand in the presence of the holy God, save in and by the grace and mercy of God in

Jesus Christ. We come assured of God's desire and will to forgive, and we finish with the assurance that God is faithful to the promise that in Jesus Christ we are forgiven. While writing such a prayer should be within the scope of the abilities of every minister, and while there are many contemporary compositions from which to choose, the classic prayers of the church are far too rich and beautiful and powerful in their composition and historic use to be overlooked. A brief period of silence may be provided just before or following the corporate prayer in order to allow worshipers the opportunity to make private confession before God. Silence in corporate worship is sometimes awkward for us, and we are tempted to fill it with something—words, music, anything. Times of silence, though, are both appropriate and useful. Rather than being wasted or empty time, they provide an opportunity for us to listen for the sound of the "still small voice" speaking to us.

Kyrie or Agnus Dei

A spoken or sung Kyrie or Agnus Dei may follow the prayer. *Kyrie eleison* was a widespread secular and religious shout of praise, not unlike the Hebrew acclamation *Hosanna,* "Save now!" In the liturgy of the early church, the Kyrie was an acclamation by the people at the conclusion of the litany. In time the use of the litany was lost, but the Kyrie as a sung response was retained and took on a penitential tone. Used as a response to confession, as it would be here in the liturgy, it serves as a plea for forgiveness. Used as a response in the prayers of the people, as it may be later in the service, it stands as a plea for God's active response to the petitions of the people, a cry to God for the fulfillment of the Holy One's good purpose.[58] The use of the Agnus Dei in Christian liturgy reaches back to the sixth century and before. It was sung during the celebrant's Communion. The practice continued in the 1570 Roman Mass. The 1524 Reformed rite at Strasbourg retained it as well. During the penitential season of Lent, and especially during Holy Week, singing the Agnus Dei prior to the distribution of the elements is quite appropriate. At other times, however, its use in relation to the Eucharist, our thanksgiving, shifts the focus from mercy received to a plea for mercy more appropriate at the conclusion of the confession.

Assurance of Pardon

A scriptural assurance of God's forgiveness is spoken by the worship leader, and the people respond with a spoken *Amen*, which concludes the act of confession. The prayer, Kyrie, silence, and assurance of pardon are all seen as individual parts of a whole, so that the *Amen* is spoken at the conclusion of the whole rather than at the end of the corporate prayer. What we give assent to is both the reality of our sin and the promise of God's gracious forgiveness.

Guidelines for Righteous Living

The Commandments may be sung or said at this point in their capacity as a guide for righteous living, or a summary of the Law (Matt. 22:37–40) may be said. Having been assured of God's gracious forgiveness in Jesus Christ, we are now reminded of the quality of life God calls us to live within the covenant of grace. A unison setting of the commandments is found in the "Preparation for Worship" section of the *Book of Common Worship*. Another option would be, after the example of *The Book of Common Prayer*, to have the congregation respond in litany form saying, "*Amen. Lord, have mercy,*" or "*O Lord, write these words on our hearts,*" after each of the commandments is read aloud by the leader. Calvin's 1542 liturgy included the Kyrie as a response after each of the commandments, although it was later dropped.

Sharing the Gift

Assured of God's forgiving and renewing grace, the members of the congregation are invited to offer that same gift to one another. This is not simply a time for friendly greeting, but a time when we extend to one another what we ourselves have received from God in Christ. It is appropriate for members to say to one another, "*The peace of Christ be with you,*" or simply, "*Peace be with you,*" the greeting of our Lord to his disciples on the day of resurrection. In the early church "passing the peace" was more than a handshake or a friendly embrace. The "holy kiss" was exchanged. The men kissed one another, as men still do in Eastern cultures, and the women kissed one another. In the second- and third-century church this kiss of peace followed the prayers of the people and marked the transition from the service of the Word to the service of the Table. It is still appropriate to share the peace at this juncture in the service as a sign of our unity in approaching the Lord's Table. Another option is to pass the peace at the conclusion of the sacrament of baptism, a service of ordination and installation, or on the recognition of new members in the church community.

A Response of Thanksgiving

The whole act of confession is summed up in a glad song of celebration: a biblical canticle, a hymn or verse of a hymn, or a psalm of praise. The Gloria Patri or Gloria in Excelsis are especially appropriate. Hymns that might be used include "O for a Thousand Tongues to Sing," "Great Is Thy Faithfulness," "Amazing Grace, How Sweet the Sound," "Now Thank We All Our God," or "God, Whose Giving Knows No Ending." The third stanza of "O Sacred Head, Now Wounded" provides a very suitable response during the Sundays of Lent, when the music of worship is generally more subdued.

> What language shall I borrow
> To thank Thee, dearest friend,
> For this Thy dying sorrow,
> Thy pity without end?
> O make me Thine forever;
> And should I fainting be,
> Lord, let me never, never
> Outlive my love to Thee.

One of the advantages, however, of using the Gloria at this point is that children who have not yet learned to read may participate in the praise of the congregation. One option to consider is using the Gloria Patri during the Sundays of Ordinary Time and other responses during special seasons. Whatever the case, this is an act of celebration, of praise, of thanksgiving by people who, having been forgiven, are freed to forgive.

Up to this point, where practical, the liturgy will have been conducted from behind the Communion table. This is in keeping both with the earliest Reformed practice and the practice of the early church. It also helps to affirm the unity of Word and sacrament in our tradition. The people have also been standing since the call to worship. Standing was the generally accepted posture for prayer from the very first gatherings of the church, a practice taken over from the synagogue worship and continued for the first one thousand years of the church's life. Worshipers stood with arms extended and palms upward or crossed their hands on the breast. Kneeling did not come into general use until later, and then was limited to penitential seasons. Even until the nineteenth century, Presbyterians traditionally stood to pray. Harold Daniels writes: "The old formula, kneel to pray, stand to praise, and sit to receive instruction, still has merit. One can still make a case for kneeling to confess sin, and standing for all other prayer. But if restoration of kneeling is unlikely, at least standing for all prayer in the most ancient tradition would help impress upon us that prayer is an action to engage in. Sitting for prayer hardly impresses upon us our being in the presence of a holy God. It fails to convey the offering of ourselves to God. Sitting is passive, implying a sense of waiting for something to be done for us. Would we remain comfortably seated if Christ were to visibly appear in our midst? No, some would kneel, some would stand in his presence. Then why do we sit casually back in our pews when we address God, the creator of all, the fountain of all goodness?"[59]

The Word

Scripture Readings

The focus shifts from our gathering before God to hearing anew the Word of God. The leader moves to the pulpit or lectern and offers a prayer for illumination. This short prayer reflects the conviction that God's Word can neither be rightly proclaimed nor rightly understood apart from the illuminating power of the Holy Spirit. The Common Lectionary appoints three lessons to be read each Lord's Day: an Old Testament reading, an Epistle lesson, and a reading from the Gospel (which is the traditional order of the readings). Even if the lectionary is not followed, it is appropriate and desirable to have at least two lessons, one from the Old Testament and one from the New, to help ensure that the full biblical witness is plumbed in the corporate worship of the church. That is especially true when you consider that many who sit in the pews on Sunday morning are, for the most part, biblically illiterate and may not be inclined to read or to study the Bible on their own. Consequently, what they do hear of God's Word is heard in the corporate worship of the church.

Ironically, in a tradition that has emphasized the centrality of the Word of God in the worship and work of the church, the use of Scripture in worship has actually declined in this century. Fred Holper noted in his keynote address for the 1993–94 Festivals of Worship introducing the *Book of Common Worship* that "for the pioneers of our tradition, Scripture was not only a sword with which to purge the church's worship of corruption and superstition, it was the taproot of the church's piety and the only fitting source for its sung praise of God in worship. No worship service in Geneva or Edinburgh ever began without acknowledging God's grace and power in the words of Scripture. Unfortunately Scripture's generative role in our tradition of worship has diminished over time. Prayers have too often become arguments for the correctness of a particular doctrinal position couched in the abstract language of theology, instead of a recital of God's mighty acts in history drawn from the concrete images of Scripture. The discipline of reading and preaching through entire books of both Testaments Sunday after Sunday has too often given way to topical preaching, sometimes with only a verse or two of Scripture being read. In this century, congregations stopped singing the psalms in worship altogether, and started reading them, and by the 1970s, psalms had all but disappeared from our servicebook and hymnal."[60] A people starving for the biblical word are reduced to little more than subsistence rations. If we are indeed a people of the Word, restoring Scripture's central role in the worship of the church is a matter of vital importance to us and to the generations that will come after us.

There are two different schools of thought about the passages that are chosen to be read in worship. The use of a lectionary based on the church's year, *lectio selecta,* has a long history in the church and has much to commend its use. It will reflect the rhythms and emphases of the seasons of the year and the great themes of the faith. It can bring discipline to one's preaching and it helps ensure that the congregation will hear from the total testimony of Scripture. The other school of thought, *lectio continua,* also reflects a time-honored tradition and may also ensure both discipline in preaching from a variety of texts and reading from the total witness of Scripture. John Calvin routinely preached through entire books of the Bible, on the average of three to six verses at a time. Both approaches have much to commend them and either is appropriate in a Presbyterian congregation. The Revised Common Lectionary combines the best of both worlds occasionally during Ordinary Time, when there is a semicontinuous reading through one of the books of the Bible on a succession of Sundays. Whatever the case, the first lesson of the day will be from the Old Testament, except for the Sundays of Easter when the first lesson is traditionally drawn from the Acts of the Apostles.

The psalm that follows the first lesson in the lectionary readings is not technically one of the lessons for the day but a response to the Old Testament reading, and it is chosen for the way in which it reflects or continues the theme of the first lesson. This use of the psalm represents the oldest regular use of psalmody in Christian liturgy. Ordinarily the psalm should be sung, as has been the church's custom for nearly all of its history and the practice of the people of Israel from time immemorial. The responsorial singing of the psalm—a leader intones the words of the psalm and the people respond with a refrain after each section—was the way in which the psalms were first sung in Christian worship, and the form flourished until the fourth century. *The Psalter: Psalms and Canticles for Singing* is an excellent resource for tones and refrains. The *Book of Common Worship* also contains eight tones and an equal number of antiphons. Metrical psalmody was one of the primary contributions of our Reformed tradition to the Reformation of the sixteenth century and a valuable gift to the church in general. While Luther and his followers pursued hymnody as the preferred form of Christian praise, Calvin favored the psalms and canticles of Scripture. Unlike psalm texts that are intoned, metrical settings are, by necessity, paraphrases of the biblical word. If the psalm is not sung, it may be read in unison; as a responsive reading between leader and people; or, in keeping with earlier Reformed practice, antiphonally between sides of the congregation, male and female voices, or the choir and the congregation. The psalm for the day functions not only as a response to the Old Testament reading, but also as a bridge to the second lesson, the reading from the Epistle. A hymn, canticle, or anthem may follow the Epistle reading and should reflect the theme of the Epistle or anticipate that of the Gospel to follow.

Elders or others may be chosen to serve as readers or lectors of one or more of the lessons for the day. Care should be given in choosing these volunteers in order to ensure that they possess the necessary gifts for public reading and speaking. Readers should be given the texts well in advance and offered the opportunity to rehearse their readings. The Gospel lection is traditionally read by the clergy.

At the conclusion of the lesson, the lector declares, "The Word of the Lord," and the people respond, *Thanks be to God.* Or, following the gospel: "The Gospel of the Lord," to which the people respond, *Praise to you, O Christ.* Not only does the use of these liturgical formulas tie us to the ancient practice of the church, but it also allows those who hear the Word to claim or affirm through an audible and public response the authority of that Word in their own lives.

Sermon

The sermon that follows the readings concludes with a biblical ascription of praise, which reminds both preacher and listeners that preaching is not merely for the edification of the listener or even the enjoyment of the listener, or a means of displaying the knowledge and homiletical skills of the preacher, but for the glorification of God. The sermon, like the rest of worship, is offered up to God.

Response to the Word

An invitation to discipleship may follow the ascription. It too is drawn from the biblical word. A hymn, canticle, or psalm is sung in response to the Word proclaimed and should reflect the general theme or the concluding point of the sermon. While standing, the members of the congregation affirm their faith in the words of a Scriptural declaration of faith, or a creed (one that bears ecclesiastical endorsement and/or the approbation of the larger church). The Nicene Creed is traditionally used on Sundays when the Lord's Supper is celebrated, and the Apostles' Creed is especially appropriate on Sundays when the sacrament of baptism is administered. The *Book of Common Worship* provides several other options. Another excellent resource, of course, is the *Book of Confessions*. Portions of the Confession of 1967, the Theological Declaration of Barmen, the Scots Confession, and the Heidelberg Catechism lend themselves well to this use. It is important, however, to choose with care. A

Brief Statement of Faith also is a wonderful resource. The entire Statement is a bit long for use in its totality, but the three sections work well independently. When using only a portion of the Statement, the opening paragraph and the concluding sentences should be included.

If the sacrament of baptism is to be administered, this is the appropriate place in the liturgy, as a response to the Word. Here, too, would be included any pastoral rites such as the recognition of new members, the ordination and installation of officers, or the commissioning of members for special service (Sunday school teachers, mission trip participants, and so on).

Prayers of the People

The prayers of the people follow. The prayers of adoration and confession have already been offered. Now the people turn to God in intercession and supplication, praying for both international and local concerns, for the church, and for those in particular need. The prayer traditionally begins with the widest scope of universal concerns then narrows in focus. Following the call to prayer, the leader should pause for a moment before beginning the prayer. This moment of silence allows all present the opportunity to center their thoughts and their hearts on the work of prayer that is to follow. The prayer itself may take a variety of forms. The traditional pastoral prayer, that is, with the pastor or worship leader speaking alone, is for most Presbyterians the customary form. Even so, this is not the *pastor's* prayer, but the prayers of the *people*. The pastor offers the prayer on behalf of all. Seven different models are presented in the *Book of Common Worship*. The first, example A, is a directed prayer that, having begun with a general collect asking for God's guidance in praying, continues with the leader inviting prayer for particular persons or situations. This is followed by silence so that the people may offer their own prayers, and is concluded with a brief collect and the people's response of *Amen*. Prayers of the People B follows the same pattern, except that each collect concludes with the leader saying, "God of mercy," to which the people respond, *Hear our prayer.* The third model (Prayers of the People C) omits the periods of silence and replaces them with brief petitions to which the people respond, *Hear our prayer.* Model D follows the same pattern, but concludes with the leader saying, "Lord, in your mercy," and the people responding, *Hear our prayer.* Prayers of the People E is a litany based on the liturgies of St. Basil and St. John Chrysostom. It may be intoned, using the musical setting provided. Model F continues the litany form by having the people respond, *Lord, have mercy,* to each petition. Prayers of the People G provides a responsive format that, unlike those which precede it, requires a large portion of the prayer to be printed. Each of the preceding forms provides for a key phrase that alerts the congregation to their response.

While this form of prayer is ancient in its practice, reaching back to the very beginning of the church's life, it is nonetheless foreign to many Presbyterians. It is important, therefore, to explain not only that through their audible participation members of the congregation are afforded the opportunity to claim the prayer as their own, but that Christians have been praying like this from the very beginning. Initially, too, it is advisable to print the leader's concluding words and the people's response in the service bulletin. After a while, however, a simple introductory word in the invitation to prayer will alert the congregation to their participation. For example, Model D introduces the prayer with these words: "Let us bring the needs of the church, the world, and all in need, to God's loving care, saying: Lord, in your mercy, hear our prayer." Initially something more to the point may be desirable. "Let us bring the needs of the church, the world, and all in need, to God's loving care. I invite your participation in the prayer, asking you to respond to my words, 'Lord, in your mercy,' by saying together, *Hear our prayer.*" Then say, "Let us pray to the Lord saying, 'Lord, in your mercy,'" and, raising both arms slightly in a gesture of invitation, say with the people, *"Hear our prayer."* When people understand what they are being asked to do and why, they ordinarily respond without too much hesitation. In the beginning it may also be wise to request the choir's assistance. A group of voices offering the response bolsters the courage of others to speak out.

Whatever form is employed, it is traditional for the prayers of the people to conclude with a "Commemoration of Those Who Have Died in the Faith" (a prayer for the communion of the saints) and a brief concluding collect. The people should be encouraged in every way possible to claim every prayer offered by joining in declaring *Amen* at the end. The word, which in Hebrew means "firm" or "established," or as an adverb "certainly" or "assuredly," serves as the community's response of affirmation. "*Amen,*" "So may it be," the people say together. Congregations need to be encouraged to reclaim this ancient practice. William D. Maxwell is most blunt in his opinion in the matter. "It is morose sacerdotalism of an acute sort to allow the minister alone to say the *Amen.* Meaning 'So be it', it is a latinized Hebrew word which from remote antiquity has been the people's assent to prayer and praise. It occurs throughout the Old Testament, and its use by the people in Christian worship is mentioned by St. Paul in the New Testament. . . . Such sacerdotalism has no defence in history or reason; it is not only an impoverishment but a perversion of worship which should cease."[61]

The Eucharist

Receiving the Offering and Preparing the Table

The offering of the people's tithes and gifts follows the intercessions as yet another response to the Word of God. Having heard again the Gospel of the Lord, having remembered the abundant goodness and kindness of the author of all grace, we are called on to respond in gratitude. These gifts, which come from the resources we rely on to sustain our lives, become in the giving symbols not simply of our support for the church's ministry, but, more importantly, of the offering of ourselves in response to God's own self-offering for us in Christ. In the early church this included gifts for the poor as well as the bread and wine for Communion. In keeping with the most ancient practice of the church, our thanksgiving, our Eucharist, begins with the offering of our own gifts. As the people's gifts are being received, the table is made ready. In some congregations, in which the people actually bring the bread for Communion, the loaves are presented, perhaps in baskets, by the ushers as they come forward to receive the plates for the offering. (Bread not used in the sacrament might be given to a soup kitchen, homeless shelter, or food bank.) Then, as the offering is made, the table is set by the elders and pastor. In the Reformation centers of both Geneva and Scotland, the table was never prepared in advance and covered, but was prepared in the sight of the people during the singing of the creed after the sermon or immediately following the creed. If the table is prepared prior to the service and covered, it may be uncovered as the offerings are received. The offering is presented during the singing of the Doxology, a psalm, or a hymn, and a brief prayer of dedication follows.

Invitation to the Lord's Table

While the people are still standing, and with the minister facing them from behind the table, an invitation to the Lord's table is given. It is the *Lord's* table to which we are being invited, which makes it all the more appropriate, indeed necessary, that the invitation be extended in the language of Scripture. Several Scriptural invitations are provided in the *Book of Common Worship*. Others, of course, may be drawn from Scripture. The biblical invitation does not preclude other words of invitation clarifying, for instance, that the Eucharist is the Lord's Supper and not a Presbyterian meal, and that the Lord invites all those who believe and who trust in him to share in the feast. To this the church has historically added the requirement of baptism, the sign of one's belonging to the body of Christ. From the beginning only the baptized participated in this sacred meal, and *all* the baptized participated, from the youngest to the oldest. The ticket of admission is not how much we ourselves know or how righteous we may be, but the gift of God's grace in Jesus Christ that has drawn us into the circle of the church's life and given us a place at the table. Unfortunately, the Reformed tradition, more than any other, has preserved in the sacramental celebration the penitential nature that marked the medieval Mass. Indeed, we have so much emphasized the unworthiness of those who gather at the Table that we sometimes forget that the primary emphasis is God's grace and not our worthiness. In his book *The Preaching Event,* John Claypool writes: "We do not partake of Christ's body and blood because we have earned the right to do so by our dazzling performance. We come there as patients who go to a hospital because they are sick, or people who go to a table because they are hungry. We partake of those sacraments because of our need, not our worthiness. The love of God is the power that makes perfection possible. It is not that which awaits perfection before it is given."[62] This is our eucharist, literally our "thanksgiving." The second-century *Didache* directs: "Now about the Eucharist: This is how to give thanks." It is thanksgiving for mercy clearly received and mercy yet promised; for love that has embraced us before we could embrace it in return; for grace that equips and strengthens us to live as those who belong to the realm of God's gracious rule in Jesus Christ.

If instructions are needed regarding the mode of reception, they are best stated here, succinctly, rather than after the fraction and before the distribution. Printed instructions in the service bulletin are helpful as well. Clarity about the mode of reception saves worshipers and those serving from any potential embarrassments.

The Great Prayer of Thanksgiving

The Great Thanksgiving follows the words of invitation. This primary prayer of the sacrament has been called by several names. In the rite of the Eastern Church it has historically been referred to as the Anaphora. The Canon of the Mass is the name given to it in Roman Catholic practice. Among Protestants it has been known as the prayer of consecration or the Communion prayer. The Great Thanksgiving, the Great Prayer, the Prayer of Thanksgiving, or the Eucharistic Prayer are names that have gained popular usage in more recent years. These titles grow out of the emergence of the ancient term *eucharist* for the supper itself. This is our thanksgiving, the whole of the meal. Since the time of Hippolytus in the third century, this prayer has begun with the same dialogue inviting the people to give thanks to God. Traditionally the people have stood for the dialogue and the prayer. The dialogue begins with a mutual greeting: "The Lord be with you. *And also with you.*" The leader then invites all to lift their hearts to God, and the people respond that they are prepared to do just that. "Lift up your hearts. *We lift them to the Lord.*" The third and final versicle explains the reason for the dialogue. "Let us give thanks to the Lord our God. *It is right to give our thanks and praise.*" Before the one offering the prayer on behalf of the whole community may proceed to give thanks, the consent of the whole assembly is needed.

The prayer that follows is clearly Trinitarian in its structure, beginning with praise to God the Father for the Father's mighty acts of redemption in the past. The work of creation, the deliverance of the people from bondage in Egypt, the work of the prophets are among those acts of God's grace that are recalled. This first part of the prayer is called the Preface, from the Latin word *praefatio,* which means "preliminary" or "proclamation." While the preface stands at the beginning of the prayer, its meaning here does not refer to its position, but to its content. This is proclamation. The preface may be general in character, or may be specific to the day or season in which it is used, a "proper preface." The conclusion of the preface unites the praise of the preface to the holy song of the whole company of heaven. "Therefore we praise you, joining our voices with choirs of angels, with prophets, apostles, and martyrs, and with all the faithful of every time and place, who forever sing to the glory of your name." And then the people sing or say:

> Holy, holy, holy Lord, God of power and might,
> heaven and earth are full of your glory.
> Hosanna in the highest.
> Blessed is he who comes in the name of the Lord.
> Hosanna in the highest.

The Sanctus has been sung by Christians as a part of the Great Thanksgiving since the earliest years of the church. Its use here joins our voices with all those past and present who have gathered at the table of our Lord in thanksgiving for grace received and anticipation of the fulfillment of God's eternal realm in Jesus Christ. The song is composed of the hymn of the heavenly court from Isaiah's vision (Isa. 6:3) and the cry of welcome with which the crowds greeted the Lord on his entry into Jerusalem (Matt. 21:9), taken from Psalm 118:26. It really should be sung rather than simply recited. *The Presbyterian Hymnal* contains several settings, as do other denominational hymnals. (Be sure to secure permission to copy before printing any music in the service bulletin.)

The second section of the prayer, referred to as the post-sanctus, begins with reference to the holiness of God and thus picks up the theme of the Sanctus: "You are holy, O God of majesty." And the thanksgiving is continued with reference to Christ's life and saving work: "And blessed is Jesus Christ, your Son, our Lord." In some rites, rather than continuing the theme of thanksgiving, this second portion of the prayer turns to asking for the blessing of the Holy Spirit's power in the gifts of bread and wine and is referred to as the "preliminary epiclesis."

The words of institution traditionally follow the post-sanctus, and have for nearly all of the church's life. Although the early church viewed the entire prayer as effecting the consecration of the elements, by the time of the Reformation the institution narrative alone had come to be understood as having the power to transform the bread and wine into the very body and blood of our Lord. John Calvin, concerned to remove any reference to this doctrine of the medieval church, moved the words of institution from the eucharistic prayer and had them read separately as proclamation and warrant for the sacrament. Consequently, the words are bracketed in the Great Thanksgiving in the *Book of Common Worship*. They may be spoken in conjunction with the invitation to the table, within the Great Thanksgiving, or in conjunction with the fraction, but they are spoken only once.

The second section of the eucharistic prayer concludes with what is termed the anamnesis, which is derived from Jesus' command "do this for my *anamnesis*." It is a difficult word to translate adequately into English. It means memorial, commemoration, remembrance, but it also means more. These words refer to something that is past and finished. Anamnesis, though, means not only to remember but in a sense to reenact what is past. "Biblically and liturgically when one remembers, the past, brought into the here and now, is made present. What was past becomes a living contemporary experience. The whole Eucharist is *anamnesis,* for in the Eucharist we recall before the Father the saving deeds of the Son, and in fulfillment of his promise Christ makes himself present to the congregation in all his redeeming activity. The anamnesis is the statement that the church, in obedience to the Lord's command, offers the bread and cup to remember and proclaim the death-resurrection of Christ in all its accomplished fullness."[63] The congregation may respond with one of several suggested memorial acclamations, which provide a way of saying that we do, indeed, remember. The memorial acclamation may be sung or spoken.

The third section of the Great Prayer is known as the epiclesis, and asks for the presence and the power of the Holy Spirit within and among the community gathered, "that the bread we break and the cup we bless may be the communion of the body and blood of Christ." It is the Spirit's presence and power that make the sacrament effective in our lives and in the life of all the church. The epiclesis also often includes a statement on the self-offering of those who participate and a plea for the Spirit's power in the church. Intercessions for the church and the world may follow at this point in the prayer, if they have not already been offered in the form of the Prayers of the People. The prayer concludes with a joyful doxology and the people's audible *Amen,* by which they express their assent to all that has been said and done. The Great Amen said by all the people loudly and clearly has been a part of the prayer since the time of Justin Martyr in the second century. The Lord's Prayer follows.

The Fraction

The prayer having ended, the minister takes the bread in hand and, using the words of institution unless they have previously been recited, breaks the bread in full view of the people. Some congregations use wafers, others small cubes of precut bread, and others loaves from which worshipers break a piece. Whatever the form used, the bread that is broken ought to be a loaf large enough that when it is held up and then broken, the bread itself will be clearly visible in the minister's hands. As the loaf is fractured and held out to the congregation, the minister says: "The Lord Jesus, on the night of his arrest, took bread, and after giving thanks to God, he broke it, and gave it to his disciples, saying: 'Take, eat. This is my body, given for you. Do this in remembrance of me.'" The pieces are placed again on the table and the minister takes a chalice and holds it up and forward to the congregation as the remainder of the words are spoken. Or the minister may choose to pour the wine from a pitcher into the chalice as the words are said: "In the same way he took the cup, saying: 'This cup is the new covenant sealed in my blood, shed for you for the forgiveness of sins. Whenever you drink it, do this in remembrance of me.'" And then, holding the chalice aloft to the congregation and gesturing to the bread on the table, the minister says, "Every time you eat this bread and drink this cup, you proclaim the saving death of the risen Lord, until he comes." This bread and cup are the visible signs of the Lord's body broken and blood shed for us. That being the case, the symbols need to be clearly visible to all. In a smaller sanctuary or worship space the movement related to the breaking and pouring and lifting may be quite the same as one would do at table in a home, but in a larger setting, the actions and the movement need to be more expansive—not forced or overly dramatic, but with a sweep large enough to be seen by all. After the breaking of the bread and the pouring of the cup, the minister may lift the cup in one hand and the bread in the other and declare: "The gifts of God for the people of God." Or with the bread and cup remaining on the table, the minister may extend both hands to the table and then lift them gently toward the congregation, speaking the words.

Sharing the Feast

The minister and the elders serving the people may commune first, providing, as it were, an example for the people to follow and symbolizing the fact that this spiritual food of the Eucharist nurtures us for the service of Christian discipleship. As we are nurtured, so we go forth to nurture. As we are served, so we go forth to serve. The elements may be shared while standing around the table before the elders go forth to serve the people. On the other hand, it has been argued that as the celebrant serves in the name of Christ, the host of the meal, he or she and others assisting in serving the people ought to commune last. What host of a dinner party would eat before serving the guests who have been invited? One way is not inherently better than the other. As much as anything, local custom, familiarity, even personal preference, can be the deciding factor here. One thing to avoid, however, is any form or ceremonial that would infer that the few who are served first or last are somehow more important than the many. We eat and drink as one people, one body in Christ.

Most Presbyterian congregations practice pew communion, with the elements being brought to the worshipers where they are sitting in the pews. While this may seem to be "the way that we have always done it," history teaches otherwise. In Martin Bucer's rite in Strasbourg, the people went forward to the Table, receiving the bread at one end of the table and the cup at the other. Worshipers formed a continuous line down the center aisle and waited. It was Huldrych Zwingli who began the custom of sitting for communion. The people came forward and took their places in the choir of the sanctuary and were served from a simple wooden plate and wooden cup. In Calvin's rite the people came to the Table and received the bread and wine either standing or kneeling. In the Reformed Church in Scotland the people received sitting as well, but sitting at a long Communion table placed in the choir or the nave. It is still possible, though in larger churches perhaps unreasonable as far as time is concerned, for worshipers to stand around the table to receive the sacrament. Sitting at table may be more difficult, for most sanctuaries are not built to accommodate that kind of action. The use of one or more stations to which the people may come at will to receive the bread and the wine is finding wider acceptance in Presbyterian congregations. The physical response of standing and walking to receive in response to the invitation is much more meaningful and powerful for most people than remaining in a pew and waiting to be served. If the people are invited to come to the table or to one of several stations to receive the elements, it is important to provide for some means of serving those who may be physically prevented from coming to the Table. Two elders or deacons may be prepared to serve these where they are in the pews, as others walk to the Table. As the bread is given into the hands of the worshiper, the minister or elder may say, "The body of Christ, given for you." To which the worshiper responds, *Amen.* And with the cup, "The blood of Christ, shed for you." And again, *Amen.*

It is important that the people be served, or in the case of pew communion that they serve one another. This is not a self-serve, eat-on-the-run meal. Christ is the host at the Table who serves us, and we, in his name, serve one another. For those who value the symbolism of the common cup but who prefer not to drink from the cup—especially if grape juice is used— the practice of intinction is recommended. Intinction developed sometime after the fourth century in the East. The use of wafers, which may be purchased in bulk from church supply houses, is suggested if intinction is employed. While they do not have the consistency of bread, they do not break up as they are dipped into the cup as ordinary bread will. Wheat wafers are also available today and have more the consistency and texture of bread. Pita bread also works well, and has the advantage of actually being able to be broken as it is given to the worshiper. The worshipers should be served, the celebrant or another placing the bread in the hands and offering the cup as well. Where pew communion is observed, it is preferable that the bread and wine be distributed in close proximity to each other. These are not two courses or two different meals, but one supper, one action. Elders serving wine might come to the table immediately after those serving bread have turned to serve the congregation.

Some congregations practice a unison eating of the bread or sharing of the cup as a symbol of their unity as the body of Christ. The practice is really rather artificial and is fraught with difficulty, especially for those who may have trouble holding a piece of bread or a thimble-size cup of juice for a long period of time. We do not eat and drink in unison at any other meal. The one exception would be a toast at a wedding, retirement party, or New Year's Eve, but this is no toast! Rather, our unity is symbolized by the very fact that we are eating and drinking together as God's redeemed and reconciled people in Jesus Christ. A much more powerful experience of unity is, instead of merely passing the tray with bread and the tray with the cups to the person sitting next to you, to serve that person, calling him or her by name, and saying, "The body of Christ broken for you," and "The blood of Christ shed for you." To which the other may respond, *Amen.* So let it be. After all have communed and the Communion vessels have been returned to their place on the table, the Eucharist concludes with a short prayer of thanksgiving

Sending

The service ends with an act of sending forth into the world to live out our worship in our daily lives. A hymn or psalm follows the concluding prayer of thanksgiving in the Eucharist, and this is followed by the charge and blessing. The benediction is God's blessing on the people. The minister is simply the medium through which the blessing is communicated. This is *not* a prayer asking for God's blessing, but a *declaration* of a blessing given, and therefore it should be drawn from Scripture. The blessing is pronounced with both arms raised and eyes focused on the people.

Chapter 6

Worshiping through the Year

*F*or Christians there are two ways of marking time. There is time on the secular calendar measured in months, weeks, and days—January through December—with special days that stand out, like New Year's Day, Presidents' Day, Martin Luther King Jr.'s Birthday, Valentine's Day, and Independence Day. This way of telling time honors the story of cultural heroes and the history of our secular heritage. There is also the time of the church's calendar; it too has both ordinary and special times. The church year begins not with January 1, but with the first Sunday in Advent, four Sundays prior to Christmas Day. This way of keeping time tells the story of God's saving work in and beyond human history in the life, death, and resurrection of Jesus Christ.

We Christians live in both these time zones, and we see and understand human life through both. We are part of this world. We have responsibilities within it, are shaped by it, and help to shape it. God made us this way, and as believers God calls us not *out* of this world but deeper *into* it, there to bear witness to the other reality that shapes us, the sphere of God's gracious rule in Jesus Christ. In the midst of this world that resists God's will and purpose for creation lives the church, God's new creation in Jesus Christ. It is in telling and retelling the story of God's faithfulness in the past and God's promises for the future that we begin to understand more and more who we are, what we are called to do, and how we are called to live as people who belong to both time zones. The story, in its telling and retelling, shapes our lives, our perspectives, our conduct. It also opens our eyes to see and our hearts and minds to respond to God's acting in our present. Laurence Hull Stookey writes that "the Christian story reaches back to the Exodus of ancient Israel and before and stretches forward to the descent of a new heaven and a new earth and beyond. Indeed, it can be said that Christians are called to assume a cruciform posture: Standing upright with feet firmly planted in the present, we stretch out one arm to grasp our heritage and the other arm to lay hold of our hope; standing thus, we assume the shape of our central symbol of faith: the cross. If either hand releases its grip, spiritual disaster threatens as the sign of the cross becomes misformed."[64]

The church year is one of the most effective ways of telling that story. Its structure, movement, colors, special rites, and services underscore the complexity and the richness of God's amazing grace. Keeping the year in worship is an especially helpful way of teaching children the story of God's love in Jesus Christ and emphasizing the distinctiveness of the Christian faith and commitment in the midst of the secular world. Robert Webber, an evangelical Christian, writes: "I am deeply concerned that evangelicals who are alarmed over the pervasiveness of secularism in our schools, on television, and in contemporary music seem unaware of a similar trend in our churches. Often, we operate with a secular calendar in mind, adjusting our schedules according to the academic calendar and the national calendar of holidays. . . . We celebrate Boy Scouts' Day, Girl Scouts' Day, Mother's Day, Father's Day, and the like. But few evangelical churches follow the Christian calendar of Advent, Christmas, Epiphany, Lent, Holy Week, Easter, Pentecost, and Trinity season except on a few special days such as Christmas and Easter."[65] Webber proposes that some of the sixteenth-century Reformers rejected the church year because Christ himself had become lost in the plethora of saints' days that cluttered the calendar. "But today we face another problem. By not following the Christian calendar we have come to adopt secular guidelines for our spiritual time. Christ has again become lost in our celebration of time, not because of too many saints' days and feasts, but because of our celebration in worship of too many other days—national holidays like Independence Day and special events like Mother's Day."[66] Only in recent years have Presbyterians begun to rediscover the liturgical year and to celebrate at least the major seasons. There was a time when we did not even celebrate Christmas. Now not only has Christmas become commonplace in our annual cycle of celebrations, but Advent is beginning to be a part of it as well. Not only do we celebrate Easter, but we are becoming acquainted with the whole of the Lenten journey, the days of Holy Week, and the historic Triduum, the most ancient of all the Christian festivals (Maundy Thursday evening through Easter Day). The Great Fifty Days of Easter, which culminate in Pentecost, are also becoming a part of our vocabulary and practice. There are tremendous possibilities in the rediscovery of this part of our liturgical heritage, not only for the nurture of children but for the nurture of all of us who make up the household of faith.

The Lord's Day

The church's year moves from anticipation to fulfillment, from promise to renewed hope for the future. The year, of course, did not appear full-grown on the liturgical landscape, but developed over a number of centuries. The basic unit of the church year is Sunday, the Lord's Day. The first Christians, being Jewish, attended synagogue on the Sabbath and then gathered for distinctive Christian worship on Sunday, the first day of the week and the day of the Lord's resurrection. Early Christians saw Sunday as a sort of eighth day of creation. In six days God created the heavens and the earth and all that is in them, and on the seventh God rested. On the eighth day of God's creative work, in the resurrection of Christ from death to life, God began a new creation. Sunday, the Lord's Day, is the principal feast of the church. For the first three hundred years of the church's life, this weekly celebration of the death and resurrection of the Savior, along with the annual celebration of Easter, constituted the full extent of the church's liturgical calendar.[67] The Easter celebration began with the Easter Vigil kept on Saturday night. In the fourth century, the Saturday night through Easter Eve celebration that covered the whole passion and resurrection story began to expand, and the three-day observance of the Holy Triduum (Maundy Thursday evening through Easter evening) began to take shape. This most ancient feast of the church is often referred to as the "paschal mystery," because the Lord's crucifixion and resurrection occurred during the feast of the Passover. The root word for paschal, *pasch,* is a transliteration of the Aramaic form of the Hebrew word for Passover. Just as the angel of death passed over the homes of the Hebrew slaves in Egypt, and as they passed through the sea into freedom, so Jesus by his passage through the suffering and death of the cross delivered the people of the new Israel out of the bondage of sin and death and into the sphere of God's new creation.[68] The use of the term "mystery" to describe the *pasch* is not intended to imply anything hidden or obscure, but refers to the richness of God's mercy and grace in this sacrificial act of love that reaches far beyond the limits of our human minds fully to comprehend and our words adequately to describe. When we speak of the paschal mystery, we are speaking not only of the Lord's passion, but also of his victory in the resurrection.

Lent

As early as the second century, Christians were observing a two-day fast in preparation for the celebration of Easter. In the third century, the fast was extended to include the entire week prior to Easter. A forty-day fast had developed by the first quarter of the fourth century and was recognized by the Council of Nicaea in 325. The forty days were intended to imitate Jesus' forty days of temptation in the wilderness. They were also reminiscent of Israel's forty years of wilderness wandering. It is this fast that we know as the season of Lent, a time of preparation for the celebration of the paschal mystery. The forty-day period began on the sixth Sunday before Easter and lasted until Maundy Thursday, when the restoration of the penitents took place. There was no fasting on Sundays, so the actual number of fast days was only thirty-four. By the fifth century, efforts were under way to increase the number to forty. This was accomplished in two stages. First, Good Friday and Holy Saturday were separated from the Easter Triduum and added to the Lenten fast, bringing the number up to thirty-six. Next, the four days prior to the first Sunday in Lent were added to raise the number to forty, making Wednesday the first day of Lent. The fast provided for several things. It was seen as a way of preparing for the reception of the Holy Spirit. It was understood as a weapon in the fight against evil. It served as a period of preparation for those desiring to be baptized. (Catechumens were baptized and received Communion for the first time during the Easter Vigil.) And finally, it was, quite pragmatically, a way of helping the poor by giving them money not spent on food.[69]

The ashes that mark the beginning of the Lenten fast were originally imposed on those guilty of a serious enough sin to require special penance. Penitents donned special garments and had ashes sprinkled on them. They were then expelled from the church.[70] "In the fourth century those undergoing church discipline had to endure several stages of excommunication and reinstatement: *weepers,* who stood outside the church door asking the prayers of those who went in; *hearers,* who were allowed in the narthex; *kneelers,* who were required to kneel with the standing congregation; *standers* who stood with the congregation but who had to leave before the Communion. Several years might be spent in each of the stages. In succeeding centuries, however, this public penitence was joined to Lent; and at the beginning of Lent (Sunday) or on the Wednesday before Lent (40 days before Easter), the penitents were placed under discipline. (The time was called *quarantine,* for 'forty.') They were admonished, prayed for, given the laying-on of hands, and expelled from the church before the Eucharist."[71] This rite of public ecclesiastical penance disappeared around the end of the first millennium, but the rite of ashes was retained and applied now to all believers. Men had the ashes sprinkled on them, and women had a sign of the cross made with ashes on their foreheads. The rule of using ashes obtained from burning the previous year's Palm Sunday branches appeared in the twelfth century.[72]

Ash Wednesday brings us face to face with our disobedience, our sin, and our need for forgiveness. It also brings us face to face with our mortality. We will die, every one of us. The words from Genesis repeated as the ashes are imposed remind us of that again and again: "Remember that you are dust, and to dust you shall return." The ashes, however, are made in the sign of the cross, which reminds us that even though each of us is to die, we may also die in Christ Jesus, whose death for us transforms our end from death to life. The season of Lent, though, is not about dying. It is about living as those who are being raised to new life in Christ Jesus. Lent provides us with an opportunity to reflect on the shape and conduct of our lives, to repent (literally "to turn") of those things that detract from our Christian commitment, and by the grace of God to grow more into the new life that is ours in Christ. We keep Lent in order to become better people and more faithful disciples.

Historically, Lent has contained three primary foci. For those guilty of "capital sins," it was a time of expulsion, public penance, and preparation to be welcomed back into the church. For those who were preparing to be baptized and to take their place in the Christian community, it was a time of preparation, learning, and study. For believers it was and is a time of introspection, confession, and repentance in preparation for the celebration of new life in Christ in the resurrection of Easter. Lent is a time for us to remember our own baptisms and our own baptismal vows, a time for us to renew our commitment to Christ and to his service.

Holy Week

Lent concludes in Holy Week, which begins with Passion/Palm Sunday and concludes with the Easter Vigil on Saturday evening. On Passion/Palm Sunday we hail the Lord's triumphal entry into Jerusalem, but we also know that the parade was short-lived. The one hailed as Messiah would die a criminal's death in less than a week. So the service itself moves from the pomp and exuberance of the triumphal entry to the story of the Lord's passion very early in the liturgy. Monday, Tuesday, and Wednesday of Holy Week may be marked by services of morning or evening prayer, providing an opportunity for the faithful to reflect on the sacrifice to come. Maundy Thursday evening, so named because of the "new mandate" Jesus gave his disciples, begins the Holy Triduum. Triduum is a Latin word meaning "three days," and is used to emphasize the unity of the events in these three holy days that begin with Maundy Thursday evening and conclude with the Easter Vigil on Saturday evening. The unity is further emphasized by the fact that services on Thursday and Friday nights end without benedictions. Actually, they do not end at all, but carry over into the next day, when they are resumed. The benediction or blessing is not heard until the shout of resurrection has been made.

The color for Lent is violet, symbolic of penitence. The color continues in use throughout Holy Week. Red is sometimes used as an optional color for the week. White may be used on Maundy Thursday. No color is used on Good Friday, for no paraments or stoles are used on this day.

Easter

The Lenten season culminates in the glorious celebration of Christ's resurrection from death to life on Easter Day. Easter, however, is not simply one day; it is the first and primary day of a fifty-day season of celebration. The forty days of Lent serve to prepare us not simply for a one-day celebration, but for a season of celebration. Many denominational calendars have begun to emphasize this by designating the Sundays following Easter Day as Sundays *of* Easter rather than Sundays *after* Easter.[73] We need to discover and to incorporate into our worship during these Great Fifty Days of Easter ways of keeping the energy up, the spirit enlivened, so that when we come to the end of them on the Day of Pentecost, our celebration is not like a spent Roman candle on New Year's Day. The color for all of Easter is white.

Ascension

The fortieth day after Easter Day has for centuries been observed as Ascension Day. Because it always falls on a Thursday, the Ascension may be celebrated on the Sunday following the day itself. The Ascension explained for the disciples the end of the resurrection appearances of Jesus. It also stands as a witness to the faithfulness of God. What God begins, God always brings to completion. "Men of Galilee, why do you stand looking up toward heaven? This Jesus, who has been taken up from you into heaven, will come in the same way as you saw him go into heaven" (Acts 1:11). The end of Jesus' earthly appearances did not mean the end of Jesus, but the exaltation of Jesus. The story of God's redemptive work in human history continues and will be brought to fulfillment in God's own good time. The church bears special responsibility in that undertaking, and the theme of the Day of Ascension alerts us to what is to come on the Day of Pentecost.

Pentecost

Pentecost concludes the celebration of the season of Easter in the church's calendar. The Day of Pentecost, writes Laurence Stookey, "is not about the work of the Spirit in the hearts of individual believers; there is ample opportunity to deal with that work throughout the year. The Day of Pentecost is about the formation of the church out of a frightened band of followers; that tight-lipped crowd, which had huddled timidly behind closed doors, is thrust by the Spirit into the streets of Jerusalem to proclaim the gospel in terms everyone can understand. How are we to account for this change? Only by recognizing that the Spirit is the One who forms the church by making the Risen Christ manifest in power."[74] That same Spirit continues to be bestowed on the church; that same Spirit continues to empower, equip, and enliven us for the work of speaking the gospel and living the gospel in the world today. Pentecost needs to be a day of great celebration in the church, a day when we focus on our empowerment for ministry and renew our commitment to the work of being the church of the risen Christ in the world. The color for Pentecost is red, for flames of fire, for the enlivening power of the Holy Spirit.

Trinity Sunday

The Sunday after Pentecost is traditionally celebrated as Trinity Sunday. The color is white. Trinity marks the transition from Lent-Easter-Pentecost to Ordinary Time, which will continue until the beginning of Advent, four Sundays prior to Christmas. Trinity Sunday is the only feast day in the liturgical year that is based solely on a theological doctrine, and is the most recent of all the special days.

Ordinary Time

The liturgical color for Ordinary Time is green. The term "ordinary" is not intended to imply that these Sundays are any less special than the other Sundays in the year, only that their focus is not as finely tuned. In the two cycles of Ordinary Time that mark the Christian calendar, our attention turns to the whole witness of the gospel. Christ the King Sunday provides the transition from the extended season of Ordinary Time to the other great cycle of extraordinary time. On this Sunday, as we prepare to begin the cycle anew, we celebrate the reign of the risen Christ in the church, in human life, in the world of God's creation. The color is white.

Advent

The second great cycle of time in the church's year, Advent-Christmas-Epiphany, begins the annual cycle. By the year 336, December 25 had begun to be celebrated in the West as Christmas, the day of the Savior's birth, and the seed for the development of a second cycle for the church's year had been sown.[75] There are two theories for the choice of this date. One is that the date, the day of the winter solstice, was already set aside for the feast of the "Unconquered Sun-God," a Syrian deity for which Roman Emperor Aurelian established an empirewide holiday in 274 in an effort to unite and strengthen his far-flung empire. The Church of Rome then established a feast of Christ's birth on the same day, to provide Christians an alternative celebration and to give the church the opportunity to proclaim that on this day the Christian community was celebrating the birth of him who alone is the light and the salvation of the world. A second theory is drawn from the fact that as early as the third century, Christian theologians were trying to calculate the date of the Lord's birth. One theory held that John the Baptist was conceived at the autumn equinox and born at the summer solstice. Since Luke 1:26 relates that Jesus was conceived six months after John, it was concluded that he was conceived at the spring equinox, March 25, and born on December 25, the winter solstice.[76] Whatever the case, Christmas had found widespread acceptance in the Western Church by the middle of the fourth century.

Like Easter, Christmas developed a season of preparation. The earliest witness to Advent as a season of preparation for Christmas is found in the regulations for fasting as issued by Bishop Perpetuus of Tours (A.D. 490). Reference is made to a three-day fast kept weekly from the Feast of St. Martin, November 11, until Christmas. This was tied to what was previously known as St. Martin's Lent, which lasted from November 11 until the day of Epiphany, January 6, a period of eight weeks or fifty-six days. However, since there was no fasting on Saturday or Sunday, the actual number of fast days was forty, the same as the number of Lenten fast days. The motive behind this fast before Epiphany was the same one associated with Lent—the preparation of catechumens for baptism and participation in the Holy Eucharist. By the tenth and eleventh centuries, the four-week Advent season had found general acceptance and came to mark the beginning of the church year. The four Sundays of Advent comprise a period of preparation for the celebration of the incarnation of God in the child of Bethlehem, and a renewal of the church's anticipation that the work God has begun in Jesus Christ will be brought to completion in him in the fullness of time. Our vision is directed both to the past and to the future. Consequently, the tone of Advent is one of eager anticipation and penitential self-examination. How shall we greet this One who comes to us both in humility and in power, in weakness and vulnerability, as the Lord of all?

The traditional color for Advent is purple, which may be traced to a translation of the Latin word *violaceus* in the Roman rubrics to "violet" in English. In common usage, violet and purple are considered the same. The Latin name, however, was used to describe a blue-purple.[77] Consequently, some congregations are reviving the historical use of blue, the color for royalty, for Advent. One advantage to using blue rather than purple is that it distinguishes Advent from the more penitential season of Lent, in which purple is also used.

Christmas

As with Easter, we tend to think of Christmas as a single day or a several-week season that culminates on December 25. Actually, Christmas begins on December 25 and concludes twelve days later on January 6, the day of the Epiphany of the Lord. The celebration of Christmas as a season in the church's liturgy has for the most part been lost. By the Sunday after Christmas, most people are ready to get on with the new year. The Christmas decorations at home have been taken down and put away, and it's time to put Christmas away too. It is hard for us to imagine today, but under the Puritan influence Christmas, either as a single day or a season, was not even celebrated by many Christians, Presbyterians in particular, in the early years of this country. The Christmas "season" now begins some weeks before the day (during Advent) and ends on the day. Keeping Christmas alive for eleven days after December 25 in the church's worship may be difficult, but it can also be well worth the effort.

Epiphany

The twelfth day of Christmas, the day of Epiphany, was the original feast of the Lord's birth in the East. In antiquity an epiphany referred to a visible manifestation of a deity or the visit of a ruler who was regarded as divine.[78] Originally the feast day drew together four events in the life of Christ: his birth, the visit of the Magi, his baptism, and his first miracle at the wedding feast in Cana. In the West, the visit of the Magi came to dominate the celebration of Epiphany. The feast focuses on the manifestation of the nature of this child born in Bethlehem. He is the one who is "born king of the Jews" (Matt. 2:2). He is "my Son, the Beloved, with whom I am well pleased" (Matt. 3:17). And, in turning the water into wine at the wedding feast in Cana he "revealed his glory; and his disciples believed in him" (John 2:11b). Because Epiphany always falls on January 6, which more often than not is a weekday, it may be celebrated on the Sunday preceding the actual day. The Sunday after Epiphany is celebrated as the Baptism of the Lord and provides the transition to Ordinary Time.

The fully developed liturgical year is based on two cycles of extraordinary time (Lent-Easter-Pentecost, and Advent-Christmas-Epiphany) linked by two periods of regular or Ordinary Time. Each cycle of extraordinary time begins with a period of preparation. In addition, both have at their beginning and their end Sundays bearing special designations that serve as transition points into the new time of celebration.

The Church Year

Christmas Cycle

Advent—Four Sundays before Christmas

Christmas Day

Sundays after Christmas

Epiphany (January 6)

Ordinary Time

Baptism of the Lord (the Sunday following Epiphany)—begins
    Ordinary Time

Sundays in Ordinary Time

Transfiguration of the Lord (Sunday before Ash Wednesday)—
    concludes Ordinary Time

Easter Cycle

Ash Wednesday—begins the forty weekdays and six Sundays of
    preparation for Easter

Six Sundays of Lent

Holy Week

    Palm/Passion Sunday

    Maundy Thursday

Good Friday

Holy Saturday—concludes Lent

Easter Day

Sundays of Easter (the fifty days of Easter)

Ascension of the Lord

Pentecost

Ordinary Time

Trinity Sunday—begins Ordinary Time

Sundays in Ordinary Time

All Saints' Day (November 1)

Christ the King Sunday (the Sunday before First Sunday of Advent)—ends Ordinary Time

Chapter 7

Celebrating Advent, Christmas, and Epiphany

Advent

*I*t is sometimes difficult to maintain the integrity of the church's season of Advent when the secular celebration of "the Christmas season" begins the day after Thanksgiving, if not before. It is hard to resist the pressure to begin singing Christmas carols the first Sunday in December. Parishioners sometimes complain that the church is not helping them "get into the Christmas spirit" when we stick to our resolve in observing a season of preparation. Christmas, though, is much more than a feeling, a spirit to be created and enjoyed during a three- or four-week time frame, and the complaint itself indicates how seriously the Christian community's celebration of one of its principal religious feasts has been compromised by the pressures of the marketplace and social custom. It is unlikely that the secular world will back off from the Christmas hype. Too much of our economy depends on it. It is possible, however, for the Christian community to resist the pressure to conform, and instead to hold fast to its unique identity and to the importance of a season of spiritual preparation in anticipation of Christmas.

If a congregation has not observed Advent, it would be unwise, if not altogether foolish, to begin abruptly. A more gradual approach will receive a warmer reception and have a better chance of success. Obtain the worship committee's cooperation in introducing the observance of Advent in your congregation's worship. Obtain the session's endorsement, and be sure that the congregation's music leaders are accepting of the idea and share your understanding of the importance of observing Advent. Several weeks before the First Sunday of Advent, begin a series of short newsletter and/or bulletin articles on the history and significance of the season and on the benefits of observing a time of spiritual preparation for Christmas. We prepare our homes, should we not prepare our souls? Sing only Advent hymns for the first two Sundays in the season. Begin the third and fourth Sundays with Advent hymns but then use one or two carols later in the services. Ease the congregation into the practice of an Advent observance. Remind the congregation that many Christmas carols will be sung during the Christmas Eve service(s). During the second and third Sundays, use metrical settings of the psalm for the day that can be sung to reasonably familiar Christmas melodies. Most of all, educate the congregation in the meaning of Advent.

An Advent Festival

On the Sunday or a weekday evening before the First Sunday of Advent, hold an *Advent festival*. Begin with a congregational meal using the color of Advent, purple or blue—whichever will be used in the sanctuary—for decorations. Include a workshop on Advent hymns, and centers for making banners, Advent wreaths, Advent calendars, simple crèches, and the like. The possibilities are many, but the focus should be single-minded: getting ready to celebrate Advent. The worship committee or another group in the church may choose to take on the task of compiling a booklet of short Advent devotionals written by members of the church family for use during the season. These could be distributed as a part of the festival. Preparations for this kind of project, however, need to begin far in advance. Writers need to be carefully chosen and thoroughly informed as to the length and focus of their devotionals.

Advent Wreath

On the First Sunday of Advent, begin the service by lighting the first candle in the *Advent wreath*. The wreath, which includes four purple (or blue) candles, is an excellent way of marking the Sundays of Advent and the progression of time toward Christmas. Children in particular find the tradition meaningful, especially when what we do in church on Sunday mornings is replicated at home with a family Advent wreath. The *Book of Common Worship* provides Scripture verses that may be read on the four Sundays of Advent, as well as verses for Christmas Eve. At each successive lighting of the candles, the texts from the previous Sundays are read in addition to the verse for the day. The candles from the previous Sundays are lighted as well. The central white candle, the Christ candle, is not lighted until Christmas Eve. Some traditions identify the candles with titles such as Hope, Peace, Joy, and Love. The tradition of lighting a pink candle on the Third Sunday of Advent dates from the Middle Ages, when the reading from the Epistle appointed for that day was Philippians 4:4–6, which in the New Revised Standard Version reads, "Rejoice in the Lord always; again I will say, Rejoice. Let your

gentleness be known to everyone. The Lord is near. Do not worry about anything, but in everything by prayer and supplication with thanksgiving let your
requests be made known to God." In Latin the first word in this passage is
Gaudete ("rejoice"), and in time the Sunday became known as Gaudete Sunday. The note of joy provided a bright moment of release from the otherwise
penitential mood of the season, and this was signified by the use of pink.[79] Different families, individuals, or groups might be invited to light the candles and
to offer the readings. The candles may be lighted during the reading or during the singing of an opening hymn that follows. The lighting of the candles
might also serve as the call to worship. Another option would be to place the
lighting after the opening hymn and before the prayer of confession, where
the collect for the day might otherwise be offered. A sung response, such as a
stanza of "O Come, O Come, Emmanuel" may be sung by the congregation
at the conclusion to act as a bridge from adoration to confession.

The Advent wreath is last lighted on Christmas Eve, and should be
removed from the sanctuary before any services on Christmas Day or the First
Sunday after Christmas. If a congregation uses the central Christ candle
throughout the church year, it alone should be present and burning for Christmas. While some consider the Christ candle a "liturgical novelty" and argue
against its usage beyond Advent as being potentially confusing with the
paschal candle of Easter, which is also used for baptisms and funerals, it
nonetheless offers a visible symbol of Christ's abiding presence with us, its
flame a reminder of the promise "The light shines in the darkness, and the
darkness did not overcome it" (John 1:5).

Advent Service of Lessons and Carols

Another helpful way of beginning the Advent season and helping a congregation to appreciate the wealth of spiritual opportunity in this time is with an
Advent service of lessons and carols, an adaptation of the traditional Christmas Festival of Nine Lessons and Carols. The service begins with a processional hymn such as "Come, Thou Long-Expected Jesus" or "O Come, O
Come, Emmanuel," a biblical greeting, and a bidding prayer. *The United
Methodist Book of Worship* and *The Book of Occasional Services* of the Episcopal Church both offer services that may be adapted for Presbyterian use.
The prayer is followed by the reading of nine lessons interspersed with hymns
and anthems of Advent. The lessons should be read by members of the congregation. Readers should be recruited well in advance, provided with a copy
of the lessons they will be reading (so as to ensure that all read from the same
translation), and given clear instructions about when they will read, where

they will stand for the readings, and how and when to walk there. A rehearsal helps to ensure that the service will run smoothly and that all participants are familiar and comfortable with their assignments. The congregation's participation in the music should be emphasized. Most volunteer choirs will already be rather heavily involved with preparation for other services during the season and would appreciate a service in which their primary energy is invested in leading the congregation in the hymns and songs of the whole community.

Variety can be added by allowing the choir to sing alternating stanzas with the congregation, alternating male and female voices by stanza, introducing a hymn with a solo voice and having the congregation join on the second stanza or refrain, and so on. "Watchman, Tell Us of the Night" may be sung antiphonally between choir and congregation, male and female voices, or those sitting on opposite sides of the sanctuary. A child's voice might introduce "Creator of the Stars of Night" by singing the first stanza, treble voices only joining on the second stanza, and all voices joining on the last two. The possibilities are many. Instructions may be printed beneath the title of each hymn so that there is no need for verbal instructions, which would interrupt the flow of the service and detract from the focus on the biblical and musical texts. Hymns and anthems, of course, are to be chosen in light of the lesson that precedes or follows each.

Chrismon Tree

Many congregations have begun the tradition of using a *Chrismon tree* in the sanctuary as a part of the Advent and Christmas celebration. It is important, especially for children, that the distinction between this tree and the family Christmas tree be clearly made. The Chrismon tree is decorated only with clear lights and Chrismons made from white and gold material. White, the color of Christmas, is the color of purity and perfection, while gold is the color for majesty and glory. The Chrismons are ancient symbols for Christ or some part of Christ's ministry: the crown, descending dove, fish, Celtic cross, Jerusalem cross, shepherd's crook, chalice, shell, and others. Some congregations include in the Sunday bulletin, on a separate pamphlet, a description of all the Chrismons on the tree.

Service for Hanging of the Greens

Most Presbyterian churches are decorated, to one degree or another, for the season at least a couple of weeks in advance of Christmas. A service that is helpful in giving some meaning to the decorations that adorn our places of worship, as well as providing an excuse to sing Christmas carols at least once during the course of Advent, is a *service for the hanging of the greens*. The service can be as elaborate or simple, structured or relaxed as your congregation may choose to make it. Whatever the case, it should not supplant the Service for the Lord's Day. Biblical passages and other readings help explain the significance of the holly, the cedar, the Advent wreath, the Chrismon tree, and any other special decorations. The Chrismon tree may be lighted for the first time during the service. A tradition in one congregation I served is that everyone present is invited to place a Chrismon on the tree as a medley of carols is sung by all. (Ornaments may be rearranged later to ensure balance and beauty.) *The United Methodist Book of Worship* contains a service for the hanging of the greens which, with some minor modifications, works very well in a Presbyterian congregation. In the same vein as Gaudete Sunday in some traditions, this service provides a momentary break from the predominantly penitential theme of Advent.

Celebrating Christmas

On Christmas Eve, both the tone and the color for the service change. The purple or blue of Advent gives way to the glistening brilliance of white, the color of gladness, light, and joy. Some congregations now use gold as well. The time of waiting is over; the gift is given. Let the church join with the angels in heralding the birth of "a Savior, who is Christ the Lord."

While most Presbyterian congregations still do not hold a service on Christmas Day, unless it falls on Sunday, many have begun to celebrate Christmas Eve with a variety of services. Of those who attend Christmas Eve services, many may not be regular participants in the life and worship of the Christian community. For some it is part of a once- or twice-annual church visit. This is no time to "dumb down" the liturgy in order to make it appeal to the widest possible audience. It is not a secular holiday that we celebrate, but the very incarnation of God in human flesh, "God with us." The service, whatever form it takes, needs to reflect the holy awe and joyful wonder of this unparalleled event in human history, not the saccharine sweet sentimentality often associated with the "Christmas spirit."

Christmas Eve Communion

A service of Holy Communion is most appropriate to Christmas Eve, especially when we recall that the Eucharist is given to us not merely as a memorial meal, but as a means of communion with the risen Christ and a festive celebration of his promise to come again in the fullness of time. The service may begin with the lighting of the Advent wreath. On this night all five candles are lighted, and the readings for the four Sundays in Advent as well as that for Christmas Eve are read. The Litany for Christmas: A *(Book of Com-*

mon Worship, p. 178) provides the service with a resounding note of praise at its very beginning, as we join in proclaiming, *Glory to you, O Lord!* A hymn of joyful praise, "O Come, All Ye Faithful" or "Joy to the World!" continues the adoration of the gathered community. The service moves directly to the reading of the Word. The lessons for Christmas Eve do not vary: Isaiah 9:2–7, Titus 2:11–14, and Luke 2:1–14 (15–20). The psalm for Christmas Eve is Psalm 96. Carols might also be sung between the lessons. Following the sermon, a carol is sung, and then the community confesses its faith in the words of a creed of the Church. The second section of A Brief Statement of Faith, found in the *Book of Confessions,* is especially appropriate for Christmas Eve. An offering may be received, perhaps designated for some special ministry of compassion. Again, a carol such as "Hark! The Herald Angels Sing" might be used in place of the Doxology on Christmas Eve. The *Book of Common Worship* offers an excellent Great Prayer of Thanksgiving for use in this service. Rather than speaking the Sanctus or singing it to a melody used at other times of the year, consider using the following paraphrase* which may be sung to the tune of GLORIA ("Angels We Have Heard on High"):

> *Holy, holy, holy Lord,*
> *God of power and God of might,*
> *Heaven and earth your glory fills.*
> *Praise to you, O God on high.*
> *Gloria in excelsis Deo. Gloria in excelsis Deo.*
>
> *Blest is he who comes to us*
> *in the name of God most high.*
> *Glad hosannas sing we now,*
> *Jesus Christ, Emmanuel;*
> *Gloria in excelsis Deo. Gloria in excelsis Deo.*

Or this paraphrase may be sung to MENDELSSOHN ("Hark! the Herald Angels Sing"):

> *Holy, holy, holy Lord,*
> *God of power and God of might,*
> *Heaven and earth reveal your glory.*
> *Praise to you, Creator God.*
> *Blest is He who now draws nigh*
> *in the name of God Most High.*
> *Glad hosannas sing we now,*
> *Jesus Christ, Emmanuel.*
> *With the heavenly host we sing,*
> *glory to the Savior King!*

*(These paraphrases are my own and may be used if appropriate credit is given: Copyright © 2001, J. Dudley Weaver Jr. Used by permission.)

Likewise, this paraphrase set to the tune of MUELLER ("Away in a Manger") might be used for the memorial acclamation:

> *Lord Jesus, our Savior, in love we recall*
> *Your pain and your death on the cross for us all.*
> *In death you redeemed us, in rising you reign.*
> *Lord Jesus, we look for your coming again.*

Christmas Eve Communion is a good time to get Presbyterians out of their pews. Instead of pew communion, invite worshipers to come in small groups and stand around the Communion Table to receive the elements, or use two or more stations to which they may walk at will to receive the elements. Carols might be sung as the elements are shared.

Traditional to most Christmas Eve services now is the lighting of Christmas candles. The light from the Christ candle may be passed among the congregation, the minister lighting the first candle and then passing the light to the congregation. Lights are dimmed as the candlelight begins to illuminate the room and the congregation joins in singing a familiar carol, *"Silent night, holy night! All is calm, all is bright."* And the service, following the benediction, ends in a hush of holy awe.

Festival of Nine Lessons and Carols for Christmas

Another option for Christmas Eve or any of the twelve days of Christmas is to celebrate a Festival of Nine Lessons and Carols. The service originated in Truro Cathedral in England during the nineteenth century and was later adapted for use in King's College Chapel, Cambridge, in 1918. From there it found its way into general congregational use during the season of Christmas. Supplemental Liturgical Resource 7: *Liturgical Year* provides a liturgy with readings and suggested carols and anthems adapted from the King's College Chapel liturgy. While nine lessons are traditionally read, fewer may be used. However, Genesis 3:8–15 should always be used. The account of Adam and Eve's fall sets the stage for the whole story of salvation that follows, finding its culmination in the birth of the Savior. The lessons included in the service from *Liturgical Year* are Genesis 3:8–15; Genesis 22:15–18; Isaiah 9:2, 6–7; Micah 5:2–4; Luke 1:26–35, 38; Matthew 1:18–21; Luke 2:8–20; Matthew 2:1–11, and John 1:1–14. Others that might be considered are Genesis 2:4b–9, 15–25; Isaiah 40:1–11; Isaiah 35:1–10; Isaiah 7:10–15; Luke 1:5–24; Luke 1:26–58; Luke 1:39–45; Luke 1:57–80; Luke 2:21–35; and Hebrews 1:1–12.

It is appropriate for the sanctuary to be dimly lighted as the service begins, symbolizing the bewilderment and hopelessness of a world without its light, which is Christ. At the appointed time, bells may ring and lights are raised as the procession, following an acolyte, enters the sanctuary. The procession may include not only choir, liturgists, and readers, but also participants dressed as Mary and Joseph, wise men, shepherds, and angels. The traditional processional hymn is "Once in Royal David's City." The first stanza may be sung by a solo voice, perhaps a child, with the congregation and choir joining on the second stanza. The costumed members form a living crèche, around the Chrismon tree or some other appropriate space in the chancel. These leaders in the liturgy are simply there—silent witnesses to the unfolding story told in the biblical readings, the carols, and the anthems. The focus of the service is *not* on any reenactment but on the biblical Word read and sung.

When the hymn is ended, the leader greets the people with an appropriate biblical greeting: "The grace of our Lord Jesus Christ be with you all." And the people respond: *And also with you.* The opening sentences or call to worship follows immediately: "The people who walked in darkness have seen a great light; those who lived in a land of deep darkness—on them light has shined" (Isa. 9:2). Response: *"Glory to God in the highest, and peace to God's people on earth"* (Luke 2:14).

If the Advent wreath has been a part of the Advent worship, the central Christ candle is lighted at this time. (The acolyte will have lighted the other candles on the wreath as well as any others used in the chancel area when he or she arrived.)

It is traditional that a bidding prayer follows. The prayer begins with a greeting:

> Friends in Christ, in this Christmas season we delight to hear again the message of the angels, to go to Bethlehem and see the Son of God lying in a manger.

And the prayer continues with an invitation:

> Let us therefore open the Holy Scriptures and read the story of the loving purpose of God from the time of our rebellion against God until the glorious redemption brought to us by this holy child, and let us make this place glad with carols of praise.

The intercessions then follow:

> But first, let us pray for the needs of the whole world:
> for peace and justice on earth . . .
> For the unity and mission of the church for which Christ died . . .
> And because Christ particularly loves them, let us remember in his name:
> the poor and helpless . . .

>the cold, the hungry and the oppressed . . .
>the sick and those who mourn . . .
>the lonely and unloved . . .
>the aged and little children . . .
>and all who do not know and love the Lord Jesus Christ. . . .
>   Finally, let us remember before God that multitude which no one can number, whose hope was in the Word made flesh, and with whom, in Jesus, we are one for evermore. . . .
>   And now, to sum up all these petitions, let us pray in the words which Christ himself has taught us. . . .[80]

The Lord's Prayer follows. The prayer bids us celebrate with joy the glad news of the birth of the Savior and the gift of our salvation. The prayer also reminds us that not all the world is wrapped in the light and life of the Christmas event. The darkness still stalks the world of God's creation, and the new creation begun in Jesus is yet to be fulfilled. And so we begin our celebration remembering a gift already given and anticipating a gift yet to be received, the gift of a new creation in Christ Jesus.

A hymn or carol serves as a transition from prayer to the reading of the lessons. "Of the Father's Love Begotten," with its reference to Christ the "Alpha and Omega" and its concluding doxological stanza is especially effective. Each lesson is introduced by a single sentence summarizing the content of the reading. Following the lesson, the reader may simply end or may mark the ending with: *Thanks be to God.* Effort should be made to minimize attention drawn to the physical movement of the readers or singers. The lessons are read by nine different lectors, who should be chosen as representative of the whole congregation, for their gifts and skills for public reading, and for the quality and intelligibility of their speaking voices. Anthems, hymns, or carols appropriate to the readings are placed after each. While choirs have much to offer in this service and in all services of Christian worship, their greatest gift, especially in a service such as this, is in leading the people in their sung praise and prayer. Allow the congregation the opportunity to sing as many of the carols of the season as possible. Alternating stanzas between choir and congregation, soloists and organ, using alternative harmonizations, and employing various instruments in accompanying the choir and congregation add color and diversity to the music of the service.

Ordinarily there is no sermon with this service, but Presbyterian preachers may not want to pass up the opportunity for proclaiming, however briefly, some word of the gospel on this very special occasion in the worship of the church. Bear in mind the story that has just been told in the words of Scripture and through the powerful combination of poetry and music in the hymns and carols is one that cannot be improved on. The best that can be expected is a homily that reflects some of the holy awe and reverence of the incredible event remembered. This is one time when less is more.

The service may conclude with the lighting of Christmas candles, the light from the Christ candle being passed among the people, and then the blessing. It is appropriate for the readers, choir, other participants, and clergy to process from the sanctuary during the hymn that follows the benediction.

Baptism of the Lord

Reaffirmation of the Baptismal Covenant

On the Sunday after Epiphany, the Baptism of the Lord is celebrated and marks the transition from the Advent-Christmas-Epiphany cycle to the first cycle of Ordinary Time in the church year (formerly known as Sundays after Epiphany). The Baptism of the Lord, with its emphasis on Jesus' empowerment and commissioning for his ministry, provides an excellent opportunity for the ordination and installation of elders and deacons, which ordinarily occurs at this time of year. It also provides a wonderful opportunity for a service for the reaffirmation of baptismal vows. The renewal of baptismal vows reminds us here at the beginning of a new year of our unique identity and calling in the world and of our need of daily grace to live in faithfulness to both. We make New Year's resolutions. This is one of the most important resolutions that we can make. The rite is ordinarily included in the order for the Service for the Lord's Day and follows the sermon. It is conducted from the baptismal font. Traditionally the Reaffirmation of Baptismal Vows is a part of the Easter Vigil when there is no celebration of the sacrament itself. Other occasions when the rite is appropriate include the Day of Pentecost, Sundays in Lent, Sundays in Easter, and All Saints' Day. It might also be observed as a part of any service planned for New Year's Eve or New Year's Day. Of course, the session's approval should be received and the congregation should be apprised ahead of time when the service is used. Careful explanation is owed to the congregation prior to the event so that they may participate with understanding.

The liturgy begins with scriptural sentences related to baptism and living within the baptismal covenant. The congregation stands and is invited "once again to reject sin, to profess your faith in Christ Jesus, and to confess the faith of the church, the faith in which we were baptized." The renunciations follow, the congregation answering as one the questions previously addressed to them or to their parents on the occasion of their baptism into the community of faith. The interrogatory form of the Apostles' Creed is used, as it is in the sacrament of baptism. Water is poured into the font. A large earthenware or silver pitcher may be used. The central element of baptism needs to be clearly visible and the sound of that element splashing into the font ought to be clearly audible to all. Raise the pitcher high enough that the water can be seen by all and heard by all. A prayer of thanksgiving for baptism follows. As with the prayer of thanksgiving over the water in the baptismal liturgy, this prayer recalls with thanksgiving the ways in which God has acted in the past in the history of the people of Israel and especially in the life, death, and resurrection of Jesus Christ, to nourish, sustain, and enliven human life. It concludes with a petition that the Holy Spirit will lead all who have passed through the waters of baptism in the way of faithful obedience. The minister then reaches his or her hand into the font and lifts some of the water high, allowing it to fall back into the font. The water should *not* be sprinkled or thrown in the direction of the people or indiscriminately around the room. This is not a mass rebaptism. The sign of the cross is then made over the people while the pastor charges: "Remember your baptism and be thankful. In the name of the Father and of the Son and of the Holy Spirit." And all respond, *Amen.*

Making the sign of the cross may be a bit uncomfortable for some Presbyterians. Historically our tradition has incorporated little ritual action in the liturgy. Much of the ritual of the sixteenth-century liturgy was eliminated by the Reformers because it was surrounded by superstition and misunderstanding and did not serve to edify the faithful. Huldrych Zwingli, for instance, removed all statues and images from the churches as well as the pipe organs. The liturgy took on a drab austerity. Zwingli believed that no external element or ritual could be of use in edifying us in spiritual things. Calvin, on the other hand, understood how God can and does use material things, signs and symbols, to bestow spiritual blessings. The sacraments, and especially their elements, were understood as physical signs of spiritual grace.[81] What is important in our tradition is not maintaining a ban on ritual action, but maintaining a clear perspective. It is not the use of symbol and ritual to which the tradition objects so much as it is the misuse of these in worship. Do they serve to edify? Do they point us in the direction of God? The liturgy itself can become idolatrous when we see it as an end in itself rather than as a means to an end, an avenue that leads us to an encounter with God. Ritual is extremely important to us as created beings. We all have daily rituals and rituals that mark special occasions in our lives. They help bring structure to our lives, give a sense of connectedness to the disparate experiences of our lives, and provide a kind of comfort zone for a life and world constantly in the process of change. Harold Daniels noted that "we live in a vastly different setting from the situation in the sixteenth century. Overwhelmed with secularism, we need to restore ceremonial acts that build us up in the faith, and make them a significant part of the liturgy. To fail to do so is to fail to recognize that worship is more than words, but also movement, gesture, posture, and action. We pray with the body as well as with the lips and minds."[82]

The use of the sign of the cross here in the service of Reaffirmation of the Baptismal Covenant ties this act to our baptisms when, after the washing with water, the sign of the cross is made on the forehead and the pastor declares, "Child of the covenant, you have been sealed by the Holy Spirit in baptism, and marked as Christ's own forever." It ties us to our confirmation when as we kneel before God's people, hands are placed upon the head, the pastor says, "O Lord, uphold [name] by your Holy Spirit. Daily increase in *him/her* your gifts of grace: the spirit of wisdom and understanding, the spirit of counsel and might, the spirit of knowledge and the fear of the Lord, the spirit of joy in your presence, both now and forever," and the sign of the cross is traced on the forehead. This visible symbol reminds us that we, each of us, bear within ourselves the mark of the Crucified and Risen One.

An option in the service is to provide persons who wish to receive the laying on of hands an opportunity to come and kneel beside the font. This may not be possible during the Service for the Lord's Day, but certainly is an option at other times. The minister lays both hands on the head of the person kneeling. The blessing is the same as that which is pronounced on those being confirmed in their baptismal vows and, with the exception of two words, the same as that pronounced on those who are baptized. Following the blessing, the sign of the cross may be traced on the person's forehead with or without oil. The use of oil in anointing at baptism reaches back to as early as the second century, perhaps before, and thus has a long history in the rite of Christian baptism. The liturgy for the Reaffirmation of the Baptismal Covenant concludes with the passing of the peace.

Ordinary Time extends from the Sunday after Epiphany (Baptism of the Lord) until Ash Wednesday, when Lent begins. The Transfiguration of the Lord, which occurs the Sunday before Ash Wednesday, marks the conclusion of Ordinary Time and anticipates the beginning of Lent.

Chapter 8

Celebrating Lent, Easter, and Pentecost

Ash Wednesday

Ash Wednesday marks the beginning of Lent, and is probably the most somber day in all the church year. It begins, appropriately, in silence. There is no organ or other instrumental prelude. Worshipers are to be encouraged, on this occasion especially, to enter the sanctuary in silence and to keep that silence in the minutes preceding the call to worship. The minister(s), choir, and other worship leaders also enter in silence. A silent procession provides a powerful way of beginning this service and reinforcing the mood of solemnity. There is no greeting, but all are instructed to stand on the entrance of the worship leaders, either through printed instructions in the service bulletin or with a silent gesture of raised arms by the minister or another. It is helpful on occasions of this kind, when a congregation is asked to do something a bit different from the norm, to recruit several members ahead of time to stand at the appropriate time. Others will then follow their example.

The call to worship is taken from John 3:17 and Psalm 46, and reminds us of the enduring nature of God's love. The prayer of the day continues the theme of the constancy of God's love and confesses our own failure in love. A hymn or metrical psalm of a penitential tone is sung. "Lord, Who throughout These Forty Days" expresses well the focus and intent of the season of preparation on which we are embarking with the Ash Wednesday service. The liturgy then moves directly to the service of the Word. The lessons do not vary. While two options are offered for the Old Testament reading, Joel 2:1–2, 12–17 or Isaiah 58:1–12, the Epistle is always 2 Corinthians 5:20b–6:10, and the Gospel is Matthew 6:1–6, 16–21. The Joel passage begins with a cry of alarm and moves to a call to repentance: "Yet even now, says the LORD, return to me with all your heart." Isaiah speaks of the fast that God finds acceptable. Second Corinthians continues the theme of repentance that leads to reconciliation with God, while the Gospel turns our attention both to the quality of life we are called to live as those who abide within the sphere of God's rule in Christ and to the meaning of true repentance. While the lections point clearly to the reality of our human condition, they also point beyond that to the hope extended to us through God's love and mercy in Jesus Christ.

An invitation to observe a holy Lent, a time of disciplined preparation for the celebration of Easter, is extended. It begins with a brief explanation of the meaning of Lent and the reason for using ashes to mark the beginning of the Lenten journey, and then invites all "to observe a holy Lent" specifically "by self-examination and penitence, by prayer and fasting, by works of love, and by reading and meditating on the Word of God." Following a period of silence, Psalm 51:1–17 is read, sung, or intoned. The psalm may be read in unison, responsively between leader and people, or antiphonally between segments of the congregation or the congregation and choir. *The Presbyterian Hymnal* contains both metrical and responsorial settings of Psalm 51. The psalm serves as the beginning of an extended act of confession. While the *Lutheran Book of Worship* places the confession prior to the service of Word and sacrament, the *Book of Common Worship* follows the practice of both *The Book of Common Prayer* (1979) and the Roman rite in placing the confession within the context of the service and as a prelude to the Eucharist. A prayer of confession or the litany of penitence provided in the Ash Wednesday liturgy is said following Psalm 51:1–17.

The imposition of ashes should be presented to the congregation as something in which all are invited and encouraged to participate, but worshipers should not be made to feel pressured to receive the ashes. A note in the bulletin might simply state that "those who do not wish to receive the imposition of ashes may remain in their seats and use the time for silent prayer and meditation." The congregation is invited to come forward to receive the ashes. The station(s) should *not* be located at the Communion table—this is not a part of the Eucharist—but perhaps at the foot of the chancel steps or beside the baptismal font. (Ashes were sometimes associated with cleansing in antiquity, and the font stands as a reminder of our cleansing from sin and resurrection to new life.) As the sign of the cross is made on the forehead of each worshiper, the minister or elder administering the rite says, "Remember that you are dust, and to dust you shall return." It is *not* appropriate to call individuals by name. The focus is not on any one person's sin and mortality but on the common condition in which we all share. The sign of the cross is made by using the thumb and index finger as the words are spoken. The ashes that are used may be obtained by burning the palm branches from the previous year's

Palm Sunday celebration, or, if they are not available, ashes may be purchased through a number of church supply houses. Other ashes, of course, are always readily available. The rubrics of the *Book of Common Worship* suggest that hymns or psalms may be sung or a silence may be kept. The sound of the words of imposition being repeated again and again in an otherwise silent room has a powerful impact on all. Silence is preferred to music, sung or instrumental.

The Lord's Supper follows. The table is prepared as a hymn is sung by the congregation. The use of the Agnus Dei, "Jesus, Lamb of God," is suggested in this service prior to the distribution and is particularly appropriate. We come to the Eucharist, on this night in particular, aware of our unworthiness and of our dependence on grace. This also is an occasion when pew communion, the preferred form for Presbyterians, should be discarded and members of the community invited to walk to one or more stations to receive the elements. At this time the pastor and elders serving may and should call the members of the community of faith by name, saying, "The body of Christ, given for you," and "The blood of Christ, shed for you," to which the one receiving replies, *Amen,* that is, So may it be. The service ends as quietly as it began.

The Sundays in Lent

The Lord's Day service during Lent is more restrained and somber than during the other seasons of the year, and yet it is the Lord's Day service, a witness not only to the Lord's passion and death, but also to his victory over sin and death. Even so, hymns, anthems, and service music containing "alleluia" are traditionally not sung during these weeks. Rather than using the Gloria Patri or Gloria in Excelsis as a response of thanksgiving following the declaration of pardon, consider using a verse of a hymn with a penitential theme. One possibility is the stanza from "O Sacred Head, Now Wounded," which begins "What language shall I borrow / To thank Thee, dearest friend?" Another appropriate response is the first stanza of "What Wondrous Love Is This." There are others, of course, but it is important to use the same stanza or refrain throughout the season. It becomes the ordinary for the season. People grow accustomed to it. Nonsingers can learn to sing it, and, most importantly, children can and do learn the words and melody.

Lent is also a good time to use the summary of the Law (Matt. 22:37–40) or the Ten Commandments following the declaration of pardon, in their function as a guide for righteous living. Both are found in the "Preparation for Worship" section of the *Book of Common Worship.*

During these weeks, consider also the possibility of changing the mode of entrance to the sanctuary by the clergy, choir, and other worship leaders. Ask an elder or other member of the church to bring the Bible into the sanctuary in procession before the clergy and other worship leaders. The minister(s) stand(s) at the foot of the chancel steps or before the pulpit while the elder places the Bible on the pulpit and opens it to the first lesson of the day. A tradition that comes from the Church of Scotland, the rite reminds us that the Scriptures belong to *all* the people and not simply to the clergy or any other group, and that the Bible is given into the care of the clergy with the expectation that they will faithfully endeavor, through the gift of preaching, to open the Word of God to our understanding and to application in our lives. During a season when we emphasize meditation on the Scriptures as one way of keeping a holy Lent, this practice seems particularly appropriate. To that end, if your congregation does not already observe a service of daily prayer, a service that focuses on prayer and Scripture, Lent is an excellent time to introduce the custom. The service might be held one or more days each week in the morning, at noon, or in the evening, depending on your congregation's particular needs and patterns.

Passion/Palm Sunday

Passion/Palm Sunday marks the beginning of Holy Week. The service begins on a note of jubilant triumph. The congregation is invited to gather at a place other than the sanctuary to walk in procession to the place of worship. Palm fronds are distributed to all. Following the call to worship and a prayer, a member of the congregation reads the account of the Lord's entrance into Jerusalem from one of the Gospels, and the congregation, led by the clergy, walks in procession to the sanctuary singing Psalm 118:1–2, 19–29, or Theodulf of Orléans's ninth-century hymn written for the Palm Sunday procession, "All Glory, Laud, and Honor." The procession concludes with Psalm 118:26. The worship leader exclaims: "Blessed is he who comes in the name of the Lord," and the people respond: *Hosanna in the highest!*

If it is not practical for the congregation to process from one location to the next, they may be invited to join in a procession around the interior of the building. Ask everyone to stand in or toward the center aisle. When the reading is completed and the hymn begins, proceed down the center aisle to the chancel, turn and move down the side aisles, and so on around. At the very least, the children of the church, the choirs, and clergy ought to join in a procession with palms at the beginning of the service. This first part of the liturgy then concludes with the prayer of the day.

There is no act of confession on Passion/Palm Sunday, but the tone of the service nonetheless changes radically as the liturgy of the Word begins. The festive, celebrative mood shifts to one of muted awe and wonder as we turn our attention away from the palms and to the passion. The Old Testament and Epistle lessons do not vary from year to year, but the Gospel reading rotates among the Synoptic Gospels. A shorter or longer form is suggested for each of the years in the three-year lectionary. The reading in either form is longer than the ordinary Gospel lection, but this may be the one time in the course of Holy Week when many worshipers will avail themselves of the opportunity to hear this story read. One option that has been received well in many churches is to read the lesson as a dramatic reading, assigning parts to various readers and the parts of the crowd and the religious leaders to the congregation. An insert in the bulletin with the parts printed in various fonts will help facilitate the readings. Another would be to involve several persons in reading selected verses of the narrative so that different voices are heard. Readers should be chosen with care and ought to rehearse their parts carefully, so that they not only have a sense of familiarity with the words themselves but a sensitivity to and deepened appreciation for the unfolding drama of God's act of salvation in Jesus Christ. Time as well as care should be given to reading this passage. Above all, don't rush the reading or abbreviate it to save time. This is the story of God's saving grace. Take time to tell it and give the people time to hear it.

In some traditions the sermon is replaced by an extended period of silence following the Gospel reading. But you should consider that not to preach at all is to miss a golden opportunity. The majority of worshipers will not be back to worship again until Easter. Maundy Thursday Communion, Good Friday worship, and the Saturday evening Easter Vigil will not be nearly as well attended as the Lord's Day service of Passion/Palm Sunday and Easter Sunday. The day is simply too ripe with opportunity to allow it to pass without preaching. Here we stand on the edge of the greatest of all mysteries. It cannot be explained, and the preacher who tries is foolish, but the depths of its riches can be explored with awe and wonder and praise.

A hymn focusing on Christ's passion follows the sermon, and the people may affirm their faith in a creed of the church or an affirmation taken from Scripture. Some traditions omit the recitation of a creed on this day, seeing it as being too festive for this occasion. The prayers of the people are then said. If there is not a Good Friday service, the Solemn Reproaches of the Cross may be said here in place of the prayers. The language used in the reproaches is reminiscent of Micah 6:3ff.:

"O my people, what have I done to you?
In what have I wearied you? Answer me!
For I brought you up from the land of Egypt. . . . "

The reproaches are addressed to us, the church, and serve to remind us of God's grace and mercy and our continuing need of both because of our failure to be the people God has called us to be. God has been faithful to us, but we have failed God. Evidence of the Reproaches in the liturgy appear as early as the seventh century. There are two parts to the hymn in its fully developed form. The first three verses date from the ninth and early tenth centuries, and the second part from the eleventh.[83] After each verse the people may respond by saying or singing *"Lord, have mercy or Holy God, Holy and mighty, Holy immortal One, have mercy upon us!"*

If the Lord's Supper is celebrated on Passion/Palm Sunday, the passing of the peace is placed just prior to the invitation to the Lord's Table. As in the third-century liturgy of Hippolytus and before, the peace serves as a bridge from the service of the Word to the service of the Table. We gather at the table, a redeemed and reconciled people. In keeping with historic practice, the Great Thanksgiving in the *Book of Common Worship* includes the option of reciting the words of institution as a part of the prayer. If the words are not said here, they may be recited at the fraction. The prayers of intercession are included in the Great Thanksgiving rather than separately in the liturgy. If they are offered earlier, after the sermon, they should not be repeated here. A hymn of passion follows the prayer after communion, and the service concludes on a much quieter, reflective, somber note than it began. Any choral response to the benediction or organ postlude should reflect the mood of the passion rather than that of the triumphal entry. The journey to the cross has begun in earnest. We travel through the week as people who know that beyond the cross is an empty tomb and the glad news "The Lord is risen! He is risen indeed!" But first we stand in the shadow of the cross.

A Service of Stations of the Cross

Some congregations may want to consider observing a service of the stations of the cross sometime during the first part of Holy Week. The service tracks the journey of the Lord from Pilate's hall to Golgotha, the "Place of the Skull," outside Jerusalem. The Roman Catholic and Episcopal services provide for fourteen stations, but only eight of these have Biblical references. The "stations" ordinarily feature a rough-hewn cross, and may also include artistic renderings of the theme of the particular station. The congregation moves from one station to the next, figuratively walking with Jesus to the cross. If

the number of worshipers is too large to allow for movement, the congregation may remain seated while the readers and the clergy move from one station to the next. The lections are traditionally read by different members of
the congregation, while the minister(s) lead in the versicle that follows and
the concluding prayer. One possibility would be to ask the youth group or a
Sunday school class to study the readings associated with the stations, to
design the artistic renderings that accompany the cross at each station, and to
provide readers for each of the lections. The "Stabat Mater" is traditionally
used in relation to the stations, although that is not required. In the model
included with this resource, "The Way of the Cross," Appendix B, each station concludes with the singing of the Trisagion, which provides a unifying
theme for the whole journey. Trisagion is taken from the Greek word meaning "thrice holy." "Holy God, Holy immortal, Holy and mighty One, have
mercy upon us." Hymns sung by the congregation, a solo voice, or a small
ensemble provide music for moving from one station to the next, or the walk
may be made in silence. The hymn texts should be printed in the bulletin so
that people do not have to carry hymnals with them. The service should be
rehearsed carefully, and instructions ought to be given to the congregation
before the call to worship.

Maundy Thursday

The name is derived from the new *mandate* of John 13:34: "I give you a new
commandment, that you love one another. Just as I have loved you, you also
should love one another." Measuring time according to the Hebrew pattern of
the day, beginning at sunset, Maundy Thursday evening begins the Holy
Triduum (holy three days of Jesus' passion and resurrection). The service is
actually the beginning of one service spread over three days. The Maundy
Thursday service is continued in the liturgies of Good Friday and the Easter
Vigil. This is emphasized by the fact that there is no benediction on Thursday
or Friday evening. The benediction comes only when the shout of the resurrection has been heard at the Easter Vigil and the Eucharist celebrated. The
color for Maundy Thursday is violet or red, although white may be used.

Some congregations may choose to celebrate this Eucharist in conjunction
with an Agape meal, sharing dinner around the tables in the social hall and
then celebrating the holy meal at the same tables. A few congregations have
begun to celebrate a kind of modified Seder in conjunction with the Eucharist
on Maundy Thursday. There are, however, problems with this practice. One
is that the Synoptic Gospels and the Gospel of John present differing
chronologies, and it is a matter of debate whether the meal in which the Lord's

Supper was instituted was actually a Seder. Furthermore, a Jewish feast presided over by Christians, even if accurately replicated, does not convey authenticity—it will carry connotations foreign to a true Seder. The practice may also be offensive to devout Jews. Christians, no doubt, would find offense in the Jewish community's copying the Eucharist in order to know what it might be like to be Christian.[84]

The service is best held in the sanctuary, where it is allowed to stand on its own. The congregation is asked to gather in silence. Any musical prelude should serve to enhance the quiet, reflective tone of the service. The liturgy begins with a biblical summons to worship in the words of John 13:34, followed by a brief statement on the meaning of the day. The statement recalls how Jesus "gave himself into the hands of those who would slay him," reminding us that this sacrifice was not coerced but was freely offered in obedience to God's will and purpose. It also recalls how Jesus gathered with his disciples in the upper room and washed their feet, "giving us an example that we should do to others as he has done to us." His model of humble service is one that we are called to follow. And finally we are reminded that it was on this day that the Lord gave to us the gift of this holy feast, so that through it "we who eat this bread and drink this cup may here proclaim his holy sacrifice and be partakers of his resurrection, and at the last day may reign with him in heaven."[85] The statement reminds us that this meal is not simply a memorial, a time of remembrance, but also a time of anticipation. We look to the past, but we also anticipate the future.

A brief prayer of the day follows the statement. The *Book of Common Worship* offers two options, both of which reflect the Gospel lection. One focuses on the gift of the new commandment and asks for grace to keep the mandate. The other centers on the symbol of washing, and prays that we might be washed clean of our sin and strengthened to follow Christ faithfully in the times of trial and danger. A congregational hymn is sung. There are any number of possibilities, to be sure, but Fred Pratt Green's "An Upper Room Did Our Lord Prepare," set to John Weaver's harmonization of the English folk melody O WALY WALY, works especially well. As the congregation continues to stand, all join in a prayer of confession and sing the Kyrie. The declaration of forgiveness is followed by the peace, and the confession concludes with another congregational song. "What Wondrous Love Is This, " an early American folk hymn, is an excellent choice.

In usual fashion, a prayer for illumination precedes the readings. The lessons for the day do not change. The Roman Catholic lectionary, *The Book of Common Prayer* (1979), and *The United Methodist Book of Worship* follow the same practice. Exodus 12:1–14, the institution of the Passover, is the Old

Testament reading. Psalm 116:1–2, 12–19 is the response to the Old Testament. The psalm may be intoned using Presbyterian Psalm tone 6 from the *Book of Common Worship*. There are also two responsorial settings of the psalm in *The Psalter: Psalms and Canticles for Singing*. *The Presbyterian Hymnal* contains a common meter setting of the psalm, "O Thou, My Soul, Return in Peace,*"* to the early American hymn tune of MARTYRDOM. The Epistle lesson is Paul's account of the institution of the Lord's Supper (1 Cor. 11:23–26), and the Gospel is, of course, John's account of the footwashing that occurred during the supper and the giving of the "new commandment." Following the sermon, the congregation may stand and join in affirming faith in a creed of the church or one drawn from Scripture. The use of an affirmation of faith is bracketed in the liturgy to indicate that it is an optional act in this service. Some congregations in some traditions omit the creed in the Maundy Thursday liturgy because it is thought of as being too festive for the occasion. The Roman, Lutheran, Episcopalian, and Methodist liturgies all omit the creed.

A service of footwashing may also be included in the service, here before the celebration of the Supper. All may be invited to participate in washing one another's feet. Basins, pitchers with water, towels, and chairs will need to be provided, and those participating should be reminded ahead of time to remove footwear, socks, or hose before the rite begins. One kneels before another, pours water over the feet, and then dries them with a towel. The whole act may be done in silence, or the rubrics suggest that "Where Charity and Love Prevail" ("Ubi Caritas") may be sung by the congregation. The full text of the ninth-century hymn is found in *The Worshipbook*. Another, set to a common meter tune, may be found in *The Lutheran Hymnal*. (The paraphrase is copyrighted, so if you choose to use it, be sure to receive permission.) *The Psalter: Psalms and Canticles for Singing* contains a beautiful setting from the Taizé Community. This melodic and very singable refrain may be reprinted for one-time use in a congregational service at no cost and without further permission from the publisher.

The rite may well be awkward and rather uncomfortable for many, and, if utilized, it should be clear that worshipers are free to participate or merely to observe. A representative group of members might be selected to participate in the footwashing to be done by the pastor and one or two elders. The washing should always be mutual, however: the minister and assisting elders ought to have their feet washed as well. Ours is a shared ministry, and we serve one another. The Lutheran rubrics direct that the minister should lay aside his or her vestments and put on an apron or towel for this work. The Roman rites suggest that the priest may remove his chasuble if necessary.[86] The *Book of*

Common Worship, like *The Book of Common Prayer,* does not give any specific instructions in this regard. However, it would be appropriate for the pastor to remove clerical robe or other clerical vestments for this service, as a symbol of the equality we share in our common life and service. The prayers of the people follow unless they are to be incorporated in the Great Thanksgiving.

An offering may be received, and as the gifts are being offered the table is prepared with bread and wine. If an offering is not received, the table may be set following the prayers of the people, as the congregation sings a hymn, canticle, or psalm. A setting of John 6 from the Taizé Community, utilizing the refrain "Eat this bread, drink this cup, come to me and never be hungry; Eat this bread, drink this cup, come to me and you will not thirst," works very effectively as an introduction to the spoken invitation to the Lord's Table. In this service the invitation consists of the words of institution. Having been spoken here, they are not repeated in the Great Thanksgiving or at the fraction. The words from 1 Corinthians 10:16–17 are said in relation to the breaking of the bread and the pouring of the cup and underscore the communal and unifying nature of this sacrament. The bread is broken in clear view of the people, and the cup is likewise filled. This done, the minister lifts cup and bread toward the people and declares, "The gifts of God for the people of God." Or the elements may be left upon the table, and the pastor, with both arms extended, points first to the table and then, arms raised in a gesture of invitation toward the congregation, speaks the declaration.

Maundy Thursday is an excellent time to forgo pew communion in favor of a different mode of reception. Coming to stand around the table, or, if there is space, actually sitting at table are two good options, both of which have precedent in our Reformed tradition. However it is done, this Eucharist, in particular, is one in which the communal nature of the sacrament is stressed and the mode of reception ought to stress the same. Standing or sitting at table, serving one another, is one of the best ways to accomplish this. As the people serve one another—serve, not simply pass the elements—each is encouraged to say to the other: "The body of Christ given for you," and "The blood of Christ shed for you." To each of which the recipient responds, *Amen.*

Lighting may be dimmed and candles placed on the table. It was evening when Jesus and his disciples shared this meal, and in the rhythm of our Holy Week observance evening has come in yet another, more symbolic way. Hymns may be sung by the congregation as the sacrament is shared, or a silence may be kept. The rubrics suggest that an Agnus Dei may be said or sung as the elements are shared. If a silence is kept or if it is otherwise desired to use this ancient song of the church, it may be spoken or sung responsively immediately after the fraction and before the declaration "The gifts of God for the people of God." After all have communed, a prayer is offered.

The stripping of the church concludes the service. This ceremonial "undressing" of the sanctuary symbolizes the stripping of Christ before his crucifixion and his separation from all those who loved and followed him. In a powerfully effective way it impresses on us the desolation and loneliness of Jesus in the darkness of Gethsemane and what was to follow. Alone, the Savior goes forth to die. Elders who assisted in Communion, ushers, or others may be designated ahead of time to remove all linens, candles, paraments, banners, flowers, Communion service, and so on, as Psalm 22 is read. In the Roman rite the cross is removed or covered. The action should not be rushed, but done with reverence and dignity. Likewise, the pastor or other person reading the psalm should read with deliberation and appropriate emphasis. Be sure that those who are doing the "stripping" know what items to remove and where to place them. Written instructions help. The sanctuary remains bare until "dressed" again during the Easter Vigil or, if there is no Vigil, prior to the first service on Easter Day. The service ends in silence—no benediction, no instrumental or choral music—and all are asked to depart in silence after the clergy and other worship leaders. These instructions may be printed in the bulletin. It is better that they not be spoken. The last words heard should be the words of Psalm 22.

Good Friday

The term is derived from an early name for the second day of the Holy Triduum, God's Friday, but for those of us who see it from this side of the resurrection the day is indeed "good" Friday, for in the events of this day, painful as they are, the saving work that Christ set forth to do in obedience to the Father's will is brought to completion. It is also God's Friday, for even though Jesus' enemies appear to seize control and to direct his destiny, even though they succeed in causing his death, it is God who is in control and God's will that is being fulfilled. As Jesus himself said to Pilate: "You would have no power over me unless it had been given you from above" (John 19:11a). It is with this understanding that we observe God's Good Friday.

The service continues from Maundy Thursday. The people once again gather in silence. No prelude is played. A silent procession of clergy, choir, and other worship leaders with acolyte if needed signals the beginning of the service. The call to worship reminds us of the focus of the service. A prayer of the day follows or, as the rubrics suggest, the Litany for Good Friday (*Book of Common Worship,* p. 292) may be said. This is followed by a congregational hymn or psalm. "O Sacred Head, Now Wounded," "Deep Were His Wounds, and Red," and "Were You There When They Crucified My Lord?" are all hymns appropriate for the day.

Following a prayer for illumination, the lessons are read. Isaiah 52:13–53:12 as the Old Testament lesson does not vary. Psalm 22, read the night before, is again read or intoned as the response to this lesson. *The Psalter: Psalms and Canticles for Singing* contains three settings for the psalm, two of which are appropriate for the day. The setting by Hal Hopson is especially effective for Good Friday. The cantor will need to prepare carefully. The psalm should be rendered without flaw, but should not draw attention to the cantor. The words of the psalm are raw with pain, physical and spiritual suffering, angst, and desolation. This is no time to try to make the cross more palatable. A brief reading from Hebrews serves as the Epistle lesson, and may be followed by an anthem or congregational hymn or song.

The centerpiece of this liturgy is the reading of the passion narrative from John's Gospel. John 18:1–19:42 is a long reading, but should nonetheless be read without haste, with appropriate dramatic emphasis, and by one intimately familiar with the text. Again, the intention is not to draw attention to the reader, but to what is read. The reader should know the text well enough to allow himself or herself to be drawn into it, even as those who listen may be drawn into its story.

One option is to incorporate into the reading the extinguishing of candles at particular points in the narrative. This action is drawn from the Tenebrae service. The candles may be placed on the otherwise empty Communion table and extinguished by an acolyte. (They would have been lighted as the service began by the acolyte who led the silent processional.) Lighting in the sanctuary might also be diminished as the candles are extinguished. The gradual darkening of the room can serve to remind us of the increasing isolation experienced by Jesus in the hours before his death. Fourteen candles may be used, along with the large central Christ candle, which is never extinguished. When the reading is complete, only the light of the Christ candle is burning.

A brief sermon may be given, but this is one time when the sound of silence, in which the words of the passion narrative may echo, speaks much more eloquently than any words the preacher can utter. A hymn on the passion may follow, and the people remain standing for the bidding prayer (the Solemn Intercession) that follows. The Good Friday intercessions date from the time of Leo the Great in the fifth century.[87] The collects in the bidding prayer from the *Book of Common Worship* are patterned after those from *The Book of Common Prayer* (1979). The United Methodist service omits the solemn intercessions, and the Lutheran and Roman prayers bear a marked similarity. The prayer concludes with the Lord's Prayer.

A large wooden, rough-hewn cross may be brought into the church. The crucifer, or crossbearer, pauses inside the front doors and the pastor declares: "Behold the cross on which was hung the salvation of the whole world." And the people respond, *Come, let us worship.* The crossbearer walks midway down the aisle and stops. Again the exchange is spoken. The crossbearer then proceeds to the steps of the chancel, or within a few feet of the Communion table if it is on floor level, and the exchange is made a third time. The cross is then placed in a stand in front of the table or leaned against the table. At the Easter Vigil the new light of the paschal candle will be brought into the sanctuary in a similar fashion. The Solemn Reproaches of the Cross follow. (See the commentary on the Passion/Palm Sunday liturgy.)

The service concludes with a hymn and, once more, all depart in silence.

Other Options for Good Friday

If desired, there are, of course, other options that may be employed in worship on Good Friday. One is a service of meditations on the "Words" of Christ from the cross. This service, traditionally held from noon until 3:00 P.M. in remembrance of Jesus' time on the cross, centers on the "seven last words of Christ" from the cross. The "words" or phrases are gleaned from a harmonizing of the passion narratives in the four Gospels and serve as the focal point of brief meditations or other presentations. The words are:

Luke 23:34	"Father, forgive them."
Luke 23:43	"Today you will be with me in Paradise."
John 19:26–27	"Woman, here is your son. . . . Here is your mother."
Mark 15:34 (Matt. 27:46)	"My God, why have you forsaken me?"
John 19:28	"I am thirsty."
John 19:30a	"It is finished."
Luke 23:46	"Into your hands I commend my spirit."

Another option is a form of the ancient Tenebrae service, or service of "Darkness." The service has its roots in a complex monastic service from the Middle Ages. Fifteen candles were used and fourteen were extinguished individually over a three-day period from Wednesday through Friday evenings as a part of the traditional monastic offices (prayer services).[88] Morning and evening the candles were lighted and extinguished—nine candles in the morning and five in the evening—but one candle always remained burning. This candle would be hidden, leaving the community in darkness. A loud crashing sound would be heard, and the lighted candle would be restored to its place in anticipation of the resurrection.[89] *Liturgical Year: Supplemental Liturgical Resource 7* offers a form of the Tenebrae that focuses on the psalms and various readings from Lamentations. *The Book of Common Prayer* also contains a liturgy for observing a Tenebrae. *The United Methodist Book of Worship* contains a Tenebrae service that may be incorporated into the Maundy Thursday service or celebrated on Good Friday.

Easter Vigil

The Easter Vigil, the oldest of all the church's annual observances, provides an impressive and spiritually enriching transition from Lent to Easter. The vigil moves us from the darkness of Holy Saturday to the brilliance of Easter, from bondage and death to freedom and life. To keep the vigil is to be joined with the worship and witness of Christian mothers and fathers since the very beginning of the church's life.

In the ancient church, the vigil stood as the culmination of an extended time of preparation for catechumens (those preparing for baptism and profession of their faith). The candidates for membership in the church participated in a day of fasting from Friday night through Saturday and then spent Saturday night with the community of faith in a vigil of prayer, Scripture, and shared silence. From four to twelve readings were shared, interspersed with psalms, canticles, and prayers. The readings, which tell the story of God's redemptive work in human history from creation to Christ, served as a kind of last-minute instruction for the catechumens and as a reminder to the faithful of the mercy and grace of God as they told the story of God's redemptive work in human history from creation to Christ. Together the community waited for the dawn of Easter Day. As the sun began to rise, the catechumens renounced Satan and evil, professed their faith in Jesus Christ, were baptized, anointed with oil, blessed by the bishop, clothed in a new white garment, and joined the community in the celebration of the Eucharist. The preparatory fast disappeared after Christianity became the official religion of the realm in the latter part of the fourth century. In time, the primary means of entrance into the church came to be through baptism in infancy rather than adult conversion, and as the practice of baptizing infants shortly after birth began to become the norm, the need for the fast disappeared. The vigil, though, continued.

During the medieval period the vigil became more and more clericalized and the proclamation of the gospel almost entirely suppressed, so that at the time of the sixteenth-century Reformation, the Reformers saw little of worth to be continued in this practice and abandoned it. It has only been in this century that interest in the vigil has been revived and Protestant churches have begun keeping this most ancient of all the church's liturgical celebrations.

The Easter Vigil consists of four parts: the Service of Light, the service of Readings (the Word), the celebration of Baptism, and the celebration of the Lord's Supper. The entire paschal mystery finds expression in the readings, music, movements, and symbols of this service. The vigil begins in complete darkness. Christ is still in the tomb. Ideally, the service begins around 10:30 P.M., with the celebration of the Eucharist taking place at midnight, on Easter Day. It can run for two hours or more in length or may be abbreviated for a shorter time. It may be scheduled earlier in the evening on Saturday and conclude before midnight. Another option is to observe the service of Light and the service of the Word on Saturday evening, and then continue the service at dawn on Easter Day with the service of Baptism and the celebration of the Lord's Supper. A festive Easter breakfast celebrating the end of the Lenten fast may follow. A number of factors, many of them unique to each local situation, need to be taken into consideration in planning the service. The important thing is that the vigil begin *after* dark and that it begin outside the church sanctuary, if at all possible.

The Service of Light

The people gather in silence at a place where a small fire has been made ready. Each is given a small candle. The wood for the fire has been prepared ahead of time and treated so that it lights easily. A metal brazier on legs might be used, so that when the lighting is completed and the procession into the sanctuary has begun it may be covered with a lid to smother the fire. The Episcopal, Lutheran, and United Methodist services all provide for the lighting of the fire before the people have gathered or as they are gathering. This Service of Light (*lucernarium*) has its roots in the Jewish custom of blessing the household lamp at the beginning of the Sabbath (Friday evening). Households in the early church continued the practice, moving it to Saturday evening, the beginning of the Christian Sabbath, and translating it into a thanksgiving for Christ, the Light of the world. In later times, the household practice disappeared, but the rite continued as a part of the daily office on Saturdays and at the Easter Vigil.

The Service of Light begins with a biblical greeting and an introduction that explains what we are remembering and what we are about in this service. We are reminded that this is the Passover of Jesus Christ, a passover in which we all participate. As we share in his death, so we also participate in his resurrection to new life. The introduction concludes with the words from the prologue of John's Gospel reminding us that "the light shines in the darkness, and the darkness has not overcome it." If it has not been lighted previously, the fire is lighted at this time.

A prayer of blessing for the fire is said and the paschal candle is lighted from it. Both the fire and the candle symbolize the victory of light over darkness, specifically the light of Christ that "shines in the darkness" and which the darkness has not overcome. The paschal candle reaches back to the sixth century, and at one time was as tall as and sometimes several times taller than a human being. The candle today is at least two inches in diameter and at least two feet tall. It is inscribed with a cross bearing the Greek letters *alpha* above and *omega* beneath. The date of the current year is inscribed in the corners formed by the crossbars. In the Roman and Lutheran rites this inscription is made with a stylus just before the lighting of the candle, and is accompanied by these words: "Christ yesterday and today, the beginning and the end, Alpha and Omega, all time belongs to him and all the ages, to him be glory and power through every age forever. Amen." Five grains of incense are inserted in the cross in the form of a cross and the priest says: "By his holy and glorious wounds may Christ our Lord guard us and keep us. Amen." The Lutheran rite also uses incense, but the grains are inserted in the candle during the Exsultet. In the Presbyterian service, the inscription may be made prior to the service, and the incense is not ordinarily used, although there is no prohibition to its use. A smaller taper may be used to pass the light from the fire to the paschal candle. As the candle is lighted, the minister or another declares: "The light of Christ rises in glory, overcoming the darkness of sin and death." (The same declaration is made in the Lutheran, Roman, and United Methodist rites, but omitted in the Episcopal.) The candle is then raised for all to see, and the light bearer says or sings: "The light of Christ," and the people respond by saying or singing: *Thanks be to God.* The *Book of Common Worship* contains a musical setting for the exchange that rises in pitch each time it is sung. The elevation in pitch enhances the sense of anticipation, the emerging energy of the service, as it moves physically and liturgically toward the bright dawn of the resurrection.

Before the procession into the church begins, the light from the paschal candle is passed among the people as their individual candles are lighted. (In the Lutheran service this is done at the church doors with the second exchange. The Episcopal service has the congregational candles lighted at the conclusion of the procession.) The group then processes in silence to the church. At the doors to the church, the procession pauses, and the silence is broken as the exchange, "The light of Christ. *Thanks be to God,*" is said or sung again. Inside, when all have taken their places, the candle is raised and the exchange is made a third time. The only light in the sanctuary is the light from the paschal candle and the candles of the people. When the procession is concluded, the paschal candle is placed in its stand, either in the center of the chancel or next to the pulpit or lectern, wherever the Exsultet will be sung. *The United Methodist Book of Worship* service provides that a hymn to Christ the light, such as "Christ, Whose Glory Fills the Skies," might be sung during the procession rather than the sung declaration and response. The Episcopal *Book of Common Prayer* provides that it is the privilege of the deacon to carry the paschal candle and to sing the Exsultet that follows. The light may be carried by any baptized member of the church and the Exsultet sung by any member with the requisite musical gifts. If a confirmation class is being received, a member or members of the class may be invited to carry the paschal candle in procession.

The second part of the Service of Light is the Easter proclamation or Exsultet, so called because *exsultet* is the first word in the Latin form of the song. The song is very old in its origin, incorporating the thought of Ambrose and Augustine and even older texts. The present form of the Easter proclamation dates from the seventh century. It is sung by a cantor or choir and, in the song as it is included in the *Book of Common Worship* and *The United Methodist Book of Worship,* is interspersed with a refrain sung by all. The cantor or choir sings the refrain once, the congregation responds, and the cantor or choir then begins the Exsultet. The refrain is repeated after each section of the song. *The United Methodist Book of Worship* provides that the song may be read by several readers and the refrain sung or said by the congregation. However it is done and by whomever it is done, the Easter declaration is said or sung in the light of the paschal candle. The song begins by addressing the heavenly powers, the choirs of angels, inviting them to join in the praise of Christ's resurrection, and then descends in ever smaller circles to embrace the whole of creation, the church, and in the Episcopal, Lutheran, and Roman rites all those who stand in the light of the paschal candle in the local church. While the first half of the song serves as an invitation to join in praising Christ's victory, the second half proclaims his triumph. It begins with the traditional dialogue for prayer. The Lutheran and Episcopal liturgies use the first and the third portions of the three-part dialogue, reserving the second for use in the Eucharist only. Presbyterian and Roman rites employ the full dialogue. The United Methodist service omits it altogether. The bracketed words in the second half may be omitted to provide for a shorter prayer. The prayer resonates with Old Testament themes (Adam's sin, the Passover feast and sacrificial lamb, the deliverance from bondage in Egypt), but the themes are seen and celebrated in light of the glad news of Christ's glorious resurrection. This is the night we remember and give thanks for our redemption and deliverance from sin and death through Christ, "the true Lamb," of sacrifice. The song concludes with the petition that Christ the Morning Star whose light never fades may "find this flame still burning"—an allusion not simply to the flame of the paschal candle but to the light that shines from within all those who share in Christ's death and resurrection. After the Exsultet has been sung, the candles of the people are extinguished, the paschal candle is carried in procession to the place where the liturgy of the Word will take place, if different, and lights in the church are turned on, but only partially.

The Liturgy of the Word

An introductory statement explains that what we give our attention to now is the story of God's saving work in human history, which has culminated in the Word made flesh, Jesus Christ our Redeemer. There are nine Old Testament lessons. All or as few as three may be read, but Exodus 14 is always included. The lessons may be read by different readers. Each reading is followed by a brief silence, the singing of a psalm, canticle, or hymn reflecting the theme of the reading, and a concluding collect. If your congregation has not had considerable exposure to responsorial psalmody, as you introduce this service you may want to rely more on metrical settings of the psalms listed or hymns that reflect the reading and that are familiar to the congregation. The use of all three adds variety and freshness to the service, which may be useful in enabling people to focus on what is a rather long list of lengthy readings. When the Old Testament lessons are completed, a hymn or canticle provides the transition from the Old Testament witness to the New. Bells can be rung following the hymn and the remainder of the church lights illuminated so that now the sanctuary is flooded with light. Any remnants of Holy Week are removed at this time. Crosses that may have been draped or removed are uncovered or replaced. The white paraments of Easter are placed where they belong. Flowers, Easter lilies if they are traditionally used, are brought in, and so forth. Just as the sanctuary was stripped on Maundy Thursday, now is it dressed anew in the colors and symbols of resurrection to new life. The whole environment is transformed. Careful coordination and planning will need to be made so that everything moves smoothly. The activity may take place as the hymn is sung. If there is not adequate time, the process may be begun here and completed during the extended "alleluia" or the hymn following Psalm 114. It is preferable, however, that all the action take place at once. If not, in the first segment the sanctuary may be returned to its normal appearance, and in the second it may be further adorned for Easter.

The Prayer of the Day is said and marks the transition from Lent to Easter, from the old life to the new. The Epistle lesson for Easter Day is read. The passage, Romans 6:3–11, has a double significance in this service, as it sounds the note of Christ's resurrection from death to life and speaks boldly of our own death and resurrection to new life in him through the waters of baptism. The lesson is followed by Psalm 114. The psalm should be sung. The responsorial setting of the psalm in *The Psalter: Psalms and Canticles for Singing* is especially appropriate for use in this service because of its use of the alleluia refrain. The alleluia is traditionally not sung during Lent, and, here at the first service of Easter, it is at last reintroduced to the church's liturgy. If this setting of the psalm is not used, an alleluia may be sung following the conclusion of a metrical setting of the psalm. The refrain from "Alleluia, Alleluia! Give Thanks" (*The Presbyterian Hymnal,* no. 106), with its flowing accompaniment and soaring soprano descant, can be used very effectively. "All Creatures of Our God and King" (*The Presbyterian Hymnal,* no. 455), with its call for all creation to praise God and its recurring "alleluia," is another excellent choice. Either of these hymns would also work well as the hymn following the sermon.

The Gospel lesson for the day is read, and a brief sermon may be preached. The sermon is followed by a hymn, psalm, or canticle, during which the paschal candle is carried in procession to the baptismal font, from which the third section of the vigil is led.

The Sacrament of Baptism

If there are candidates for baptism, the service continues with the baptismal liturgy found in the *Book of Common Worship*. The *Lutheran Book of Worship* provides that when the sacrament is celebrated, the members of the congregation may be invited to participate in the renunciations and affirmations as a way of reaffirming their own baptismal vows. It is a practice worthy of emulation. If there are no candidates for baptism, the liturgy for the Reaffirmation of the Baptismal Covenant for a Congregation in the *Book of Common Worship* may be used here. (See author's commentary at pp. 85–87 in this resource.)

The Easter Vigil provides an excellent opportunity for confirmation/ commissioning. If the confirmation class does not begin earlier in the year, it could commence with the beginning of Lent, and the Easter Vigil could serve as the climax of the class members' preparation. Part of the class time might be spent in learning about this ancient liturgy of the church, the meaning of baptism, and living as people who have been buried with Christ in baptism to be raised with him to new life. The youth could prepare for leadership roles in the vigil. Two or three could accept responsibility for preparing the new fire from which the paschal candle is lighted, carrying the candle in procession into the church, and processing with the candle to its various stations during the service. Others might serve as lectors for the Old Testament readings in the service of the Word. Members of the class could have baked the bread and assisted in the preparation of the elements for the Eucharist. They could take an active role in the "dressing" of the sanctuary for Easter during the service. The possibilities are many. Too often we are inclined to toss young people in the church an annual "youth service" as a means of highlighting their presence and promoting this one area of the church's ministry. Here is an opportunity—and there are *many* others throughout the year—when young people and children can provide liturgical leadership that has integrity and meaning and which contributes to the whole worship of the church.

A hymn follows the service of Baptism or Reaffirmation of the Baptismal Covenant, and the paschal candle is carried in procession to the Communion table. (It is not until this point in the Lutheran service that the lights are turned up, bells are rung, and any remaining signs of Holy Week are removed.)

The Eucharist

Presbyterians, especially, have been noted for retaining the medieval penitential focus of the Eucharist, but this is certainly one time when our hearts and minds and voices and physical movement can give expression to the broader understanding of this meal as a feast of thanksgiving. This is our eucharist. Not only does it point us to the passion of our Lord, but it opens our eyes and our hearts to his abiding presence with us, and turns our vision to the fulfillment of his promise to come again to complete the work of the earth's redemption wrought in him. This is our victory banquet in advance. This is also our food and drink for the life on which we entered in our baptism. So we eat and drink with joy and thanksgiving and hopeful anticipation. This needs to be clearly communicated to all. The sermon that is preached prior to the baptismal liturgy provides just such an opportunity. The music played and sung since the prayer of the day, especially the *alleluia,* helps to undergird this sense of joyful celebration. The very demeanor of the clergy and elders who participate in serving the meal also helps to set the tone of rejoicing. The invitation to the Lord's Table reminds us that "this is the joyful feast of the people of God!" Let us then rejoice with heart and soul and mind and strength! The Great Thanksgiving for Easter is recommended. The rubrics in the *Book of Common Worship* also suggest that Great Thanksgiving F might be employed, if preferred. The Sanctus and memorial acclamation should be sung in this liturgy and sung to glad tunes. The settings by Joseph Roff (*The Presbyterian Hymnal,* nos. 581, 582) are especially recommended. *The United Methodist*

Book of Worship also contains settings by James A. Kreiwald that can be sung responsively, and which are bright and lively. Easter hymns may be sung during the serving of the elements or various *alleluias* may be sung by all. This is not a time for silence in the Eucharist. Let vocal and instrumental music abound. Also, this is not a time to let people sit passively in their pews and wait for the elements to be brought to them. Set up two or three stations (depending on the number of worshipers anticipated) to which the people may come to receive the elements.

The service concludes with a bright, glad, and glorious hymn of praise for the Lord's resurrection, a charge, and a blessing, which is followed by the pastor and people exclaiming responsively, loudly, and joyfully, "Christ is risen! *Christ is risen!*" And the last words are a shout of *"Alleluia! Alleluia!"*

Easter Day

The restrained tone of Lent and Holy Week gives way to an exuberant celebration of God's victory over sin and death on Easter. Christian churches welcome their largest number of worshipers on this day. People gather with the community of faith on this particular day for a variety of reasons. But no doubt at the heart of them all is the need to be reassured and to give witness to the conviction that by the power of God at work in the life, death, and resurrection of Jesus Christ, the way things are is not the way they will always be: that the power of sin and death does not have the last word, but God does, and God's word for our lives and the life of the world is *life*. This, then, is a day of unfettered celebration. Let organ and brass and human voices resound together in praise to God, for Christ who was dead has risen!

The service begins with a glad shout: "Alleluia! Christ is risen! *The Lord is risen indeed. Alleluia!*" Of all days, this is the day for a festive liturgical procession. Children from one or more of the Sunday school classes might lead the procession, carrying a banner of their own making. Choirs and clergy follow. The *Book of Common Worship* offers a prayer of the day as well as a prayer of adoration that may be used throughout the season of Easter. A prayer of confession is also provided, but the Responsive Prayer for Easter or the Litany for Easter may be used instead. Both acknowledge our frailty and need for grace, but do so in the context of the celebration of a victory already won. After the extended period of penitence in Lent, it is appropriate on Easter Day, if not all the Sundays of Easter, to forgo the act of corporate confession. The Council of Nicaea in 325 forbade two practices common to the rest of the year: fasting and kneeling for prayer—both of which were and are associated with a posture and attitude of penitence.

If the Lord's Supper was not celebrated during an Easter Vigil, the first service of the day (or at least one of the services of the day) should include a festive celebration of the Eucharist. Considering the penitential nature that has traditionally characterized the Reformed celebration of the sacrament, it may at first be difficult for some worshipers to understand why the "last" supper of Jesus is being observed on the day when his victory over sin and death is celebrated. Keeping the Eucharist on Easter will be greeted with more understanding and will be more willingly embraced if throughout the year the sacrament is celebrated and not simply observed, that is, if the theme of joyful thanksgiving and eschatological anticipation have been expressed, as well as the remembrance of the Savior's sacrifice. If, however, we remember that many who sit in the pews on this Sunday may not be regular participants in the church's worship throughout the rest of the year, a printed explanation such as this may be helpful: "In our celebration of the Lord's Supper we remember with thanksgiving our Savior's suffering and death on the cross for the redemption of the world. We celebrate as well the risen Christ's presence with us in the breaking of the bread and sharing of the cup, and we anticipate the fulfillment of the promise of his coming again to bring to completion the work of redemption already begun. Baptized members of all Christian churches are invited to partake of the sacrament." It will also be helpful in the Great Thanksgiving to use settings of the Sanctus and memorial acclamation that are bright and festive rather than somber. Joseph Roff's settings in *The Presbyterian Hymnal* serve this purpose well. The congregation may also be invited to join in singing Easter hymns as the elements are shared. Consider also changing the mode of reception as a means of helping worshipers to think of the meal not merely as a memorial, but as a feast of the risen and reigning Lord. Invite worshipers to leave the pews and to come to one of several stations to receive the elements. Use intinction as the mode of reception. Not only may this be different from the rest of the year, but it has the added practical benefit of speeding up the mechanics of serving a much larger than usual congregation.

The Season of Easter

Easter continues for fifty days. During these seven Sundays the church continues in its worship to acclaim Christ's victory and, by faith, our participation in that victory. Maintaining the "high" of Easter Day is not feasible or even desirable for the Fifty Days of Easter, but maintaining the focus of the season is. We do that, of course, in prayers, in sermons, and in the choice of hymns, choral anthems, and instrumental music for the service. Another means for helping to maintain the focus of the season is through the use of the paschal or Easter candle. The candle would have already been brought into the sanctuary during the Easter Vigil. If a vigil is not kept, the candle may simply be placed in the sanctuary on Easter morning. It remains lighted during the Fifty Days of Easter, and also remains in its place near the Communion table. After the Day of Pentecost the candle is moved to a place near the baptismal font, where it remains for the balance of the year, but is lighted only when the sacrament of baptism is celebrated. The paschal candle is also lighted at all funerals. If the body of the deceased is present, the candle is placed in a position near the casket.

The Ascension of the Lord comes on the fortieth day of Easter, always a Thursday, and may be celebrated on the Seventh Sunday of Easter. On this day the church joins with the saints from throughout the ages in affirming that the crucified and risen Christ is also the Christ who reigns in eternal glory.

The Day of Pentecost, the fiftieth day of Easter, marks the close of the Easter season. It celebrates the gift of the Holy Spirit to the church and the church's empowerment for its mission to be the risen Lord's witnesses "in Jerusalem, in all Judea and Samaria, and to the ends of the earth." The color for Pentecost is red, reminiscent of the tongues of flame that rested on the disciples on this day. Early in the church's history this day also stood as an optional time for the baptism of those who could not be baptized during the Easter Vigil. It is both liturgically and historically an appropriate time for the service of confirmation and commissioning.

The next Sunday, Trinity Sunday, provides the transition from the Great Fifty Days of Easter to Ordinary Time. Trinity Sunday originated in the tenth century and spread slowly in the Western Church. It finally received the approval of Rome in the fourteenth century. Unlike the other feasts in the liturgical year, which focus on the historical events of God's saving work, Trinity focuses on a theological doctrine. The color is white.

Ordinary Time

Ordinary Time, interrupted by Lent/Holy Week/Easter, resumes with Trinity Sunday and continues until the First Sunday of Advent. Two Sundays in particular during this extended time hold special possibilities for us.

Reformation Sunday

The last Sunday in October has traditionally been observed as Reformation Sunday in many Presbyterian and Lutheran congregations. The date was chosen because of its proximity to All Hallow's Eve, October 30, the day on which Martin Luther nailed his Ninety-Five Theses to the castle door at Wittenberg. The day provides a wonderful occasion for Reformed Christians to focus on our understanding of the Reformation, not simply as an accomplished historical fact, but as an ongoing process in which we are still involved. This is a day to draw on some of the rich liturgical tradition that is ours in the Reformed tradition.

Have an elder or other member of the church present the Bible at the beginning of worship. The practice is observed in many Presbyterian congregations in Scotland and reminds us of the historical link of American Presbyterianism to our Scottish forebears. The Bible's being brought in by a layperson emphasizes that the Word of God is not the sole possession of the clergy but belongs to all God's people. The one carrying the Bible walks ahead of the choir and clergy. The Bible is placed on the pulpit and opened to the first lesson for the day.

Use Psalm 124:8 as the opening sentences or the first words in the opening sentences for the day. "Our help is in the name of the LORD, who made heaven and earth" were the words that comprised the call to worship for Presbyterians in Geneva (1542) and Strasbourg (1545), and they remind us, as they did them, that apart from the help of the Lord our worship, our lives, are in vain. The One who made heaven and earth is our help in the midst of all of life.

Include the Ten Commandments in the service at the conclusion of the act of confession. In Calvin's liturgies the commandments were sung at this place in the worship. Positioned here, the reading of the Law is in keeping with the third understanding of the Decalogue: a guide for righteous living. Having confessed our sins and having been assured of God's forgiveness, we are reminded of the life that God has called us to live. The commandments may be read in litany form with the congregation responding, "Amen, Lord have mercy," or "Help us to keep your law, O Lord," after each.

Consider also using as an affirmation of faith a portion of the Brief Statement of Faith or a selection from one of the other distinctively Reformed confessional statements in the *Book of Confessions*. At least one metrical psalm from our Reformed heritage ought to be included in the service, and hymns related to our heritage also ought to fill the service. *The Presbyterian Hymnal Companion,* by LindaJo McKim, is a helpful resource in identifying music and musical texts deriving from the Reformed tradition.

Finally, include a page in the Sunday bulletin explaining the significance of various parts of the service, as well as information about the authors and composers of the hymns and metrical psalm settings.

All Saints' Day

All Saints' Day falls on November 1 and, if not celebrated on the day on which it falls, may be celebrated on the first Sunday after November 1. On this day the church remembers and gives thanks to God for "all the saints who from their labors rest." All Saints' Day grew out of the need to recognize those saints who could not be accorded a day specifically their own. In the Roman Catholic tradition, only those saints who have been officially canonized are recognized on November 1, and the remainder of the faithful departed are remembered on November 2. Protestant Churches have traditionally combined the two into one day of recognition, November 1, and while all the saints are remembered, the emphasis is ordinarily placed more on the dead whom we have known and loved than on historically distant figures of note.

The color is white, symbolic of victory and life. Although a sense of solemnity pervades the service, it is not morose or somber, for what we affirm is not merely the memory of faithful lives but the victory they and we share in Jesus Christ. On this Sunday it is appropriate to include in the service, immediately following the sermon, the Naming of the Saints. The congregation is asked to stand as the names of those who have died in the last year are called. A minute of silence follows at the conclusion, and a brief collect concludes the prayer. Not only does this remind us of the living and unbroken connection we share with all the saints who have gone before us, but it also provides family members and friends the opportunity to celebrate the lives of loved ones especially dear to them at a time when grief is passing and healing is taking place.

The service, whether observed on All Saints' Day or the Sunday afterward, ought to include the celebration of the Lord's Supper. In Communion we not only remember a sacrifice once made, but also anticipate the heavenly banquet toward which we all journey.

One possibility for personalizing the service is to precede worship with a congregational gathering in which members and friends are invited to move among tables on which have been placed paper banners bearing the names of the saints who are remembered, and encouraged to write brief remembrances of the person named on each. These may then be carried in procession into the sanctuary.

Families of individuals being remembered might receive a special invitation to the service. Also, along with the announcement of the service in the church bulletin, notice might be given inviting members of the congregation to add the names of friends and relatives who were not members to the list of names called in the service.

Christ the King or the Reign of Christ

This Sunday marks the transition from Ordinary Time to Advent and falls on the Sunday preceding the First Sunday of Advent. The color is white, and the day serves as a kind of summary of the entire year. The sovereign reign of the risen Christ over all things and all time is the theme of the day.

Appendix A

Readings for the Advent Wreath

First Sunday of Advent

Today we begin the celebration of Advent, a time in which we prepare ourselves to celebrate anew God's gift of himself to us in the child of Bethlehem, and when we renew our faith in the fulfillment of the Lord's promise to come again to complete the work of the world's redemption begun in him.

Hear the words of the prophet Isaiah: "Darkness shall cover the earth, and thick darkness the peoples; but the LORD will arise upon you, and his glory will appear over you. Nations shall come to your light, and kings to the brightness of your dawn" (Isa. 60:2–3).

We light this candle as a symbol of the light of Christ which is coming into the world. With Christ comes the light of hope. Let us walk in the light of the Lord, who is our hope.

Light one purple candle.

Second Sunday of Advent

The candle lighted on the previous Sunday will have been lighted before the service.

On this Second Sunday of Advent we are called to repentance in the words of John the Baptist. We know that all is not right with us or with our world. There is too much strife, too much brokenness, yet we live in hope.

Hear the words of the prophet Isaiah: "A child has been born for us, a son given to us; authority rests upon his shoulders; and he is named Wonderful Counselor, Mighty God, Everlasting Father, Prince of Peace. His authority shall grow continually, and there shall be endless peace for the throne of David and his kingdom. He will establish and uphold it with justice and with righteousness from this time onward and forevermore" (Isa. 9:6–7).

We light this candle as a symbol of the light of Christ which is coming into the world. With Christ comes the light of peace, which is wholeness. Let us walk in the light of the Lord, who is our hope and peace.

Light one purple candle.

Third Sunday of Advent

The candles lighted on the previous Sunday will have been lighted before the service.

This season of preparation is half over. We have heard John the Baptist's call to repentance. The day of Christ's birth approaches, and we wait in joyful anticipation, for Christ is not only our hope and our peace, Christ is also our joy.

Hear the words of the prophet Isaiah: "The ransomed of the LORD shall return, and come to Zion with singing; everlasting joy shall be upon their heads; they shall obtain joy and gladness, and sorrow and sighing shall flee away" (Isa. 35:10).

We light this candle as a symbol of the light of Christ which is coming into the world. With Christ there comes the light of joy, joy that is ours not only at Christmas but always. Let us walk in the light of the Lord, who is our hope, our peace, and our joy.

Light the one pink candle.

Fourth Sunday of Advent

The candles lighted on the previous Sundays will have been lighted before the service.

Advent is drawing to a close. The time of anticipation and preparation is about to end. Soon we shall celebrate the birth of Jesus, the very incarnation of God, who is love. This is how God has shown us his love for us: in the gift of the Son.

Here the words of John: "God's love was revealed among us in this way: God sent his only Son into the world so that we might live through him. In this is love, not that we loved God but that he loved us and sent his Son to be the atoning sacrifice for our sins. Beloved, since God loved us so much, we also ought to love one another" (1 John 4:9–11).

We light this candle as a symbol of the light of Christ, which is coming into the world. His light has brought us love. Let us walk in the light of the Lord, who is our hope, our peace, our joy, the gift of God's love.

Light the fourth candle on the circle.

Christmas Eve

The candles lighted on the four Sundays in Advent will have been lighted before the service.

On this Christmas Eve we are gathered as God's people to celebrate again what Christ's coming means to the world and to each of us. Tonight we join with Christians from all over the world in celebrating the gift of God's love and life to us in the birth of Jesus in Bethlehem.

A different person may read each passage.

Hear the words of Isaiah: "For a child has been born for us, a son given to us; authority rests upon his shoulders; and he is named Wonderful Counselor, Mighty God, Everlasting Father, Prince of Peace" (Isa. 9:6).

Hear also these words from Luke's Gospel: "The angel said to them, 'Do not be afraid; for see—I am bringing you good news of great joy for all the people: to you is born this day in the city of David a Savior, who is the Messiah, the Lord. . . . And suddenly there was with the angel a multitude of the heavenly host, praising God and saying, 'Glory to God in the highest heaven, and on earth peace among those whom he favors!'" (Luke 2:10–11;13–14).

We light this central Christ candle as a symbol of Christ's abiding presence with us. In him is our hope, our peace, our joy, the gift of God's love. Always he is with us. Thanks be to God!

Light the central candle.

Appendix B

The Way of the Cross

The congregation gathers in silence.

Greeting

The grace of our Lord Jesus Christ be with you all.
And also with you.

Hymn

"Go to Dark Gethsemane" REDHEAD 76

The congregation gathers around the Communion table as the hymn is sung.

Litany for Lent

O Christ,
out of your fullness we have all received grace upon grace.
You are our eternal hope;
you are patient and full of mercy;
you are generous to all who call upon you.
Save us, Lord.
O Christ, fountain of life and holiness,
you have taken away our sins.
On the cross you were wounded for our transgressions
and were bruised for our iniquities.
Save us, Lord.
O Christ, obedient unto death,
source of all comfort,
our life and our resurrection,
our peace and reconciliation:
Save us, Lord.

O Christ, Savior of all who trust you,
hope of all who die for you,
and joy of all the saints:
Save us, Lord.
Jesus, Lamb of God,
have mercy on us.
Jesus, bearer of our sins,
have mercy on us.
Jesus, redeemer of the world,
grant us peace.

After a brief silence, the leader concludes the litany.

God of love, as in Jesus Christ you gave yourself to us, so may we give ourselves
to you, living according to your holy will. Keep our feet firmly in the way where
Christ leads us; make our mouths speak the truth that Christ teaches us; fill our
bodies with the life that is Christ within us. In his holy name we pray. **Amen.**[90]

The Lord's Prayer

Invitation to a Journey to the Cross

Let us this night walk with Jesus from Pilate's hall to Golgotha. Let us hear
the story of his suffering and death, and remember, in the words of Scripture,
that "while we were still weak, at the right time Christ died for the ungodly.
Indeed, rarely will anyone die for a righteous person—though perhaps for a
good person someone might actually dare to die. But God proves his love for
us in that while we still were sinners Christ died for us" (Rom. 5:6–8).

The First Station:
Jesus Is Condemned to Death

The congregation sings while walking:

"Were You There When They Crucified My Lord?"   WERE YOU THERE

The Reading:
Matthew 27:1–2, 11–26

When morning came, all the chief priests and the elders of the people con-
ferred together against Jesus in order to bring about his death. They bound
him, led him away, and handed him over to Pilate the governor. . . .

Now Jesus stood before the governor; and the governor asked him, "Are you the King of the Jews?" Jesus said, "You say so." But when he was accused by the chief priests and elders, he did not answer. Then Pilate said to him, "Do you not hear how many accusations they make against you?" But he gave him no answer, not even to a single charge, so that the governor was greatly amazed.

Now at the festival the governor was accustomed to release a prisoner for the crowd, anyone whom they wanted. At that time they had a notorious prisoner, called Jesus Barabbas. So after they had gathered, Pilate said to them, "Whom do you want me to release for you, Jesus Barabbas or Jesus who is called the Messiah?" For he realized that it was out of jealousy that they had handed him over. While he was sitting on the judgment seat, his wife sent word to him, "Have nothing to do with that innocent man, for today I have suffered a great deal because of a dream about him." Now the chief priests and the elders persuaded the crowds to ask for Barabbas and to have Jesus killed. The governor again said to them, "Which of the two do you want me to release for you?" And they said, "Barabbas." Pilate said to them, "Then what should I do with Jesus who is called the Messiah?" All of them said, "Let him be crucified!" Then he asked, "Why, what evil has he done?" But they shouted all the more, "Let him be crucified!"

So, when Pilate saw that he could do nothing, but rather that a riot was beginning, he took some water and washed his hands before the crowd, saying, "I am innocent of this man's blood; see to it yourselves." Then the people as a whole answered, "His blood be on us and on our children!" So he released Barabbas for them; and after flogging Jesus, he handed him over to be crucified.

A silence is kept.

God did not spare his own Son:
But delivered him up for us all.

Prayer

Let us pray. *(Silence)*
Gracious God, whose Son stood toe to toe with the power of unjust rulers, endured the torment of the crowd and their cries for his death, and took upon himself the pain of the cross for the sake of all people: Grant that we, walking in the way of his cross, may discover the life that is promised those who follow him in faith and in obedience; through Jesus Christ your Son, our Savior. **Amen.**

The congregation says or sings three times:

Holy God, Holy immortal, Holy and mighty One, have mercy upon us.

Second Station:
Jesus Takes Up His Cross

The congregation sings while walking:

"Jesus Walked This Lonesome Valley"   LONESOME VALLEY

The Reading:
John 19:16b–17

They took Jesus; and carrying the cross by himself, he went out to what is called The Place of the Skull, which in Hebrew is called Golgotha.

Isaiah 53:4–7

Surely he has borne our infirmities and carried our diseases; yet we accounted him stricken, struck down by God, and afflicted. But he was wounded for our transgressions, crushed for our iniquities; upon him was the punishment that made us whole, and by his bruises we are healed. All we like sheep have gone astray; we have all turned to our own way, and the Lord has laid on him the iniquity of us all. He was oppressed, and he was afflicted, yet he did not open his mouth; like a lamb that is led to the slaughter, and like a sheep that before its shearers is silent, so he did not open his mouth.

A silence is kept.

He was wounded for our transgressions, crushed for our iniquities;
Upon him was the punishment that made us whole, and by his bruises we are healed.

Prayer

Let us pray. *(Silence)*
Gracious and loving God, as Jesus our Lord took up the cross of suffering and death for our redemption, grant that we in obedience to his command may take up the cross of self-denial and service, and by your grace in each day die more and more to sin and rise to newer and fuller life; through Jesus Christ our Lord. **Amen.**

The congregation says or sings three times:

Holy God, Holy immortal, Holy and mighty One, have mercy upon us.

The Third Station:
The Cross Is Laid on Simon of Cyrene

A solo voice sings a cappella as the congregation walks:

"Take Up Your Cross, the Savior Said"   BOURBON

The Reading:
Luke 23:26

As they led him away, they seized a man, Simon of Cyrene, who was coming from the country, and they laid the cross on him, and made him carry it behind Jesus.

Luke 9:23–25

"If any want to become my followers, let them deny themselves and take up their cross daily and follow me. For those who want to save their life will lose it, and those who lose their life for my sake will save it. What does it profit them if they gain the whole world, but lose or forfeit themselves?"

A silence is kept.

"I am the way, and the truth, and the life," said Jesus.
"No one comes to the Father except through me."

Prayer

Let us pray. *(Silence)*
Gracious Father, whose Son came among us not to be served but to serve and to give his life as a ransom for many: We remember with gratitude all those who have served us and who have allowed us to be of service to them. Grant that like Simon we may take up the cross of suffering not only for those we know and love, but for those who are strangers among us, even those who are despised; through Jesus Christ our Lord. **Amen.**

The congregation says or sings three times:

Holy God, Holy immortal, Holy and mighty One, have mercy upon us.

Fourth Station:
Jesus Meets the Women of Jerusalem

A solo, a cappella voice sings as the congregation walks:

"O Lamb of God Most Holy!"   O LAMM GOTTES

The Reading:
Luke 23:27–31

A great number of the people followed him, and among them were women who were beating their breasts and wailing for him. But Jesus turned to them and said, "Daughters of Jerusalem, do not weep for me, but weep for yourselves and for your children. For the days are surely coming when they will say, 'Blessed are the barren, and the wombs that never bore, and the breasts that never nursed.' Then they will begin to say to the mountains, 'Fall on us'; and to the hills, 'Cover us.' For if they do this when the wood is green, what will happen when it is dry?"

A silence is kept.

Blessed are those who mourn their sins,
For they will be comforted.

Prayer

Let us pray. *(Silence)*
Merciful God, grant us grace to see within ourselves, to mourn our sins, and to seek the blessing of your forgiving, life-renewing grace, that we may live as your faithful and obedient children throughout all our days; in Jesus Christ our Lord. **Amen.**

The congregation says or sings three times:

Holy God, Holy immortal, Holy and mighty One, have mercy upon us.

Fifth Station:
Jesus Is Stripped of His Garments

The congregation sings while walking:

"What Wondrous Love Is This"   WONDROUS LOVE

The Reading:
Mark 15:22–24

Then they brought Jesus to the place called Golgotha (which means the place of a skull). And they offered him wine mixed with myrrh; but he did not take it. And they crucified him, and divided his clothes among them, casting lots to decide what each should take.

A silence is kept.

I can count all my bones. My enemies stare and gloat over me;
They divide my clothes among themselves, and for my clothing they cast lots.

Prayer

Let us pray. *(Silence)*
Eternal God, how deeply Jesus humbled himself, accepting the scorn of those who hated him, bearing the shame of those who looked upon him. Grant us grace to bear the pains that we ourselves encounter, the indignities we may have to endure, with hope in your good promises and confidence in the glory that is to be ours; through Jesus Christ our Lord. **Amen.**

The congregation says or sings three times:

Holy God, Holy immortal, Holy and mighty One, have mercy upon us.

The Sixth Station:
Jesus Is Nailed to the Cross

As the congregation walks, a solo voice sings:

"Deep Were His Wounds, and Red"   MARLEE

The Reading:
Luke 23:32–33, 35

Two others also, who were criminals, were led away to be put to death with him. When they came to the place that is called The Skull, they crucified Jesus there with the criminals, one on his right and one on his left. . . . And the people stood by, watching; but the leaders scoffed at him, saying, "He saved others; let him save himself if he is the Messiah of God, his chosen one!"

A silence is kept.

They made his grave with the wicked and his tomb with the rich,
Although he had done no violence, and there was no deceit in his mouth.

Prayer

Let us pray. *(Silence)*
Lord Jesus Christ, you stretched out your arms on the wood of the cross that all might come within the reach of your saving embrace. Grant that we, your disciples, may reach out to those around us who do not know your love and bring them to the knowledge of your love and saving grace, that they may share in your life with us; through Jesus Christ our Lord. **Amen.**

The congregation says or sings three times:

Holy God, Holy immortal, Holy and mighty One, have mercy upon us.

Seventh Station:
Jesus Dies on the Cross

The congregation sings while walking:

"When I Survey the Wondrous Cross"   HAMBURG

The Reading:
John 19:25b–30

Meanwhile, standing near the cross of Jesus were his mother, and his mother's sister, Mary the wife of Clopas, and Mary Magdalene. When Jesus saw his mother and the disciple whom he loved standing beside her, he said to his mother, "Woman, here is your son." Then he said to the disciple, "Here is your mother." And from that hour the disciple took her into his own home.

After this, when Jesus knew that all was now finished, he said (in order to fulfill the scripture), "I am thirsty." A jar full of sour wine was standing there. So they put a sponge full of the wine on a branch of hyssop and held it to his mouth. When Jesus had received the wine, he said, "It is finished." Then he bowed his head and gave up his spirit.

A silence is kept.

Let the same mind be in you that was in Christ Jesus, who, though he was in the form of God, did not regard equality with God as something to be exploited, but emptied himself, taking the form of a slave, being born in human likeness.

And being found in human form, he humbled himself and became obedient to the point of death—even death on a cross.

Prayer

Let us pray. *(Silence)*
Lord Jesus, we stand in awe of your grace and mercy, your love that knows no limits. As we have been forgiven, grant that we might forgive; as we have been loved, grant that we might also love one another; through Jesus Christ our Lord. **Amen.**

The congregation says or sings three times:

Holy God, Holy immortal, Holy and mighty One, have mercy upon us.

Eighth Station:
Jesus Is Laid in the Tomb

The congregation sings while walking:

"Beneath the Cross of Jesus"   ST. CHRISTOPHER

The Reading:
Mark 15:42–46

When evening had come, and since it was the day of Preparation, that is, the day before the sabbath, Joseph of Arimathea, a respected member of the council, who was also himself waiting expectantly for the kingdom of God, went boldly to Pilate and asked for the body of Jesus. Then Pilate wondered if he were already dead; and summoning the centurion, he asked him whether he had been dead for some time. When he learned from the centurion that he was dead, he granted the body to Joseph. Then Joseph bought a linen cloth, and taking down the body, wrapped it in the linen cloth, and laid it in a tomb that had been hewn out of the rock. He then rolled a stone against the door of the tomb.

A silence is kept.

For he was cut off from the land of the living, stricken for the transgression of my people.
They made his grave with the wicked and his tomb with the rich, although he had done no violence, and there was no deceit in his mouth.

Prayer

Let us pray. *(Silence)*
Gracious God, the tomb is sealed, darkness descends, and we wait—wait in hope for the fulfillment of the promise of resurrection to new life. In our own days of darkness, whenever they may fall, grant us grace to remember and to trust that the light of Christ's own love and life still shines even in the darkness, and the darkness will not overcome it. **Amen.**

The congregation says or sings three times:

Holy God, Holy immortal, Holy and mighty One, have mercy upon us.

Concluding Prayer around the Communion Table

Hymn

"My Faith Looks Up to Thee"   OLIVET

Benediction

All depart in silence.

Notes

1. Donald Wilson Stake, *The ABCs of Worship: A Concise Dictionary* (Louisville, Ky.: Westminster/John Knox Press, 1992), pp. 187–88.
2. Marva J. Dawn, *Reaching Out without Dumbing Down: A Theology of Worship for the Turn-of-the-Century Culture* (Grand Rapids: William B. Eerdmans Publishing Co., 1995), p. 119.
3. Tim Wright, *A Community of Joy: How to Create Contemporary Worship,* ed. Herb Miller (Nashville: Abingdon Press, 1994), p. 56.
4. Gail Ramshaw, *Liturgical Language: Keeping It Metaphoric, Making It Inclusive,* American Essays in Liturgy (Collegeville, Minn.: Liturgical Press, 1996), p. 15.
5. David B. Batchelder, "Counting the Cost: Assessing What's at Stake in the 'Worship Wars,'" *Reformed Liturgy & Music,* vol. 30, no. 2 (1996), p. 89.
6. Stanley Hauerwas and William H. Willimon, *Where Resident Aliens Live: Exercises for Christian Practice* (Nashville: Abingdon Press, 1996), pp. 59–60.
7. Daniel B. Stevick, *The Crafting of Liturgy: A Guide for Preparers* (New York: Church Hymnal Corporation, 1990), p. 51.
8. *The Constitution of the Presbyterian Church (U.S.A.),* Part II, *Book of Order* (Louisville, Ky.: Office of the General Assembly, Presbyterian Church (U.S.A.), 2000), G-2.0200.
9. Don E. Saliers, *Worship as Theology: Foretaste of Glory Divine* (Nashville: Abingdon Press, 1994), p. 154.
10. Stevick, *Crafting of Liturgy,* pp. 65, 66.
11. Cheslyn Jones, et al., eds., *The Study of Liturgy,* rev. ed. (New York: Oxford University Press, 1992), p. 80.
12. Adolf Adam, *The Liturgical Year: Its History & Its Meaning after the Reform of the Liturgy,* trans. Matthew J. O'Connell (New York: Pueblo Publishing Company, 1981), p. 37.
13. Cyril C. Richardson, ed. and trans., *Early Christian Fathers,* The Library of Christian Classics, vol. 1 (Philadelphia: Westminster Press, 1953), pp. 175–76.
14. Ibid., p. 178.
15. Ibid., p. 287.
16. Saliers, *Worship as Theology,* p. 93.
17. James F. White, *Introduction to Christian Worship* (Nashville: Abingdon Press, 1980), p. 212.

18. William D. Maxwell, *An Outline of Christian Worship: Its Developments and Forms* (London: Oxford University Press, 1936), pp. 16–17.

19. Frank C. Senn, *Christian Liturgy: Catholic and Evangelical* (Minneapolis: Augsburg Fortress, 1997), p. 114.

20. Adolf Adam, *Foundations of Liturgy: An Introduction to Its History and Practice,* trans. Matthew J. O'Connell (Collegeville, Minn.: Liturgical Press, 1992), p. 18.

21. Maxwell, *Outline of Christian Worship*, p. 45.

22. Jones, et al., *Study of Liturgy,* pp. 281–82.

23. Paul Westermeyer, *Te Deum: The Church and Music* (Minneapolis: Fortress Press, 1998), p. 122.

24. Ibid., p. 123.

25. John Calvin, *Institutes of the Christian Religion,* 4.17.44; Library of Christian Classics, ed. John T. McNeill, trans. Ford Lewis Battles (Philadelphia: Westminster Press, 1960), 21:1422.

26. Maxwell, *Outline of Christian Worship,* p. 117.

27. Bard Thompson, *Liturgies of the Western Church* (New York: World Publishing Company, 1961), pp. 197–98.

28. John H. Leith, *An Introduction to the Reformed Tradition: A Way of Being the Christian Community,* rev. ed. (Atlanta: John Knox Press, 1981), p. 192.

29. Julius Melton, *Presbyterian Worship in America: Changing Patterns since 1787* (Richmond: John Knox Press, 1967), pp. 21–22.

30. Ibid., pp. 35–36.

31. Westermeyer, *Te Deum,* p. 248.

32. Stevick, *Crafting of Liturgy,* p. 34.

33. Melton, *Presbyterian Worship,* p. 47.

34. James F. White, *Protestant Worship: Traditions in Transition* (Louisville, Ky.: Westminster/John Knox Press, 1989), p. 73.

35. Carol Doran and Thomas H. Troeger, *Open to Glory: Renewing Worship in the Congregation* (Valley Forge, Pa.: Judson Press, 1983), p. 73.

36. Melton, *Presbyterian Worship,* pp. 28–29.

37. Ernest Trice Thompson, *Presbyterians in the South,* vol. 2, *1861–1890* (Richmond: John Knox Press, 1973), pp. 426–29.

38. Maurice W. Armstrong, Lefferts A. Loetscher, and Charles A. Anderson, eds., *The Presbyterian Enterprise: Sources of American Presbyterian History* (Philadelphia: Westminster Press, 1956), pp. 254–55.

39. Presbyterian Church (U.S.A.), *Book of Common Worship* (Louisville, Ky.: Westminster/John Knox Press, 1993), p. 7.

40. Jones, et al., *Study of Liturgy,* p. 288.

41. Philip H. Pfatteicher, *Commentary on the Lutheran Book of Worship: Lutheran Liturgy in Its Ecumenical Context* (Minneapolis: Augsburg Fortress, 1990), p. 1.

42. White, *Protestant Worship,* p. 34.

43. White, *Introduction to Christian Worship,* pp. 23–24.

44. *Book of Order,* W-1.4001.

45. Ibid., W-1.4004.

46. Ibid., W-1.4005.

47. John H. Leith, *From Generation to Generation: The Renewal of the Church according to Its Own Theology and Practice* (Louisville, Ky.: Westminster/John Knox Press, 1990), p. 87.

48. Stevick, *Crafting of Liturgy*, p.7.
49. C. S. Lewis, *Letters to Malcolm, Chiefly on Prayer* (London: Harcourt Brace Jovanovich, 1964), p. 4.
50. Saliers, *Worship as Theology*, p. 158.
51. Stevick, *Crafting of Liturgy*, p. 6.
52. Robin A. Leaver, "The Hymnbook as a Book of Practical Theology," *Reformed Liturgy & Music,* vol. 24, no. 2 (1990), p. 55.
53. Yme Woensdregt, "The Pastor as Liturgist," *Reformed Liturgy & Music*, vol. 30, no. 4, 1996, p. 169.
54. Ibid., p. 168.
55. Carol Doran and Thomas H. Troeger, *Trouble at the Table: Gathering the Tribes for Worship* (Nashville: Abingdon Press, 1992), pp. 100–101.
56. Stevick, *Crafting of Liturgy,* p. 139.
57. Dawn, *Reaching Out*, p. 87.
58. Pfatteicher, *Commentary,* pp. 117–18.
59. Harold Daniels, "The Languages of Worship," *Reformed Liturgy & Music*, vol. 30, no. 4 (1996), p. 202.
60. Fred Holper, *Praying in Common: The Promise of Presbyterian Liturgical Renewal.* Keynote address from Festival of Worship, Evanston, Illinois, September 1993.
61. Maxwell, *Outline of Christian Worship*, pp. 180–81.
62. John R. Claypool, *The Preaching Event* (San Francisco: Harper & Row, 1989), pp. 132–33.
63. Pfatteicher, *Commentary*, p. 166.
64. Laurence Hull Stookey, *Calendar: Christ's Time for the Church* (Nashville: Abingdon Press) p. 22.
65. Robert E. Webber, *Worship Is a Verb: Eight Principles for Transforming Worship* (Peabody, Mass: Hendrickson Publishers, 1992), p. 158.
66. Ibid., p. 170.
67. Adam, *The Liturgical Year,* p. 40.
68. Ibid., p. 20.
69. Ibid., pp. 92–93.
70. Ibid., p. 97.
71. Philip H. Pfatteicher and Carlos R. Messerli, *Manual on the Liturgy: Lutheran Book of Worship* (Minneapolis: Augsburg Publishing House, 1979), p. 306.
72. Adam, *Liturgical Year*, p. 98.
73. Stookey, *Calendar*, p. 56.
74. Ibid., p. 74.
75. Ibid., p. 180, note 1, for p. 121.
76. Adam, *Liturgical Year*, pp. 122–23.
77. Pfatteicher, *Commentary*, pp. 208–9.
78. Adam, *Liturgical Year*, pp. 144–45.
79. Presbyterian Church (U.S.A.) and the Cumberland Presbyterian Church, *Liturgical Year: The Worship of God,* Supplemental Liturgical Resource 7 (Louisville, Ky.: Westminster/John Knox Press, 1992), p. 282.
80. Ibid., p. 83.
81. White, *Protestant Worship*, pp. 61–64.
82. Daniels, "The Languages of Worship," p. 201.
83. Pfatteicher, *Commentary,* pp. 251–52.

84. Stookey, *Calendar,* pp. 92–93.
85. *Book of Common Worship,* p. 269.
86. Pfatteicher, *Commentary*, p. 242.
87. Ibid., p. 247.
88. Stookey, *Calendar*, p. 93.
89. *Liturgical Year:* Resource 7, p. 301.
90. *Book of Common Worship,* pp. 235–36. Reprinted by permission from *Book of Common Worship,* © 1993 Westminster/John Knox Press.